GOODNIGHT, BEAUTIFUL

Childhood friends Nova and Mal would do anything for each other. So, when Mal asks her to have a baby for him and his wife, Stephanie, Nova agrees.

Months into the pregnancy, Stephanie finds a text from Mal to Nova saying 'Goodnight, Beautiful'. Terrified she is losing her husband, Stephanie begs Mal to cut all ties to Nova and his unborn child.

Eight years later, Leo—Nova's son—is critically ill and she decides Mal needs to get to know their child before it's too late. But as they all discover, losing someone you love can happen at any time...

GOODNIGHT, BEAUTIFUL

Dorothy Koomson

WINDSOR
PARAGON

First published 2008
by Sphere
This Large Print edition published 2008
by BBC Audiobooks Ltd
by arrangement with
Little, Brown Book Group

Hardcover ISBN: 978 1 408 41405 7
Softcover   ISBN: 978 1 408 41406 4

British Library Cataloguing in Publication Data available

Printed and bound in Great Britain by
CPI Antony Rowe, Chippenham, Wiltshire

For
Pebble

ACKNOWLEDGEMENTS

I have so many people to thank, and not enough space to do it in. But, I'll give most things a try, so here goes:

To my family, one and all, thank you; you have been, and continue to be, fabulous.

To Jo, Kirsteen, Emma, Jenny and everyone at Little, Brown, thanks for everything. That's a small word, but everything you've done means so much to me.

To Ant and James—you're so much more than agents to me, and thanks for indulging my looooooonnngggg phone calls.

To my lovely friends—you all know who you are—I love your enthusiasm, and support, and thanks for continuing to like me despite my 'misappropriation' of pieces of your personalities and stories to create my characters.

And last, but not least, to 'The Children', thank you for letting me live with you for six months. I had the best time.

PROLOGUE

He cries all the time.

Even when there are no tears, his eyes have the haunted hollowness of someone who is sobbing inside.

I want to help him but he won't let me near. The crying he does alone, shut away in the room that was once going to be the nursery. He sleeps with his back to me, like a solid wall of flesh that keeps the world out. He talks to me with empty words, in sentences that hold no deeper meaning. He used to weave everything he said with the strands of the depth of his love. Now, he talks to me because he has to. Now, everything he says is flat and meaningless.

The grief is so huge, so immense that he is floundering in it. Swimming blind as he would in a raging sea at night. Swimming against the crashing waves and getting nowhere. Every day he is dragged further down, into those depths. Away from the surface. Away from life. Away from me. All he clings to is the loss. Nothing else matters. I want to take his hand, swim us both to safety. To make him whole again; to soothe his wounds and help him heal.

But he will not reach for me. Instead, he flinches away, preferring to do this alone. He blames me, you see. He blames himself. And he blames me.

I blame myself, as well. But I also blame her. Nova. This is her fault, her responsibility, too. If not for her . . .

Mostly, I blame myself. Mostly, I want him to

stop crying, to stop hurting, to stop grieving with every piece of his soul.

I don't understand this loss that he and Nova share. I doubt I ever will. But I understand my husband. And soon, I'll lose him. The one thing I tried to stop by doing what I did, saying what I said, will happen. But this time I won't lose him to another woman and her unborn baby, I won't lose him to her and her child, I'll lose him to himself.

I can see it happening: he's going to drown in his grief, he's going to be pulled so far down he won't be able to break the surface. He'll be dragged down to those bleak, grey depths and will never start living again. And all I'll be able to do is stand on the shore and watch.

She fumbled at his shoes, took them off, and he watched her roll off his sock and then it was cold under his toes. Like in the bath, before his wash, cold.

And there is water.

A big, big, BIG bath.

'This is the beach,' Mummy said.

'Beach!' he said.

'And that's the sea.'

'Sea!'

'Come on, let's get our feet wet.'

He pointed. 'Toes?'

'Yeah,' she said. 'Toes in the sea.'

She took his hand, it was warm like always. Her hand warm, his toes cold. She walked with him to the sea.

'It's going to be cold,' she said.

'Cold!'

Then his toes were gone. No more toes, just sea.

'Whoa!' Mummy screamed—her toes were under the sea, too.

'Whoa!' he screamed.

'Whoa!' they screamed together. 'Whoa!'

Leo, age 18 months

part one

CHAPTER ONE

'Hey, Marm.'

It's going to be one of those days.

I knew it when I opened my eyes this morning. I had that strong pervasive feeling of everything being skew-whiff, off-key. That I'd have to endure a day of it. I was hoping I was wrong as I showered, as I got dressed, as I flicked on the radio to keep me company whilst I stirred porridge and cut up fruit.

But Leo has just confirmed it for me. It's going to be one of *those* days. Nothing will go right, tempers will be frayed, life will play nasty tricks on me. My seven-year-old will play nasty tricks on me. Or try to aggravate me.

He only calls me 'Marm' when he is trying to rile me. He knows how much I hate it; he knows that he could call me 'Nova' and I'd hate it less than 'Marm'. He picked it up from watching American TV shows, their intonation when they say 'Mum' ('Mom') and every time it reminds me that he could be one step away from saying 'rowt' instead of 'route', 'aloominum' instead of 'aluminium'. That he could start talking with a stateside inflection.

I stand at the sink, filling the porridge saucepan with soapy water, and through the reflection in the window I watch Leo saunter across the room to the solid oak wood table, climb up on to his chair and settle himself in front of his bowl. He's going all out to wind me up today. Not only has he called me 'Marm', he is wearing his Teen League Fighter

3

costume. On a school morning.

I turn off the tap and spin away from the sink to face him. Fully ingest him in all his glory: the costume is bright green with a detachable red cape that currently hangs at an awkward angle from the corner of his left shoulder by a small square of Velcro. He's tied on his red mask, which serves to emphasise his huge, long-lashed eyes, just as it disguises part of his face.

He's a four-foot-nothing, seven-year-old superhero with bulging biceps, rippling chest, six-pack abdomen and sculpted bottom.

Deep breath in, I think. *Deep breath out*.

I close my eyes. Count to ten. Count the memories that make me love him: two days old when he smiled at me as I held him in the crook of my arm. Eighteen months old when we first stood on the beach and watched the sea foam up to shore and effortlessly swallow our feet, then just as easily spit them out again. Five years old when he took my hands in his and told me earnestly, 'You're the best mummy in the world' because I'd made him cheesy beans on toast for his birthday dinner.

This is the way I have to deal with Leo sometimes. This is the only way to remind myself not to lose it. There are only two people on earth who can slip through the layers of my calm and push my buttons; who can make me shout. Leo is the one who does it most regularly.

I open my eyes. He is still wearing the suit. It is still a school morning. I am still unimpressed.

'So, Marm, is this all there is for breakfast?' he drawls, spoon raised, his head on one side as he stares at me.

The blood rises in my veins, heat rushing first to

4

my throat, then to my cheeks. Very soon, I'm going to start crying. If I shout at him, I'll feel awful and will have to go to my room and cry. If I don't shout at him, I'll probably have to do something else like ban him from the PlayStation until the weekend, which will make him cry. Which will, of course, make me cry—silently, privately, but certainly—because I can't bear to make him cry. Either way, I'm going to be crying at some point this morning if I can't reason with him.

'Leo, you need to go and get ready,' I say, calmly. 'Put on your uniform.'

'I am ready,' he says.

'No, you're not.'

He nods, furrows his brow. 'I am ready,' he insists. 'This is what I'm wearing.'

'I don't want to argue, go and get ready. *Now!*'

'This is what I'm wearing. This is what I have to wear.'

'*Leo.*' I grit my teeth as I continue. 'Ple—'

DING-DONG! chimes the doorbell. Leo's dark eyes light up as if it's his birthday and he's expecting the usual glut of presents to be handed to him by the postman. He's out of his seat and racing through the kitchen door before I can completely comprehend what he's doing. I dash out after him with 'Don't you—' on my lips.

But even as the words leave my mouth, he is doing what he knows he's not supposed to do. He is reaching up, his wide, chubby hand closing around the knob, and he is pulling the door wide open.

Suddenly the hallway is flooded with light. A brilliant, glorious white light. I raise my arm, use my hand to shield my eyes from the brightness that is drenching the hallway, making everything around us luminescent.

There is no postman on the other side of the door, in the white light. Just a tall, rakishly thin man wearing a white suit with white shirt, white tie and white shoes. He glows with the light surrounding us. His hair is black and neatly combed, with a perfectly straight side parting and a lock of black hair that lays across his forehead; his skin is a pale white that highlights his large, walnut-brown eyes; his mature features are friendly and open. He smiles at me, reassuring and friendly, then turns his attention to Leo, the smile becoming wider and more affectionate.

'Are you ready, young man?' he asks Leo. He speaks without moving his lips. He talks straight into my head, my heart. I know him, I realise. I know him, he knows me, but the full memory of him is out of reach and I cannot place him.

'Yes,' Leo says with a nod and a grin. 'Yes, I am.' Leo speaks with his mouth.

'What's happening?' I ask.

'You do look ready,' the man says to Leo.

'You're not going anywhere with him,' I say.

The man looks up at me again, fixes me with his warm, friendly brown eyes. A stare that is kind but firm. Definite. 'It's time, Nova,' he says, again without moving his lips.

Leo runs to me, throws his arms around my waist, buries his head in the area above my stomach, snuggles me for a moment, then pulls away. 'I miss you, Mum,' Leo says, looking up at me, a smile on his face. 'I miss you lots.'

I reach out to hold him, to keep him near, but I'm reaching for air; clutching at nothingness. Leo

6

is with the man, holding the man's hand. They are so different, but so similar. I know Leo will be safe with him. But I can't let him go. How can I let him go?

'Where are you taking him?' I ask. 'He's not even dressed. Where are you taking him?'

'It's OK, Mum,' Leo says, 'I want to go. I'm ready. I told you, I'm ready. This is what I'm wearing.'

I shake my head. No. He's not ready. How can my little boy be ready to go somewhere without me? How? He's not ready. I'm not ready. 'I'll come with you,' I say.

Leo grins, raises his hand and waves. 'Bye, Mum. Bye.'

'No—'

*　　*　　*

My eyes snap open and I am still—startled and confused—for a moment as my mind scrabbles around, trying to get my bearings, trying to remember where I am. The room is in virtual darkness; slivers of orange street lighting creeping in through the horizontal blinds, and white light shining in from the corridor outside through the squares of safety glass in the door make it not quite black in here. I was asleep, but I wasn't lying down. My eyes move around the room, finding it full of unknown angles and shapes.

Then I hear them, the bleeps. The rhythmical bleeps in the background that remind me where I am, and my eyes fly to the bed.

He is still here. Still there. Still in the bed. I sit forwards in the chair, and gasp as every muscle and

7

sinew in my back and neck screams in agony. I brush away the pain, trying to see if there is any change, if Leo has moved while I was sleeping.

Leo still lies on his back, his eyes gently pressed together as he remains in that world he inhabits now. That between world: not awake, not on the other side. I sit further forwards in my chair so I can examine his face closer. The dream was so vivid. He'd been active. Walking, talking. Surely that must have translated into the here and now? *Surely?*

His eyes rest lightly together. His lips are soft and slightly parted. His features are smooth and expressionless, not like when he is usually asleep. I can remember in detail the many expressions he has when he is asleep, the way he is animated, his muscles moving and twitching as he lives out as exciting a sleeping life as the one he has when he is awake. This, this sleep, is so unlike him: he is rarely still for long, something always happens to make him light up or speak or want to run around. He never stops for this long.

'It's OK, Mum. I want to go.' This time he had taken the man's hand. In the dream, this time, he was really going to go.

My eyes flick over the bed to Keith; his muscular, six-foot-five frame is slumped in the chair on the other side, his shaved head lolling to one side on his shoulder as he sleeps, still wearing his police uniform. He obviously came straight from his shift and found me deeply asleep because I hadn't stirred when he came in. Usually I'm awake when he arrives, and he asks me about my day before I go home to bed, but today I was spark out. The vague memories of his lips on my forehead, his fingers stroking my cheek, drift across my mind. I'd been out of it, but I'd been aware of him.

I turn back to Leo, wondering if he is aware we are here all the time. One of us always sitting beside him, watching, waiting. Waiting.

Do the sounds of the machines penetrate through to him? What about the hellos, the chats, the books I read, the goodnights? Does he know it's Thursday? His second Thursday here? Do all these little pieces of our reality slither through the cracks in his sleep and make him aware of the world going on around him? Or is he locked away from it all? Hidden. Removed. Somewhere separate. I couldn't bear it if it was like that. If he is all alone and doesn't know I am here, waiting for him to come back.

'I'm ready, Mum. I want to go.'

I rub the base of my thumbs over my eyes, removing the crystals of grit, trying to massage wakefulness and life into my face.

'I'm ready to go.'

After thirteen days of this, I'd have thought my body would get used to being in that chair for hours on end; it wouldn't be as sore and stiff, protesting with long snaps of pain every time I try to move. I get up, go to the bed, instinctively shutting out the IV drips, the electrodes attaching him to machines, and stare down at my boy. My boy. He's been the reason I have opened my eyes and climbed out of bed every day for the past seven-and-a-half years; even when I haven't wanted to, I've done it. My world started to rotate around him from the moment he was born, and now it is off-kilter.

9

I stroke his forehead with the very tips of my fingers, gently, so as not to disturb him. Even now, my instinct is to be gentle so I don't disturb him. Even though disturbing him, waking him, is exactly what we want.

His head is shorn, a fine covering of his black hair slowly growing back. They'd done that, clipped and shaved away all his beautiful, thick black curls, eight days ago. His mocha-caramel skin is smooth on his head, except at that point on his lower skull, where they drilled into him to clamp off three blood vessels, to try to prevent a haemorrhage. The operation had been a complete success, they told me.

I'd stared at the surgeon, with his green cap on his head, his mask around his neck, his green operating scrubs surprisingly clean. 'Success?' I'd echoed.

He'd nodded. Explained that the other aneurysm they'd been worried about hadn't ruptured, and was now no longer a threat.

'Success,' I'd repeated, my voice far away and disconnected. Keith had put his hand on my forearm to steady me. That word obviously had different meanings to the surgeon and to me. My boy was still asleep, was still more 'there' than here, he wasn't talking or walking, his eyes weren't open, his face wasn't moving, but still, it'd been a success. 'Thank you,' I'd said as Keith's large, warm hand closed around mine. It wasn't the surgeon's fault he didn't understand what the word success actually meant. It meant Leo would be back to normal. It meant, at the very least, that they would be able to tell me when he would be waking up.

I return to my brown padded chair and curl my legs up under me, rest my head back and watch Leo.

This is the world I live in now. A world where success means this. A world where I know those dreams are born of the feeling, the knowledge that has been stealthily and determinedly uncoiling itself bit by bit inside me every day.

The feeling that maybe Leo is ready.

Maybe I might have to let him go.

'Look at that woman's stomach!' he said.

He saw Mummy close her eyes before she said, 'Shhh,' and kissed his head while rocking him on her lap.

'Look at that woman's stomach!' he said again. He pointed. She had a big one. It was round like his football, but big like Mummy's big, big cushion.

'Shush-shush,' Mummy said. She took his finger and kissed it.

'Mummy! Look at that woman's stomach!'

Mummy didn't look, she pressed the button and it happened again, the sound of the bell like on his fire car. Then the bus stopped like always. Mummy got his pram and her big bag and she let him jump on every step to get off.

She opened the pram and moved the straps for him to sit down, but he wanted to walk. 'I just walk,' he told her. 'I just walk.'

Mummy carried on looking in his pram and when the bus went away she stood up. 'Leo, why do you have to keep pointing out people's stomachs? Or that small man? Or that woman's big milk boobies? Or

11

that man's funny hair?' she said to him. 'That's the third time in two days you've done that. I'm going to have to learn to drive cos I am never getting a bus with you again.'

She put her bag in his pram. 'Someday someone's going to smack me one.'

'Are you naughty?' he asked. Was Mummy a naughty girl like he was a naughty boy so she would get a smack?

Mummy stared at him with her head on one side. 'I sometimes wonder if I was in a former life.' She started pushing the pram with one hand, held his hand in the other. 'Come on, we have a very long walk ahead of us.'

A woman who was old like Grandma smiled at him. 'My mummy's naughty,' he told her.

The woman looked at Mummy. 'I'm sure she is,' the woman said and walked on.

He smiled at Mummy, but she didn't see—she was staring at the woman with her mouth open.

Leo, age 2 years

CHAPTER TWO

'Have you seen how much that girl with locker 117 runs?'

'The blonde?'

'Yeah. She's here every day. Sometimes she does yoga or Pilates, then runs. It's mad!'

My locker is 117. I had been about to throw the bolt on the toilet cubicle door when I heard the woman on the other side mention my locker, mention me. Now my hand is hovering over the lock, unsure whether to go ahead and leave or stay here. I'm already running a little late to meet Mal to go to this dinner party, I haven't got time to sit here, a prisoner of their gossip.

'I'm not surprised,' the other woman replies.

Well obviously I am not going anywhere now. I quietly lower the toilet lid and sit down. I have to know why she isn't surprised that I'm here every day. My hands are trembling slightly, my mouth is dry, my heart a little jumpy in my chest. I absently fiddle with the strap of my black dress as I wait to find out.

'Have you seen her husband? He is ab-so-lutely *gorgeous*. I'd run a million miles every day if it meant it'd stop his eyes wandering.'

'Oh my God, I've seen him when he comes to pick her up sometimes . . . And bloody hell! I know what you mean. I could eat him up!'

'Do you think she's one of those women who would balloon if she didn't do all those things?'

'*Yeah!* You can see it in her face.'

They have no idea I am listening to their words echo around the marble floor and walls in the gym toilets. I recognise their voices, they are the two women who do everything together: use the equipment, have their mats next to each other in yoga and Pilates. I was on nodding terms with them and I thought they liked me. Maybe that was overstating the tenuous, fleeting nature of our association—I hadn't thought they *didn't* like me, I didn't imagine for even one minute they did this: talked about me.

I fear this. Probably more than most rational adults, I fear people talking about me. Dissecting

13

me in private, peeling back the layers I so carefully and painstakingly present to the world and finding truths and half-truths, as they interpret them; I am scared of people creating a reality that is different to the beautiful home, the perfect husband, the successful friends who invite me to dinner parties that actually make up my life.

'But you've got to give it to her, she was probably a bit of a porker when she was younger and now she's shaped up.'

I wasn't! I want to shout through the door at them. I really wasn't. I was always this shape, and this size. Now I'm just firmer. In any case, I do not exercise to keep my looks, to fend off rolls of fat, nor to keep my husband faithful. I need it to keep grounded. Safe. Stable. Me.

If I don't feel the push of blood chasing endorphins and adrenalin at a hundred miles an hour through my veins every day, things start to slip. My grip on reality begins to numb and the slow decline to feeling out of control begins. That's why I run every day—even on a Friday night. What's their excuse for being here? When most people who don't *need* to run are out in the pub, why aren't they?

'Yeah, not as if either of us has got there. Alan keeps asking me why I bother coming to the gym when the second I get in I light up and head straight to the fridge.'

'Yeah, my Ian asks me the same thing. His eyes would be out on stalks if he saw *her.*'

When I was younger, people used to gossip about my family, and especially about me. It became a pastime in the town where we lived. People spoke in whispers, cast disapproving looks, hushed themselves whenever one of us went past. I felt every whisper, nudge and look. We all did, they were like shards of glass, lacerating the skin. That's why as an adult I do my best to not give anyone things to gossip about. Great job, beautiful home, gorgeous husband, group of friends. Why would you gossip about that? Envy that, maybe, but not find fault with.

'Do you fancy a pint?' one of the girls on the other side says.

'Oh, go on then. I've been fantasising about salt and vinegar crisps all day. If I do extra time on the machines next week, it won't matter so much, will it?'

'If that's the game we're playing right now, then I'll say yes. Extra time—in other words five more minutes—on the machines will make the extra fat just magically melt away.'

'You are such a bitch! Hey, shall we ask Miss Locker 117?'

The other woman smirks: nasty and cruel, perfectly expressive. 'She probably doesn't drink or eat.'

'I know!'

My mother always dealt with vicious smirks and bitchy comments by praying. 'Let he who is without sin cast the first stone,' she would say, as if that would make it stop; or even stem the rivers of pain that it caused. Whenever my sister, Mary, would cry about the things she heard, my mother would say, 'Remember them in your prayers, Mary.' *Remember to ask God to make bad things happen to them*, I would think but never say. Nothing bad ever did happen to those accusers who were with and without sin, and they still cast stones at us;

15

they still called me a slut and a whore and a host of other things behind my back, to my face; on all available walls. Praying didn't help; but neither did crying. Nothing helped. Nothing made it stop.

Time passes and the two women fall silent, then their footsteps, loud and magnified like their words have been, echo around the room as they retreat, the door slamming shut behind them. I wait a few more minutes, even though I'm really quite late for Mal, just to make sure they're really gone. When I can hear nothing, no sound from outside the cubicle, I unlock the door and release myself from my self-imposed prison into the marbled bathroom, with its wide mirror strip above the sinks opposite the cubicles.

My body stops short and my heart halts at exactly the same moment: they're still here. They're still here and now they know that I know what they were saying. That I have been sitting in the cubicle, listening to them rip me apart.

One of them, a tall blonde with her hair tucked behind her ears, is leaning over the bank of sinks applying a thick layer of eyeliner; the other, a small brunette, is perched on the edge of the sinks, rolling up a cigarette on her thigh.

All our eyes collide and everything becomes unnaturally, eerily still, a death shroud of stunned silence thrown over us. The one now frozen in applying make-up drains of all colour until her face is an ashen-grey mask of horror; the other now paused in rolling her cigarette fills up with red until her face resembles a pulsating, puce tomato.

Lowering my eyes, I move to the nearest basin, squirt blue gel handwash between my palms and rub them together under the sensor-operated tap. I

16

had wanted to apply lipstick, check my eye make-up and foundation before I went to meet Mal. Now, I dare not look up from the blue gel slipping and foaming through my fingers, not even a glance to see if my hair is in place.

I dry my hands on two scratchy paper towels, crush them in one hand and drop them into the bin under the sink. I'm sure the women can hear the thrash of my heart in my chest, the throbbing of my pulse in my throat because the slightest movement is magnified in here, and they have not moved at all since they saw me.

Their words and the cruel little smirk reverberate all around us as I start my epic journey to the door. The door, by the way, seems to have moved to the other side of London, and every step towards it in these six-inch heels sounds like an anvil being dropped through a glass roof.

RING! RING! RING! goes my mobile and it sounds like I have a miniature Hunchback of Notre Dame crammed into my bag, clanging 'the bells, the bells' for all he's worth. It's Mal's ringtone. Probably asking why I am not there, when I warned him—repeatedly—I'd skin him alive if he dared to work late tonight.

RING! RING! RING! insists my phone as I continue to walk to the door. I can't answer it, of course. If I stop for even a fraction of a moment of a second, something bad will happen. Something more bad than what has just happened will happen. I don't know what, but I know it will.

RING! RING! RING! I just have to get out of here. Out of this bathroom, out of this gym. Once I do that, it'll all be fine.

RING! RING! RING! I'm nearly there. Just

17

one more step. Two at the most. And then I'm home free.

RING! RIN—! The final ring is cut short and the sudden silence causes my heart to leap to my throat and my legs to wobble. But it's OK, I'm here, at the door.

I push it open and step outside, feeling the sweet rush of freedom crash like a welcome wave over me.

I do not know what happens after I am gone: if they fall about laughing, if they wither up and die in shame or if they decide to do what I have to do—look for another gym.

CHAPTER THREE

It's 11 p.m. and Keith isn't here.

He usually gets here by eight, sometimes nine, but never this late. Not without calling. Normally, I wouldn't worry even if he hasn't called because he's Keith and he does the job he does and he always turns up. Sometimes a little worse for wear and full of affection, sometimes because he couldn't get to a phone, sometimes because he's Keith and he does the job he does. That was before our lives became about this hospital room, about taking it in 'shifts' to sit here and keep our son company, and before I started to believe that even the smallest mishap could escalate into something unmanageable and terrifying. That was before I discovered you could bring your son to hospital because of a gusher of a nosebleed and find he has an aneurysm that is hours away from rupturing, and needs a life-saving operation that leaves him in a coma.

Now, I worry about everything.

I flip over the book I was reading, splaying it open in my lap, and try to avoid looking at my watch.

'Where's your dad?' I ask Leo in my head. I don't want to worry him so I don't say it out loud. I don't like to think of him listening to everything going on around him and panicking because he can't ask the questions whose answers will reassure him it will be OK. Worrying is my job. He just needs to concentrate on getting better. Because it's all up to him now.

The medically induced coma they put him in after the first operation should have worn off by now. They've removed all sedation, they've attempted to wake him, he's had multiple MRI scans all of which show he has brain activity, but he is still asleep.

He is still asleep.

Which means Leo, my seven-year-old who would choose to wear his Teen League Fighter costume all day every day, who would choose cheesy beans over broccoli but not spinach, who is still trying to find proof that Keith is a spy, decides from now on when he will wake up. His fate is in his chubby, perfectly formed hands.

I gnaw on the first knuckle of my thumb; the worry is like a multi-barrelled lock, each barrel moving slowly and precisely into position until every one clicks into place and the lock is set. Fused shut with no key to open it up again.

11:03 p.m. my watch shows me. 11:03. You'd think he'd call. If not to reassure me that he is OK,

19

which he's never had to do, but to at least ask how Leo is. If there's been any change.

His mobile was off when I tried him earlier. *Off or crushed in the smouldering carcass of his car?* I'd asked myself. *Off or sitting in his locker at work, waiting for someone to find it and call his next of kin with the news? Off for now or off for ever?*

What would I do if something happened to him? How would I cope? *Would* I cope? Probably, but how would I divide my time between Leo and Keith? Your husband and your son, how do you carve yourself up so you can be with both of them at the same time?

This is the anatomy of worry: becoming extremely irrational, very quickly, playing scenario after scenario out until the normal option, the probable option, seems fantastical rather than likely.

I'm a qualified clinical psychologist, I know better, I should behave better. But I can't. Not right now. It simply isn't in me. If I prepare for the worst-case scenario, then anything less than that will seem trivial, something I can shrug a shoulder at, can become Zen and stoic about. Besides, I don't use my 'Doctor' title enough according to my parents, and the job of restaurant manager I took to fund my studies somehow became my career.

I check my watch again at the exact same moment that *BUZZZZ* rises up from my bag. *BUZZ-BUZZ-BUZZ*, insists my mobile and I snatch it up, press the 'answer' button and put it to my ear without checking the caller display.

'Come outside,' Keith says. As if he hasn't caused me hours of worry, as if it's the normal way to start a phone call. The relief, however, is incredible. My heart starts beating normally again, my lungs are untwisting themselves, the feeling is returning to my muscles.

'I can't leave Leo,' I say, whispering so Leo won't hear.

'It'll only take a few minutes, come outside.'

I hesitate. *Why does he want me to come outside? Why hasn't he been in? Have I been a bit too hasty in being relieved?*

'Get a nurse to watch him, but come outside.'

He is trying to hide something by forcing his tone to come out even and flat: something is going on.

'Is it important?' I ask, feeling the barrels of the worry lock starting to spin again.

'Life or death,' he replies seriously.

I jerk myself upright, ignoring my vertebrae complaining as they try to click into place, ignoring the book falling off my lap on to my bag with a dull thud, and the blanket pooling over the top of my bag and the book. 'Where are you?'

'By the main entrance.'

I open the door to Leo's hospital room and peek out, looking for a nurse. One, who often sits with Leo when I need a break for food or the loo, is walking past. Melissa is her name. She is curvy and pretty, with a mane of curly red hair she always pins back and a beautiful Welsh accent. Leo would be enchanted by her; he would follow her around with his eyes out on stalks, trying to get her to talk so he could copy her accent. Nurse Melissa arches an eyebrow at me then glances pointedly at the sign with the mobile crossed out on the wall opposite.

'I'll be right there,' I say to Keith, cutting the

line. My heart is already galloping in that familiar, sickening way it does when I fear something bad is about to happen. 'Can you watch Leo for a few minutes?' I ask Melissa. 'My husband needs me.'

Suddenly concerned, she nods as she pulls at her plastic apron and deposits it in the nearest bin. She washes her hands with the gel from the dispenser on the wall, and steps into the room. I set off, walking quickly towards the exit. At the end of the corridor, after a left turn, is the door to that ward. I know this place so well I could navigate it with my eyes shut. Often it feels as if I have, because I rarely sleep for more than two hours when I go home. No one knows this, but I actually use my doctor status to get access to online medical journals and spend most of the hours away from here reading up on comas, haemorrhages and aneurysms. I try to find out as much as I can so I can help Leo. I don't tell Keith what I do because he would tell me I am stressing myself out unnecessarily, I don't tell the doctors because I don't want them to think I am trying to take over, and I don't tell my family because they don't yet know how serious all this is.

I squirt a little antibacterial cleaner on to my left palm, 'wash' the slippery gel over my hands. Out of the door, I'm into the corridor with the lifts and I hit the call button. As I wait for one to arrive, I run through the possible scenarios: someone has crashed into my car in the car park; someone has broken into the café and Amy had forgotten to cash up the day's takings; Keith has been injured on his shift and doesn't want to tell me in front of Leo . . . *Oh, God, what's happened? What else is going to be heaped upon us?*

22

On the first floor, I start running. Down the long corridor, around the corner, down another flight of steps—I cannot wait for another lift—past the security desk and out the main entrance. The heat of the air hits me as I run out into the warm, muggy May night. This is the type of night we've had, in recent years, during September. But tonight it is warm.

And it is snowing.

Over the small whir of an engine and through the warmth of the air, it is snowing. In May, it is snowing. Small flakes of it fall from the sky, covering the world around me in a thin film of white. I stop, stand still and watch the snowflakes dance around me in the warm breeze. It's a miracle. A pure, momentary miracle.

I love snow. The way it makes everything it touches seem softer. There are no sharp edges when snow has fallen; everything is smooth and soft. A road is not long and difficult, but velvety and inviting, as short as you want it to be. I hate the cold, I love snow. And now, I have it all: snow, without the cold. I stick out my hands, trying to catch the snowflakes. I spin in delight as I tip my head up to gaze at the sky, which is not just lit by orange street lights, but illuminated by the pin-pricks of stars, by the glittering of falling snowflakes.

The snow is warm on my skin, it doesn't melt on contact, it sticks to my hands, my oversized, chunky-knit cream cardigan, my navy-blue jeans and my black hair.

'Happy anniversary,' Keith says, stepping out from the shadows beside the entrance to the hospital. He's been standing there, observing me.

He walks towards me while I still watch the white flakes land on me and blanket the ground, making it soft and gentle. Transforming it from the hard path I have to walk up every day to see my son into something soothing.

'You did this?' I ask him as he comes closer, until he can encompass me in his strong, muscled arms. Suddenly I am caught up in him, protected and safe. 'For me?'

He nods. 'Happy anniversary,' he whispers against my hair.

Anniversary? As a couple, Keith and I have more than our fair share of anniversaries. We met when I was nineteen and I applied for a job in the bar he managed in Oxford city centre. He was nearly ten years older than me and didn't look twice at me, of course. Two years later, days after my twenty-first birthday, when I no longer even worked in the bar, he called me up and asked me out. 'I had to wait until you'd completely cleared your teens before I could come near you,' he explained. We had two first dates. On the first first date I was so nervous I self-medicated with a little too much Dutch courage and passed out in the front seat of Keith's car before we got to the end of the road, and he had to carry me back to my shared house and hand me over to my flatmates. The second first date, which I had been surprised had happened, was a week later and I didn't drink at all. Then there were other notable dates for our diaries: when we split up for the first time because I thought he was too old for me; when we got back together; when we split up again after five months before his need for commitment made me break up with him again. We got back together and split up many

24

times over the years, until the last time he left me, eight years ago. And then three years ago we got back together for the final time, and two more memorable dates were created: the day he moved in with Leo and me, and the day we got married. I have a memory for dates, and I know, across the spread of the twelve months that make up a year, none of the dates worth remembering fall in May.

'It's not our anniversary,' I say.

'Not our wedding anniversary, no,' he agrees.

'It's not our anniversary,' I reassure him. 'I'd remember.'

One of his hands moves down to cup my left bum cheek, and he yanks me closer to him as he places his lips against my ear, his warm, fragrant breath tickling my cheek and my neck. 'It's the anniversary of our first fuck.' He draws out the last word, somehow making it seductive and dirty, romantic and loving all at the same time.

'Of all our anniversaries to choose from, this is the one you thought needed such public celebration?' I say, laughing.

'It's a reminder that miracles do happen to the same person twice.'

'You'd better mean that it's a miracle that I slept with you rather than the other way around, or you're in trouble, mate.'

'But of course,' he says, squeezing my bum again.

I smile at him. 'I can't believe you did all this for me.'

'Who else would I do this for?' He drops a kiss on my forehead. 'I, of course, have to thank my supporting cast—Peter, who actually got out of bed to open his shop so that I could hire the snow

25

machine; the security guard who went up to a higher level to work said snow machine; and, of course, you for reacting so perfectly.'

'Thank you,' I say to him. 'No one has ever given me a miracle before.'

At that moment, if there was anything I could wish for it was a miracle. A miracle that would bring Leo round, a miracle that would return my life to how it was. It didn't have to be a divine miracle that brought Leo back to me, it could be a human-created one. The dreams are settling into my sleep at a rate now of one a day, always moving him a little further and further away from me; a miracle is exactly what I need.

'Lucks,' Keith says gently, holding me closer. I only vaguely hear him calling me, using the name he gave me when we first met in the bar (Nova . . . exploding star . . . lucky star . . . Lucks).

'Lucks,' he repeats more urgently. 'Stop it, please. Stop thinking about it for the next two minutes. After that, we'll go back and deal with it. We'll go back to all that. But right now, just be here with me in this moment, and enjoy the snow. OK?'

Two minutes.

Two minutes is a lifetime. Every second Leo is asleep is a lifetime. Is like living a hundred and twenty lives without having a heart beating in my chest or blood running through my veins.

Two minutes is the blink of an eye. Is the time in which everything can change. He could wake up in those two minutes. He could take thirty seconds to come back, and then spend a minute and a half wondering why I am not there to welcome him back, like I promised him I would be before he

26

went to sleep. Keith isn't asking for two minutes, he is asking for a lifetime and for a nanosecond; he is asking for the whole of space and time. He's made it snow for me, now all I have to do is give him back the whole of space and time.

'OK?' he repeats. 'Two minutes. For me. For us. Let's just enjoy the snow, enjoy these two minutes of our anniversary, and then once we've done that, we'll be stronger. We'll find it easier to go back there. OK?'

My gaze goes to his face, and for the first time since we started this life I see my husband. He is a relative stranger. His black eyes, his wide nose, his full lips, his mahogany-brown skin are all alien to me. I'm probably a stranger to him as well because the seams of our relationship are being unpicked.

I know that couples are often split by the loss of a child, but I didn't realise until this that an illness can divide you as well, much more slowly, much more insidiously but just as decisively. For better or worse, we vowed, but we didn't realise it was for powerlessness as well. We deal with problems in different ways, Keith and I. He needs to divide up the time to deal with a crisis. To deal with Leo being in suspended animation, he needs to step away, recharge himself, and then he can head back into battle, he can face and fight whatever is thrown at him. I have to immerse myself in it. To make it all I think about all the time, to keep wishing and hoping and wanting it to be OK because I know it is in the moment I don't that something awful will happen.

That is why we are coming apart. Our two coping mechanisms are incompatible, so while we're aware of the other's pain, we do little more

27

than acknowledge it. That is why, seam by seam, stitch by stitch, the fabric of us is being undone. And that is why Keith has made it snow for me. He wants me to try it his way, to see if it can possibly work for me, and if we can stop what is happening to us.

I nod. 'OK,' I say, smiling at him. 'OK.'

Two minutes. I can give him that. It might work. It might save us. After all, it's only two minutes to stand and enjoy the May snow.

He watched her, her head looking down at the book when she should be looking at the TV.

She was being naughty. She was being a naughty girl. Mummy put on Bob the Builder, *now she had to watch it, too. He was happy in his room, drawing on the wall with the big pen, but she picked him up and sat him on the sofa beside her and put* Bob the Builder *on the TV. He didn't like* Bob the Builder *all the every time, but Mummy did, she put it on all the every time, so she had to watch it.*

'Mummy, no book, watch Bob the Builder,*' he told her.*

She looked at him. 'Pardon?' she asked.

He pushed the book away. 'No book, watch Bob the Builder.*'*

'I just want to finish this chap—' She stopped talking because he was looking at her. 'OK. I'll watch Bob the Builder.*' She put down the book and turned towards the TV.*

He patted her leg. 'Good girl, Mummy. Good girl.'

Leo, age 2 years and 6 months
28

CHAPTER FOUR

I really need a cigarette.

More than anything in the world right now, I need a cigarette. It will help to turn the temperature down on my blood, which is hovering somewhere around boiling point. And the smoke will erect a physical barrier between Mal and me, although the current mental one that separates us in the car is amazingly effective. I'm not sure who isn't talking to who, who is more angry with who, but it's clear: we are not talking. It's been fifteen minutes since we left the dinner party and so far the drive has been in total silence. Even the purr of the engine, our breathing, the little clicks and ticks that make up the sound of our car have been smothered by the anger that has created the silence. We have at least another fifteen minutes to go until we get home, and we are not going to be talking for the entire drive. That's a promise.

The worst part—the part that slides into the space between my ribs and jabs at my core like a blunt knife trying to find a partially healed wound to reopen—is that he thinks he's done nothing wrong. He seriously thinks he's done nothing wrong.

I glance sideways at him. His jaw is set, his teeth are gritted, his russet eyes have darkened and stay fixed on the road ahead. His body is a straight, rigid line that could have been carved from rock, and his hands are almost bone-white from how hard he grips the steering wheel. Every time he changes gear, I expect him to wrench the stick out of its socket.

He showed us up in front of all those people and *he* is angry.

I really *need* a cigarette.

I call them up in my mind: hidden in the pack of Tampax under the sink in the bathroom, waiting for me to light them up and suck them down. Waiting to do their duty and hug me on the inside. Mal doesn't know I smoke anything more than the odd one or two in social situations, or to keep my boss company during working hours. He doesn't know that every three or four days I have to buy a new pack of twenty, that there's a crystal ashtray hidden in the bushes outside the house, and that I use breath freshener to hide the evidence. And he *certainly* doesn't have the slightest inkling that those cigarettes are probably the only things that are going to stop me taking an axe to his head tonight.

*   *   *

'So, Steph, Mal, when are you two going to have kids?' Vince asked us.

We'd all settled down to dinner and had, for the most part, been enduring Vince's brand of party entertainment—picking on people—with relative good humour, because he was the co-host (his wife Carole, who is lovely, had invited us), and this was what Vince did. He didn't mean anything by it, he was just a moderately belligerent drunk. Even at his most obnoxious he usually stayed away from this subject with us, though. Just like no one mentioned the war, no one mentioned our childlessness. From the way the room stilled after he spoke, the way a few heads dipped to stare at their plates while a few more tried to master a look of vague interest, I knew instantly they had all been talking about this before Mal and I arrived.

That was always the danger of turning up last at a gathering of friends, they talked about you. Discussed and dissected your life, relationship, looks, and decided they knew everything about everything. They knew where you were going wrong, what you could do to work it out, how you could fix the chasms in your life. They'd obviously discussed Mal and me and decided what was missing in our lives was a baby. Ten years of marriage meant nothing, as far as they were concerned, because we did not have a child.

They knew me better than they knew Mal, they knew how I loved to be around children, so they decided that our childlessness was Mal's doing. And what they, as my friends, could do about it was to publicly shame Mal into doing the right thing: show him that they could all see my baby pain and he should ease it.

None of them knew the truth of it. Not even Mal. But I didn't think about that. I couldn't think about that. If I did, then . . . Mal didn't know. Mal could never know. Neither could any of them.

My eyes darted to Carole—she was one of the head-dippers. She did that a lot where her husband was concerned: he opened his mouth, she cringed and dipped her head, wanting nothing more than for him to stem the stream of outrageous offensiveness that was no doubt flowing from his lips. Ruth was struggling and failing to look mildly interested as she looked at me, her lips curled together in a supportive smile. Opposite Ruth,

Graeme, her husband, was sipping on his wine and openly watching Mal. Dyan was another head-dipper—even though I couldn't see her face, I knew her cheeks were red with embarrassment. She hated this type of questioning that Vince subjected us to. She and Dan, her husband, had got together at college in our final year. Dan and Vince were best friends, so he was backing Vince up by leaning forwards and staring at me. Julian was another head-dipper, although his head was dipped probably because he listened more than he watched. He studied the intonation of people's voices, the words they emphasised and those they flitted over. His girlfriend, Frankie, was smiling benignly at everyone. 'Vacant' was the word we most used about her. We couldn't understand why ultra-intelligent, slightly superior Julian had been with her for six years. Although, at that moment, I could see the spark of interest in her eye. She was twirling a long lock of her black hair around her finger, as usual, but she was definitely in the room, following what was going on. They must have been talking about this for a long time before our arrival to get even her to pay attention. And finally Nicole and Jeremy—the fifth couple—both looking vaguely interested, were waiting eagerly to see what either of us would say.

I hadn't been on the receiving end of a Vince interrogation for months. Mainly because I was usually the first to arrive at these things so no one had the chance to properly discuss me. Us. Unfortunately, hiding from those women in the toilets had taken away precious time. Also, Vince and I had a history that meant I knew more about him than most people at the table. If he got out of hand, I could stop him with a look. A reminder that I knew things about him that he didn't want shared around. Things that not even Dan knew.

I lowered my eyes to my plate, stared at my dinner, wondering how to react. Too defensive and they would assume it was a subject to pursue. Too casual and they would think that I was faking it. I had to pitch my reply just right.

Raising my gaze to Vince, I shrugged a little, smiled a little more. 'I don't know. Maybe never,' I said, my voice skimming on the serious side of glib.

'But you'd be such a great mum,' Carole gushed. 'I can't imagine you not ever having kids, you're wonderful with our two.'

The corners of my mouth edged up into a bigger smile, I couldn't help it. It was a such a compliment. 'Thank you,' I cooed. 'That's such a lovely thing to say. They are wonderful kids, though.'

'They *adore* you. They're always wanting to see their Aunty Steph. That's why . . . Well, you'd be a great mum.'

'Thank you,' I said again, still glowing from the compliment. A second or two later, I felt rather than saw Mal's body stiffen across the table. Everyone not privy to my thoughts probably assumed I was grinning about the idea of me being a great mother, they did not realise that I collected compliments like other people collected oxygen molecules to breathe. I craved external validation of my self-worth. It soothed a deep part of me like very little else could. However, to anyone outside of my mind, it must have seemed that I was desperate to have a baby, I was desperate to become a mother. And Mal . . . Mal obviously thought I was basking in this, that I was so caught up in the idea of parenthood that I'd forgotten what happened eight years ago.

I had to stop this. I had to change the conversation otherwise it would become explosive. Mal's explosion would be quiet, subdued, but destructive. He wouldn't shout, he wouldn't rant and rave, he would do something far worse: he would get up and leave.

He would not say anything to anyone, he would simply get up, go outside and wait in the car for me. He'd done it several times before, and I couldn't bear it if he did it tonight. It made people think he was some sort of uncouth brute who couldn't express himself. It made our friends think they had to worry about me and that maybe, just maybe, he might one day hurt me. Physically. He never would. I knew that, but none of those at the table did.

'You haven't answered the question, Stephie, dear, when are we going to hear the patter of little Wacken feet?' Vince pressed. 'How long are we going to have to wait?'

All eyes were on me by then; even the head-dippers were focused on me.

I'd known most of these people since we were eighteen or nineteen, but we were not close. The reason we had all got on for so many years was because our friendships were impressively shallow. We enjoyed our time together, but I wouldn't call any of the people sitting around the table during a crisis. After the crisis had passed, to tell them what could be a then-funny anecdote, yes. *During*, when one of them had to take charge and offer comfort, never.

34

I opened my mouth to repeat that we'd maybe never have children, to put a firmness into the words that would shut Vince up and would tell the rest of them that they had to end this interrogation.

'You can hear the patter of tiny Wacken feet whenever you want,' Mal said for me. 'I've already got a child.'

Everyone at the table drew back, a couple of people gasped quietly. Internally, I gasped, too. Out of everyone there, I was most jolted: I *never* thought he'd say that.

'A son,' Mal continued, seemingly oblivious to the horror he had unleashed. Even Vince, cocky, mouthy Vince, was stunned to silence.

Carole found her voice first. 'Was this from a previous relationship?' she asked, keeping her shock in check. She raised her hand, brushed a brown lock from her face as she looked to Mal for his answer. A tremulous silence settled as everyone looked to him for an answer. *Lie*, I pleaded telepathically with him across the table. *Please lie. For me, lie.*

'He's coming up to eight,' Mal said. 'He's called Leo, in case you're interested. He's got black hair, brown eyes. He likes the green Teen League Fighter superhero the best and he plays *Star Wars* on the PlayStation all the time.' Was that pride in his voice? He was proud. *Proud*. He hadn't told me these trivial details and we had agreed . . . Now, he was revealing unknown secrets to our friends. And he was *proud*.

All eyes shifted back to me. Truly horrified as they were. My husband had cheated on me, had impregnated another woman while cheating and was so unabashed about it. Even vacant Frankie was agog: her eyes wide and incredulous, her mouth hanging open as her gaze swung between Mal and me, trying to work out who to stare at.

I gathered my senses together, inhaled and exhaled a few times before I attempted to speak. 'It's not as simple as Mal is making out.' I began the damage limitation process. 'Someone very close to us desperately wanted a baby. It was heartbreaking. Mal loved her so much he'd do anything for her. And he agreed to father her child.' The absolute truth.

Mal stared at me across the table. His eyes were a piercing glare, slicing me open, cutting me apart, trying to expose the way I was lying without lying.

'Do you still see the child and mother?' Frankie asked. Frankie, who would previously have been smiling benignly and playing with her hair, was fully engaged and asking questions.

Mal's glare intensified, I could feel it on my skin so I didn't look at him. He was daring me to misdirect my way out of that question. He was accusing me, too. Accusing me because we both knew I was guilty. Of course I was.

'No,' I said. 'She moved away before the baby was born. Went to live on the coast, rarely comes to London. We never see them.'

His chair made no sound as he pushed it back. He made no sound as he dropped his cream napkin on his half eaten meal. Poor Carole had probably spent hours handmaking the pastry for the salmon en croute, scrubbing the new potatoes, baking the goat's cheese and chilli-topped vegetables. And Mal had hardly touched it. Mal made no sound as he left the dining room. The only sound from his exit was the click of the front door as it shut behind him.

I stared down at my plate, tears collecting at the corners of my eyes, a lump bulging in my throat. I had hardly touched my food, either, and it all looked so beautiful. So delicious. And I could not even think of eating another crumb. In the candlelight and the shocked hush, everyone was watching me. Everyone was watching me and I was so ashamed. About now. About then.

I pushed out my chair, told Carole I would call her in the morning, told everyone it was good to see them, and left. And for the second time in less than six hours, I had to leave a room, knowing that the second the door shut behind me, people would be talking about me.

*   *   *

Mal marches into the house without so much as a backward glance. After slamming the door I run up the stairs straight to the bathroom. I clatter open the bathroom window, get a cigarette and then empty my bag on the tiled floor to find my lighter. I suck the life out of a cigarette, leaning out of the window to let the evidence escape. I draw the innards out of a second cigarette in four or five inhalations, too. After I am done, after I am calmer, I wrap the ends in a wad of toilet roll and flush the telltale signs that I am a liar. It's only a little lie, one of action not words, and it's necessary because now I can talk to him without shouting.

He isn't in the living room, sprawled on the sofa, angrily flicking through TV stations, as I thought he might be. He isn't in the dining room, rummaging through our CD collection, looking for something loud and thrashy he can play at full volume to rile the neighbours and hurt my ears. He is in the dark kitchen, standing in front of the open fridge door so he is illuminated by its light, chugging down a beer as though it is water.

'I can't believe you did that,' I say to Mal.

The last of the pale gold liquid slides out of the clear glass bottle and down my husband's throat. He slams the bottle back on to the shelf in the fridge, hard enough to crack the bottle or the shelf, and reaches for the next beer, twists off the top, flicks the top back into the fridge, puts the glass lip of the bottle to his mouth, starts to gulp. It's him ignoring me. In the car, I thought I had been ignoring him right back, but now it is obvious that it's definitely this way around.

'Don't you dare ignore me, Mal Wacken. I'm not the one in the wrong here.'

He halts as he tips the bottle to his lips, lowers it and turns to me for the first time. His hooded eyes settle on me but are focused somewhere inside my head, as though he is trying to ransack my mind for information on what makes me tick.

'I did nothing wrong,' he states. 'I simply told the truth.'

'We agreed—'

'We agreed I wouldn't have any contact,' Mal cuts in. 'That's all we agreed. We didn't say I wasn't to talk about them. Him.'

He is right, of course. Just because we don't talk about it, about her, about him, about them, I have assumed that he wouldn't talk about it at all. To anyone. Not to his mother (who he must have been getting all that information from), to his friends, to his work colleagues, to our friends. The world might know all about Mal's son and I would be none the wiser. 'But you didn't have to do that,' I insist.

'Don't you ever feel guilty, Steph?' he asks suddenly, the tone of his voice dropping to a low level that makes his words reverberate through me, like a low bass on a speaker moving sound through a body. 'Don't you walk around with a huge anvil of guilt sitting just there?' He presses his beer to the area over his heart. A million times he has silently and vocally asked me that, and every time the same thought flies through my mind: you have no idea how it feels to be me. To feel so guilty all the time that you aren't sure where you begin and the guilt ends. 'I never forced you to do anything,' I reply, deliberately avoiding the question. My guilt is not like an anvil, it is a small, determined, lethal parasite that has gnawed its way through my mind, my body, my heart, my spirit. My guilt has hollowed me out and left me dead inside.

'I know. It was my choice.' He clutches the bottle over his heart, a brand of his guilt as well as that anvil. 'And I'd make the same choice again. I'd always make that choice.'

I move across the room to him, all anger gone. I wrap my arms around him, the bottle, his symbol of remorse, still between us, separating our hearts.

'There's something I meant to say to you earlier,' I tell him, trying to bridge the gap.

'Yeah?' he asks, still clutching the bottle between us.

'It's a little weird that we both forgot,' I said.

'Forgot what?'

'It's our anniversary.'

39

He closes his eyes, exhales deeply. 'I did forget. With work and everything . . . I'm sorry.'

'I forgot, too,' I remind him. 'If I hadn't, we wouldn't have gone to dinner with a lot of other people tonight. I only remembered as we sat down to eat.' I lower one of my arms, and with my hand I find the space on his body reserved just for me, that only I am allowed to touch in this way. 'We could always make it up to each other.' I flatten my hand more firmly against him, but there is no response, his body hasn't replied that he wants what I am doing to him. I continue talking, keeping my voice low, a suggestive smile on my lips—if I can get him to respond it will be fine. We'll be fine again. 'You know how good we are at making things up to each other.' Nothing. Absolutely nothing from his body. Absolutely nothing from his face: his eyes stare blankly down at me, as though I am a person he does not recognise, as though I am speaking a language he does not understand nor wants to learn. My fingers find his zip and slowly draw it open. He shifts away from me then. Only a fraction, but it tells me his answer very clearly: no.

'I forgot,' he repeats, fumbling with his free hand to redo his zip.

'Happy anniversary, Mal,' I say, and with a strength I didn't know I possessed, I keep the tremble of tears out of my voice and off my face.

'Steph, happy anniversary.' His lips are brief and distanced as he touches something approximating a kiss on my forehead. He carefully untangles himself from me and leaves me to stand rejected and humiliated in the darkened kitchen.

My fingers curl into my hands, my nails dig into my palms and I close my eyes to stop the panic.

Breathe. All I have to do is stand here and breathe. It will be fine, it will be OK if I can breathe.

I know he means it. I know he means it when he says he'd make the same choice again. Between Nova, his oldest friend, and me, he would choose me. Between his son and me, Mal would choose me. Always, he'd choose me.

I know this. But I also know that at no point in the last eight years has Mal said he doesn't regret the choice he made with every bit of his guilt-heavy heart.

'Why you crying?'

Mummy was sitting on the sofa with her head in her hands and she was crying. She was crying and crying and crying. She looked up at him and she had a wet face, and funny eyes and she kept crying.

'Why you crying?' he asked.

'Because I'm tired, Leo. I'm really, really tired. The house is a mess, and I don't know where to start. Amy's on holiday for another week, so I have to run the café on my own because that girl who was covering for her kept stealing from the till. I'm scared to close my eyes and go to sleep at night because you keep climbing out of your cot and I'm terrified that if you're not turning on the gas downstairs, you're going to work out how to unhook the chain and then you'll disappear out the front door. And I'm sick of doing this on my own. I'm sick of having no one to talk to, no one to rely on, of having to be everything all the time. That's why I'm crying, Leo, I'm tired.'

He stared at her. Poor Mummy. From the box on the table, he pulled out a tissue. He put it on her arm

41

*and held it there, like she did to him when he had a
bump and he cried. He held it and held it and then he
took it away and kissed her arm.*

'All better,' he said. 'No cry any more. All better.'

'I suppose it has to be, doesn't it?' Mummy said.

He nodded at her. All better now.

Leo, age 3 years

CHAPTER FIVE

'He's been good as gold,' Nurse Melissa says as we
return to Leo's hospital room.

She has switched on the lights and is thumbing
through my book—*Methods in Experimental
Psychology.* I wonder for a moment if she finds it
interesting or if, as is most likely, she thinks it's
dull.

'Thanks, Melissa,' I reply, until I realise she is
looking at, and talking to—in fact, completely
focused on—Keith. I roll my eyes as I take my seat
and start to examine Leo for any signs—no matter
how small—of change. I often wonder if Nurse
Melissa is so eager to watch over Leo because she
fancies my husband. A disproportionate number of
women do, Nurse Melissa is simply a shade more
unsubtle than most.

Over the years, I've watched otherwise sane,
rational and professional women lose their minds
and, frankly, their self-respect around Keith—it
happens all the time, in shops, in banks, in
restaurants, at airports, in this hospital. It's his
looks, his height, his job, his persona, and his

presence. He is like a fantasy. Even if you didn't know he had once been in the Army, you only have to look at him to know he's the type of guy who would take a bullet for one of his men in battle, and would go on to lead a group of villagers to safety by putting himself between them and life-threatening danger. You spoke to him and his voice would turn your knees to mush, he smiled at you and you felt like the most beautiful woman in the world. He might not be someone you would normally fancy on paper, but in the flesh he would make you turn a little bit silly. I know, because that's exactly how I felt about him when I first worked with him at the bar. I had a huge crush but I got over it. Then two years later he asked me out. And the fantasy became an altogether different reality.

The first time I'd seen him naked, the anniversary we'd just been 'celebrating', I had become frozen. His body had been carved from the most perfect block of dark mahogany, every line of him smooth and unblemished. I'd lost my nerve at that point, and my eyes started scanning the room for the clothes I'd already shed, as I decided *not* to take anything else off. I couldn't, I just couldn't. Not when he looked like that, like a Michelangelo statue, and I was ordinary and, up until that moment, more than happy with myself. He'd taken my wrist and, gently but firmly, had placed the flat of my hand just left of the centre of his bare chest, held it there. I'd immediately felt the rhythm of his heart: strong, steady, fast. Incredibly fast. 'You're the only person who's ever been able to make my heart beat that fast without trying,' he'd said. 'Do you understand now why I love you?' In his dark

43

eyes, in his smooth voice, rang sincerity. Plain, simple, honest. I'd smiled, he'd grinned back and the big dipper feeling that swelled and plummeted inside me told me I was going to fall in love with him. I wasn't then, not like he was with me, but it would happen. It would absolutely happen.

'You've arrived quite late,' Melissa says to Keith. I don't have to look at her to know she's probably twirling a lock of hair around her fingers, sticking out her chest, just-so to sit in his line of sight, while she simpers up at him from under her eyelashes.

'I suppose I have,' Keith replies. 'I didn't really notice the time.'

I have no real need to be bothered by the women who flirt with my husband, even if I was the jealous type. He's aware of their attention—he's a man, after all—but he isn't interested. In his post-Army, bar manager days, he slept with any woman who looked in his direction and had no shame about it. He was like a sugar addict let loose in a world full of every variety of cake and he did not restrain himself. He sampled, devoured, indulged in—basically gorged himself on—every crumb that came his way, so by the time we went on our first first date, he had decided he wanted steady, filling, home cooking. He had lost his taste for sugary, empty goodies and was ready to settle down, get married and have children. Even though I wasn't, he was very open about being willing to wait for me to catch him up.

During the breaks in our relationship, I expected him to go back to his old ways but he never did. And that was why he never flirted with any of these women: he really had lost his appetite for cake.

44

'Did you just come off shift?' Melissa asks him.

'Yeah,' Keith mumbles uncomfortably. Keith doesn't talk about his work—not even to me. I know he works in the police force and that he sometimes wears a uniform and walks the beat. I also know he, more often than not, doesn't walk the beat. Once a year, I don my finery and accompany him to the annual police ball, which is held up in London. But I couldn't tell anyone his job title, I couldn't give even a basic answer to what he does on a day-to-day basis. He leaves work behind when he leaves work. He refuses to carry the weight of what he has seen and experienced with him into our lives. (It's this secretiveness that makes Leo think he's a spy.)

'Do you think Leo will want to be a policeman when he grows up?' Melissa asks. 'Take after his father in more ways than one?'

There is a puzzled pause from Keith. 'Leo's my stepson, you know that, right?' Keith asks her, his tone serious and slightly concerned. 'He might act like me sometimes, but he doesn't take after me. Not genetically.' I feel him look from her to me. 'I'm right, aren't I, Lucks, he doesn't take after me?'

'Apart from the PlayStation obsession and the fascination with farts and fart jokes, no, he doesn't take after you,' I supply without looking away from Leo.

'If anyone, he's more like you, and your dad, isn't he?' Keith says to me.

He's more like his father, I think as I say, 'I suppose.'

'Nova would never go into the army or join the police, can't see her father ever doing that either,

45

so I doubt Leo would join the police because he's not like me.' My husband, steadfast and practical and romantic, is oblivious to the fact that Nurse Melissa obviously wishes the ground below her feet would open up and swallow her.

Any irritation I feel towards her is replaced with pity, because I know what's coming: a riveting lecture on Keith's theories about the types of people who feel compelled by their personality to serve their country and society, as opposed to those who find themselves forced into those jobs. I've heard the theory several times, but that's what I get for living with the fantasy—along with his inability to watch a soap without judging the characters because they are flawed and he has a strong sense of right and wrong that he cannot suspend even to watch fiction; him dismissing my strong belief in the esoteric world; and him secretly believing I should be responsible for the housework because I'm a woman. Even though Nurse Melissa has been flirting with my husband, right in front of me, I decide to rescue her. No one deserves the lecture if they're not at least going to get a shag out of him. 'Thanks, Melissa, for staying with Leo,' I cut in, 'we'll see you later.'

'Oh, yes, yes, see you later,' she says eagerly and dashes out of the room.

Keith takes his seat on the opposite side of Leo's bed. We always sit in the same places, even when the other one isn't here; we wouldn't dream of sitting in the other's seat, just like at home we wouldn't sleep on the other's side of the bed. It would feel like an invasion, trespassing on someone else's sacred space.

'Does he take after him?' Keith asks, tearing his

eyes away from our boy to focus on me. 'Does he take after his father?'

He's never asked me this before, and it's not something we ever talk about. When we got back together for the final time after the break-up of five years, I told him that I had a son and that he was four years old. Keith knew immediately whose son he was. It had been the reason he left me that last time: when I told him what I was going to do, Keith had thrown in the towel. It was not something he could understand, and he couldn't watch me carry a child only to give it away, so he left me.

'Yeah,' I say to Keith, 'I suppose he does.'

He never questioned why I ended up with the child when we got back together. He assumed that keeping Leo was a choice I made; that I had come to my senses and realised what he suspected about all women who agreed to have a baby for someone else: that you could never live with yourself afterwards; the guilt and the loss would be too much so you would almost always choose to keep the baby. I never felt compelled enough to enlighten him as to what really happened.

Keith shrugs. 'I suppose that's no bad thing,' he says. 'Leo could do worse than take after him. He's a good man.'

I nod. *You can believe that*, I think at Keith, *because you don't know what he did.*

They're ready for launch.

He was sitting in his special seat, so he could see everything.

Moving forwards, slowly. Three . . . two . . . one!

The water splashed all over their subm'ine. Everywhere! It was all over them, all around them. They were underwater and they both cheered as it happened.

Crash! Captain Leo jumped as a big wave hit the top of their subm'ine. They both cheered again.

'Go forwards!' Captain Leo shouted, as another big white foam wave hit them.

'Aye, aye, Cap'n,' she shouted back. 'Going forwards.'

'Dive!' Captain Leo shouted over the sound of the water. 'Dive! We need to dive!'

'I cannae change the laws of physics, Cap'n,' she said.

'You can!' Captain Leo replied. 'Dive!'

'OK, here we go . . .' she said. 'Three . . . . two . . . one!'

They both screamed as more water splashed over them, and then they laughed. And screamed. And laughed. And screamed. Even as they came out of the water, and then they were being dried off, they continued to laugh and scream. And at the end, they were free. They were on dry land again and their subm'ine could work on the ground. And he wasn't a captain, and she didn't have a silly voice.

'Can we go again?' he asked her.

'No, sweetheart. We can go again next week.'

'OK,' he said, staring out of the window at the other people who wanted to go play subm'ines as

well. None of theirs was as good as theirs. And no one was as good a captain as he was. Ever.

Leo, age 4 years

part two

CHAPTER SIX

I hate leaving him.

Every night, when Keith can convince me to go home and get some sleep, I always linger over his bed, saying goodnight, looking for change, wondering if I should stay a little bit longer. But I need to be there during the day, and sleeping on the bed that folds down from one of the panels in the wall of his hospital room is not viable every night. Every night, when I kiss him goodnight and wish silently for him to wake up, I leave the hospital with a deep, throbbing ache in the centre of my soul that only Leo can soothe by getting better.

I sit in my car in the dark, partially empty car park, with the doors locked—Keith would murder me himself if he thought I didn't first check the car was empty before I got in and didn't immediately lock the doors—but I don't reach for the ignition. I leave my keys in my lap and rest my forehead on the padded leather steering wheel.

I want to call him.

I want to pick up the phone and call him.

He most likely won't be awake, he most likely won't be alone, and he most likely won't answer my call, but I want to call him. I want to hear his voice, I want to slip into that warm comfortable place in the world where I used to fit, where he used to talk to me and the most confusing things would suddenly make sense.

Even now, after all this time, I want to call him. Tell him what's happened, tell him about the dreams, and tell him without having to tell him that he has to make everything all right. Even now, after everything, Mal, Leo's father, is the one person I want to be with. When I should theoretically hate him, most of the time, all I can do is miss him. I hate myself for it sometimes.

*   *   *

Today's the day Malvolio's daddy is coming home. For real.

My mummy said that he had been working far, far away from home and that was why we had never seen him in real, proper life. Malvolio's mummy, Aunty Merry, had lots of pictures and we looked at them all the time. Sometimes Malvolio looked like his daddy when Malvolio frowned really hard.

My mummy told me Malvolio's daddy had seen us both when we were little babies and just borned—he came to the hospital and had a look at us. There's a picture of Malvolio's daddy holding him and looking at Malvolio instead of at the camera like everyone else did in photos. Right behind him there was a man with a hat and clothes like a policeman who looked very cross and had a big moustache that covered the whole of his top lip. When I asked who that was, Aunty Merry started crying and Mummy said it was a friend of Uncle Victor's. I didn't understand why that made Aunty Merry cry, but I think it was because she didn't like Uncle Victor having friends who weren't her friend as well.

My mummy said it was five years ago that Malvolio's daddy had seen us.

54

I was allowed to wear my special church dress. It was red with a white collar and buttons all the way up to the top at the back. And I had white socks that Mummy kept telling me to pull up—it wasn't my fault they kept falling down—and my favourite black, shiny church shoes. Mummy had plaited my hair into four, which was my favourite, and told me not to mess it up. Uncle Victor probably didn't like children to look messy. Cordelia was only two but she had the same dress as me but hers was blue. She was sitting on the floor by the table that we had put in Aunty Merry's front room and she was playing with Malvolio's favourite car. He didn't mind. He let Cordelia play with all his toys because he said she was only a little baby and it didn't matter. 'Not baby!' Cordelia always said. 'Big girl.'

Malvolio was wearing his church suit, which was dark blue and had a white shirt and red tie that looked like two triangles with the points stuck together. He looked *hasome*, Mummy said when he came down earlier. Just like a little man. Aunty Merry had put special stuff on his hair and combed it so it looked like his daddy's.

Mummy and Daddy and Aunty Merry were all wearing their church clothes, too. And my mummy made lots and lots of food for Uncle Victor. I helped. I put *ray-suns* in the bowl so Mummy could make her big, big, big hot cross buns. And I put the *new-meg* in the cake so it would taste like Mummy's cake. It was her secret she told me. All the food was all on the big table in the front room, and there was a white tablecloth Mummy had *crow-chayed*. We weren't allowed to have anything, not even cherryade, until Malvolio's daddy came home.

We were all in the front room waiting for Malvolio's daddy to come home. I didn't know the time, but Mummy and Daddy kept looking at each other. I knew they were worried about him. Maybe he missed the bus. Sometimes when my daddy's car wouldn't work properly he had to catch the bus and he was cross when he missed it because it made him late for his work. Malvolio was sitting next to his mummy and she kept kissing his hand and saying, 'My beautiful boy,' and looking out the window to see if Uncle Victor was coming.

I kept looking at the sandwiches. I wanted one. Mummy put Sandwich Spread on them. That was my favourite. I was so hungry. I moved closer to the table. I could take a bite from one of the sandwiches and put it back. Mummy and Daddy and Aunty Merry wouldn't see. I stood next to the table and slowly put my hand near the sandwiches. I was going to get a bite really soon. My mouth was all wet inside. I pulled the sandwich off the plate, and pulled it towards me. I would only take one bite. Then I would put it back. Just one bite. I licked my lips as I lifted the sandwich to my mouth.

'NOVA!' Mummy shouted. 'What are you doing?!'

I was so scared I dropped the sandwich. My eyes were really wide as I looked at Mummy. She was frowning at me. I was in so much trouble. I would probably have to go home and go straight to bed. Or face the wall in the corridor. Daddy was frowning at me too. Aunty Merry was looking at me but she wasn't frowning. Malvolio looked scared like me. He knew how much trouble I was in. It wasn't my fault, I was hungry.

The front door closed really loud. We all looked

at the door and Uncle Victor was there. He was really, really tall. Taller than my daddy. But he didn't look like he did in the photos. He was much skinnier, as skinny as a rake, Mummy said about people who looked like him. Tall and skinny as a rake. He had lots of lines on his face and he had a beard. It was dark and it was thick and all round his mouth and cheeks and chin. His hair wasn't combed like Malvolio's was now, it was like Malvolio's usually was—all messy. 'Like he's been dragged through a bush, backwards,' Mummy said when she was combing the twigs and leaves out of Malvolio's hair.

Uncle Victor looked at me and I smiled and waved. He looked at Mummy. He looked at Daddy. He looked at Cordelia for a bit longer, because she was new. Then he looked at Aunty Merry for even longer. He looked longest at Malvolio. He looked and looked and looked at Malvolio. My daddy looked at his Pools coupon like that. When he said if he had written down the numbers properly, he had won ten pounds. My daddy would look happy but then wasn't sure if he should be happy in case he had written the numbers down wrong when the man on the television had been saying them. That's how Uncle Victor looked at Malvolio: like he was happy but he was not sure if he should be yet.

'I need a bath,' Uncle Victor said and then went up the stairs. Nobody was talking or anything while Uncle Victor was having his bath upstairs. It was very quiet for a long, long time. Then he came downstairs again. He was wearing different clothes. He had a big thick blue jumper on, and he had tucked it into his black trousers. His black trousers looked like ones he would normally wear to church. I didn't know if Uncle Victor ever went to church. His hair was combed like it was in the pictures and he had no beard any more. He looked like the man in the pictures except old and skinny as a rake.

'Fancy a pint down the pub, Frank?' Uncle Victor said to my daddy. He didn't look at any of us this time, just Daddy.

Daddy looked at Mum, then at Aunty Merry. My daddy never went to pubs. The people at school said their daddies went to pubs and when I asked Mummy why my daddy didn't go to pubs, Mummy said men like my daddy didn't go to pubs; he didn't fit in at pubs.

'OK,' Daddy said. 'I have to stop off at home to pick up my wallet.'

Daddy said goodbye to us, Uncle Victor didn't.

As soon as the door shut behind them, Aunty Merry started crying, really loudly. She jumped up from the sofa and ran out of the room and upstairs, crying and crying, tears all over her face.

'You have to give him time,' Mummy said as she followed Aunty Merry. 'This is all new to him.'

Malvolio kept sitting on the sofa, hitting his feet on the bottom of the sofa, and staring at the carpet. I went and sat next to him. I did the same with my feet until we were doing it at the same time so our feet made a loud noise.

'My daddy doesn't like me,' Malvolio said.

His daddy *didn't* like him. My daddy had never looked at me or Cordelia or Malvolio like that and then went away to the pub. And my daddy liked us all the time. 'You have to give him time,' I said to Malvolio. 'This is all new to him.'

58

'I wanted my daddy to be my best friend when he comes home,' Malvolio said. 'You're my bestest ever friend. And so's Cordelia. I wanted my daddy to be my bestest friend, too.'

I patted Malvolio on the shoulder. That's what you had to do when someone cried. I saw it: Mummy did it to Aunty Merry when she cried and Daddy did it to Mummy when she cried. Malvolio was going to cry so I had to pat his shoulder.

'NICE!' Cordelia shouted.

I was in so much trouble. Cordelia had opened the sandwich I had dropped. She had put some under Malvolio's car and run the car over it again and again and again so it was all squishy and stuck to the carpet. She tried to eat some of it and her face was shiny from the Sandwich Spread, orange and green and yellow and red bits of it were stuck all over her face. Some of it was in her hair.

'NICE!' Cordelia shouted again. She was waving the car in one hand and some sandwich in the other.

'I'm going to get in so much trouble,' I said to Malvolio.

And because he was so sad and because his daddy didn't like him, I didn't get very cross when Malvolio started laughing.

*   *   *

There's a peculiar type of silence that hits you when you come into a Leo-less house. It's like a short, sharp blast of extremely cold air that takes your breath away the second you step over the threshold. Then the eerie, unnatural cold seeps slowly into your body and mind as you walk around

59

turning on lights, checking the post, checking the answer machine messages, and finally ending up in the kitchen where you flick on the kettle to make a cup of coffee, only to realise it's empty and you're probably going to burn down the house, but you listen to it crackle and complain on its stand, unable to move. Unable to do what is necessary because you feel so powerless. In all things, frozen and powerless. Unable to create or effect change in any way.

As the kettle's fizzing becomes louder, something in me snaps to attention and I reach out and flick it off. That'd be great, wouldn't it, for Leo to come home to a blackened, charred shell of a home? Actually, he'd probably think it was really cool. He'd probably tell me that I was the coolest mum in the world for giving him a burnt-down house as a welcome home present—until he discovered all his toys, his books and the precious PlayStation had gone up in the blaze. Then he and Keith would probably join forces in having me prosecuted for crimes against humanity.

I massage my eyes, I can't get Mal out of my mind. Maybe I should call him. My eyes flick to the kitchen clock: midnight. Yeah, maybe I should call, get the stunned silence on the end of the phone, then the mouthful, then the dialling tone as he hangs up. *Then* maybe I'd be able to concentrate on something else. Maybe I'd be able to sit down and think how I'm going to tell my family that Leo isn't being kept in for routine observation. That he's actually very ill. That although the doctors haven't said this to me directly, they're very worried about him. Maybe if I can shift Mal from my mind, I can get on with the stuff that needs to

60

be done in the present.

*   *   *

Mal, Cordelia and I turned the corner to our road and saw the ambulance outside my and Cordelia's house, and in unison we all stopped.

The ambulance was usually outside Mal's house. But this time, it was outside ours. I started running first, Mal caught me up, then outran me because his legs were that bit longer and he was that bit stronger. Cordelia, who was six, was strides behind us. We ran and ran but it still took for ever to reach our house.

As we arrived, we saw my mum being helped into the back of the ambulance. She looked fine, fit and healthy. It must be my dad. I could run a hundred metres in very quick time and my heart was always racing afterwards, but not like this. It had never raced as much as this.

I was scared of lots of things: the dark, the monster Mal had convinced me lived in the outdoor toilet, the fluffy toys I told Cordelia came to life every full moon (I did such a good job convincing her that I became terrified of them, too), of something happening to Aunt Mer. But I'd never been this scared before. I'd never been so scared that something would happen to my dad like it had happened to Uncle Victor and I wouldn't see him again.

We stopped in front of the ambulance and tried to see in. My whole body began to tremble. 'Children,' Dad said. Behind us. He was behind us, in front of our house. We all turned towards him. He was wearing the pinstripe grey suit he wore for work with a light blue shirt, his blue tie slightly undone. I wanted to run to him and hug him and kiss his face and tell him I was glad he was all right, and that I'd never been happier to see him in all my life, but I didn't. He wouldn't like it. My dad wasn't like that. In his arms, he held three-year-old Victoria, Mal's sister. She was staring at the ambulance, her face dry, her eyes wide. Her hair was in perfect bunches with a perfectly straight centre parting, the kind of style Aunt Mer used to spend hours brushing and brushing until everything was even. Everything was neat. We all knew that was a sign. That she was unwell. That we should be scared.

'Come inside and eat your dinner.' We were all looking at Dad so we were all startled when the back of the ambulance slammed shut.

It was Aunt Mer.

Like always, it was Aunt Mer.

The siren started up on the ambulance and it began to move down the narrow street, lined on both sides by parked cars. We all watched it bump down the uneven road and turn the corner.

'Come inside,' Dad said more sternly. I knew why: all the neighbours on that part of our street were standing outside their houses or peeking out of their windows, watching. They were always watching. I sometimes used to think that if they could, they'd pull up chairs and sit and watch us because we were better than *Coronation Street*. Better than anything they could ever see in the cinema. Mum and Dad hated it. 'Like being a goldfish,' Mum had said to Dad once. It wasn't that my parents begrudged people looking, it was the comforting pleasure these people seemed to get from the knowledge that if they were standing on a cold, damp pavement watching it happen to someone else, it was very unlikely to happen to them.

Mum often told us that when she and Dad moved into this street about eleven years ago, those very same neighbours wouldn't talk to them. The women would often stand in groups in the street, gossiping, but would stop talking when Mum walked past; they stared at her if she smiled at them in the shops; they refused to take parcels in for her from the postman. This was alien behaviour to two African people who always tried to welcome newcomers to their community. The neighbours had shunned Aunt Mer and Uncle Victor when they moved in six months later, so Mum had gone over and taken them a casserole. That was how their friendship began, that was how our families became intertwined, and that was why Mum always went to the hospital with Aunt Mer.

Dad struggled trying to get dinner together because Victoria wouldn't let him put her down, so he had to work single-handed. Every time I tried to help, as I did when Mum made dinner, he waved me away. He was scared, but pretending not to be. We could all tell, even Cordelia.

'Your mother has had to go to hospital,' he said, whilst trying to transfer fish fingers on to a plate with boiled potatoes and bright green peas. 'It's only for a little while,' he said to Mal. 'You two will stay here until she comes home. We will go and get your pyjamas and some toys for Victoria later.'

Mal, Cordelia and I sat at the dining table in silence. It was the deathly silence that we often sat in. It was the silence of afterwards. Afterwards always felt like this: stiff, sore, quiet. Every breath a painful reminder of what could have happened.

We ate in silence, each of us imagining what had happened. My mum and dad wouldn't tell us anything of course, we were only nine, Mal and I, too young to hear from them directly. We, instead, heard it from what the people at school taunted us with, and what we found out from creeping out of bed late at night and listening to my parents talking. That was how we found out that Uncle Victor hadn't been working away for the five years after we were born, he had been in prison. We still didn't know what for, everyone at school would chant at us that he had been anything from a murderer to a burglar. But no one *knew*. And Mum and Dad never seemed to talk about it.

A few days later they did talk about Aunt Mer and I found out.

She had dressed up in her best dress, put on her fur coat that Uncle Victor had bought her years and years ago, and brushed her hair just so. She had brushed Victoria's hair, and dressed her up in her party dress. And then she had put Victoria downstairs in front of the television, while upstairs she took almost a whole bottle of paracetamol and cut her wrists, then lay down on the bed to sleep.

Uncle Victor had died six months ago, so Mum had started going to the Wackens' several times a day: first thing in the morning to check Mal was ready for school and had his packed lunch, and that Victoria got her breakfast; once at lunchtime to check Aunt Mer and Victoria had eaten and if they wanted to go to the shops or the park; then again in the evening to check Mal and Victoria had eaten dinner, Mal had done his homework and they were in bed. That day, Dad had come home early from work, so Mum thought she'd drop in early to see Aunt Mer. She had knocked for a while, then she got scared and used her spare key to let herself in. The ambulance had parked outside our house because there was nowhere else for it to park.

The hospital were keeping her in for a while because, I heard, this time was the worst yet. She'd tried it before, we all knew that. But this time she was serious. This time, with what she had done, how she had timed it, it meant that she didn't want to be here any more.

*   *   *

I wake up to find the kitchen light on, the grain of the wood from the kitchen table imprinted on my cheek and five text messages on my mobile from Keith:

All fine here. Love you. K x

Go to bed. Love you. K x

I mean it, go to bed. Love you. K x

And don't even think about going on the computer. K x

I said bed, not the kitchen table. K x

Keith thinks I go on the computer because I can't sleep or because I am looking for alternative therapies that will wake up Leo. He'd prefer that to me reading medical journals, he doesn't want me trying to learn technical jargon and about the doctors' procedures because he thinks that will make me feel worse. He believes that in this instance, ignorance is bliss, and I should leave it all in the hands of the doctors; that if I must, I should look at my nice little alternative therapies that he can dismiss as nonsense, and leave the rest to the professionals. He doesn't want me talking in terms he cannot understand, making him feel more powerless than he already does.

I can understand why he feels like that. Keith has always been in control in his life. He has always been strong and self-assured, his sense of right and wrong has always seen him through. This has stranded him in an unknown place where he has nothing tangible to fight; nothing wrong that can be brought to justice. He hates it. Me knowing more than him would make him feel even more insubstantial, insecure, weak.

If I can do anything for him, it's to not add to his pain.

*   *   *

We, all six of us, were squeezed around our dining table because Mum and Dad wanted to talk to us.

It was serious because Mum and Dad rarely sat us all down together to talk to us. Ever since they had called Mal and me downstairs from where we were doing our homework in my bedroom, I had been running through the list of things I could possibly have done wrong. I couldn't think of anything that would mean all of us sitting down like this. Mal and I weren't like other fourteen-year-olds: we didn't smoke; we didn't hang around in the park; we didn't try to get our hands on alcohol; we weren't 'in' enough to be invited to parties—even if we were, Mum and Dad wouldn't have let Mal or me go. The only thing I could think of was that I hadn't got an A on my last history project.

'We want to talk to you children,' Mum said.

I realised suddenly how old my mum looked. Weary, actually, rather than old. She was beautiful, my mum. She had her hair in nice, big, bouncy curls that came from wearing rollers every night; she had wonderful cheekbones and huge, nearly black eyes, and really, really long eyelashes. She used to have virtually no wrinkles on her deep, dark brown, smooth skin but now some were appearing around her mouth, around her eyes. They weren't laughter lines, as I'd seen them called in magazines, either. Dad's hair was turning white. I hadn't noticed until now, but the sides were grey and would probably soon be white, and the jet-black areas would soon be grey. I knew he used to dye his hair but he hadn't done so for a while. His once smooth dark brown skin was now wrinkling across the forehead, too.

They weren't old, they were weary: the most recent incident with Aunt Mer had taken it out of them. It had taken it out of all of us, but especially them. On top of everything, they must have been feeling guilty as well. They hadn't noticed the signs, none of us had really. Or maybe it was because she had become better at hiding it over the years. But she wasn't here at the moment and none of us children knew if and when she was coming back.

Which meant that Mum and Dad were raising four children when they had only intended to have two. One of them had to stay over with Mal and Victoria every night or the two of them would have to sleep over with us—Cordy in bed with me, Mal on a mattress on the floor in Cordy's room with Victoria in Cordy's bed. Mum had gone back to nursing and Dad did as many extra shifts at the college lab as he could so they could afford to feed and clothe and house us all. I hadn't noticed how much of a toll it had taken on them until I saw it carved into their faces as wrinkles, and etched into their eyes as sadness.

'We've decided that Malvolio and Victoria will go away to school,' Mum said, a waver in her voice.

Dad placed his hand on her shoulder to steady her, silently telling her he would do this. He focused on Mal and Victoria. 'Your mother's brother, who lives in Birmingham, said he will look after you both if you go and live with him. He will pay for you to go to boarding school. The two schools are very near each other so you will be able to see each other often. And for the holidays you can spend time with your uncle. You can get to know his family.'

'You're splitting us up?' I asked. There was a tone of anger in my voice that I never used with my parents, but I couldn't believe what I was hearing.

'Malvolio will be starting his O-levels soon, he needs to concentrate, and Victoria will be able to catch up with her school work.'

'You can't split us up.' I was outraged they'd even consider this. It was unthinkable. Waking up every morning knowing I wouldn't see Mal or Victoria would be like knowing I wouldn't see

Mum, Dad or Cordy. It would be like waking up to find the sun had forgotten to rise. We didn't have much that was stable or predictable in our lives except the six of us always being together. This was not going to happen. 'You can't send them away. What about me and Cordelia? How can you split us up?'

Mum's shoulders fell as she lowered her head. She was going to start crying for real.

'Nova, this isn't what we want to do, but we have to,' Dad said reasonably. I may have looked like my mum, but I usually took after my dad. I was of the same temperament, Mum was always saying. Always trying to be reasonable. Until now, of course, when I was faced with losing my family. 'With Malvolio and Victoria being looked after, we can look after your Aunt Meredith.'

She was coming out of hospital, then. I wondered for a moment if they knew when. If they were going to move Mal and Victoria before she came back or after. It was May, now; they would have to start school in September. Would Aunt Mer be back by then?

She had promised, promised, promised Mal when he last saw her that she hadn't been trying to kill herself. Not this time. She just needed some sleep. She had taken the sleeping pills because she had been awake for so long that she needed sleep. Nothing she did would make her tired. Her body would sometimes feel tired and she'd be too exhausted to get out of bed, but she couldn't stop her mind from racing. She'd tried writing down her thoughts to get them out of her head, she said, but her hand wouldn't keep up with them. She had tried speaking her thoughts into a tape recorder but the sound of the tape whirring had driven her to distraction. She had tried reading but she couldn't take in the words. She had tried cleaning the house from top to bottom but she still had energy. She had tried running around and around the garden to make herself tired but it didn't work. Nothing worked. She knew that if she didn't get some sleep soon, she would go crazy. That's why she went to the doctor and got some sleeping tablets. Just in case it carried on for too long. The doctor was new to the surgery and didn't know her, and had been very sympathetic and had given her the tablets. (He was an idiot, I had raged inside as Mal told me. Simply glancing at her notes would have told him that you didn't give someone with Aunt Mer's history sleeping tablets; you didn't make it easy for her to end it all.)

Aunt Mer had promised, promised, promised Mal that she had only meant to take a couple, like it said on the side of the bottle. She thought taking them with a little vodka instead of water would make them work faster. She'd been so long without sleep, she decided to take a couple more to make sure they worked. And then she'd forgotten how many she'd taken so she took another one to make sure she'd taken enough. And then another.

She'd been able to sleep then. The first she knew that she'd taken too many and used too much vodka to help them down was when she woke up in the hospital to find she was back on suicide watch. And even then it'd taken a while to understand what was going on because she was so fuzzy from not having slept.

I understood perfectly why my parents thought this was the best way to handle this. I'd heard them talking about it one night: Mal and Victoria shouldn't have to suffer because their mother was ill, they'd said. I hadn't realised separating us was their solution.

'It's not fair,' I said. 'We all have to stay together. It's not fair if they have to go away. We won't see them any more and that's not fair. We haven't done anything wrong.'

'No one has done anything wrong,' Dad said. 'This is just the best way.'

I opened my mouth to disagree, when Mal moved in his seat beside me and then pressed his hand on to my forearm, telling me to stop. I glanced at him to ask him why, and saw he was watching Victoria. She had her head bowed, her long wavy blonde hair hiding her face, but not the tears that had puddled on top of the mahogany table. She was eight but her height, her mannerisms, her deeply ingrained sadness, made her seem so much older.

Mal pushed out his chair, went around the table and took his little sister's hand. 'Come on, let's go for a walk,' he said to her. He used to say that to Cordy when she was being 'difficult', which was pretty much all the time. He used to say that to Victoria when she would slink into silence at the dinner table. He used to say that to me whenever he had done something to annoy me and wanted me to still be his friend. This was the first time he'd said it and looked so heartbroken and scared as he spoke.

They were gone for about half an hour and in that time Mum had made herself a cup of tea, Dad a cup of coffee, and Cordy and me a cup of Ovaltine each. Cordy had been singing the tune to the Ovaltine advert ever since and even though it was extremely annoying, especially because she filled in the bits she didn't know with 'da-de-da-da', no one told her to stop.

'Victoria has gone for a lie-down in Nova's bedroom,' Mal said as he sat down in the seat he had occupied earlier. He sounded so grown up that I blinked a few times at him. 'She wants to go to Birmingham. She wants to go away to school. Thank you, Uncle Frank and Aunt Hope, it's what she needs. She doesn't want to be here any more, but she doesn't want us to be cross with her because of it.'

'No one would ever be cross with her,' I said at exactly the same time as Dad. Mum smiled to herself.

'But I'm going to stay,' Mal continued. 'I can't leave Mum. I can't ever leave Mum.'

The words he said, his tone of voice, the slight shake of his head, told everyone he was serious, that no one could put asunder him and his mother.

'We understand,' Mum said.

'Yes, we do,' Dad agreed.

Silence came to us as we all digested what this would mean for us. Once Victoria left, she would no longer be a part of our family. Once we didn't see her every day, create memories and jokes and feuds with her every day, it'd be difficult to connect with her. We'd be a different type of close. No matter how many times she visited physically, she would always have grown up somewhere else. Somewhere other. With some others.

'So,' Cordy said after a while, 'if Malvolio's not going away to school, can I go instead?'

Later, much later, Mal said to me, 'I wish my

dad was here.' We had sneaked out of bed and were sitting side by side in the dark on the back step, staring into the garden and the railings that backed on to the railway line that ran past our house. (Mum and Dad probably knew that we were out here: apart from the fact we both had the grace of stampeding elephants, Mum and Dad seemed to know pretty much everything about everything. Which was why, I suppose, they'd been so upset about the sleeping tablets and vodka Aunt Mer had been able to get her hands on.)

Mal never talked about his father. It was an unacknowledged agreement that Uncle Victor was something we never spoke about. This was a revelation to me that Mal not only thought about his dad—although I always suspected he did—but also missed him enough to want him here.

'Do you?' I said.

'I wish he was here so I wouldn't have to do this alone. I know your mum and dad look after Mum, but it should be Dad. And then Victoria wouldn't have to go away.'

I understood at that moment why he could let Victoria go. He couldn't take care of both of them as well as his mother, and if going to boarding school meant Victoria would be looked after, that she wouldn't have to go through every moment of worry and fear that he had to, then he'd do that. He didn't want to lose his sister, but if that was the price he had to pay to stop her going through the agony we all went through every time his mother struggled or slipped or spun out into psychosis, then he would pay it. These were adult choices he had to make. He knew that I would have fought my parents to keep us together. I would have made life

73

a misery for all concerned until they realised that we couldn't be split up. But Mal had decided to let Victoria go to give her the chance to grow up 'normal'.

'Why us, Nova?' he asked. 'Why us? Why my mum? Why'd God pick on my mum?' I didn't think he wanted an answer. He was just asking. Even if he did want or need a solid answer, I didn't have one. I didn't know who got chosen to go through life suffering. Having things happen to them. Putting up with things and not having any choice in the matter.

I doubted I'd ever understand why them and not anyone else. Or maybe I would. Maybe at some point I would grow up. Not in the sense of being old enough to vote, get married, leave home, get a job. But in the sense of being able to understand the world more. Being able to pinpoint why some are chosen, some are not. Why some are blessed and others seem to suffer. Maybe that was what being a grown-up truly meant. You finally understood the ways of the world. You were finally given insight into the truth of life. Maybe you could do all those other things, live as though you were grown up, but you would never *be* grown up until you had that kind of understanding and knowledge. Until you had that kind of enlightenment. Maybe that's what enlightenment was. Maybe it wasn't being able to sit cross-legged while wearing white robes and chanting and feeling 'at one with the world', as I had been reading about; maybe enlightenment was simply being able to understand.

I put my arm around him and was surprised when he crumpled against me like a cola can being

74

crushed. All fight and strength went out of his body and I realised that what had been meant as a one-armed hug was now holding him up. His whole bodyweight was resting on me. He looked skinny as a rake, but he was heavy so it took me a while to move him off my shoulder and pull him on to my lap. His head rested on my thigh as my eyes became more accustomed to the dark and could make out shapes in the small rectangle of our back garden, and through the black rails into the overgrown green that separated the end of our garden from the train track.

Mal had climbed over that fence so many times to retrieve our footballs, shuttlecocks and tennis balls. And the time our budgie, Birdie, flew over there, he'd climbed over to catch it. He'd gently covered it with his T-shirt to stop it flying away whilst he scrambled back over the fence to bring it home. The wild, spiky weeds scratched his back and chest, but he hadn't cared, all he cared about was bringing the terrified budgie home.

He was ten at the time. Mum had told him not to climb over that fence but to wait instead for Dad to come back so he could use the ladder to get over the fence and up the tree. The second she went back into the house to check on dinner, he'd scaled the railings, jumped down on to the other side and shimmied up the tree. He'd only disobeyed Mum because it was Aunt Mer who had let out Birdie. She'd said she wanted to see Birdie fly. She was working on a design for wings for humans and she needed to see how budgies flew. It was a sign. We all knew that, we all knew that there'd be a visit to the doctor soon. Mal at that time hadn't been able to do anything about making his mother well, but he did what he could, and that was to fix things. In this case, rescuing Birdie. Mal had done this as long as I could remember: anything she did, he tried to set right.

A slither of wetness ran down my bare thigh and I instinctively checked the sky for rain. The sky, a beautiful, rich, velvet blue-black, didn't have any clouds in it, and the air didn't hold the heavy, musky scent of rain. Another slither crawled down my thigh and I realised what was happening. I wanted to place one hand on his back in comfort and to use the other to wipe away his tears. I wanted to love him better, but I knew that was what I wanted. What he needed was for me to pretend it wasn't happening. For me to overlook the fact that he wasn't being strong and capable and wise beyond his years, that he was going to allow himself to cry.

I rested back on my elbows, leant my body back and stared up at the sky. What he needed me to do was to be there, but to leave him be. So I did the one thing I did best—I talked. I talked and talked and talked.

*　　　*　　　*

The door to Leo's bedroom is open.

It has been since he went to hospital. I always resist the temptation to go in, smell his clothes, run my fingers over the lines of his furniture, lie down on his bed. That is the sort of thing that the bereaved do. When they are trying to cling on to what they have lost. And that hasn't happened. It won't happen. This is only a pause, a break while he gets better.

I've been spoilt with Leo, really. I've had him all to myself for so many years, I suppose I've forgotten that many single mothers have to share their children with their biological fathers. That some women are forced to live without their children for half the summer holidays and weekends, that their children have two families and get to make a set of memories that don't include them.

Until now, I've spent maybe ten nights without Leo. Mostly when he goes to stay with his cousins up near Crawley or with my parents for the night, but other than that my life has revolved around him, and his life around me. He even came on honeymoon with Keith and me to Spain. Lots of people—Mum, Dad, Cordy and Aunt Mer included—had asked if I was sure I didn't want time alone with my new husband, a holiday from it all, a break. Of course I did, and I was going to get one. With Leo. Keith had come into his life as well, he needed a break to get to know Keith in that different context. Besides, I told them, what's a holiday without Leo? I might as well leave my right arm at home as well.

His room is an organised mess. He has books on the floor, and anyone who doesn't know my son would think they'd just been dropped there casually after reading. But no, he has put them there in special places to fool the burglars. One book squeaks, so if the burglar steps on it, it'll wake Leo up. Another book has a bell on it, so if the burglar moves it aside, it'll do the same job as the squeaking book. The other books and a couple of toys are placed in a pattern that will make it complicated and treacherous for someone to navigate. We've never been burgled, he's never known anyone who's been burgled, it's just Keith's job that makes him conscious of such things. I've had to memorise the pattern and then come in during the night once he's asleep, remove them all and then replace them in exactly the same place in the morning before he gets up. It doesn't occur to him when he's laying his traps at night that he might trip and hurt himself if he wakes up to go to the toilet, or to come into our room to tell us something important that has come to him in a dream.

Leo had been in hospital three days before I remembered not to go to his room and replace the traps. I did it automatically, without even noticing his bed was empty. Now I've left the traps in place so that when Leo wakes up, I'll be able to tell him that his room is safe, there have been no burglars because the traps are all there, laid in perfect, innocent-looking formation, waiting to trip up the unsuspecting.

*　　　*　　　*

'Do you mind if we go?'
It was barely midnight and the dancing had only just started at the uni disco, but Mal wanted to leave. He was up in Oxford visiting me for the weekend and for some reason he hadn't brought Cordy with him. The last two times he had driven up—three weeks after I first started here, and then to collect me for the Christmas holidays—he had brought my sister because she was still at home and he had chosen to go to college in London so he could live at home.

When he'd climbed out of the car without her, I'd wondered if she was being punished because apart from that, the only other way he would have come alone would have been to sneak off without her knowledge while she was at school. I didn't envy him the wrath of Cordy when he returned if that was what he'd done.

I peered up at him through the dense fog of smoky air mingled with the heady musk of people trying to get together in the union disco, wondering why he wasn't having a good time.

He took my hand, laced his fingers through the gaps between mine. 'I've hardly spoken to you,' he explained. 'I want to talk to you.'

'OK,' I replied with a shrug—he had a point: after he arrived we'd gone straight to the canteen for an early dinner, then, still hungry, had walked into town for a pizza, then had been dragged out to the bar for drinks by a couple of my friends. I moved to take my hand back so we could find my friends to tell them we were leaving, but he didn't let go. He held on like he was worried about losing me in the crowd. When I said we were leaving to Rebecca and Lucy, they looked from me to him a few times and in unison broke out into huge smiles. They obviously thought . . . And they couldn't be more wrong. 'See you tomorrow,' they chorused drunkenly as we navigated our way through the virtually mating bodies on the dance floor.

He didn't let go of my hand until I shut my room door behind us, and then he seemed to think it was safe, that I wouldn't disappear.

'Do you want to top-to-toe it like Cordy and me usually do, or use your sleeping bag?' I asked him as I grabbed my T-shirt and pyjama bottoms to start changing.

'I don't mind sharing the bed,' he said. 'If you don't mind?'

'Course not.'

As soon as our bodies touched when we squeezed into my narrow, single bed, everything changed. He wasn't my best friend/brother any longer. I didn't have a name for him, a role in my life, but what we were to each other was different.

His scent had changed. He smelt like the guys I had kissed since I'd been at college: of heat and desire and physical need. He smelt of something unnamed that I suddenly wanted. Without thinking, we rearranged ourselves in the bed, his slightly bent legs slotted perfectly behind mine, his arm across my stomach, his other arm under his head. He moved again, pressing our bodies closer, nestling his chin against the curve of my neck, the slight beginnings of his beard gently prickling my skin, his breath, deep and slow, moving softly over my cheek.

I could feel he was interested, *down there*. I'd felt it when kissing men before, but this was different. It was more than this being part of the normal urges of two people who were sharing a space made for one. I wanted him to kiss me. I wanted him to touch me. And if he did, I would. I would do it with him.

I knew that I was slightly odd, that I was one of the few girls at university who, even after all this time and kissing a few men, still hadn't—what was it Rebecca called it?—still hadn't 'taken the first bite of womanhood'.

No one, not even Rebecca and Lucy, understood

that I was waiting for someone special. I was waiting for someone who I was in love with and who was in love with me before I did that. They thought I was a little scared of sex, when really, I wanted to wait. You only get one first time, I wanted it to be with someone special. I wanted to look back and know that physically it may not have been great, but it had been with the right person. I didn't realise until we were two curls in my narrow college bed that I had been waiting for Mal.

Through the walls of my room I could hear chatter, laughter, people ransacking the communal kitchens that were located on every floor for food to satisfy middle-of-the-night, drug-induced munchies. There was music, too. The girl in the room next door had her stereo on a bit too loud, and the sound seeped through the brickwork into my room. She had probably come in, pressed play on her tape deck, and passed out fully clothed on the bed as she did most Friday nights. This Friday it was Roxy Music. She'd been playing it to death all week, and everyone was sick of it. Which was probably why she kept playing it.

Above the beginning beat of 'Dance Away' Mal's breathing slowed. He shifted a fraction closer, too close for it to be accidental. As the metronomic beat of the song got louder, more insistent around us, he slid his hand under my T-shirt and rested it on my stomach. My eyes slipped shut. His palm lay over my skin, imprinting the heat of his body, of desire, on me. I inhaled him, drew deep on the scent of him and became slightly drunk and giddy. Slowly, his thumb stroked across the dip of my navel.

Bryan Ferry's voice began. Mal sighed and his

81

hand moved lower, to the top of my pyjama trousers.

With all the other men I had kissed, I'd never felt this. The crush of longing that was bearing down on my chest; the tight ball of yearning that was unfurling between my legs; the craving of excitement swirling in my bloodstream. It made perfect sense that he was the one this would happen with. I'd never regret it with Mal. He'd been around for so many of my other firsts—tooth, step, crush on a TV star, kiss with Jason Butterworth at the sixth-form disco—of course he'd be the first one for this.

His fingers tentatively reached below the lip of my bottoms and all breath left my body in one steady stream of expectation. I felt his fingers brush slowly over my pubic hair, his head moved towards my neck and I opened my legs a fraction, waiting for him. His hand moved lower still, reaching for me, closer towards where he would become a part of me.

As his lips reached the curve of my neck, he gave a small, strangled, guttural cry at the back of his throat and took his hand away, the elastic waistband of my pyjama trousers snapping unceremoniously back into place. He moved his body away from me, took his face away from mine, dropped his head heavily on the corner of pillow I had left for him.

What happened?

I could hear him breathing heavily behind me, but couldn't turn around. I knew he wanted me, I had felt it in the electric sensations of his body, the hardness that had been pressed against me.

What did I do wrong? Why did he change his

82

mind?

Loud and fast, as though he had just crossed the finish line of a 200-metre sprint, his breathing filled the room, some of it falling on the back of my neck.

Is he scared that he won't be experienced enough? He has done it before, so is that why he stopped? Or is he scared of being my first?

He pulled aside the covers and slipped out of bed. The room was dark, but light still filtered in from the corridor lights, which were garish and harsh and permanently on so the rooms were never truly blacked out.

Is it my body? Isn't it as good as the other girls he's been with?

He went to the bank of wardrobes that stood, a big, tall, oak monstrosity, in the corner. Behind one set of doors, a space for my clothes and shoes; behind the next set, a sink and mirror. I heard the water running, I heard him splash his face with water, I heard the stillness of him standing motionless in front of the mirror, his breathing still loud and uncontrolled in the darkness. I didn't have the courage to turn around, to see what he was doing. Instead, slowly and carefully, avoiding moving the bed, I curled towards the wall, making myself as small as possible while tugging down my T-shirt to cover my stomach.

I heard him rustling by the other wardrobe, where he'd dumped his belongings, then the sharp rip of Velcro being opened and the soft nylon hush of his sleeping bag being laid out on the floor beside the bed.

'There's not much space in the bed,' he whispered, over the sound of undoing the zip on the sleeping bag.

In response, I closed my eyes and started to breathe deeply, as though I was asleep. Speaking to him was not an option; embarrassment and humiliation had made me mute.

Why did I think he'd want to, with me?

'I'll sleep on the floor,' he whispered. 'Goodnight.'

The dying strains of 'Dance Away' filled the room, then petered out to silence. It'd taken less time than a song took to play itself out for all that to happen. For us to come so close and then . . .

Neither of us slept very much. I could tell by the rhythm of his breathing, by his stillness, that he, like me, spent most of the night wide awake, staring into the partial dark. Neither of us brought it up the next morning. We went about the business of a normal weekend as though nothing had happened. But I did catch him staring at me, as though trying to work out something, trying to make a decision.

I knew Mal—I didn't know why he had changed his mind, but I did know there was a deeper reason for what had happened, what had gone wrong; something he couldn't explain to me yet.

'Cordy's going to murder me when I get home,' he said as he was leaving on Sunday evening.

'Yup, I don't know why you didn't bring her along.'

'I wanted you all to myself, didn't I?' he replied. 'I never get you alone any more.'

'Well, I hope for your sake it was worth it,' I said. 'Cos she is going to make you *suffer*.'

He took me in his arms and I didn't melt into them as usual, he didn't hold me as close—we

84

hadn't talked about what happened but our bodies hadn't forgotten that we were meant to be awkward, stiff, uncomfortable with each other.

'Of course it was,' he said. 'Every second with you is worth it.'

I stepped back first, unable to stay that close for too long. 'Tell that to Cordy, I'm sure she'll forgive you,' I smirked.

'Yeah, I'm sure.' He opened his car door, stopped and turned to me. 'I miss you, Nova,' he said before he got in. 'I'll see you soon.'

'Yeah,' I replied.

As his car disappeared in the traffic heading for London, I realised that I had to tell him I loved him.

*   *   *

I haven't cried.

Since Leo started sleeping at the hospital, I haven't cried. I think the only person who'd be more surprised than me at that is Leo. He thinks I cry all the time at the most ridiculous things. He's right, I do. But then, I don't. Not really. He's the person who experiences me crying the most, because, like me shouting, he's the one who causes it the most.

Very few people can make me cry. Leo often does it without trying. When he was four and had just started nursery school, there was an 'incident'. In one of the lessons, the children had been asked 'what does your mum or dad do?'—I think they meant for a job. Leo had said, 'She cries' about me. The teacher had asked him about it and he had repeated, 'My mum cries. All the time.' Before too long I was 'invited' in to speak to the teacher. The school nurse sat in on the meeting as well and it took an incredible amount of time to convince them that, yes, although I was a lone parent I had a lot of support, I wasn't feeling isolated and lonely; yes, Leo was exaggerating and I didn't cry all the time. And, yes, if I was feeling depressed, or even a little down, I would seek help. They pressed upon me the numbers of several excellent counsellors—obviously they didn't realise the irony of that—and told me to get in touch if I needed anything. Absolutely anything.

When I'd asked Leo later why he'd told them that, he looked at me and said, confused as anything, 'But you do, Mum. You cry.' When I told my mum she asked me if I had told them I was a doctor. When I said no, her silence basically said, 'Well, it's your own fault, then'. Mum thinks that my Ph.D. can protect me from virtually anything so I should brandish it a little more often. Cordy laughed so much she dropped the phone. I'm sure somewhere there is a file that still has a note in it for people to keep an eye on me because I cry. All the time.

Keith and I have agreed that we're not allowed to be anything but normal in front of Leo right now. We have to talk as normal, as though nothing is wrong. And that means no crying. I don't want him worrying because I am sure he can hear us. Even if I wasn't, crying around him would change the energy of the room, would make it sad and heavy and not at all the sort of place he would want to return to.

But away from there, I don't cry. I don't even feel the inclination. Crying, I suppose, would be admitting I'm scared. More scared than I am. I'm terrified, of course I am, but crying about it would be like showing Keith, the universe, myself that I think this is all out of our control. That I think there is a chance . . .

He *is* coming back to us. He is.

And when he does, he's going to go back to doing what he does best: making me laugh, making me crazy, making me shout, making me cry.

When you're as close as Leo and me, it's something you can expect. It's the ones you love the most who can lift you in an instant, and destroy you without trying.

*   *   *

Mal's car spluttered its way into a parking space beside King's Cross train station, where I was getting the coach back to Oxford.

His car was very little more than scrap metal, but he'd bought it with the money his dad had left him. It was almost as though his dad had given him the car himself, the love Mal heaped upon it. Given that he professed to hate his father for everything he put his mother through, *everyone* thought it odd that he would not let it go. There was so much wrong with it, and he'd had it repaired so many times, I often wondered how much of the original vehicle actually still existed. It was forbidden to say anything against the car, especially not that he could have bought a new car for the amount he had spent having it fixed.

We climbed out and he took my black rucksack from the back seat—the boot wouldn't open for some mysterious reason—and hefted it on to his

87

shoulder. I had come to visit with very little: a few clothes, underwear, toothbrush, face wash and moisturiser, and two pairs of shoes. I was leaving with three Pyrex bowls of food (rice, stew and plantain), a cake wrapped in foil, a blanket, a bottle of Vimto and two framed photos Aunt Mer had given me of Mal, Mum, Dad and Cordy that she'd taken at our house the day I left to go back to college after Christmas. Cordy, of course, was centre stage in both of them.

Last Night, in all its glory, climbed out of the car as well—it had accompanied us for the entire drive here, sitting between us on the gear stick like a third person, and now it chose to accompany us to the coach station. Very few times in our lives had Mal and I been so awkward with each other. Not even when he walked in on me getting changed in the bathroom at his house over Christmas, after I had removed my knickers and had just taken my bra off. He'd blinked at me, blinked at my bare body, then quickly turned away, slamming the door shut behind him. I'd thought I'd locked it, but hadn't pushed the bolt into place firmly. It wasn't even this awkward after what happened during that last visit, three weeks ago. Now, Last Night slung one of its arms around each of us and hugged us close as we walked beside each other.

I suppose I'd never done what I did last night, before.

On Friday night I had travelled down from Oxford to allegedly visit my family but in reality it was to see Mal. Because when I saw him, I'd know if I had come to the right decision to tell him I loved him or if I was absolutely out of my mind even contemplating it.

In the last three weeks, he had called me every day, which was unusual even for us. Every phone call he would ask if I'd met any new people, if anyone had asked me out, if there was anyone I was interested in. Whenever I said no, I would hear the relief in his voice, for the most part hidden, but there, as clear and true as the ringing of a bell.

Once I saw him, it would all become obvious what I had to do. When he had dragged me out of bed at 8 a.m. on Saturday morning to 'do stuff', I knew I had to tell him.

I tried to tell him as we stumbled through the frozen wastelands of Wimbledon Common. I tried to tell him when we proved how grown up we were and played Knockdown Ginger at one of the big houses in Raynes Park and stood around the corner laughing and puffing from our quick getaway. I tried again when he bought us ice cream at the petrol station on the way back home. I tried to tell him again as we stood outside my house, chatting as though we weren't simply going in to shower and change before we met again in an hour to go out clubbing.

It was simple. It was easy. All I had to do was say: 'Mal, I've fallen in love with you.' 'Mal, I'm in love with you.' 'Mal, I love you, but not just like that any more.'

But every time, *every* time I looked into his eyes, my mind went blank. Now that I knew how I felt, I couldn't look at him and not think about what I wanted. What we could mean to each other. And I wanted some time to enjoy the thrill of it. The thrill of being with the first person I was in love with.

89

As it was, I blurted it out. Someone bumped him in the club we ended up in, his drink went all down my white T-shirt, making it instantly see-through as it clung to the lacy edges of the black bra I wore underneath. He grabbed some napkins from the bar and started to dab me down, apologising profusely as though I was a stranger, not the person he'd actually been throwing food at for most of his life.

'God, I'm sorry,' he said, dabbing at my right breast again. 'We have to go home, get you changed.'

I smiled up at him. His beautiful, honey-blond hair, his dark eyes so genuinely concerned, his beautiful mouth.

'I love you so much,' I said without thinking.

He blinked, like he had blinked when he saw me naked. 'I love you too,' he said.

I grinned, warmed by the heat of his easy, instant reply; wobbly and giddy with happiness.

'You're the best friend I've got,' he added. 'It's funny, someone was talking about this new film that came out just before Christmas.' He spoke quickly, not giving me space to speak. 'It's about how men and women can't be friends without sex getting in the way. One of the girls in my class was going on and on about it and saying it was true. And I said to her my best friend is a girl and it's never been an issue. And it never will be. Because the quickest way to damage a great friendship is to talk—or even think—about sex. But the most certain way to end that friendship is to talk about love in any other terms.'

He stopped then, but wouldn't look at me, instead choosing to fiddle and play with the sodden napkins wadded together in his hands. I said nothing, just watched his bowed head, his nervous hands.

'No sensible people would ever do that,' he eventually continued. 'I told this girl, the one in my class who's so opinionated, I'd never do that. I could never be interested in that way in a girl who is my friend. I would never confuse friendship for *that* love. Because friends aren't meant to be lovers. If they were, they'd be frovers. Lo-ends. Don't you think?'

I had the sudden urge to run. To tear blindly out into the street and not stop running until I was as far away from here as possible. My next urge was to crawl under the nearest table and hide. My final urge, the one I went with, was to say, 'I need to get out of this top before I catch my death of cold.' I had substituted the word 'top' for 'club' and 'cold' for 'humiliation'.

'Oh, yeah.' He dumped the napkins on the bar, brushed his hands clean on his trousers. 'You wait here, I'll go get the coats.'

'You don't have to leave now,' I said. 'I'll be all right getting home by myself. I do it all the time in Oxford.'

'What kind of friend would I be if I let you go home all alone?' he replied.

'One who's as subtle as a brick smacked around your head,' I mumbled as he disappeared into the crowd.

We got the night bus home and we tried. We really tried to be normal. To be us. But the magic that had showered our day with happiness, fun, laughter and all that hope I had for the future was gone. In its place gestated the uncomfortable

91

creature that had finally been born this morning, and had named itself 'Last Night'.

'You know that you'll always be my number one girl, yeah?' Mal said to me as we stood by the coach I would be catching, the two of us still and awkward amongst the frantic comings and goings of the coach station.

I stood on tiptoes, took his face in both hands. 'And you'll always be my number one cutey doggy, yeah?' I replied, shaking his head as I would a dog. I'd started doing that to him when Mum and Dad said we couldn't get a dog. 'What do you need a dog for, we've got Malvolio?' Cordy had said. I'd decided the instant she said it that he probably was a pooch in a previous life: I could vividly picture him as a big, gangly Labrador that would bound all over you to cheer you up when you were sad; or would lie mournfully by your side, its features drooping to show it was sad too, depending on the type of sadness it was.

We had to joke about it. I had read the whole thing wrong and if I wasn't careful, this could come between us. It wasn't his fault he didn't feel that way for me. That I wasn't good enough in his eyes. We had so much else—a shared history, a family, so many years together—that was far more important than some misguided romantic notion of us getting together, having a long-distance relationship for the next two years and then what, getting married? At our age? No, he was right. Friends shouldn't be lovers. Friends shouldn't even entertain the idea of it.

If I could keep doing that, keep rationalising it, then I would be safe, at least until I got away from London. If I dared to feel about it, for even a fraction of a second, the chasm of pain would open up and swallow me whole. I had to consign it to the realm of the mind. To logic. To seeing the bigger picture. And make a joke of it.

'Are you getting on this coach, love?' the driver asked.

'Oh, yes,' I replied. Mal slung my rucksack off his shoulder and handed it carefully to the driver. The middle-aged, portly driver, with his white, short-sleeved shirt and tie, took my bag as though it was the most precious item he'd ever been handed, then flung it into the coach's luggage compartment, before approaching another couple to ask if they were getting on board. I shook my head and looked away, unable to believe what I'd just seen. The framed photos Aunt Mer gave me would be in pieces, as would the Pyrex bowls of food, while the Vimto bottle Mum had pressed upon me would be leaking sticky liquid all over my clothes. All in all a wonderful thing to be taking back to Oxford after everything. I could hear Last Night smirking at me.

'Now, does the cutey doggy want to play a quick game of fetch before I leave, or give me a hug?' I asked in my speaking-to-a-dog voice.

Rolling his eyes, he came into my open arms. We hugged and I counted the seconds, each one a lifetime, before I could reasonably end this part of the torture. I had to play the game. Be normal. If I tried hard enough to be normal, it would be normal again. Soon. Soon I wouldn't have to think twice about hugging him, touching him, looking him in the eye.

'I'll come see you soon, yeah?' he said as we came out of the hug.

'No, don't,' I said.

His eyes searched mine, desperate to know why I was rejecting him.

'I know what you're thinking,' I said, with a huge grin. 'And you're completely right. I don't want you to visit because no blokes will come near me because they think I'm attached. And all the really annoying girls want to be my friend because they think they've got a chance with you. I don't need that nonsense to be honest.' I added a laugh, hollow and pitiful, but necessary. *Please give me space*, I was subliminally begging him. *Please let me go away and have the chance to get over this.*

The bulge of his Adam's apple moved up and down as he swallowed hard, and he pressed his lips together as he nodded.

'I'll be home for summer,' I said. 'That'll come around in no time.'

'But it's Easter in a few weeks,' he protested.

'We're thinking of staying up there, a group of us. Someone's got a houseshare that will be free over the holidays. We're going to move in. It'll be a laugh.' For a moment I thought he might ask if he could come so added, 'But room will be tight. I'll see you during the summer, all right?'

'Look—' he began.

'All right?' I insisted.

He pressed his lips together again, they whitened under the pressure, his eyes narrowing. It wasn't all right. Slowly, he shook his head, once, twice, three times. 'All right,' he eventually said.

I ruffled the sides of his head. 'Good dog,' I said. 'There's a good Mal. There's a good Mal.'

'Ah, gerroff,' he said, brushing my hands away. 'One of these days I will actually bite you, and then

94

you'll have to go for a rabies injection. Then you'll be sorry.'

'But then they'd have to lock you up so you'd be more sorry.'

Unexpectedly, because we'd already hugged, he scooped me into his arms, lifted me off my feet. 'I miss you,' he whispered, soft as an angel's sigh. 'I miss you so much it hurts.'

So why don't you love me? I asked inside. *Why don't you love me?*

'Any more, for any more?' shouted the coach driver, resting his foot on the bottom step of the stairs leading up to the coach. He was shouting at me, I realised; he was glaring his impatience right at me. I glanced up at the coach: every window seat seemed to be taken, no one else was getting ready to board. Everyone else was ready to go. Except me, of course.

'Oh, yes, me!' I called.

'I knew that,' he mumbled loudly.

I spun back to Mal. 'I'll see you in the summer,' I said, then hurried towards the coach driver. Mal raised his right hand, the one that had slid below the waist of my pyjama trousers three weeks ago, but he didn't wave when I paused to smile at him at the top of the steps.

The next time we saw each other everything would be different, I decided. I wouldn't be a virgin, I was determined about that. I would find someone to take that first bite with. They didn't have to be special, that special person didn't want me, didn't love me, and no one would ever live up to him, so someone nice enough would have to do.

I would make more friends, now that I needed more people in my life because I wouldn't be able

95

to run back to London on a whim any longer.

Most importantly, the next time I saw Mal again, I wouldn't be in love with him any more. I wasn't sure how I was going to do it, but I knew if I still wanted him to be in my life, if our friendship was going to survive this, then more than anything I had to make that true. Or hide it so well it would be as if it had never existed.

*   *   *

One time, I found a note Leo wrote. I don't know why he wrote it, but it had made me sit down on his bed in shock and read it over and over.

i hav too dads. one is a spy and livs at my huse. the uver one isnt ded. i dont no where he livs. mum lovs my to dads. she lovs me. by Leo.

He must have written it a while ago because his spelling is so much better now, but I couldn't work out how he knew so much. He's always known that Keith isn't his 'real' dad, even though he chose to call him Dad straight away. I hadn't guessed he gave much thought to who his 'real' dad was. That he knew this dad person wasn't dead. That he assumed I loved this other dad.

I hadn't been sure what to do about it. Leo had never shown any real interest in his father, had never asked any questions about him. But it was clearly something he thought about.

I'd never wanted it to be like this. I'd never planned for him to grow up without knowing his father. He was meant, when he was conceived, to have two parents who would love and care for and raise him. I wasn't meant to be one of those parents, of course: I was going to be the aunt, the birth mother, the person who had helped give him life—but he was always meant to know his father.

And then I became his mother, and Leo was left wondering about his dad. He was left thinking about his uver one but never saying anything. Maybe because he thought it'd make me cry. Maybe because he wasn't sure if I would tell him. If he asked I don't know what I would have told him. It's not as if I had told anyone else. My family all suspected, but no one had ever asked so I had never told them.

It wasn't as if, once I told Leo about his dad, I could finish it by saying, 'You can go and see him if you want.'

I hadn't been sure what to do, so I did what I did every time I didn't know what to do for the best, I put the note back where I found it, and blocked it out by making us all something to eat.

I stand in the doorway of Leo's room, wondering if there are any other notes he has written.

*   *   *

His plane landed hours ago.
OK, it wasn't quite hours ago, but it felt like it. Every minute that he was queuing up to get through immigration, to get his passport stamped, waiting for his bags (how many can he have when he's a boy who's always travelled and lived light?) to appear on the carousel and wrestle them off, felt like an hour to me.

97

Put in context, the fact that I hadn't seen him in eight months, three weeks and four days should have stayed my impatience. But this was Mal. Mal. My most favourite person in the whole world. The person I had known longest in the whole world. I was barely restraining myself from climbing over the barrier and running through the double doors of the Arrivals lounge, leapfrogging over a couple of (armed) security guards, whilst shouting his name. I had visions that he'd missed his plane. He'd called me two days ago to make sure I could still come and meet him at the airport. It was all meant to be a big surprise for our family; they weren't expecting him back for another five months at least, so I was to meet him, then we'd show up at his mother's. Bless Mal, though, he wasn't exactly the most organised of men when there were women involved. It wouldn't surprise me if he'd gone out for a few beers the night before his plane left, got talking to someone pretty and Antipodean and decided that his future did indeed lie in Australia, and that he might just stay. Then in a week or so, he'd be back on the phone, telling me that he'd changed his mind and was coming home after all.

That was the thing about my pal Mal, he fell in love at the same rate he fell in lust, then he spent an inordinate amount of time—usually longer than it took for him to fall for said woman—trying to make it work, before giving it up as a bad lot and leaving.

The last time I saw him it had been at this very airport, but I hadn't been able to see him properly because I was crying so much. I don't think his mother had cried that much and she, Victoria,

Cordy, Mum and Dad had all discreetly blended into the background whilst we said our goodbyes. He'd put down his small rucksack and gathered me up in his arms. 'Please stop crying,' he whispered into my ear.

I nodded, tears still streaming down my face despite my valiant effort to hold them in, which involved sniffing back a large globule of snot before it left my nose. 'You're going to make me cry,' he said.

I hadn't approved of this plan to go off and explore the world. Who did he think he was, Christopher Columbus? Captain Cook? Captain Kirk? What did he need to see out there that he couldn't find right here in London? What was so great about 'out there'? Beautiful beaches, glorious sunshine, an outdoor lifestyle, stunning scenery and the chance to reinvent yourself—yes, Australia had all that going for it, but still.

The double doors opened and I felt the level of expectation and excitement leap up around me. All of us were in the same position: desperate to see that face, to see that person again. As though choreographed, we, the group of strangers at the barriers, strained forwards as the edge of a trolley, laden with suitcases, pushed through the doors. My eyes flew up to see the pusher. He was tall, white, but in his fifties with silver, thinning hair. All around me, people sagged in disappointment.

The worst part of him going away was that we had originally planned to do it together. I'd never wanted to travel, but Mal had convinced me it would be just the thing I needed to get some life experience before I started my psychology doctorate.

'You have to take care of Mum,' he had said, stroking away my tears.

That was why I couldn't go. I had the money saved up, but we couldn't both go and leave his mother behind. We wouldn't have felt right. It was his dream to see the world, he was the one who had lived with his mother all the way through university to take care of her, he was the one who never had the chance to have an adventure, to do what I did when I went to Oxford. I would have been the sidekick, along for the ride but not appreciating it as much as someone who had never known freedom, independence, what it means to be young. I'd known that was his worry as we made plans, so I'd said to him I wanted to start my course that year and, since I was studying in London, I would keep an eye on Aunt Mer. My parents would do most of the looking after, they always had, but I would let him know regularly what was happening.

'You promise?' he had asked me.

I'd swallowed the big lump of emotion clogging up my throat. 'Promise.'

'Thank you,' he'd breathed, cupping my face in his hand. He'd pressed his lips against my wet cheek and hugged me close. He smelt of what I thought love felt like. True love. He smelt of nothing and everything. Inhaling him made me smile inside. He reminded me of every good thing that had ever happened to me. When he'd finally pulled away, his dark, rust-brown eyes were glistening. I took a mental picture of him. Tall, the marginally bulkier side of lanky, with long, streamlined muscles. He'd cut his honey-blond curls short so he looked older around the face. His large, veiny hands with long, thick fingers. His oval face with his slightly long nose. His large, awestruck eyes. He hadn't shaved, despite his mum telling him to do so, so he had stubble that sat around his chin, reaching up to his sideburns.

Touching him reminded me of feeling safe, of knowing that no matter what, there was someone out there who relied on me. Always. I'd pressed my head against his chest, listening to his heart. I knew that rhythm, that beat, better than any other heart. I'd heard it more times than I'd heard my own. It'd keep me going for the fifteen months he was going to be away: twelve in Australia until his visa ran out, then three months to make his way home.

'I've got to go,' he'd said. His voice. I took in his voice. I'd almost forgotten to take an imprint of that. I clung tighter to him.

'F-ing 'ell, Nove, what you trying to do, break a rib?' he'd gasped.

'Yeah, if it'll stop you going,' I'd said.

'I'll be back before you know it,' he'd replied. 'You won't even have the chance to miss me.' He sounded so casual about it, I almost believed he meant it, until he stepped back and I saw fresh tears glistening in his eyes.

He'd raised a hand, waved at our family, turned to me. I saw his face tremble, and then I saw him struggle to control himself; his thumb and forefinger went to the inner corners of his eyes and he pinched the bridge of his nose as he lowered his head. 'I'll see you,' he'd said, picking up his rucksack. 'I'll see you really soon.' He started to walk away and I quailed inside. That was it. He was walking out of my life and all he'd said was 'I'll see you.'

Two steps away, he turned, his face lit up as he grinned at me. I grinned too, before he was back in front of me, grabbing me into a bear hug, lifting me off my feet and then putting me down again. Then he kissed me on the mouth. For the first time ever. He kissed me on the mouth. His soft, sensual lips covering mine, moving over them, his tongue pushing gently into my mouth. It seemed to last for ever. This feeling of flying, this feeling of floating on a different plane with the person I loved more than anything. We were friends, best friends, and everyone was always asking if there was anything more between us, but there wasn't. After all that stuff from four years ago, I had all but consigned my feelings to nonsense, to me being silly. But he still kissed me on the mouth in the middle of a crowded London airport, in front of our family. He broke away. Too soon, I thought. How many years had I wanted that to happen? Always knowing after the weekend he had told me he could never love me that it never would. 'Now, try explaining to them lot,' he had nodded towards our family, 'that we're just friends and you weren't sobbing your heart out because the love of your life was walking away.'

'You—' I'd begun, realising what he'd done, why he'd done it. Now they were all going to think . . . 'You—'

'Bye, Nova,' he'd said with a wide cheeky grin (one that I snapped up and stowed away carefully in my heart with all the other images of him I had), 'good luck with that,' and walked away.

More and more people were pouring into the Arrivals area. The noise level in the airport was at a deafening high: people squealing and crying as

102

they saw each other; talking loudly and excitedly as they tried to catch up on everything that had happened during their separation. Making up for lost time in the seconds they'd been reunited. I watched couples leaping into each other's arms, clinging to each other, kissing and crying and kissing, repeating how they'd missed each other. I saw relatives who lived thousands of miles apart, hugging and promising they wouldn't leave it so long next time. I noticed friends, dancing around, holding on to each other, so excited to be together they could hardly stand still.

And then I saw him. Sauntering out of the double doors, a huge, black, many-pocketed rucksack on his back. His hair long and wild, his face still smattered with stubble. He seemed bigger than the last time I saw him. Despite his tan, he was grey with jetlag, dark circles ringed his eyes. His travelling clothes—long surfer shorts and a pink surfer T-shirt under a white overshirt—were all creased.

Mal. *Mal*.

He saw me and started walking quickly towards the Arrivals barriers; I pushed my way towards the end, shooing people aside as though they were flies. He shed his rucksack, dropped his bag and bent with his arms open as I leapt on to him. In the Olympics of leaping, I would have scored a perfect ten. He caught me and I wrapped my legs around his waist, my arms around his neck. Even though I wasn't waif-like, he was strong enough to hold me. Solid enough to keep on holding me as my senses reacquainted themselves with him. He smelt of sunshine and adventures; he felt solid and strong; with my ear pressed against his neck, his heart sounded exactly the same.

'You smell so good,' he whispered. His voice hadn't developed an Australian inflection, it was the same one that I had replayed over and over whilst he'd been gone. 'You look so good. You feel so good.' His lips pressed against the space between my neck and cheek, lingering there. 'I'm so glad I'm back.'

I couldn't speak. I was overwhelmed by having him home. Safe. Looking ridiculous, but safe. So many things had happened since he'd been gone, stuff I couldn't tell him about on the phone. Stuff that could keep for now, stuff that I'd often struggled to handle all on my own, but would be all right now he was back.

'You look ridiculous,' I said to him as he settled me down on the ground.

He glanced down at himself, then returned his gaze to me. He didn't seem to have noticed until I pointed it out. 'I came straight from the beach—we had a party,' he explained. 'My flight was so early there was no point going to sleep.'

'You're going to freeze out there.'

'Yeah, you're right, I'd better change.'

I looked around for signs to the men's. They were located to the left, just beyond the car hire desks. I turned around to tell him and saw that he'd opened his rucksack right there. He started rummaging inside, retrieved a pair of jeans and the thick blue jumper his mother had made for him when he was sixteen. Oblivious to the open-mouthed stares of people around him, Mal stepped into his jeans, buttoned them on. Then he struggled into his jumper, which had been way too big for him when he'd first got it but was now just a tad too small and was moulded to him like a second skin. It was the only thing Aunt Mer had ever finished and he was obviously loath to be parted from it. He kicked off his flip-flops—thongs, he'd told me they were called in Australia—and pulled out a pair of boots from each of the large pockets on the sides of his rucksack. Rolled up in the boots were thick socks. He tugged on his socks and boots, then stood up, holding his arms out in a 't'dah!' gesture. 'Better?' he asked.

I laughed. 'Yeah, better.'

'Good,' he said through his smile. He took a step towards me, staring down at me. I felt my heart flip, my stomach dance. *He's back, he's really back.*

He leant down, kissed me briefly on the mouth. 'You taste amazing, like home,' he said. 'You don't know how glad I am to be back.'

I couldn't help but touch my lips. All the nights I'd spent breaking my heart over him came flooding back. All those years when I had been so convinced that I was in love with him, that he was my soul mate, he was my future and I didn't want anyone else, gushed through my mind. I could never understand why he didn't want me. Why he could be so open about loving me as a friend but didn't find me attractive. Never wanted to kiss me. Except that one time at the airport to get me into strife, and now, this brief homecoming kiss. I'd always longed for him to look at me like he was doing now. Except this was clearly a look that was all about him being home. Nothing to do with wanting me in *that* way. Thankfully I'd grown out of wanting that. Mostly.

His grin was wide and bright because of his tan. 'Did you spend all your time on the beach?' I asked him, noticing the string of shell fragments he wore around his neck. I bet if someone held him upside down, sand would pour out of him.

He shook his head, his grin getting wider. 'Not all my time. Beach, bars, snowboarding, hiking. Seeking enlightenment.'

'Oh, so you don't think all that is nonsense any more?'

'Did I ever say it was nonsense? I must have been winding you up. I developed a particular interest in crystals.'

'Crystals, huh? Really?' I replied. I was waiting for the punchline. He was always doing this. Pretending to me that he was interested in the 'out there' stuff I was passionate about and then would have some way to make a joke of it. This time, with the crystals, I was sure the words 'hard' and 'stiff' were about to come out of his mouth.

'I found out what they are used for. I found out that diamonds are a stone of purity. They bond relationships and are seen as a sign of,' he closed one eye, looking upwards as though trying hard to remember, 'commitment and fidelity. That's why they're used so often in engagement rings. And then there's rose quartz, the stone of love and romance.'

I raised my eyebrows, he'd clearly used those lines to get women into bed. They were pretty inspired chat-up lines—he'd be hinting at love and a long-term relationship—things you'd probably never get, but they seemed to reveal a deep, thoughtful side to him; showed that he felt things intensely. He did, but you only found that out once you'd known him years.

'Aren't you impressed with what I learned?' he asked.

'Very,' I admitted.

'Sooooo, I was thinking,' he began, just as Keith arrived and said: 'Found you!' as he came to a standstill beside us. 'Not doing too well on the location front,' he said. 'First I couldn't find a parking spot that wasn't all the way back on the motorway, and then I couldn't find you. You wouldn't think I used to do orienteering in the Army, would you?'

Mal stopped talking as shock passed across his face. I hadn't told him I was back with Keith. That after a year apart, we'd bumped into each other in a supermarket and had gone for a coffee, which turned into a drink, which turned into dinner, which turned into dating again because we'd only split up because I'd decided he was too old for me. I hadn't told Mal because I always suspected he didn't think Keith was right for me.

'All right, mate,' Keith said, suddenly remembering why we were at the airport in the first place. He took Mal's hand, shook it. 'Good time away?'

Mal nodded, conjured up a smile for his face as he said, 'Yeah.' I'd hoped that Keith giving us a lift back from the airport would endear him to Mal.

'Nothing's changed, I still can't drive—despite what I said about maybe taking lessons—so Keith offered to come pick you up with me.'

'Thanks,' Mal said in a monotone. 'Disgruntled' could have been his middle name at that moment. He was probably narked with me for telling my boyfriend he was back when his own mother didn't know.

'OK, shall we go?' I said brightly, trying to rescue the good mood we'd had. 'I've got lots of treats planned for you. All your favourite foods and a few tinnies. We can get a cab round to your mum's later, if you like?'

Mal hoisted his rucksack on to his shoulder, even though he was still wearing his new middle name like a thick heavy cloak. I picked up his smaller bag and linked my arm through his. Keith wouldn't mind, he understood about me and Mal; Mal, on the other hand, did mind. He stiffened at my touch. *This is going to be fun*, I thought as we followed Keith towards the car park.

While Keith went to do battle with the queues for the paying machines, Mal and I waited by his car.

Mal hadn't spoken since the two words he'd said to Keith. Strong and silent type he may be, but this was bordering on the ridiculous. I didn't want to get cross with him, but if he kept it up, I'd give him a telling off when we got to my place.

'Look, I'm sorry if it's annoyed you that—' I began.

'Is he what you really want, Nova?' Mal cut in.

Ah, so this was about whether Keith was right for me. He was older, but he was incredible to me. He told me all the time how much he adored me. We laughed a lot, we liked the same things. He listened to me—not when I talked about psychics and crystals and the like—but about everything else. And he was gorgeous. He had the presence of a statesman, the looks of a film star and the biggest heart. Yes, he was what I wanted. He made me smile. When I was alone, I could think of Keith and smile. And that's why I knew I'd (mostly) grown out of my obsession with Mal. There was someone else on earth who could make me smile like Mal used to.

'I'd marry him tomorrow if he asked me,' I replied.

Mal inhaled deeply. Nodded. He exhaled just as deeply as he ran his hand through his hair, still nodding. 'OK,' he said eventually. Smiling grimly but still nodding his head. 'OK, that's good enough for me.' His cloak of disgruntlement seemed to fall away and his face became the sunshine that I'd seen earlier in the Arrivals area. 'You have my blessing, little one,' he said.

'Well that's a relief,' I said, sarcastically. Although it was. It'd be difficult to date someone who Mal didn't approve of. I'd do it, but it would feel as if I was cheating myself, lying to myself about whether I was truly in love with that person. 'Just wait, I'm going to make sure that whoever you end up with thinks Hercules' labours were nothing compared with the challenges I set her before she can get my approval. You watch, I'm going to make her go on a quest to find the Golden Fleece.'

*   *   *

I leave my clothes in a pile on the floor by the bed and don't bother to wrap my hair or even put on my pyjamas. It's far too much effort to reach under my pillow for my nightclothes or my scarf.

Maybe I haven't been thinking about Mal because I still miss him. After all, I've done that every day for the past eight years or so. Maybe it's because Leo is missing him. Leo doesn't know his dad, but that doesn't mean he can't miss him. Want to know what he's like, who he is, how he fits into the huge jigsaw puzzle that is Leo's life. Maybe, when Leo wakes up, I can talk to him about Mal. Maybe I can let him know without having to say the words that, if he could, his dad would love him very much. How could he not, when Leo is the best thing he's ever done?

CHAPTER SEVEN

'Open your eyes, Steph,' he says.

I do not want to open my eyes. I have only just fallen asleep, it seems, and I do not want to return to the place where I have recently left.

Angry Mal is there and I do not want to face him. It's too much for a weekend, for the day after my tenth wedding anniversary. I want to stay here, half asleep, half awake, completely nowhere all at once.

Here, I don't dream like I do when I'm asleep, and I don't fret like I do when I'm completely awake.

Last night, surprisingly, he'd come to bed at the same time as me. But unlike usual, when we'd chat about what we'd do the next day, he'd stripped off his clothes in silence with his back to me, standing on his side of the bed, dropping each item on the floor as he exposed his strong body. Each muscle long and toned, smooth and sleek under his pale-cream skin.

I'd watched him strip down to nothing and then slide under the covers as though I wasn't there.

110

'Goodnight,' he'd mumbled, before turning to face the window.

I'd undressed in the silence, placing my dress and bra and knickers into the laundry basket straight away. I'd tried, I'd really tried, I'd even pulled aside the sheets on my side of the bed—but I couldn't. I had to go over to Mal's side of the bed and pick up his clothes. There was no way I could leave his pile of things lying on the floor. It made the room look untidy. And if the room was untidy, it made *everything* feel untidy. It didn't take much to make things tidy, it took a lot less to let things slide. If you controlled your surroundings, made sure everything was perfect, bad things were less likely to happen to you. If you didn't let things slide, things didn't fall apart. And if things did start to crumble, they would soon be fixed because chaos wouldn't last long in the presence of perfect order.

I picked up Mal's clothes, but he really did know better—dropping them on the floor was obviously a way of getting at me. Yes, maybe he hadn't consciously done it to needle me, maybe he just couldn't be bothered walking to the laundry basket, which was on the other side of the room, but we'd been together long enough for him to know it would be like an elbow in the ribs to me.

As I crossed the carpet, I stopped, brought his bundle of clothes to my nose, inhaled. Mal, the essence of him, filled my senses. He was one of my favourite smells. Clean like rosemary, soothing like thyme, spicy like cinnamon, undercut with a sharp tanginess like oranges. Without really thinking, I dropped the jacket and trousers into the basket, then buttoned on his dark cream shirt over my

111

naked body. It was one of his more expensive shirts, its cotton was thick and the fabric tightly woven, the stitching durable, and it smelt of him. I wanted—*needed*—to go to sleep with the smell of him on me, pretending he was there with me. Pretending that he had been inside me and was now lying curled up beside me. Pretending we hadn't both forgotten our wedding anniversary, pretending I hadn't seen this played out many, many times before—that this wasn't the first step on the road to divorce.

It was the thought of that word that had conjured up the night terrors. Huge, sweeping tides of panic moved through me every time I wondered if this was it, whether he would leave. *When* he would leave.

Then a similar tide would crash through me as I wondered what would become of us if he didn't leave. If we would have to keep on living with huge unspoken truths between us. Then, I had begun to wonder if he still loved me. He stayed with me, but is he here because he loves me, or because he feels duty-bound, obligated?

At some point, when the terrors had snaked their icy tentacles over every inch of my mind, and in some places twisted back in on themselves, I fell asleep. And then I woke up again, but not fully. Which is how I like it. Floating in nothingness, too asleep to think, too awake to dream. Just floating here.

And now he's trying to bring me round. Why he thinks I would want to come back here, I have no idea.

'Come on, babe, I know you're not asleep, please open your eyes.'

112

Well, when he's called me babe and asked me so nicely . . . Slowly I prise my eyes apart. It is still dark, still the middle of the night, because the sun hasn't started to rise and the birds haven't begun their dawn chorus.

He is on his side, leaning over me, a smile on his face, sparkles in his eyes, a completely different person to the one I went to bed with. *What has happened to transform him in the past few hours?*

He strokes his thumb over my cheek and I bite my lower lip, wondering why he is behaving as though he loves me again. 'I was thinking,' he says, his eyes never leaving my face. 'If we get going in the next couple of hours, at the crack of dawn, we could go to Paris.'

'Paris?'

'Yeah. And if we take an overnight bag, we'll see if we can find somewhere nice to stay last minute. If not, we'll come back, try to find somewhere to stay up in central London.'

I frown at him. 'Why?' I ask.

'To celebrate our anniversary.'

'I thought you were working today.'

'Nope, I'll call them from the train. I'll even leave my laptop and BlackBerry at home.'

'Why?' I ask again.

'To celebrate our anniversary,' he repeats. 'Do you fancy it?'

Of course I do. 'Hmmm . . .' I say. 'Maybe.'

'Oh, maybe, huh?' He climbs on top of me, straddling me, his knees gently resting on either side of my thighs. 'Well, *maybe* I can't help but notice that you're wearing one of my shirts.' He reaches for the first button. 'And *maybe* I need a way for you to make it up to me.'

113

'Nope, don't think so,' I say, as he continues unbuttoning me. Pleasure pulses through me as he dramatically rips open the shirt. His soft fingers move over my skin, as if trying to read me, and my body comes alive with excitement.

He suddenly buries his nose in my belly button and starts to tickle me. I yelp, squirming, trying to get away from him. He holds me firmly between his legs, and soon we are both laughing as we dig at every available bit of flesh, kicking and screaming.

Mal's large hands close around my wrists, pinning them on either side of my head. 'Do you concede?' he asks, his face an inch away from mine, his chest moving rapidly.

'Yes,' I gasp. 'Yes.'

'OK,' Mal says, and his hands slip away as he sits back.

I launch myself at him, catching him off guard and in the ribs, knocking him off centre on to the bed. 'You wench!' he cries at me as he lands and I climb on top of him, pinning his wrists to the bed.

'I can't believe you fell for that,' I laugh, staring down at him. His hair, the colour of burnt butter, has grown recently, it lays in thick curls all over his scalp. His russet eyes and his mouth are all alight with mirth, his skin flushed.

'Neither can I,' he replies.

'OK, now I can do some questioning: do you really want to go to Paris?'

'Yes. I'm sorry to tell you, babe, I know the sex is fantastic between us and everything, but I am married. And I love my wife. And we've never been to Paris together so I want to go there with her.'

'Why, oh why, are the best ones taken?'

Excitement and happiness flutter around my stomach like a bird in a cage. This is how it felt between us when we first met. How I haven't felt for more than a few seconds in so long.

Mal uses my distraction, the slight loosening of my grip on his wrists, as a chance to flip me on to my back. Before I can react, he opens my legs and is making love to me. My body becomes boneless underneath him, like a fluid that moves with him, moulding myself to the curves and lines of his body. As I sigh, he buries his face in the pillow. I remember when he used to cover my mouth with his, swallowing any sigh, moan or groan—any sound I made—into himself, as though he wanted everything he could get of me while we made love. But it's only a little thing. I don't even remember when he stopped doing it. And it really is only a little thing, and it doesn't matter. We are together again. Properly. As man and wife. As woman and husband. As Steph and Mal.

And there is nothing . . . uhhhhhhhh . . . nothing as delicious as this.

In Mum's shoebox in the bottom drawer at the bottom of her wardrobe, he found the pictures. Lots of them, when everyone wore funny clothes. And then there was one of him, but it wasn't him.

The boy had hair the colour of the pebbles on the beach, and he was white like Nana Mer, and his school tie was a different colour to his. He ran to Mum in the kitchen and showed it to her.

'Who is this, Mum?' He held the photo in front of her.

115

Mum wiped her hands on her apron and took the photo from him and stared at it for the longest time. For ages and ages and ages. Then she looked up at him and her eyes were wet. His tummy went funny because he knew Mum was going to start crying.

'He's a boy I grew up with,' she said. 'But he turned into a man I don't know.'

Mum handed the photo back to him.

'Why does he look like me?'

She did that thing where she rubbed her fingers on the side of his head, then stroked them down his face. 'Because God likes to play jokes on me sometimes,' she said. 'Not always funny ones.'

Leo nodded at Mum, but he knew that wasn't the reason. He knew it was because this man was his dad. Dad wasn't his real dad and he didn't look like him. But Mum looked like Grandma. And David looked like his dad. And Richard looked like his dad. He knew, just knew, that this boy looked like him because he grew up and became his dad.

'OK, Mum,' he said and smiled at her. He didn't say he knew that this man was his dad because he knew that it would make Mum cry.

He ran upstairs to his bedroom and hid the photo at the bottom of the book box under his bed. He liked to know it was there.

Leo, age 5 years

part three

CHAPTER EIGHT

So far, these past four days, I have managed to avoid those two women who were gossiping about me.

It had all been pretty tame compared to the half-truths and stories people used to tell about me, but it's such a shock to have it happen as an adult. When I've all but convinced myself there is nothing wrong with me.

I program an hour on the running machine on a steep incline and hit the 'go' button. I need to run. I hadn't been able to come early today, before work—my way of avoiding my two critics—because Mal, for some reason, had wanted me this morning.

Being so desperately wanted by him is such a rare occurrence that I hadn't resisted. We didn't make it to Paris on Saturday, we spent the day in bed, watching DVDs and eating junk food. After that first time, first thing, we didn't make love again; we snuggled but that was as far as it went. But this morning, he had pounced on me the second the alarm went off and I opened my eyes. It wasn't once, either, he'd been like a man on heat. Twice in the bedroom, then in the shower, then, as I was leaning over the kitchen counter reading the paper and waiting for my toast to pop up, he had popped up instead. He'd actually ripped the seam of my favourite pair of (*very* expensive) knickers in his haste. Then in the shower again. Five times in one morning is unheard of. He'd only left because his BlackBerry had bleeped, reminding him about a meeting with the board members he absolutely could not miss.

Each time had been fast, frantic and unexpectedly hard, a vague sense of detachment lingering afterwards. If I didn't know better, I would have thought he was having an affair or thinking of having an affair, and this was his guilt sex.

But, he wouldn't. I know that now. *Now*, when it's too late, I know he wouldn't ever do that.

The terrain starts to rise beneath my feet, and I feel it coming, my lungs pushing harder, my heart thudding faster, the blood starting to race in my veins. I love this. The build-up. The rush towards ecstasy.

I shouldn't really complain about Mal being all over me. Sometimes for months he doesn't seem to know I'm female, let alone someone who's meant to turn him on. And those times never coincide with the times I don't feel up to it, and I have to either close my eyes and let him get on with it, or find excuses to get out of it.

Not that he'd mind if I said, 'Mal, I'm not feeling a hundred per cent right now, can I just go to bed on my own?' He'd probably appreciate it. It would mean I was being honest. He wouldn't spend his time wondering if it was a symptom, because it would be. I suppose I don't confide in him because I can't stand the way he changes. Subtly, but definitely, if I do tell the absolute truth.

The way he starts checking the medicine cabinet, and looking for evidence, and 'disappearing' the razors and painkillers, and turning up at work to pick me up, and talking to my doctor behind my back. Honestly, you have one little slip every now and again and your husband acts as though you're some sort of nut job. When really, like every other woman out there, you're just moody. I'm just moody.

I was a moody child.

I was a moody teenager.

I am a moody adult.

No big deal if you ask me. HUGE deal if you ask my husband.

As I near the peak of my hill, I feel the sweat pouring off me, just how I like it. I feel cleansed after a run, tamed and cleansed. Anything bad sweated away with a good, old-fashioned workout.

I start to speed up for the last few hundred metres.

Maybe he is feeling guilty after Friday night. For telling on me—on us—in front of all our friends. I've had to avoid all their phone calls and emails since. I'm bracing myself for Carole or Ruth to show up at my work. Or maybe, like my steep-incline running, sex has become Mal's displacement activity because—like me—all he can do is think about them.

I've been on the internet for hours searching and searching. I'd found out a few scraps of information. She hadn't used her doctorate to become a practising clinical psychologist as planned, she had opened a so-called psychic café— get your aura cleansed or something with your coffee—near Brighton. But there were no pictures of her. And most importantly, no pictures of him.

When I come out of the showers, bundled up in a towel, my hair in clumpy tangles around my face, those women are in the locker room.

Automatically my heart skips a beat, and I

hesitate in the doorway for a moment, wondering if I should turn around and go away before they see me.

The brunette looks up from lacing a pink and white trainer and catches my eye—she drains of all colour, like last Friday. If I walk away now, I'll seem cowardly, and as if I have done something wrong. And where would I go? Back to the showers and lurk around, making other women think I'm spying on them? Essentially giving more people more reasons to talk about me?

Focusing on the wall opposite, I walk in and head for my locker. I type in the code and pull open the door, and keeping it ajar to afford myself a little privacy I pull out my knickers. Hooking the towel over my shoulders, I pull them on, then fasten on my bra.

I know they're still in here, that they're probably watching me, trying to find more things to add to the list of inaccuracies they've made up about me. I can hear them whispering, I can feel them nudging each other. In about three seconds, I'm going to spin round and tell them to say whatever it is they've got to say to my face.

'We're really sorry,' one of them says. 'About last Friday, we're really sorry.'

I pull on my hipster denim skirt and button it up, pretending not to have heard.

'We didn't mean for you to overhear,' the other says as I tug on my top. Usually I would at least towel dry my hair but I have to get out of here as soon as possible.

'It's just cos we're jealous,' the first one says.

'Yeah, you've done amazingly well and we're still stuck here with our goal weights nothing more than pie in the sky numbers,' the other adds.

'We're truly sorry.'

I slip on my jacket, pull my bag from my locker and drop my trainers on the ground, shoving each foot into them without socks. I don't even bother to pull out the backs, so I have to wear them like heavy flip-flops on my feet.

I have anger, pure unadulterated rage fizzing in my veins. What am I supposed to do, tell them it's OK? Agree with them? Try to make them feel better by telling them it doesn't matter? That I completely understand?

How did their bad behaviour become my problem? At least the people who used to write that I was a 'slut whore' and a 'crazy slag' on toilet walls never expected me to forgive them for it.

I slam shut my locker with such force that the whole bank of lockers sways violently, threatening to topple over. I spin around and face them, stand frozen for a second, glaring at each of them. They both shrink back a little. My nostrils are probably flaring, my eyes narrow and fierce.

The backs of my trainers dig into my soles as I march out of the locker room. Seconds later I march back in, my trainers still like flip-flops. I stop in front of the women.

'Just because someone's husband is good-looking, it doesn't make him perfect,' I say. 'Doesn't mean being thin is enough to make your marriage work. Just because he's good-looking doesn't mean he isn't flawed in every way possible.'

*   *   *

I was wearing black.

123

I was wearing a black designer shift dress I'd found in one of the charity shops in central London where all the celebs leave their cast-offs. It was last season, but I knew I could pull it off if I wore it with ironic casualness: with my hair in a slightly messy side chignon, and flats, it would seem that I had this season's clothes but I was fashionable enough to wear what I want, when I want, and know that I still looked good in it. Once I bought it, I couldn't afford to eat for a week, but I had to have it. Between fashion and food, there was no contest. When something suited me I had to have it, no matter what I needed to sacrifice to get it. It was a simple case of self-esteem economics: once I looked good, I would feel good. Sometimes looking good, being groomed on the outside, was all that kept me going on the inside. Some women filled the hole inside them with food, their work, alcohol, drugs, unwise sex—I knew that my vice was keeping myself 'together'. Running every morning, perfecting my make-up, wearing clothes that suited me—looking the part so I would feel the part.

I'd been in the bar for ten minutes on my own, waiting for a couple of the other legal secretaries I worked with to show up. I checked my watch again, suppressing a sigh as the big hand slid to the five— showing me that it was 8:25 p.m. We'd arranged to meet in this cool bar just behind Marble Arch at 7:30, and I'd arrived just after eight because I knew they were always fashionably late—we all were. This time, we'd all outdone ourselves. Some of the partners at the large law firm where we worked had those mobile phone things. Phones you took with you in your bag or briefcase, so you could ring

124

people and ask them where they were if they were late, or ring to tell them you had been delayed. But none of us were even close to being that rich. We had to make arrangements and stick to them, or make use of the payphones.

Rather than sit alone in a booth, I stood at the bar with a Sex on the Beach, surveying the other drinkers. It was quiet, empty and sedate for that time on a Friday night. Maybe Candice, who read all the gossip columns religiously, had got it wrong, maybe this wasn't the latest place to be, after all. There weren't that many men in here, nor were there the sort of women who men would come to try to bed. A smattering of after-work types sat in a couple of booths, but none that interested me. I turned back to the bar, returned my attention to my drink. I could only afford one more so was nursing the cocktail, using the stiff straw to move the ice around in the practised way of someone who didn't earn very much. I'd been known to make a drink last all night the week before payday.

I glanced up from the depths of my drink and he was there. Standing beside me, having appeared from nowhere, it seemed. 'Hello,' he said. I hadn't seen him in the bar—I would have noticed if I had. I'm sure very few people didn't notice him. He was a tall man, with dark honey-blond hair that lay in boyish curls all over his head. He had a strong jaw and sculpted body; he wore a blue, lightweight V-neck jumper and baggy brown cords that sat on his slender hips. He had a watch on his wrist and that was it. Simply dressed, devastatingly gorgeous.

I smiled a hello back because I was speechless. He was talking to me. This god of a man was talking to me. Men approached me all the time,

125

but none as . . . none like him. He was out of my league, surely. *Surely*.

'I saw you coming in here earlier, just as I was leaving, and I decided that if I got to Oxford Circus tube and I was still thinking about you then I would come back and say hello.'

My mind did a mental calculation: with his legs, it'd take him ten, fifteen minutes to walk to Oxford Circus tube station from here, the same time back, which meant he was telling me that since he saw me, I'd been on his mind for half an hour. Half an hour. It was all true, wasn't it? All the romance stories I watched and read, they were all true: there is someone perfect out there for you and you might never know it. He had been thinking about me for half an hour and after a mere glimpse of me. That sort of thing *never* happened to me. And look at him, as well. *Look* at him.

'So you've said hello,' I said. I noticed how warm his eyes were. They were a dark russet-brown that sparkled like a log fire burning gently in the hearth. 'What's your next line?' I sounded so cool and laid back; in reality my heart was racing. Our eyes met then, and all my thoughts evaporated. After his eyes had cleared my mind, they moved on to my heart, making it thump so loud and violently, it hurt.

He shook his head, his gaze locked on mine. 'I don't have one.' He smiled then, and I thought my heart would explode. 'My mate told me to remember kisses if I manage to speak to a woman I truly like.'

'Kisses?' I breathed, my gaze flitting to his lips. Pink and firm and quite probably made to fit perfectly over my mouth.

126

He nodded. 'Keep It Short, Sweet and Especially Simple. K.I.S.S.E.S.'

'Kisses,' I repeated. We were talking about kissing. We'd only just met, but kissing was on our lips.

'She's going to be insufferable after this,' he said.

She?! My thoughts of a spring wedding halted in their tracks like a needle scratched across a record. *Who's this she?! And why is my future husband talking about her? Doesn't he know that is terribly bad form?* 'Who's she?' I asked, a thin smile stretched across my face. I was trying valiantly to steel myself to hear that he had a girlfriend and was flirting with me because he couldn't help himself. A clear euphemism for: you're a quick bunk-up. Or, worse, maybe they had an open relationship so he was allowed to sleep with other women, on the understanding that he would always be with her. *Or*, I felt my whole body baulk at the horror of it, maybe they were swingers. I'd read about it in the papers and a couple of magazines. They were into partner-swapping and . . . God, help me, *threesomes*. Maybe he wanted me to join them.

'My best friend, Nova. She told me to go out tonight because she had a feeling I'd meet someone special. She gets these feelings about things. She rang me six times today to make sure I was going out. She said I'd regret it for the rest of my life if I didn't. I tried explaining to her that if I didn't go out, there'd be no way of disproving her theory, and if I did come out and didn't meet someone, she'd explain it away by saying I didn't go to the right place. Either way, she wins. But I'm glad I came out tonight.' He smiled again. All thoughts of this woman, this friend, flew from my head like dust motes flying from a room with all the windows suddenly thrown open. All I could see was the softening of the lines of his face when he turned his mouth up to smile. I knew at that moment that I didn't want any other man to smile at me ever again. I didn't want him to smile like that at any other person. I wanted him to be mine. 'Well, I will be glad I came out if I get your number.'

'Call me old-fashioned, but I think it's a good idea to know someone's name before you give them your number,' I said. 'Even if it's just so you can know who it is on the other end of the phone when you answer it.' I was being witty. That was the effect he had on me. I'd never been witty in the whole of my life and here I was, charming him with banter. I wondered for a moment who the dress had belonged to. Which celeb had given me a piece of her allure when I picked it up in the charity shop.

His small laugh brightened his already sparkling eyes.

'My name's Mal. And yours begins with an S, right?'

My eyes widened. 'How did you know that? Did your friend tell you that? Is she psychic?'

'No. People have told her that, but she won't have a bar of it.' Gently he placed his finger a few inches below the well of my throat. 'Your necklace.'

My 'S' necklace. I felt my face colour up. *How embarrassing. He must think I'm a fool.* 'Oh. Yes. My name begins with an S. Stephanie. I'm called

Stephanie. Or Steph.'

'Steph.' My name fell gently from his tongue, a short, sweet melody. Even though he'd removed his finger from my throat, I still felt the warmth of the impression it had made, a gentle little brand. 'You're cute when you blush. Cuter.'

'Mal what?' I replied, ignoring what he had said, knowing it had made me blush a little more.

'Wacken. I'm Mal Wacken. Is that enough to get your number?'

'I think so.'

My fingers were shaking with excitement and slight disbelief as I wrote down the number for the payphone outside my studio flat—I couldn't afford to have my own phoneline—on a piece of till receipt the barman had kindly given to me. 'I can't wait to tell Nova that I got the number of the most beautiful woman in London,' he said.

'You can stop the flattery now, you've got my number.'

'K.I.S.S.E.S., remember? No flattery, that'd be far too elaborate for me. Just honesty.'

I blushed a little deeper, could feel myself glowing under my carefully applied make-up.

'OK, Steph, I have to be going now. Can I call you tomorrow, or is that too soon?'

'No, that's not too soon,' I replied.

'I'll see you,' he said with a grin, but not moving from where he stood.

'Yes.' I nodded. 'You will.'

'You might have noticed that I'm still standing here,' he said. 'I'm finding it hard to move away from you.'

'I really do want to answer the phone when you call,' I said. 'But I won't if you start using lines like that. Remember what your friend said.'

His eyes lingered on my mouth. 'Kisses,' he said. 'Yeah, kisses. Bye, Steph.'

'Bye, Mal.'

Candice and Liz descended upon me the second he left the bar.

'Oh, my God!' screeched Candice. '*Who* was he?'

I watched him raise a hand to wave, I waved back as he disappeared. 'Oh, no one,' I said, my eyes still fixed on the space he had left in the doorway. 'Just the man I'm going to marry.'

*   *   *

'And you know what? Not everybody comes to the gym to reach a goal weight or to become supermodel-thin. Some people need to come to the gym because it keeps them alive and connected, up here. In your mind. Where it really counts.'

*   *   *

He knew my body.

Every mole, every pore, every wrinkle, every crease, every lump, every bump. Every perfection, every imperfection. He had spent the past few hours mapping them out with his fingers, his mouth, his tongue, his eyes, his body.

I was always shy with a new man. Scared of how they would react, what they would think when my clothes were off and the lights were low enough to disguise, but not completely conceal, although bright enough to reveal.

130

Mal had undressed me slowly, kissing every piece of skin he exposed, touching every piece of skin he unveiled, examining every piece of skin he saw. It seemed to take hours. Hours of savouring his attention until I could barely breathe with desire. He kissed me all over when I was naked. He touched me all over when I was nude. He made love to me with his eyes first, then his fingers, then his body.

It was making love, not sex or fucking. It was expressing what I felt for him. Even though it was only two months since we met and we had, by unspoken but mutual agreement, decided to wait until now to do this for the first time, I knew I was in love with him. He was my forever. I knew it when I met him in the bar, I knew it every time we' met and spoke. I knew it now, curled up like a happy, blissed out, contented puppy in his arms.

It didn't matter that we were on an old, lumpy, back-breaking futon that someone had given to me when I moved into my studio. Nor that the tap in the sink kept dripping, and the fusty smell of mould that grew in the corners of the room was strong at the moment because it had rained earlier. None of it mattered. We were together. And he loved me. He hadn't said so, but I knew from the past few hours that he did.

'I've got something to tell you,' he whispered, as his fingers stroked through my hair.

I didn't reply. For a moment I thought of feigning sleep, so whatever it was, he couldn't say it and couldn't redefine tonight. Even if it was 'I love you', something I wanted to hear desperately (to my eternal shame), I didn't want it to take away from this. I wanted, I needed, lots of little bubbles

131

of perfect memories. They were important. When things went wrong—not that they would with Mal, but in life in general—I wanted to have as many things as possible to cling on to in my memory. To shine like beacons in my mind's eye so I could navigate my way back to happier times. I wanted to have this making-love memory. I wanted to have a separate one of him telling me he loved me. I wanted to have them to sit alongside the memory of meeting him. The memory of getting his first call. The memory of our first kiss. The memory of eating cold fish fingers and drinking warm ginger beer in Hyde Park. The memory of him taking my hand as we walked down the street and showing the world we were together—two who had become one. All those memories glittered like gems in the jewellery box of my mind. I didn't want them ruined by whatever it was he was about to say.

'Nova can't believe I haven't told you already.'

Her again. If it wasn't for her, he wouldn't have gone out the night he met me, so there was a sliver of gratitude towards her that would always live in my heart, but still, why did he have to bring her up *now*? He talked about her with alarming frequency as it was, why was she invading this time, too? I shifted in his arms so I could see his face. I used my forefinger to slowly trace the outline of his kiss-bruised lips, which were plump and red like overripe strawberries. I was trying to seal his mouth shut because this was a reminder as to why you needed to fall asleep right after you'd made love. Less chance of talking, therefore less chance of ruining things.

He took my hand gently in his large hand, kissed my fingers and then held them over his heart. He

132

wanted to speak.

'It's about my name,' he said.

'You're not called Mal Wacken?' I asked, confused and a little fearful.

'Yes and no.'

'Oh, God,' I said with a small groan, 'is this the bit where you tell me you used to be a woman and you were once called Natalie or something? Because if it is, I'd rather continue to live my days in blissful ignorance. The op worked really well, there are no scars, all the bits work, let's just pretend you were born a man and I'll die a happy, untraumatised woman.'

'No, nothing like that. My name, my full name, is Malvolio.'

I laughed, he was so funny. Not many people would get that joke, but we met on the night of the twelfth. *Twelfth Night*—Malvolio. I snuggled into him as I laughed gently at his joke. 'Very pleased to meet you, Malvolio,' I said through my giggles. 'I'm called Steph, but you can call me Sebastian if you like women in drag.'

He sighed. 'This is why Nova said I should have told you by now,' he said. 'She knew you'd think it was a joke.'

The giggles dried up in my throat and my whole body stiffened in horror as I closed my eyes. *Have I just been laughing at his name? Really?* When I dared open my eyes again, and raised them to see his face, he was staring at me without embarrassment or anger. 'Are you really called Malvolio?'

He nodded. 'No word of a lie. My mum's favourite play or something.' He shrugged, nonchalant and unbothered. 'No one really knows

133

why. Everyone tried to talk her out of it, apparently. Nova's parents said they begged her not to do that to me, but she was insistent. So, I'm called Malvolio.'

'Did you get bullied at school about your name?'

'There were far better reasons people tried to bully me at school,' he said, a shadow of resentment darkening his words. 'But most people called me Mal from when I was about nine onwards. Only my mum and Nova's parents and sometimes Nova's sister, Cordelia, when she's trying to be funny, call me Malvolio.'

I didn't know what to say. I wondered for a moment if I would have preferred the sex change thing instead. At least with that you could always hide it. With his name . . . Imagine the snickering in the church when we came to say our vows— there'd only be about five people *not* laughing. Not spending the rest of our natural lives thinking up *Twelfth Night* jokes. I didn't like to be the centre of attention, to stand out or to give anyone ammunition to make fun of me. Surprisingly, I realised, in this darkened room with its soundtrack of a leaky tap and our breathing, that didn't seem to bother Mal. He was confident in an unusual way. Not showy or arrogant, simply stable. At the core of him was stability and quiet, unshakeable strength. That was what true confidence gave you. The ability to face up to any situation because you knew without a doubt you could handle it.

Mal, *Malvolio*, could handle anything.

'So, am I allowed to test drive this man called Malvolio?' I asked, climbing on top of him, feeling the solidity of his form under me, between my thighs.

'Absolutely,' he said with a smile. His large, firm hands ran up the sides of my body, came to rest on my breasts as I arched back and gently rocked against him, teasing him to get ready to play again.

I had to tell him about me, I knew that. I'd always known that. This thing with his name was a bonus, I realised. It showed me the measure of who he was, proved he had the strength that someone would need when I told them the truth about me.

*   *   *

'And sometimes, it's not his eyes that go wandering, but his heart. And how do you stop that? How do you stop him being in love with someone else at the same time that he's in love with you? How? By being thin? Because believe me, that doesn't always work. In fact, it never works. So, how do you stop him splitting his heart in two and giving you only half? When you're meant to be the one who gets it all, how do you settle for half?'

*   *   *

Nova. Nova. Nova.
That's all I heard from him. Every other word that came out of his mouth was Nova. *Why don't you just marry her?!* I'd been tempted to say to him on more than one occasion.

What kind of a name is Nova, anyway? I thought as Mal and I wandered down a cobbled street in East London to the pool bar where we were meeting the amazing Nova.

135

Who on earth is called Nova? If you were named that, wouldn't you simply change it? Wouldn't you try to fit in with everyone else and *change* it? Unless, of course, you wanted to stand out. You wanted people to remember you. You thought you were soooooo incredibly special that you had to have such a ridiculous name.

Admittedly, Mal had an equally unusual name—probably more unusual than hers—but at least he made the effort to fit in by shortening it to Mal. She . . . she didn't.

I knew what she looked like. I hadn't met her, I hadn't seen any pictures of her, but I knew what she'd be like: tall and slender, naturally blonde hair down to her waist, perfectly applied make-up. She'd wear tight jeans—Guess because she could afford them—so they would show off her perfect bum as she leant over the pool table to sink the perfect shot.

It was obvious from the way Mal *constantly* talked about her that he was besotted with her and that she knew it. They'd grown up together, he explained, and they'd never gone out together. But he clearly wanted her. *Clearly*. It was apparent in the way he became animated, excited, *alive*, every time he talked about her. I knew, as well, that she was incredibly confident: you didn't have a name like hers, be a manager of a restaurant at twenty-five while finishing off a Ph.D. in psychology, without thinking you were God's gift to the universe. And, obviously, she used Mal's feelings to her advantage.

The only possible explanation as to why someone as incredible as him was still single was that she liked him that way. He probably told this

'*Nova*' about the newest woman he'd started dating. He'd introduce her to '*Nova*' and '*Nova*' wouldn't like the idea that she was about to be ousted as the most important person in his life, so she'd probably get dressed up in expensive, frilly bits that masqueraded as underwear, put on a rain mac and turn up at Mal's flat. They wouldn't even move from the corridor before she delivered her ultimatum: 'Dump this woman and you get to have sex with me again.' He might even resist for a little while, try to explain that he liked this latest girlfriend, more than the others, but then she'd undo her mac, letting him see the black lace, barely reining in her creamy-white breasts and barely covering her landing-strip-waxed bikini area, and he'd fold like tissue paper. He'd be pawing at her underwear, ripping it off her—she wouldn't care, she could afford lots of it—and taking her right there up against the corridor wall.

All the while, the poor unsuspecting girlfriend would be waiting for him to call, not having a clue she was being made a fool of before she was dumped.

Ever since he'd suggested I meet '*Nova*', I had been preparing myself to be removed from his life. I'd cancelled the meeting four times so I could have longer with him. So I could make sure that the sex was so great that he wouldn't be thinking of someone else. So I wouldn't have to meet my rival and find myself lacking. But I couldn't cancel again. I had to make sure that after this meeting, I didn't leave him alone long enough for her to come over and make her demands.

In the bar, there were three men—two of them playing pool at the centre table, one nursing a

137

drink at the bar, and the bartender. She was nowhere to be seen. We were a little late—my fault, I'd purposely seduced Mal against the wall in his shared flat just before we left—so she should have been here by now. My heart leapt with joy. Maybe she'd left, maybe she couldn't make it—either way, I had a stay of execution. I didn't have to face this *'Nova'* after all. I got to keep my boyfriend for another day.

Across the big smoky room with its wide circular bar and large green pool tables, the black door to the lavatories with a pink pool table symbol on it opened, and out she stepped. I knew instantly it was her. She smiled at us, gave a little wave, and right on cue, I felt Mal light up beside me as he smiled back at her. Three things occurred to me in quick succession as I rummaged around for a suitably realistic smile to paint on my face:
1. He hadn't told me she was black.
2. He hadn't told me she was so incredibly beautiful.
3. It was so over with Mal and me.

*   *   *

Mal bought us a round of drinks and went to play pool with the man sitting at the bar. They knew each other vaguely and he obviously wanted to leave us alone to bond, to quickly and suddenly become friends. As if that was going to *ever* happen.

I'd seen her eyes run over me, quickly, expertly assessing me, but I hadn't been able to read what she thought. She and Mal were similar like that, they could hide what they were thinking behind a

blank face and benign smile. I'd worn the dress I'd
been wearing when I met Mal. It was my talisman,
my good luck charm, and a way to ward off the evil
threat of this 'friend'. I'd teamed it with jeans and
these amazing jewelled sandals I'd borrowed from
Candice. I'd spent hours painstakingly applying
make-up that made me look as if I wasn't wearing
make-up. I wanted to look naturally, casually
classy.

I could tell she hadn't had similar worries about
meeting me: she had not a scrap of make-up on but
her skin glowed, and her brown eyes were huge,
with the longest natural eyelashes I'd ever seen.
Her long black plaits, woven here and there with
strands of brown and blonde, flowed loose around
her face, and all she wore on her perfectly curved
body was a grey vest top, plain jeans and a little
black cardigan with black beading across the front.

'Men are idiots, aren't they?' Nova said to me.

I rolled my eyes inside: she obviously thought it
was acceptable to slag off men as a way of bonding.

'What I should say is *that* man,' she pointed to
my boyfriend, 'is an idiot.'

I said nothing. She wasn't going to trick me into
bad-mouthing my lover so he would 'accidentally'
hear about it some time in the not too distant
future.

'Mal talks about you all the time,' she said.
'Knowing him, I'm pretty sure he talks about me
all the time, too.'

Arrogant bitch, I thought.

'It's nothing sinister, he just thinks that if he
constantly tells you how wonderful I am, and
repeats every two seconds how amazing you are to
me, that we'll take his word for it and we'll want to

spend every minute we're not with him with each other.' She smiled one of those wide open grins that I'd imagine drove most men crazy with desire—Julia Roberts had that smile in *Pretty Woman*. It illuminated her face, and would ignite every pleasure centre in a man's brain—not just the sexual ones, either. Triggering the friendship area of a man's brain whilst you looked like she did would be a one-way ticket to driving him out of his head with lust and affection. No wonder Mal was obsessed with her.

'Obviously it's going to have exactly the opposite effect,' she continued. She had amazing lips. Blowjob lips someone—I think Vince—had once called lips that full. How could any man not want those lips crushed under his in a kiss, or wrapped around his cock to create the ultimate in ecstasy? How could Mal not want that? In my head I quickly rewrote the scenario where she forced him to dump his latest girlfriend: it wasn't sex against the wall in the corridor, it was the ultimate in oral sex. With those lips. When she reached up and touched her mouth, surreptitiously trying to rub at the corners, like I did when I feared I hadn't been diligent enough with my napkin, I realised I'd been staring at her lips.

'I know you don't like me, Stephanie,' she said. She didn't grin. She was being serious. 'I'm not surprised when that idiot has probably been extolling my virtues. It'd have been a much better idea to tell you all the bad stuff about me.

'What I'm trying to say is, Mal is an idiot if he thinks that going on and on about someone being wonderful will endear them to another person. I don't know about you, but it takes a lot to call

140

someone my friend. And, thanks to Mal, if I have to earn your friendship, I'm probably starting off in the minus figures.' Another of her grins. 'I would like to get to know you, though. Maybe become friends eventually? You're the first person Mal's gone out with that . . . I've never seen him like this about anyone.'

'Not even you?' I blurted out. I didn't believe what she said.

'*Me?*' Her face was twisted in genuine surprise. 'You think Mal has ever felt that way about *me*?' She pressed her hand across her formidable chest, leant forwards, her face still painted with surprise. '*Me?*' She shook her head in disbelief, sat back and all at once looked harrowed. Sad. Dejected. It was a brief expression, but a genuine one. It came over her and then flitted away. So genuine was it that she didn't even have time to hide it behind a game face before I saw it.

'You really have nothing to worry about on that score,' she said after licking her lips and trying to return her expression to the one that she wore before. 'He's never . . .' She stopped, stared into the mid-distance as though trying to work out the best way to say it. 'I had a massive crush on him when I was eighteen. I thought he was "the one". I was so in love with him and I thought because he knew me and we'd grown up together that he would maybe feel the same way about me. I decided to tell him at one point and he stopped me before I could say anything by telling me he could never feel that way about a friend. About me, basically. It makes sense, I suppose. And I'm glad, to be honest. At the time it broke my heart, but if we had gone out with each other, we couldn't have been friends if we'd split up. And Mal, well, I need him in my life. He's always been there and it'd be a tragedy if he wasn't because we'd tried to go out with each other. So, no, he's never felt that way about me. Not even a little bit.'

Her honesty shamed me. A lot. There I was accusing her of all sorts when, secretly, she was living with a broken heart. She said it was mended, she said it was for the best, but which one of us didn't have a little piece of our heart that was for ever broken? That time would never be able to weave its magic over and heal?

I looked at Nova again, and suddenly she was even more beautiful. Before it was her sexiness that made her beautiful and a rival; now, it was her honesty. Which made her even more divine. How Mal could not be in love with her was the real mystery.

Nova stared into the mid-distance, her head slightly on one side, a gentle frown pleating her forehead as if she was calculating something, or rummaging through the rooms of her mind for some vital piece of information. She came out of her trance suddenly, and turned to me. 'Do you think other women have thought that?' she asked as though we'd been having a conversation. Her big dark eyes waited on me to catch up, to enlighten her as to what these other women had thought.

'Thought what?' I asked.

'That Mal feels that way about me? I always thought they didn't like me because he gives everyone the "love me, love my friend" routine and that gets their backs up. Now I'm thinking . . . I really hope they didn't think that me and him . . .

God, they must have *hated* me.' Her gaze wandered back to where she had recently been, sorting through the bits of information she had about Mal's past. 'What if they thought it was down to me that things never worked out?' she wondered aloud. Her eyes widened suddenly and she swung her gaze and body back towards me. 'What if they thought that I made him end things with them? That after I met them or something, I'd turn up at Mal's place and use his feelings for me to get him to finish with them. Or even offer him sexual favours to get him to dump them?'

The shame of it. My body slunk down slightly in my seat as my cheeks exploded red with the absolute bloody shame of it.

Her eyes double-took as she stared at me. She'd been looking to me for reassurance and now had seen me becoming an unflattering, unreassuring crimson. 'That's what you thought, isn't it?' she said.

I glanced away and picked up my glass of wine, sipping it with my head hung low while she groaned, slapped her hand over her eyes and shook her head.

'Do you know the very worst part of all of this?' she asked from behind her hand, her fingers cracking a fraction so she could see me as she talked to me.

I shook my head, too ashamed was I to actually speak to the woman who I had been minutes away from writing things about on toilet walls.

'Until this very moment, it never, ever occurred to me that's why none of Mal's exes liked me. I actually thought it was a combination of him going on about how close we were and my personality.'

She placed her hands on her cheeks, looked forlorn. 'My naivety annoys me sometimes. How could I have not known?' She sighed deeply, her frustration evident. 'How?'

'It's sort of a compliment, if you think about it,' I said, trying to make it up to her.

'How's that?' she asked.

'You made an impression on each of them. Imagine how insulting it would be if they met you and thought nothing of you. Mal gives you this big build-up and then they find you're plain and inconsequential. That'd be awful.'

She treated me to another of her smiles. 'You're very sweet, I'd rather people didn't hate me for the wrong reasons, but you're lovely to try.'

'It's guilt.'

'Now that you know the truth, I do hope you will give me a chance? Mal is so important to me, and I like people who make him happy. You make him happy.' She shrugged happily. 'I'd like us to try to be friends.'

Her sincerity was unnerving. She made it seem that being open, being honest, was easy, uncomplicated. It wasn't beset with a thousand million problems. Until I met Mal, and now her, I hadn't known people could be that honest and not fret about it. How could you sleep at night knowing people hadn't been presented with your best you? The you that you wanted the world to see?

I glanced over at Mal: he was watching his opponent, studying his form, learning all he could so he could win the game, win the prize. I returned my attention to Nova. She was Mal's best friend, she was a huge part of his life. My relationship with him would run a lot smoother with her on-side. Or with her not around at all.

I smiled at her. 'Yes, let's try.'

She smiled back and I knew then, her honesty, her openness, her love of Mal would probably destroy her.

*   *   *

'And you know what else? What if you do everything you can to make things perfect between you and your husband, to make your life as complete and wonderful as possible, to create a warm, inviting home and a happy, fun-filled life, because all you've ever wanted is to have your husband love you? What if you love him so much but you know it's not enough? It'll probably never be good enough because no matter how incredible everyone thinks you look on the outside, you know on the inside that you're broken. And he deserves better. He deserves the woman that he's given the other half of his heart to, but you want him *so* much you can never let him go. What do you do then?'

*   *   *

'I need to talk to you,' he said on the phone.

My fingers tightened around the handset, but I couldn't react properly because I was at work. I knew it was because of *her*.

Mal had given her my number and we'd met alone six times in the last two months for coffee, and each time she'd brought me something to eat—a cake, biscuits, flapjacks, muffins, scones, a pie. I'd eventually asked her if she thought I

145

needed fattening up or something and she had replied she liked baking for her friends. Then she'd said she didn't mean to offend me and she'd stop doing it. At which point I'd said no, of course don't do that, it's a lovely gesture. And it had *all* been an act. Just like when I first met her. That woman with a for ever broken piece of her heart routine: the carefully pitched pain sitting in her eyes, the lowered voice, the staring off, the pretending to have not known how his other girlfriends had been intimidated by her. All an act.

'Can I see you after work?' Mal was saying.

Well, I thought as I struggled to keep my voice light and not shrill and terrified as I agreed to meet him, *I'm not going quietly like the others. If it comes down to it, I will fight her, womano-a-womano. I am not losing him.*

Arriving at the pub later that day, I stood by the bar and sought him out amongst the smoke-fuzzed crowd. As always, the breath caught in my chest and my heart skipped a beat when I saw him. He stared into his pint, swimming in deep, untroubled thought. Serene. I wasn't sure if that was a word that applied to men. But it did to him. Whenever I surreptitiously watched him, I noticed he was always calm. Nothing about him seemed troubled. If he did have moments of being upset, he hid it well, disguised by a veneer of calmness and serenity.

Nova isn't having him, it's as simple as that.

'Hi,' I said, fixing a bright smile to my face, even though I was trembling as I lowered myself into the seat opposite him.

His face creased into a smile that brought all the love I felt for him rushing to the surface of my soul.

146

I couldn't imagine being without him, not for one minute. 'Steph, hi.' He stood up and kissed my cheek, the heat of him lingering long after he had been to and returned from the bar to get me a drink.

'Look,' he began, 'I'll get to the point. If I don't, I won't say what I've got to say. And as we found out with my name, that's not the best way forward.'

I didn't usually drink more than two glasses of wine. I'd spent a lot of time getting drunk as a teenager, getting my fill on the high of it, and it wasn't worth it. Not any more. But right then I wanted to down the glass of wine in front of me and then a few more. I wanted to be numb when he said whatever it was he was going to say. With a trembling hand, I picked up the glass of wine in front of me and tossed half of it back in one gulp. I needed the remaining half to make a sufficient impact should I need to throw something in his face before I walked out. That would be seconds before I slapped him, marched out into the street, hailed a cab to Nova's restaurant to deal with her. Depending on how that went, I'd either be spending the night crying myself to sleep or recovering in hospital.

'I talked it over with Nova,' he said.

I will not be in hospital, she will. For a long, long time.

'I have to tell you this. We're getting serious. That is, I feel this relationship is serious and I want you to know who I truly am before it goes any further. I think it's only fair to you that you know this and see if it's something you can handle.'

The coil of fear, anger and indignation loosened in my chest as it filtered into my worry-addled brain that he wasn't talking about ending things with me. He was talking about going further, talking as though whether our relationship continued was wholly my choice.

'I, I haven't ever told a girlfriend this. Which is why I had to talk it over with Nova first. This is her history, too, so if I reveal this about me it's about her as well. She said if I thought you felt for me what I feel for you, then I should, because she wants you to be around.'

A modicum of guilt flitted across my conscience: I'd misjudged her. Again. But the guilt was only a sliver because what should have been about us was once again about her, too. Why did he have to bring everything back to her? *Everything.* Was there a decision he had made in his life that he hadn't checked with her first?

His fingers skitted slowly across the table, laced themselves with mine. 'I love your hands,' he said, staring down at them. His eyes lifted up to meet mine. 'I love you.'

I felt my heart bubbling up again with everything I felt for him. He said it so easily. He said it as though he constantly said it; as though this wasn't the first time.

I opened my mouth and he pressed his fingers over my lips.

'No, don't say it back,' he said, before taking his hand away. 'I don't want you to feel pressured. Not when you don't know everything. I don't want you to feel trapped to stay because you've said it.' His face creased as he closed his eyes and shook his head slightly. 'I haven't said this before. Anyone who knows has always known so they don't need it to be explained.' He fixed me with a gaze, steadying himself to say what had to be said.

'My mum, who I hope you'll meet one day, is manic depressive. I know people call it bipolar these days, but we always called it manic depression, she calls it manic depression. That's it. It doesn't sound so big when I say it, but it is, of course. It's been a part of our lives since we were old enough to know. Do you know what manic depression is?' he asked, suddenly realising that I might not know what he was talking about.

I nodded. I knew.

'But she's not a psycho,' he said, suddenly angry. 'Anyone who even thinks that—'

'I don't think that,' I cut in, tightening my fingers around his to stop him. 'I'd never think that. Never.'

'But you have to know that she'll always come first. Always. That's why I had to tell you now before we got any deeper into this. I don't want this to end between us, but it wouldn't be fair to you not knowing that. Do you see what I mean?'

I nodded. Calm was flowing through my body, one cell at a time. No fear, no anxiety, nothing but calm. And then something began at my core, spreading, blossoming inside me like a baby growing. I felt it growing, taking on its own life, filling me up until my body, my heart, my mind were saturated with it. It took a few moments for me to understand what it was—for the first time in years, I knew what hope felt like.

'I know this isn't exactly what someone who's just started a relationship wants to hear, that they'll never come first, but that's the way it is. I haven't needed to do anything in years, and Nova's parents are usually the people who are there first, but if Mum needs me, I have to drop everything to go and be with her. Do you understand?'

I smiled at Mal. What he said was exactly what I needed to hear; it was what had planted the seed of hope inside me.

'I want to tell you a story,' I said to him. 'It's a true story. It's a story about me. By the time I've finished telling you the story, I hope you'll understand why I had to tell you, and why I'm glad you told me what you told me.' I sounded dramatic, but I didn't mean to. Like Mal, I was unused to telling anyone this, so in the telling it sounded dramatic. People saw me, they made assumptions, they gossiped about me. Rarely did people ask, never did I tell.

At the end of my story, where there should have been 'happily ever after' he kissed me instead. He kissed me and he made me a promise.

We all make promises. I believe we all mean to keep them. The one Mal made me he wanted to keep, but of course he didn't realise at the time—I don't think either of us did—the price he'd have to pay to do so.

*   *   *

'So it's all very well you two apologising and explaining why you did it, but the next time you're about to say something about someone, maybe you should think that you don't know all the facts. That their life may look perfect, but it may actually be fragile and sad and beset with a multitude of problems.

'And also, you might want to think how *you'd* feel if they were standing right behind you whilst you rip them to shreds. Yes, that's right, how *you'd* feel, because it's obvious you two don't care at all what other people might feel.'

I give the silent, shocked duo another mean-eyed glare and march out of the locker room again. I climb in my car and push my key in the ignition, but I do not turn it. I do not drive.

I stare out of the windscreen. Not only do I definitely have to find a new gym, I desperately have to get a new life.

'I need a dolphin.'

'OK,' Mum said.

'And where would you put it?' Dad said.

'In the bath,' he said to Dad. And turned to Mum, because Dad was going to be what Mum called 'difficult'. 'I really need a dolphin.'

'OK,' Mum said.

'What do you mean, OK?' Dad said to Mum.

'What does OK mean to you?' Mum asked him.

'You're going to get him a dolphin?'

'If he needs one, why not?'

'I can really have a dolphin? A real life dolphin?'

'Yes.'

He smiled at Mum. She was the best mum in the whole world.

'When?' he asked Mum. 'When can I have my dolphin?'

'Well, I'm going to have to save up for it so it might take a while. I can imagine them being quite expensive, cos goldfish are about £2.50, so dolphins, which are really, really big, will be loads more expensive than that. And they'll eat more. And we'll

need a bigger bath or another bath altogether because we need to have showers and things. But, if you need a dolphin, I really want to get you it. And all the money we have has to go on food, and clothes and bills. So, what I think we'll do is not go on holiday for a while, and maybe not buy any more computer games, and then we'll save all that money up towards the dolphin. Does that sound all right to you?'

Leo grinned and nodded. He really was going to get a dolphin.

'OK, it's a bit late to do it now, but tomorrow, I'll call up and cancel that trip to Portugal we had planned. It's a shame we won't get to see all that stuff there, but the dolphin's more important.'

'We can't go to Port-gal?' Leo asked. They were going on a plane and everything. And he wanted to show Richard and David and Martin the pictures Mum said she'd take of him on the plane. None of them had been on a plane. And she'd shown him pictures of their white house over there and the swimming pool—right in their back garden. He could swim in it.

'Afraid not, sweetheart. We're saving for a dolphin, remember?'

'But I want to go to Port-gal.'

'Sorry. We can't do both. Now, you're a big boy, so this is a really grown-up decision you have to make. Either we get a dolphin or we go on our holiday. Why don't you go upstairs and think about which one you want. It's fine with me either way.'

'OK,' he said and returned to his bedroom and the picture book with pictures of dolphins. Tsk. If he'd been allowed to get a dolphin, he was going to ask for a shark next.

It really wasn't fair sometimes.

CHAPTER NINE

There's no change. Another six days and there's been no change.

I have to tell my family everything today. I know the second I do, they'll be down here, a convoy of Kumalisis and one Wacken, before I've settled the phone in its cradle. I've been hoping things might have got better and that I'd be able to tell them everything when Leo is awake, but that hasn't happened. Yet. It hasn't happened *yet*. Bringing more people into this means I am accepting a small defeat. I am saying that there is something going on that Keith and I cannot handle alone. We need help.

The café is in darkness as I come in through the front door and rush through to disable the alarm—bleeping in the back like the countdown to Armageddon—before it goes off and half of East Sussex police force descends upon this place. It's happened before. Last year, Leo and I had come over to the café to get some of the giant fairy cakes I'd baked earlier for an after-dinner treat, and for some reason I had typed in the wrong number three times. Before we knew it, the world outside was illuminated by flashing blue lights and what looked like a whole platoon of officers appeared, all of them ready to deal with whichever criminal had dared to break into our little café. Leo and I had been terrified at the speedy response and the

153

number of officers that arrived, and while he thought he was clinging on to me for protection, I was clutching him just as tightly, partly to be ready to step in front of him and partly to ease my terror. Keith had been on duty at the time and he'd come with them, and had obviously been *overjoyed* that his wife had shown such utter ditziness by getting the code to her own café wrong in front of his colleagues. I could hear them all laughing, and the comments—'If it's a psychic café, how come she didn't know the code?'—all the way back to the station. Leo thought it was cool after they'd all gone but neither of us much fancied cake after that. I'd driven us to Kemp Town in Brighton to get us ice cream from a late-night supermarket instead. Later on, when I called Amy to tell her that I'd had to change the code, she said she'd already done it earlier that day because Keith had called to remind her that we hadn't changed it in a while. And had she not told me? And had he not told me? And, oh, did the police really laugh and laugh at you? And Keith never did really say you were lucky you wouldn't be charged with wasting police time, did he?

If I didn't know the pair of them better, I would have thought it was a stitch-up, but Keith has no humour in such things and it just isn't in Amy to play that sort of practical joke.

After the alarm is disabled, I dump my bag on the desk in the little broom cupboard we call the office. My keys clatter loudly in the darkness, reverberating out into the main seating area with the counter and the coffee machine.

I'm momentarily blinded as I flick on the kitchen lights and brightness bounces off all the

154

metal and white surfaces. I yank up my sleeves and from the drawer by the door I retrieve my white mesh cap and jam it on my head, before tying on my apron which hangs on a hook by the door. I move to the big metal sink and scrub my hands clean.

While Keith sits with Leo, I'm going to make some cakes and cookies so Amy doesn't have to worry about ordering them in for a few more days. Poor Amy has been running Starstruck, my café, all alone for more than two weeks now and she hasn't uttered one word of complaint. She hasn't even mentioned how tired she is, that she's been running low on supplies, that she needs cash to order more stock. She has carried on as normal, so I don't have to worry.

*   *   *

I sat at the back of a café with Leo.

'Incy wincy spider climbed up the waterspout,' I sang. Leo's big, dark russet-brown eyes stared up at me, fascinated, agog, as I leant over him, taping my fingers together while twisting my wrists. His mouth opened into a smile.

He was only three months old and I wasn't sure if he really understood that much, but he seemed to love this song and 'Round and round the garden like a teddy bear' more than the others I sang to him. His mouth would curl up at the corners and he would gurgle out the kind of laugh that made a mother's stomach flip. I was lucky, I knew. My son was an angel, a newborn miracle. He slept when he was put down, he drank his milk, he responded when I played with him. I saw so many mothers

155

struggling, cowed and broken by exhaustion and lack of support, that I knew I had been blessed. I also knew that it might not last. He might at any moment decide that I'd had it too easy for far too long and I needed to learn about motherhood by being baptised in fire. I sometimes wondered if it was because on some level he understood that there could only be one unruly newborn in our relationship, and that role was currently being filled by me. I lay awake at night fretting about our future, crying because I felt so alone. I found it hard to eat because I was so unhappy and I literally had to force food down my throat because I was breastfeeding and needed to give Leo the right nutrition. I longed more than anything to be hugged and cared for and pampered. I longed for someone to lift me up out of the crib of this life and rock me better.

The table we'd chosen was at the back of the café, not far from our house in an area of Hove called Poets Corner—the names of the roads were of the great poets; I lived on Rossetti Road, which was a ten-minute stroll from the seafront. For someone as young as me, I had been incredibly lucky with property so far. The flat in Forest Hill that I'd scraped all my cash together to buy when I was in my early twenties, when people wouldn't even think about travelling through that area of London to get somewhere else, had made me an obscene amount of money when I sold it two months before Leo was born. Forest Hill had suddenly become the place to be for those who couldn't afford to live in über-expensive Dulwich. I'd been able to buy a three-bedroom house with a garden in Rossetti Road for the money I got for my flat, and had some left over.

As I sat in the café, playing with Leo, I was thinking that I needed a job. I hadn't worked in many months and my savings were running dangerously low. We'd be able to live comfortably for at least another year, but after that, we'd have nothing. And nothing put away for the future. I'd been thinking about updating my training and going back to my original career plan to be a clinical psychologist. Although I would probably feel like a fraud. How could I listen to other people, help them, advise them where necessary, when my life was such a mess? I was the prime example for how NOT to do things. Having said that, wasn't it someone who messed up who could see where you were heading and maybe stop you? Wasn't it someone who knew of pain that could help you heal it?

The thought, though, of having to be supervised, having to reveal my secrets to someone else, was not one that appealed.

The only other thing I was qualified to do was be a waitress or restaurant manager. Which meant working odd hours that I would have to fit around Leo. *Maybe Mum won't mind coming to stay with him a few days a week*, I thought. Then I realised what a stupid thought that was: she'd be down on the next train, ready to move in permanently. She, Dad, Cordy and Aunt Mer had all been unsubtly trying to get me to move back to London.

'I don't suppose you want a job?' the tall woman with dead-straight black hair to her waist, who had served me coffee, asked.

I blinked at her. Had I been thinking aloud? She towered above me, a giant, beautiful goddess. She had clear, creamy skin, dark brown, slightly slanted eyes and a small, perfect mouth. She wore a vest top that exposed her flat stomach, and skin-tight, faded blue jeans with a big belt buckle that read 'Diva', the same name as the café. Around her belly button was an intricate tattoo that had gothic elements but also looked like Kanji-origin Japanese script.

'Do you?' she asked. 'Want a job?' She tucked her hair behind her ear, revealing a row of tiny hoop earrings.

'No,' I said. This place was rarely even half full and the coffee, cake and biscuits I'd sampled were nothing to write home about. I only came here because it was close to my house—the only café in Poets Corner—and the goddess always looked pleased to see us and would coo at Leo as though he was the most beautiful baby she had ever seen. If I did work here there'd be nothing to do and I'd probably be laid off after a few weeks. I needed stability.

'You can bring your baby to work with you,' she said. 'He can sit in the back, we'll have a baby monitor, and when we're not busy he can be out here.' She looked around the empty café and back at me. 'He'll be out here most of the time.'

'Thank you for the offer, but no.'

She sighed, chewed on her bottom lip. 'All right,' she said.

'Why did you offer me a job?' I asked. A couple of times I'd cleared plates off the tables when she was—rarely—busy and I wanted somewhere to sit. I stacked them and carried them to the side of the counter, maybe that had shown her I'd been a waitress before, but there was a wild leap from that

158

to offering me a job.

'OK,' she said, pulling out the chair opposite my little sofarette. I glanced at Leo in the carrycot beside me, his lips were pursed and his eyes kept fluttering shut. He was about to fall asleep. I pulled his blanket up to his chin, stroked his stomach a few times. 'This is going to sound completely crazy, but I had a dream and you were in it. And you were working here.'

She did sound crazy. As crazy as I sounded to people most of the time. Going along with things because of dreams and feelings.

She sat back, folded her arms triumphantly, as if my silence had just confirmed that she sounded completely mad, when in fact, I didn't say anything because I had a feeling she was going to keep talking.

'I'm always getting these things. Feelings about people. Dreams. You see, from you, I get a really strong connection to Shakespeare.'

'Most of us have a strong connection to Shakespeare,' I replied. I had seen a lot of psychics over the years and none of them had said this to me. 'Seeing as we studied at least one of his plays at school.'

'No, it's not that. With you, it's so strong. It's got this endless love thing about it, but it's nothing to do with Romeo and Juliet. That'd be too obvious. It's so strong. There's a connection to the little one as well.' The goddess stared off into space for a moment. 'I'm not very good at putting together the feelings I get, I have to admit. That's why I couldn't in good faith take money from people. My friends often tell me to start charging, you know, make a living from it, but what if I don't get anything from someone? How would I live with myself? Twelve!' She pointed at me. 'Twelve. You've got some connection to twelve.'

'I was twelve once,' I said. Why I was being so uncharitable I didn't know. Maybe it was because this woman was the genuine article. I had met many people over the years who weren't; who charged large sums and told me nothing. And this one had a conscience about her gift and wouldn't charge people because she was scared of not being able to tell them anything.

'Twelve? Twelfth? Maybe it's twelfth. Hey, are you an actress?' Her eyes lit up.

And it was going so well. 'No,' I said.

'Oh, how come I keep hearing Old Vic?'

My whole body went cold, the fingers that had been stroking Leo's stomach froze.

'Old Vic. You've got a really strong connection to the Old Vic. So has your Shakespeare thing. Maybe it's not the place. Maybe it's a man? Old Vic . . . He visits you. No, but that's silly. And you're all starry. I keep seeing you in the stars. That's why I thought you might be an actress. Famous. You know, the Old Vic, Shakespeare, stars . . . Gawd, if I had a brain I'd be dangerous!' she laughed. Threw her head back and laughed.

'Can you imagine me telling my accountant I hired someone because I had a dream about them? I don't even know if you can waitress or make coffee!' She laughed again. 'Or telling my dad! "Oh, Dad, you know that café you bought me and I've run into the ground? I've added to my financial worries by hiring some woman from my dream. Never mind the fact I dream about her because she's my most loyal customer." I can just

160

see his face now!' She carried on laughing, clutching her sides, tears rolling down her face.

You can see people, who they truly are, if you try hard enough. You listen to how your body responds to them. It may be a quiet little prod; it might be a huge red flag being waved that lights up the nerves in your body. It might be a look that you see passing across their face. It might be a note you hear in their voice. It might be them laughing at themselves in an unabashed manner.

She was an angel. This goddess was an angel. She was suddenly bathed in white and gold light, right before my eyes. She was so incredibly beautiful, she shone. I would never tell anyone that—not even her—because it did sound crazy. My friends had called me crazy, Cordy called me crazy, Mal said everything like that was bollocks.

'Oh, gawd,' said the laughing angel in front of me, wiping away her tears. 'That's really tickled me. I haven't been so tickled since I told a customer about how I'd once had a crush on that singer from Dollar and how I knew he lived in the Brighton area but I'd never seen him before. Ten minutes later in he walks. Large as life. He'd never been in before, nor since. The customer actually spat her coffee across the table. And I could hardly serve him because I was laughing so much. Probably why he never came back.'

'Would you sell me your café?' I asked her.

There were decisions I made in my life that I knew without a doubt were the right ones: not going travelling with Mal; studying for my Ph.D.; moving to Hove; buying a café.

I could see it clearly. How I would change it. How I could turn it around. How this would free

161

the angel from a cage she had never wanted to be in but her inability to say no to her family had kept her hostage. This was my future. I could do it and still be near my son.

The 'airy-fairy' side of me might have made this decision, but the business side of me, the one that had realised at a very early point that being the restaurant manager meant not only more pay but less physical grind so I could fit it around my college work, knew this would work. This was my future.

'I'll have to ask my dad,' she said cautiously.

'I'll give you a fair price for it. And I want you to stay working here if you could stand it.'

From her trouser pocket she pulled out a tiny mobile phone. How she had got it in there was a mystery. She flipped it open, pressed a couple of buttons. 'Hey, Dad,' she said when he answered. 'I'm about to make your day. OK, OK . . .' She grinned at me across the table, rolled her eyes and began talking in Japanese.

Two months later I owned a café. Leo was impressed when I showed him the keys: he burped and grinned. Cordy thought it was wonderful, until I told her about my plan to convert the upper floors into rooms for people to have tarot readings, horoscope charts done, reiki, crystal healing and massages. Then she said, 'I suppose there are as many other crazy people out there as you.' Mum and Dad had been less impressed and suggested I put under the new name of the café proprietor: DR NOVA KUMALISI so everyone would know that their daughter was a doctor, even if she was throwing away her hard-earned degree. Aunt Mer thought the same—I could tell when she came to

162

the launch party—but didn't say anything.

Amy, the angel who used to own the café, was extremely happy that she didn't have to be in charge of anything any more.

When I opened the door that first day it became mine officially, and sat alone with Leo in the café, I felt for the first time I was back in control of my life. I was doing something I had chosen to do, not going along with something because it had happened and I was reacting to it. For the first time in a while I knew I had a future. Obviously I had done the right thing because that was when Leo decided to start acting like a baby again.

*   *   *

Baking is exactly what I needed. I stand in the middle of the kitchen and survey all my labours. Every surface is covered in unbaked cakes, muffins, banana bread, pies, cookies, biscuits and hot cross buns waiting to rise.

I've probably made too much, but once I started, I couldn't stop. Being able to focus on something I could do well, and do it, had been what I needed to feel a little in control of myself again. I'll freeze some stuff and leave Amy a note to bake what is in the fridge tomorrow.

I can just imagine her face when she walks in and sees it all in the morning.

She won't instantly think that I've come in and done this—she'll think it's angels come to help her in her time of need, or those little pixie creatures from that fairy tale about the shoemaker who woke up each morning to find all his work done. *Then* she'd think it might have possibly been me. She is so gorgeous on the inside and outside, and so very often on a different plane of existence. I often wonder how her partner, Trudy, who is down to earth and practical—and as regular a proponent of the It's All Bollocks school of thought as Keith—puts up with her. I'm pretty level-headed about such things even though I'm a fervent believer, and it still drives Keith round the twist, so imagine having to live with Amy. I threaten Keith with that sometimes. When he's being annoying or 'difficult', I tell him I'll either sell him on eBay or get Amy to move in.

I free my hair from its net and untie my apron. What I need now is a hot shower and maybe a couple of hours' sleep before I go back and take over from Keith. He sent me a text earlier saying all was well and no change and that he loved me.

After locking up Starstruck, I start walking home. It's only three streets away. The café has been incredibly successful in the past few years. We gave it a complete refit, and took full advantage of being the only café around in the area with home baking and by making it child friendly. The psychic/crystal/tarot/alternative therapy side of things has also been very successful because it's part of normal everyday things. We haven't painted anything black or blood red, we haven't made it a niche thing. I don't dress in black, I don't call myself a Wicca (witch) because I'm not, and I don't believe someone is psychic just because they tell me they are. I'm constantly testing psychics and if there's ever any sign that someone is losing their touch, then I terminate their contract. I've seen far too many fakes over the years—people who charge the earth but tell you nothing, people who read

164

your reactions to their guesses and tell you what you want to hear—to allow anyone to do that to my customers.

I know there's more to life than we can see. I've known since I was eight years, eleven months, and twenty-one days old.

*   *   *

Mal, Cordy, Victoria and I were meant to stay in the garden, to play outside while all the adults were inside, talking quietly and seriously and drinking tea.

I needed to use the toilet, and now we had an inside toilet and a new bathroom, I didn't want to use the one outside any more. Mum said our new bathroom colour was called avocado, like the thing she and Dad ate.

I finished, wiped, stood up, pulled up my knickers and pushed the handle on the toilet. I was still fascinated that pushing the handle on this one did the same thing as pulling the chain on the outside loo, and watched the water swirl around the bowl and disappear for a few seconds. After I watched fresh water fill the bottom of the bowl, I turned to leave, but stopped suddenly and stared.

Standing in front of the door was Uncle Victor, Mal's dad. It was unusual that he was in the bathroom whilst I was there, but even more so because I—along with everyone else who knew him—had watched his coffin being lowered into the ground a few hours earlier. I had been sure he was in it at the time.

I stared at him.

He stared at me.

I closed my eyes, wondering if I was imagining

165

things. Like Mal said when sometimes a fish finger would disappear from my plate then come back again when I wasn't looking.

In those moments I'd stared at him before closing my eyes, he had looked real. Just like I did. He was wearing a black suit, with a white shirt and black tie. His hair was slicked and combed down with a side parting on the left, his skin was as pale and yellowy as it had been the last time I'd seen him before he died. Which hadn't been for a while. He'd been 'away' for most of the time since Mal and I had been born, then came back for a year or so when we were five, had stuck around to see Victoria born, then had gone away again. This time only coming back every six months or so for anything between a few days and a few weeks.

I opened my eyes and he was still there. He was leaning against the door, his arms crossed over his chest. I'd seen him in his coffin by accident. I had gone into Mal and Victoria's front room where the body was, so I knew he was dead. I had run out again and hid in Mal's room, scared of what I'd seen. Scared because I'd never seen Uncle Victor looking so still. Even when he fell asleep in his chair beside the fire after dinner. But I knew he was dead. And yet, he was standing in front of me. He was probably a ghost.

'I never liked your name,' he stated. His voice still rolled with his accent—Mum said it came from Yorkie-shire.

I stared at him.

'So violent. Imagine naming your child after a star that is dying—exploding,' he said. 'It could be argued that the earth started with the big bang, an exploding star that started all life as we know it,

166

but I don't see it that way. Stupid thing to name a child.'

I wasn't scared. It was Uncle Victor, after all.

'But then, not as stupid as Malvolio,' he went on. He raised a thin finger, wagged it at me. 'She did it for me. Imagine, a Yorkshire man going back to his roots and telling everyone that his son is called Malvolio. I might as well tell them I was . . . you know,' he said, jerking his head to one side. I didn't know, but I was fascinated. What might he as well have told the Yorkie-shire people he was? 'It was the first play I took her to see when we were courting. I said I felt sorry for that poor lad, Malvolio, he got a rough deal. So she names me bloomin' son after him.

'But at least he can shorten his name. Mal. Not so bad. You, on the other hand, have no such luck. You know your name is Avon spelt backwards? You'll probably end up selling the stuff.' I stared at Uncle Victor, wondering why he climbed out of his place in the cool, wet earth that he'd been lowered into earlier that day to be nasty to me about my name. Is that what happened after you did this thing called being dead? You came back to tell someone exactly what you thought of their name? 'That would serve your parents right if all you ever amounted to was selling Avon.'

His eyes raked over me, from my two neat canerows tied at the ends with yellow ribbon, to the shiny black shoes with white socks Mum had made me wear. 'Well, lass, say something,' he said.

My heart leapt in my chest. He wanted me to talk to him. Up until this moment, it wasn't necessary for me to say anything to ghost Uncle Victor. Even though he was a ghost and he wasn't being very nice to me he was still a grown-up, in other words, one who must be obeyed. *Say something. Say something.* 'Our bath's green,' I said.

His face creased up with a deep, slightly frightening frown. 'Your bath is green,' he said. 'Your. Bath. Is. Green.'

I nodded.

He shook his head. 'I didn't want you,' he said, with that tone of voice Mum used when she'd tried to make do when baking a cake without some ingredient and the cake turned out to be only fit for the bin. I, clearly to Uncle Victor, was a cake fit for the bin. 'I've been trying to talk to Hope and to Frank, but no, I get you. And your green bath.'

I started to bite on the inner lining of my cheek, while drawing small circles on the brown lino with the toe of my right shoe. I wondered if anyone would think it odd I was being told off by my Uncle Victor who everyone had thought was dead. When dead meant you were never going to wake up. Ever again.

'Stop fidgeting,' he said. 'Did you always fidget this much?'

I stopped drawing circles and stood up straight, stopped biting on my cheek and thought about his question. Did I always fidget that much? I knew what fidgeting was, of course, but did I do it more than anyone else? I didn't know. I had a feeling that if I said that to Uncle Victor, it might make him crosser than he already was.

'I suppose you aren't so bad. You're the only one who noticed me, after all,' he said, looking me up and down again. 'Very skinny though. You need to eat more.'

168

I could do that. I nodded. If it meant he'd be nicer to me, I could eat more.

'What are you, eight? Nine?'

I nodded.

'Well, which one is it, lass, eight or nine?'

'I'm nine in ten days. So is Malvolio. He's nine in eight days.'

'Oh. Yes. Well I knew that.' I thought Uncle Victor wasn't being very honest about that. I guessed he didn't know that at all. Especially since he had never once, not ever, given Mal a birthday card or a present. Not ever. Even though Aunt Mer pretended they were from his dad we knew they weren't.

'You're a bit young, but I suppose you can see me for a reason so it must be all right. Now, I want you to do something for me.'

It seemed a funny way to ask someone to do something for you, say you don't like their name, say they're too skinny and tell them to stop fidgeting. But I was all ears, eager and willing to do anything I could because I knew grown-ups were odd creatures. They could say one thing and mean something completely different and then didn't seem to notice that they had done that.

'You're to take care of Malvolio, you hear?'

Take care of Malvolio. Take care of Malvolio? Mum was always taking care of Aunt Mer when she was sick. And when Mal had measles and all of us got chicken pox Mum took care of us then. 'Is he ill?' I asked.

Uncle Victor's eyes widened for a moment, then he shook his head again, as though I was that cake only fit for the bin but he'd dropped it on the way to the bin, meaning his workload had been doubled by something that was disappointing in the first place. 'No, lass. I want you to take care of him from now until he doesn't need taking care of any more,' he said. 'And even then, you're to look out for him. That means making sure he's all right. That he's happy.' I must have looked confused because he said, 'As you get older you'll understand what I mean. But right now, just remember that I want you to take care of Malvolio. I didn't do a very good job of it.'

'But that's because you were never here,' I said to reassure him. To let him know I was more grown-up than he thought because I knew that if he was around, he would take care of Mal. And Victoria. And Aunt Mer.

'Aye, thank you, lass, I know.' He didn't sound very reassured. He sounded, if anything, crosser. 'He's a good lad—yes, I know that, even though I was never here—and he's going to need someone to take care of him.'

'What about Victoria? Won't she need someone to take care of her?'

'She's a girl, someone will always take care of her.'

How did he know someone would always take care of her? No one had really taken care of Aunt Mer until she moved into our street, as far as I knew from what Mum said. She was a girl.

My thoughts must have shown on my face because he added: 'OK, lass, take care of them both. You're just making life difficult for yourself. I was only going to ask you to take care of Malvolio. Now, I want you to take care of Malvolio and Victoria.'

'OK,' I said with a happy shrug. I generally did

whatever grown-ups told me to do. It was easier that way.

'OK? Is that it? I say something profound and important and all you can say is OK?'

Oh, have I said something wrong? I wondered. I thought that was what he wanted. 'OK, Uncle Victor?' I added.

'I expected some questions about how to do it. Maybe a bit of a fight, but all you can say is OK. I should have been given someone older to ask this of, I knew it.'

'But I said OK,' I said quietly. I didn't understand why he wasn't pleased that I was going to do what he wanted me to do. Generally, I found that grown-ups got cross because you *didn't* do as they said, because you argued back. It seemed Uncle Victor was getting cross because I *would* do as he said. I was starting to get the impression that Uncle Victor was just a cross man. Maybe being dead had made him even crosser.

'Aye, I suppose you did. Well, I'll be watching you.'

'From where?'

He blinked at me again. 'What do you mean from where? Just everywhere.'

'At the same time? You're going to be everywhere at the same time?'

'Yes.'

'Are you God?'

'What makes you say something like that?'

'God is everywhere at the same time, watching us. Are you God?'

'Don't be so bloody stupid.'

'Oh,' I said. 'Are you going to be watching me when I go to the toilet?'

'Absolutely not.'

'Or when I have my bath?'

'No, of course not.'

'So you won't be watching me all the time?'

'I suppose not,' he said, very cross again.

'But how will you know if you're not watching all the time when I'll be using the toilet or having my bath?'

'This is why I didn't want you,' he said, sounding as cross as he looked. 'You ask too many questions. I'll just be watching you. That should be enough for you to believe.'

I had been told I asked too many questions. Mum was often sending me to Dad to find out the answer to things I asked. Dad would send me to a dictionary. Or bed, if the dictionary didn't answer me. 'OK, Uncle Victor.'

'Now, run along,' he said, waving me aside with his bony hand.

'Thank you, Uncle Victor,' I said.

'Thank you?'

'For visiting me.'

He looked surprised. 'Aye, well . . .'

I smiled at him, glad for having the chance to speak to him again. That the last time I saw him wasn't him being dead in the coffin.

'Wash your hands, lass, there's a good girl.'

'Oh, OK.' I turned to our new green sink and rubbed my hands together under the water, neglecting the soap that sat on the side of the bath. When I turned back, Uncle Victor had gone.

I sneaked outside to resume the game I'd been playing and never told anyone about seeing Uncle Victor. I didn't doubt for one minute that I'd seen him, that he'd spoken to me, but I knew enough about grown-ups to know that they wouldn't like me saying it. Aunt Mer had been crying all the time since Uncle Victor had died and the doctor had to keep 'giving her something' to make her sleep. Mum and Dad were with her all the time and they wouldn't like me saying it. I couldn't tell Mal and Victoria because they wouldn't like to know their dad had visited me but not them. And Cordy would just tell Mum and Dad.

I saw Uncle Victor a few times after that. He didn't speak to me. He was just there sometimes, I'd catch a glimpse of him reflected in the dark kitchen window when I was washing up. Or I'd see him standing at the end of the garden. One time he was sitting on the edge of the bath when I went to go to the toilet, but disappeared just as soon as I opened the door a bit wider (I hadn't been able to use the loo for a good few hours after that). It was a reminder, I suppose, of what I'd promised him.

As I grew up, I became more and more interested in 'out there'. What lay beyond the ken of everyday experience. What we couldn't see or hear or experience but was still going on around us. What we might see or hear or experience if we learned to tune in to it.

My interest was about uncovering what else lay around us, in the spaces between this world and wherever we went to after we died. It was about finding out what else lay within us. What else you could perceive if you knew what you were looking for, what people could tune in to.

*   *   *

For the past few days Uncle Victor has been on my

mind, since I recognised him as the man in the dream, the one who has come to take Leo away. I'm not sure if it means anything, or if I'm just associating the two because Uncle Victor was the first—although not the last—ghost I saw. I know for definite he is on the other side, and I've always thought that leaving this life would be made easier if you had someone who loved you to meet you. And Uncle Victor would have loved Leo. Of course he would. I had been tempted to name Leo, Leo Frank Victor Kumalisi, but then that would have given the game away. Would have confirmed for everyone who Leo really was.

Maybe I'm just conjuring up that dream because of what I believe; that if Leo is ready to leave, if he wants me to let him go, he'll have someone to be with. He won't be all on his own.

Without warning, all energy leaves my body and I have to sit down on my doorstep, because I'm unable to even reach up and unlock the front door.

He has to wake up.

Leo just has to wake up.

I'm not ready to let him do that without me. He has to wake up.

He has to wake up.

CHAPTER TEN

Meredith sits in my living room, on the couch, drinking tea.

I never understood why people had such problems with their mothers-in-law. Carole, for example, avoided hers with all the deft skill of a

174

general planning a military campaign. She used her children as spies, finding out her mother-in-law's plans, then would simply be out if she came over, or would have organised to visit her family in Scotland for Christmas, Easter and birthdays. Dyan, on the other hand, had to practically go into intensive therapy every time her mother-in-law left because her self-esteem was often in shreds. My mother-in-law was a saint, in many respects. She had, essentially, been Mal's sole parent for most of his life. She had taught him about responsibility, she had shown him what life was about. If it wasn't for her, he might not have stayed with me. He may not have made the choices he made.

Our relationship is woven with many complicated strands, though. Meredith, I often think, is my own personal warning; a wake-up call in a five-foot-nine, white-haired package. Whenever she is otherwise occupied, I study her, my eyes running over the soft lines of her face and body, knowing that if I'm not careful, if I don't hang on to Mal, I could become her. I could be that woman, all alone, relying on the kindness of loved ones and strangers alike. Every time I see Meredith, I leave her company determined to get it right. To never be left sitting at home, waiting for someone to come along and allow me to live.

After the dinner party, when I worked out she is probably Mal's hotline to Nova and . . . everything else, I knew I had to talk to her. I had wanted to go to her house, to make this meeting seem far more casual and innocuous than it is, but to go to East London, to that road, would be to risk running into Nova's parents. I'd met the Kumalisis many times and at my wedding, of course, and they were the loveliest people who had welcomed me into their fold without a second thought, so the idea of making small talk with them now . . . Well, there are braver women out there. I haven't met these braver women, owing to the fact they're probably wrestling crocodiles and skinning tigers, but I am not one of them. I haven't seen Nova's parents at all in the last eight years; since what happened, I thought it best to stay away. Every time I've seen Meredith it has been here or at Victoria's place in Birmingham, just to avoid bumping into the Kumalisis.

As I fuss with pouring myself tea, I surreptitiously watch Meredith, safely ensconced on my sofa, her long, white locks severely pinned back into a pram-face bun, her brown eyes soft and unchallenging, her mouth a thin, pink line that parts frequently to receive tea and pieces of biscuit. She is fuzzy around the edges, almost as though she blends in with her surroundings whatever they may be, never wanting or needing to stand out. A little shudder thrills through me. There go I. I am sitting down with my future self: like most women dated versions of their fathers, Mal married his mother.

Being similar to her means that, in this setting, with only the two of us, I can ask her anything and she will answer it as honestly as possible.

'Do you have any pictures of Leo with you?' is the question I ask. I've always been curious, despite what I intimated to Mal—smoke and mirrors and deflection, all of it—but since I haven't been able to find out anything about them on the internet, it has started to border on obsession.

Meredith's face changes a little, a slight frown flitting around the edges of her expression.

Oh God, I shouldn't have asked her, I realise. *She has put up with me all these years, hasn't ever confronted me about what I did, but she hasn't quite forgiven me either.* The frown still on her face, she carefully puts down the cup and saucer from the tea service she gave us for a wedding present, and reaches for her bag which sits on the floor. I'd given her that bag last Christmas. It was a black-brown suede, with golden links and zip. I'd seen the forced smile that settled on her face when she unwrapped it, I'd felt the polite—but disappointed—gratitude with which she had kissed both my cheeks and knew she hated it. This was probably the first time she'd used it. Like this was the first time I had used the tea service. The pair of us are such frauds, constantly trying to curry favour with the other.

From her bag she takes out a long wallet and flips it open. I catch a glimpse of a picture of Mal and me on our wedding day, both of us laughing as we shy away from the confetti dancing around us. In the other picture square, an almost identical photo of Victoria, Mal's sister, on her wedding day. Meredith's fingers move behind the three ten-, two twenty- and four five-pound notes and pulls out three photographs.

She looks at them briefly, then gently, as though it is him, and not his image, she lays them out on the table.

The breath catches in my chest.

He's beautiful.

My heart contracts with the sudden rush of seeing him for the first time. Tears fill my eyes, and

177

his image swims in front of me. But I could close my eyes and still see him, still remember every line and curve of his face.

He's so beautiful.

My heart starts to expand in my chest, filling up with . . . with all I can describe as love. Sudden, unbidden love for this boy I have never seen before.

He's so, so beautiful.

I slip from the sofa on to my knees in front of the coffee table, staring at the photos that are laid out before me like tarot cards that show me what could have been my past, my present and my future. I reach out, gently stroke my finger over the first one, his school picture, still blurred by my tears.

Again my heart swells and contracts at the same time.

My little boy.

He has inherited Mal's big, awestruck eyes. His dark mocha skin is the blend of Mal and Nova's genes. His mouth—incredibly full for such a young boy—is probably from her. His face shape, a wonderful, plump oval, is obviously from Mal. His dark hair lies in thick curly Cs all over his head, just like Mal's honey-blond curls do.

My little boy.

He should be mine. He should be my little boy.

He is grinning crookedly, his blue, green and white striped tie a little skew-whiff, one lone curl standing to attention beside his ear, and he seems to be looking a few centimetres in the wrong direction so the image seems slightly off-centre. I am instantly curious about what is more important than looking at the camera. I remember seeing a photo of Mal that is identical to this. In it, he was about seven, too. His tie was skew-whiff, one curl stood independent of the others by his right ear, and his eyes were focused in just the wrong direction when the picture was snapped.

My finger moves to the next photo. He's wearing a lurid green superhero costume. It's far too big for him, hangs over his hands and covers his feet, but endows him with a big barrel chest and impressive six-pack. He is in the process of tying his red belt around his waist and is looking forlorn and puzzled at the camera, almost as though he wants whoever is behind the camera to stop taking photos and to help him. 'Help me, why don't you?' he seems to be saying with his expression. 'How can I be a superhero when I can't get my belt on?'

In the third picture, he's about four and laughing and laughing. He's heard the best joke in the whole world, and he's thrown his head to one side as he laughs and laughs about it. It's the same laugh that my husband wears in the wedding photo in Meredith's wallet.

A couple of tears that have been swimming at the bottom of my eyes break free, one landing with a small splat on the corner of the third photo. The tear instantly ruins that part of the photo, leeching out the colour and mottling it. I snatch up a napkin from the tray, dab away the tear, leaving behind an anaemic crescent at its bottom left-hand corner. 'Oh, God, I'm sorry,' I say to Meredith, my eyes flying up to her. 'I'm so sorry. I've ruined it. I've ruined it.' I cover my mouth with my hand. Look what I've done. I've ruined it. I've ruined it. 'I'm so sorry.'

Her hand comes to rest on my shoulder, gently

179

steadying me. 'It's fine,' she replies, quietly. 'It's only a photo. It can be replaced. I can easily get another one.'

Why is she being so lovely to me? When I've ruined her photo and I've stopped her son seeing her grandson, why is she being so kind? Another wave of tears builds up in my eyes, and I sit back to stop them falling and ruining the rest of the photographs. I press the palms of my hands on to my eyes, trying to stem the flow.

Stop it, I tell myself. *Stop it. Stop it. Stop it. Stop it*. I have to get back some control, otherwise I'll start sobbing for real. I haven't cried in an age and this would probably not be the best moment to start. And who would I be crying for? For Meredith? For Mal? For me? For the missing piece of me that at one point might possibly have been found in those photos?

We sit in silence for a few minutes while I calm myself, wrestle the out-of-control emotions back in check. A few deep breaths and I feel them recede, the feelings flowing away, like the tide going out.

I inhale deeply again, feeling myself calm down even more, enough to take my hands away and blink my eyes completely dry. How embarrassing. Doing that in front of Meredith of all people.

'Does she still hate me?' I ask quietly. It probably isn't fair to ask, to put her in the middle of this, but I have to know if Nova still curses my name.

'Does who hate you?' Meredith asks.

I turn my head to her and find her regarding me with confusion in her eyes, perplexity on her face.

'Nova. Does she still hate me?'

Meredith's face furrows with more

180

bewilderment. 'Why on earth would Nova hate you?' she asks.

'Because . . .' I point to the photographs.

Her greyed eyebrows shoot up in surprise. 'My goodness, because of Leo? I'd rather think it would be the other way around.'

'Pardon me?' I reply.

'I may not be very good at maths, dear, but I know that you have been married for ten years and Leo isn't yet eight.'

'She never told you, did she?' I say, with suddenly clarity. 'Nova didn't tell you what happened.'

I see the hackles of Meredith's body rise, the softness I know her for suddenly gone. 'Malvolio and I may be close,' she says, tartly, 'but his intimate business is his intimate business. I would never discuss it with him. Nor with Nova.'

I only partially hear what she is talking about, the rest of me is processing what I've just discovered. This is so typical of Nova. Years ago, when Mal and I announced we were getting married, she had immediately come to me and said that she didn't want to be a bridesmaid. She only wanted to be a bridesmaid once in her life and that was for her sister, so she didn't want to be a bridesmaid for me. I had thought it a bit audacious of her because I wasn't even going to ask her. After she left, I wondered if she didn't want to be in the bridal party because it would have been too painful for her to be that close to Mal when he was making the ultimate commitment to someone else. I'd let the matter pass until I discovered the real reason: Mal assumed that she would be a bridesmaid. Chief bridesmaid, of course. He just assumed. She

181

knew he would, she knew I wouldn't want her to have any part in my wedding party, so she had given me the easy way out. I could tell him that she didn't want to be a bridesmaid, which stopped the pitched battle that would have ensued between Mal and me, during which I'd have to confess my true feelings of continuing ambivalence towards her. I wasn't sure who she had done it for, but it had ultimately made my life easier. She'd done it again with this. Something much, much bigger. She could so easily have painted me as the monster I became all those years ago. The creature who ruined her life, took away her most precious friend. Even a toned-down version of what happened would have placed everyone firmly on her side and turned them against me. But she hasn't. She hadn't told anyone, I'm sure of that now.

If Meredith doesn't know, then Nova hasn't told her parents—they and Meredith are too close for that to have been kept a secret. They all probably know that Mal is Leo's father—just a glance at him reveals that—and they all probably think less of her because he was a married man when she'd conceived him. She'd taken on that shame when there was no need to. That is why Meredith had looked at me like that when I asked to see a picture of Leo. In fact, that is obviously why she tries to curry favour with me, why she walks on eggshells around me: she thinks I have been wronged, betrayed. She probably feels guilty about being in touch with her grandson, she probably feels guilty about talking to Mal about him in secret.

'Nova and Mal didn't have an affair,' I say to

Meredith, wanting to put things right for Nova. To clear her name. She's probably been secretly branded as a lying, scheming mistress, even by the people who love her. They probably all pity her a little, wonder why she has such low self-esteem that she became involved with someone who wasn't available and who couldn't love her enough to leave his wife for her. And then she got herself pregnant. They probably wondered if she'd done it on purpose to force his hand, or if it'd been an accident for which she was paying the price. They all loved Leo, were all completely enamoured by him, but there was probably a faint, enduring sense of shame of how they thought he came about.

If I put things right for her, then maybe she won't hate me as much. Maybe this noose of guilt would loosen around my heart. Maybe . . . I glance down at the photos again. Maybe . . .

'They didn't even . . .' I raise my eyebrows, twist my face a little, there is no way on earth I can say 'sex' in front of my mother-in-law—she'll have to work out what I am saying from that. 'I—I can't . . . Babies, you know? I can't. Nova agreed to help us.' My eyes are transfixed by the little boy grinning at me. *My beautiful little boy*. 'She was going to have a baby for us.'

I can't look at Meredith, but I know she is shocked. I can feel it mushroom like a nuclear cloud over us, and with every word I speak, every truth I reveal, her shock grows and spreads, until it fills the room.

'Nova was our surrogate, Leo was meant to be my son.'

183

CHAPTER ELEVEN

Keith is sitting on the four-poster bed when I come into the bedroom after my shower. A tsunami of terror erupts at my core, crashing and crushing through me.

'What's happened?' I ask as I clutch my white towel around me. I am suddenly light-headed and numb. Numb from the ends of my hair to the edges of my toenails.

'Nothing,' Keith says. 'Nothing's happened. Leo's fine.' He considers this. 'Nothing's changed,' he amends.

The relief lets me breathe again, allows blood and feeling to return to my body. 'Why are you here, then?' I ask Keith. I haven't been gone that long. At most three hours to do the baking, ten minutes sitting frozen on the doorstep, and ten minutes at the very most in the shower. 'Who's with Leo?'

'Melissa. The nurse. She's off duty, she said she'd stay with him until we get back.'

I may not be jealous of the attention my husband gets from other women, but I do object to him using the fact someone fancies him to get them to do something for him. Especially when it's something as important as this.

'Why?' I ask through gritted teeth.

He moves his long legs off the bed and sits on the edge. His eyes run up and down my body in a lascivious manner. 'We need to spend some time together,' he says. 'Once your family arrives, that'll be it. We won't get any time to be alone together.'

'We spend time together all the time,' I say, playing dumb. I know what he means. What he wants. What he probably needs.

Keith leaves the bed, comes over and circles his arms around me. Usually I melt against him at this point, lust and desire swamping me. Usually it's only seconds before we're entangled in bed— sometimes we won't make it that far. Usually, all Keith has to do is put his arms around me and I start to crave more: his touch, his kisses, his body, his eyes as they stare into mine. That is usually. This is not a usual time. I'm unmoved as he moves his hands up and down my towel-covered back.

'You know what I mean,' he says.

Yes, I know what he means.

He starts to nuzzle my neck, failing to notice that I'm not as fluid as usual. I have stopped responding to Keith. It is nothing to do with Leo's condition, I stopped responding to him about three months ago. Right after 'the conversation'. Since then, sex has become the very last thing on my mind. Way down after checking the oil in the car, checking whether the guttering needs clearing and finding a new supplier for stronger bin liners. It isn't Keith, it's me. It's how I feel about what he wants. He insisted we talk three months ago about trying for more kids—'We're not getting any younger, Lucks, and we always knew we would'— and after that I couldn't have sex. The thought of it . . .

I've always wanted three children, that was until what happened last time. This situation is completely different, and in my head I know it won't happen again, but in my heart, the fear of it runs unbridled.

185

And because Keith doesn't know everything about how I came to keep Leo, I can't explain it to him. Instead, I have avoided intimacy. Not simply sex, but also hugging, or kissing or snuggling when we're alone because it may lead to more.

As Keith continues to nuzzle my neck, my eyes slip shut, in ecstasy, Keith probably thinks. I'm trying to convince myself I can do this. I can relax and let it happen. I'm also trying to remember the last time I took the Pill. All my routines are all over the place and I can't remember popping one out of its packet and swallowing it in a while. I can't exactly ask Keith to pause while I go and check how many are left. And I can't remember when my last period was. It'll be impossible to ask him to wear a condom.

I try to relax, try to go with this. I'll go with it, then I'll get the morning after pill from the hospital pharmacy. Because I can't get pregnant again. I just can't. Not now, maybe not ever.

His lips—wonderful and full and one of the many reasons I fell for him—press a soft, gentle peck over my mouth. My heart dips a little in disappointment, he doesn't want a quickie. He wants the whole thing: caresses, soft-spoken words, nail-digging clings, lingering kisses, lazy talk afterwards. I could maybe have gone through with a quickie, anything more is too much.

His mouth moves to my neck whilst one arm holds me close; the fingers of the other hand untuck my towel and pull it away, so it falls in a pool to the ground.

'Oh, God, Lucks,' he whispers against my throat, his desire reverberating across my skin. 'It's been so long.'

186

He needs this. And he made it snow for me. And he loves me. And I love him. And we need something that will ground us together.

I reach for his shirt buttons but my fingers are numb and the buttons have shrunk, I can't get my fingers around them. Keith's kisses move to my shoulder, and I move my hand, trying to caress his neck but my fingers still can't feel the heat or smoothness of his skin. I throw my head back, it is what he expects. His hands move lower, grab me close.

I can't. I can't.

He takes my hand, presses it against his hardness, groaning as my hand makes contact. I'm numb. My whole body is completely inured to everything outside of me. My blood has run cold, my mind has switched off. I feel nothing.

'Stop, stop,' I say. In my head I am screaming it, but it comes out a whisper from my numbed lips.

Keith doesn't hear, his mouth continues to kiss me, his hand moves between my legs and his fingers push deep inside me. He groans loudly, clutches me closer.

'Please, Keith, stop,' I say, managing to raise my voice above a whisper.

He immediately stops, pulls away. 'What's the matter?' he asks.

I lean down, grab the towel, clumsily wrap it around me. 'I'm sorry, I can't,' I say.

His eyes are still aflame with desire, his chest heaving. 'What's the matter?' he repeats.

'I don't . . . I can't. I'm sorry,' I say. The feeling is returning to my body. 'Please don't be angry with me.'

'God, I'm not angry,' he says, coming towards

me. 'I'm just worried about you.' He hugs me this time, with only comfort on his mind. He rocks me, lulling me.

I press my head against his chest, feel his heart beating, steady and regular. When a heart beats like that, it shows that the world is steady and regular. Nothing bad happens, nothing good happens. It is all steady, flat, unsurprising. Normal.

That's what I want. I want Leo to wake up and for it to be normal. I want him to come home and for it to be normal. Not something out of the ordinary, something that needs celebration. Because if it is good, then something bad might happen to balance it out. I just want everything to go back to normal. Is that too much to ask?

'Tell me he's going to be OK,' I say to Keith.

'He's going to be more than OK,' Keith replies. 'Yeah? He's going to be more than OK.'

He doesn't understand. I don't want more than OK. I just want OK. We don't need any more than OK, we don't need more than normal. We just need it to be normal. OK.

'I'll go make some coffee while you get dressed. And then we can go back to the hospital,' he says.

'Yeah, that'd be great.'

He kisses the top of my head and leaves the room. Instead of moving to the wardrobe, I sit heavily on the bed, clinging to the towel.

My eyes go to the spot of crimson on the beige carpet beside the dressing table, where Leo dropped a red permanent marker pen without its lid on and I hadn't seen it for a few hours—not until it had created a spot the size of a two-pound coin. 'Do you do these things to upset me?' I'd shouted at him. It was the end of a long, ragged

188

week and this was the final straw. 'Or do you like me shouting at you?'

'I'm sorry,' Leo had said.

'But I don't think you are.'

'I am!' he'd implored. 'I'm sorry!'

'Yeah, so am I,' I'd replied. 'It's going to cost me a lot to get this stain cleaned off. So that means no more new toys, no more new computer games. I might even have to sell the PlayStation to pay for it.'

Leo had fled and I'd heard his footsteps running to his room—probably to wedge himself between his wardrobe and the window. Which is where he went when he wanted to cry and suck his thumb without anyone seeing. I had, of course, burst into tears, too. It hadn't been the carpet I was that annoyed about. I didn't in the grand scheme of things care about it—it was the fact that Leo had done something I told him over and over not to: he'd gone into my room with markers. He'd disobeyed me. Which was all a part of his growing up; growing up and growing away. Which scared me. He had always relied on me for everything, to know right from wrong, and he was starting to push the boundaries more and more. But that was normal. I knew that. I knew that then, I know that now. I wanted to lose him in a normal way. Like most mothers lost their children to time and adulthood. I don't want to lose him like this.

I want normal again. I want OK again.

Is that really too much to want? For everything to be normal.

Maybe it is, because the way Leo came about was not normal in the everyday sense. Maybe this is happening because Leo was never meant to be mine.

'I wonder how the baby gets out of the mummy's body?' he asked.

They were walking through the park. He wasn't cold even though Mum had gone on and on and on about him wearing his special coat. The one with the sticky strip and zip and buttons. They weren't even going to the beach, where it was really, really, really windy and sometimes he had to hold on to Mum because he might get blown away. He liked that idea. Being blown away. Right out to sea. But only if Mum would get blown away too. It'd be like flying.

Mum was wearing her duffel coat, which was his favourite. It was like Paddington's and she had a stripy scarf around and around and around her neck. She was wheeling his scooter along the path.

Mum looked scared when he asked her the question, like when he jumped out from behind the door. This time she didn't scream and clutch her chest, but she looked scared. Then she looked up at the trees because she was pretending she couldn't hear. It was like when he put his hands over his ears so he couldn't hear Mum when she called him to come in.

'I wonder how the baby gets out of the mummy's body?' he asked again. 'Do you know, Mum?'

She sighed, and stopped to lean on his scooter. 'Yes, I do,' she said.

His eyes widened. 'How?' he asked eagerly, ready to remember every word so he could tell Richard and David and Martin on Monday.

'Sweetheart, I really don't want to talk about it

right now,' Mum said. 'I don't think you're old enough.' At least she didn't crouch down when she said this, which would make him feel so much worse.

'I'm six!' he said.

'I know.'

'That's really old.'

'I know.'

'Why won't you tell me?'

'I know you're six and I know you're old, but as I said, I don't think you're old enough.'

He folded his arms across his chest, stamped his foot. 'That's not fair!' He frowned at Mum, scrunched his arms even tighter, lowered his head so he could glare at her through his really narrow eyes. If he narrowed them enough they might shoot laser beams, then Mum would know he was old enough. Someone who could shoot laser beams would be old enough then.

'I know,' Mum said. Then she did the worst thing in the whole world, she crouched down so they were the same height. He knew she was taller than him, almost all adults were. So why did they have to make themselves shorter when they didn't have to? 'OK, let me put it this way as well, I'm *not* old enough to tell you. How about that? Will that make you feel better?'

Leo nodded.

Mum beamed at him. He liked it when she smiled. When she smiled she looked like the sun—big and warm and beautiful. Dad always said Mum's smile lit up his world.

Mum stood up, and he heard the cracking in her knees. 'Whoa!' Leo gasped. It was cool when she did that.

They started walking again, towards the other end of the park to see if there were any ducks in the pond, *then he'd be allowed to scoot all the way along the path and go in front and Mum wouldn't run after him until he was really, really far away. She let him do things like that and it was fun. Sometimes it was extra fun when it was just her and him. Dad was great, but it was even greater when it was just him and Mum.*

Mum reached out and jokily pulled his hood up on his head. He shook it off and laughed. They walked along for a while. The quiet in the park was so cool. There weren't many people out because it was really early and cold. Mum had to go open the café soon so they went for the walk really early.

'I wonder how the baby gets into the mummy's tummy?' he asked.

Leo, age 6 years

part four

CHAPTER TWELVE

I can't look at Meredith, but I know she is shocked. I can feel it mushroom like a nuclear cloud over us, and with every word I speak, every truth I reveal, her shock grows and spreads, until it fills the room.

'Nova was our surrogate, Leo was meant to be my son.'

*   *   *

It started in the supermarket, of all places.

In the washing powder aisle. I thought it would be the sight of a young mum sharing a tender moment with her child that would ignite the maternal spark in me, but it was the exact opposite. It started with a little boy, in a blue anorak and green combats, throwing himself on the floor, writhing and twisting like a goldfish that had accidentally leapt out of its bowl on to the carpet, whilst screaming as though he was being murdered by a rusty hacksaw. Like all the other shoppers who had been down that aisle when the epic tantrum began, I stood, watching him, horrified at the spectacle and impressed at his freedom.

After a few seconds my eyes, like all the other shoppers', moved to his mother. She stood stock-still in front of the washing powder, her half-full trolley beside her, her eyes fixed on the detergents, to all intents and purposes deaf to the noise her son was creating. When we looked at her, we were all surprised because she wasn't hastily trying to

195

secrete about her person the rusty hacksaw with which the boy was being murdered. The only outward clue that she was with him and that she could hear him was that colour sat high in her face, resting on her cheekbones like two streaks of paint, and her eyes were glossy with tears.

I realised, then, that she was trying to wait out the tantrum. Giving in, even when it was causing her immense embarrassment and every witness intense discomfort, would mean he would do this again. And again. And again. He would realise that misbehaving in public would be the quickest and most effective way to get what he wanted. Having said that, it was clear that it wasn't working. He had tenacity, this young boy—his tantrum, its loud, insistent wail, was not abating.

My heart went out to her. I wanted to pick him up by the scruff of the neck, I wanted to put my arms around her. I wanted, I realised with a start, to be her. Because I would do it differently. I would give in, I would allow him what he wanted now, then take away something at home. I wouldn't allow him to embarrass me in public, I would simply punish him in private. I wanted to be her.

I wanted to be a mother.

I wanted to have a child of my own.

I abandoned my trolley there in the aisle and walked out of the supermarket, the sound of the stranger's cries and his mother's loud, silent humiliation drilling into me what I wanted and what I couldn't have.

Everything was flat after that day.

Flat and meaningless. Dull. The shine was buffed off everything, the joy drained out of life.

No matter how fast I ran at night, how far I stretched, how much weight I lifted, pushed and pulled, it was still there. The cloud. The knowledge. The unending grey that was my life. My reality.

I have moods. Like any other person I have moods. Sometimes mine last a bit longer, seem a bit deeper, but that's because I feel things with a depth most people don't allow themselves to experience. I worry, I fret, I take things to heart and I keep them there. When our dog, Duke, died when I was thirteen, everyone—my mother, my father, Mary, Peter—cried. But they all 'got over it'. They could all leave it behind. I loved Duke more than them, that was obvious, because months later I still cried for him. I still missed him. I still hurt like it had only just happened. I could feel, more than most people. Now, after the incident in the supermarket, there was nothing to feel.

The landscape of reality showed me this: there was no point to it. To anything. Don't we exist so we can create? Procreate? I couldn't. I wouldn't. Therefore, what was the point of me? What was the point of any of it?

I didn't talk to Mal about it. Why would I? This was all down to me. He could have children. He wasn't the faulty one. I was. It was all my problem, why burden him with it? When I told him originally about my history, what had happened to me, why I couldn't have children, he had accepted it like he accepted every other thing about me. He accepted that as a teenager I had been branded a slut-whore. He accepted that I'd got pregnant at fifteen. He accepted and understood about the abortion and how, because of that, because of

197

complications, I was unable to have children. He understood it as a part of who I was. He was unwavering in his support. But still, I could not tell him everything. Not *every* thing.

So I couldn't share this with him. It hurt him enough that he wouldn't be a father—he hid it, but I knew it was something he wanted—so why burden him with something that was my fault and was only now starting to hurt?

*   *   *

Grey has a sound, you know that?

It has a sound and it has a texture. It sounds like a noise so loud you can only hear it when you're quiet. It feels like huge bales of cotton wool and it smothers you. It fills up every orifice and smothers you so you drown on dry land. It deafens and drowns you.

Black is not so hard to figure out. Black isn't as bad as people make out. Blackness is just dark. Greyness is around all the time. When it's light out, when it's dark out, grey is still there, waiting to slowly, carefully, gently creep over you. To make you not exist. You never know it's happening until it's too late. Until you can't breathe and you can't see and you can't hear and you can't feel.

My life was grey.

I had to stop it.

I had to stop the greyness from taking over.

No one understood, of course. It was happening to them, I could see the grey around the edges of their lives, but they didn't notice. Or they didn't want to notice. They pretended everything was fine. They would stand by the photocopier, talking and laughing, and pretend they couldn't feel the greyness hanging over their shoulders. I could see it. I would stare at them, willing them to notice and to do something; I would stare at the greyness and will it to go away. It had already taken hold of my life, I didn't want it to take over theirs.

I didn't tell them, I had to help them. Show them the best way to do things. I wore red and yellow and green to work. I wore blue eyeshadow, red lipstick. I wore my red dress. I wore my yellow shoes. I wore my green headscarf. It showed them that they didn't have to give in to the grey. Even I, who had been invaded by it, could escape.

I didn't fit in, apparently. That's what they said when they 'let me go'. I had been a wonderful office manager for five years, but my interests obviously lay elsewhere so they were paying me a lump sum and wishing me luck in my future endeavours. It didn't matter. I was losing the battle against the grey there anyway. At home, I would be able to concentrate on my battle.

I could win against the grey.

If I didn't have to worry about other people, I could remember why the grey had started to pick on me and I could fight it. I could win if I had the time to fight back.

There was a lot of grey in the cemetery.

It stretched for miles. I walked around the place, looking at headstones. Reading them. Seeing who had lost the fight. How their battle was explained away in a few lines. A life reduced to a few lines chiselled into stone. It didn't seem right. The headstones should be proclaiming how these people lived, how they died, how they made a difference in the world. What was the point of trying if this was all that you were reduced to in the end: meaningless words on a stone.

I always lingered over the stones that said 'loving mother'. I would never be that, would I? If the grey won, they would never say that about me. What would I want them to say about me? Would I want them to even bother?

CHAPTER THIRTEEN

I want normal again. I want OK again.

Is that really too much to want? For everything to be normal.

Maybe it is, because the way Leo came about was not normal in the everyday sense. Maybe this is happening because Leo was never meant to be mine.

*   *   *

BUZZZZZZZZZZZZZZ!

BUZZZZZZ! BUZZZZZZ! BUZZZZZZZZZZZZZZZ!

My eyes snapped open, startled awake by something. The main light was on, my sweaty cheek was pressed up against the pages of a psychology tome I'd been making notes from and half the duvet was on the floor, half of it twisted around my leg. I looked at the clock: 2:07 a.m. Had I been woken up by a sound, or a dream? Sometimes my dreams did that, forced me upwards into wakefulness, where it took me a while to get my bearings.

BUZZZZZZZZZZZZ! came again and I sat up,

my eyes wide with shock. I untangled myself from the duvet and, tugging on my dressing gown, I rushed out to the wide corridor of my flat and snatched up the intercom phone.

'It's me,' Mal said.

'Oh,' I replied and pressed the key button to let him in.

Mal hadn't visited me at 2 a.m.—actually, past midnight—in years. Rarely since he'd met Stephanie and *never* since they'd moved in together and then went on to get married. It wasn't so much that I was dispensable, or that he wouldn't if the mood took him and he had something pressing to tell me, but I had explained to him at length that Stephanie wouldn't appreciate it. Keith didn't mind if he was on night duty because it would mean I wouldn't be alone. But Stephanie wasn't as secure about my friendship with Mal as Keith was. Even now, I knew, she occasionally gave me sideways looks that told me she was suspicious of me; sometimes waves of doubt about my feelings for her husband would tumble off her.

Opening the door to Mal told me that it wasn't a social visit.

He could barely stay upright. His hair stood on end, his tie was loosened and lay lopsided around his open top button. His suit jacket and trousers, although navy blue, were stiff with dark patches; his light blue shirt was also stiff and darkened. Blood. Dried blood. I reared back internally, bile gushing to my throat, my stomach spinning in on itself.

'Steph's had an accident,' he said, his voice a fragile whisper. 'She's in hospital.'

'I'll make you something to eat,' I said as I

brought him inside.

I knew he wasn't going to tell me anything else because he knew nothing else. We had a shorthand for speaking about such things. From the incidents with Aunt Mer we knew we had to give the important pieces of information as soon as possible. If he knew she was going to be OK he would have said she was fine as soon as he told me she was in hospital; if she wasn't going to make it, he would have told me straight away. He didn't know anything more than he had told me.

I didn't ask what had happened, why there was so much blood, if he had been there when it happened, because it wasn't important. He needed comfort. He needed a good feeding.

While I put on the rice, he stood in the corner of my kitchen leaning against the fridge. All the while I breathed through my mouth so I wouldn't have to inhale that sickening, dirty, metallic stench of blood. I defrosted frozen vegetables, I opened tins of tomatoes, I fried onions, I mixed in the tomatoes, I squeezed in tomato paste, and, in between, I talked. I talked about my current assignment, I talked about finishing with Keith only to get back with him hours later and start thinking of finishing with him again. I talked through my worries about who was misappropriating stock at the restaurant. I talked and talked because I talked too much. I talk too much because I had learnt from a long time ago that the last thing Mal needed in times of crisis was silence.

We didn't eat.

The plates of freshly cooked food sat on the wooden side table in the living room, while I sat on the sofa, Mal curled up with his head resting on my lap. I stroked my hand over his hair, and I talked and talked until we both fell asleep.

CHAPTER FOURTEEN

I noticed his eyes first.

Clouded over, a storm of pain and agony rolling in them.

I knew then, instantly, that something had happened to his mother. Poor Mal. I moved to comfort him, to climb out of bed and into the inviting well of his lap, to wrap my arms around him and cuddle him and love him better. I couldn't. Couldn't move. Something was holding me back. Down.

When I looked, around my forearms leather straps were secured, holding me back, holding me down. Around my wrists, bandages, holding me together. I flopped back on to the bed, stared up at the white ceiling. Sighed. Oh. Right. That. *Here*.

His eyes were still on me. I could feel them, resting gently on my profile, like he often did with his hand before he kissed me.

I don't know why you bothered, I thought at him. I couldn't say it out loud, they listened to everything you said here. Listened, wrote it down, made a big deal of it. Even throwaway lines that someone would laugh at somewhere else became as important as the Holy Grail here.

I knew what he was thinking: *What?*

Not why? What?

He knew *why*, he was thinking *what? What* was

203

the trigger? *What* made me do this? He knew why I did it, but not *what* made me do it. Yup, that was what my loving husband wanted to know: not why, what?

'I found the chocolate. And the cigarettes,' he said. He made it sound as if he'd found class A drugs or something. Every woman needed chocolate. Everyone knew that. It didn't mean anything. And if I wasn't smoking in the house, around him, if I wasn't making him inhale second-hand smoke, what was the big deal about me smoking? They were only cigarettes, not wacky baccy or anything.

'I should have noticed,' he was saying. 'I should have noticed the signs. I was so wrapped up in work and trying to get the promotion, I didn't realise how much you needed the serotonin and the nicotine. I'm sorry.'

Were you always this dramatic? I asked him inside. He made this sound like a big deal.

'Why didn't you tell me you'd left your job?' he asked.

I didn't tell you because I knew you would react like this. You wouldn't understand about the grey. You would think something was wrong and you'd bring me here.

'You've been pretending to go to work for six weeks, Steph. I don't understand why. If you weren't happy there I wouldn't have made you stay.'

No, you would have watched my every move.

My wrists were throbbing now I was awake properly, fully ensconced in the conscious world. I hadn't done the job properly. If I had, this wouldn't be happening. I wouldn't be feeling guilty and like a failure on top of everything else.

'What can I do, Steph?' he asked.

'Water,' I croaked. I didn't realise until I tried to speak that my throat was parched, scratchy. They'd probably stuck a tube down there to purge my stomach of the undigested pills. They were never gentle. I'd watched it being done, and a couple of times I'd been mostly conscious when it'd been done to me, and it's as if they didn't realise that the lining of your throat was really rather delicate and would be raw and sore from having things brutally shoved down it like that.

The water glugging into the glass was theatrically loud, it hurt my head in deep-down places. I wanted to cover my ears, but the restraints wouldn't let me. He held the straw in place so I could raise my upper body and take a few sips. The water was warm—room temperature—but good considering how dry I felt. Desiccated. I felt so dry that I might blow away like dust particles on a small gust of wind, or if he breathed a little too heavily near me.

'Did you read my diary?' I asked him carefully through my scratchy throat. If he had found the chocolate, my secret supply that kept me going, kept me happy, he must have found my diary. Tucked away in shoeboxes on the top shelf of our wardrobe. He never looked in there. He occasionally made a comment about the number of shoes I owned, but he never knew until now that along with the shoes, each of them had a few bars of chocolate, most had a packet of cigarettes, and the box with my leopard skin boots also had my diary.

When he didn't reply, I turned my head to look

at him. He was fiddling with the straw in the glass, his head bowed. He was avoiding my eyes because he was ashamed.

'You had no right,' I said to him.

He continued to play with the straw, ignoring me. 'They want you to see a psychiatrist,' he eventually said.

I frowned, shook my head in disbelief. 'There's nothing wrong with me,' I said. I had been trying to tell the doctors, nurses and orderlies this every time I woke and found I was in here and bound to a bed, but they wouldn't listen, wouldn't let me free. There really is nothing wrong with me. Over the years they'd been trying to do this to me. All of them, my mother, my doctors, and now Mal. They'd all been trying to make me go and see someone who would shrink my brain, make me talk to them and make me seem crazy. When I wasn't. I just felt things. That was all. Everyone felt things. Psychiatrists, psychologists, therapists, the whole lot of them all made a big deal out of nothing.

'They won't let you out until you talk to someone,' he said.

'They can't keep me here against my will,' I said. My voice, although raspy, sounded weak and insubstantial. I was raging against this, but I couldn't express that. I was tied down. And my voice wouldn't express my indignation.

'I signed you in here,' he explained. 'Remember, you said I should if this happened again? So I did. And I want you to comply with the treatment they suggest. I know that's what you'd want as well. If you could see clearly enough.'

One thing was certain. I was trapped here.

Stuck.

'Who have you told?' I asked. I had to find another way out. But I couldn't let Mal know that. I had to play along for now.

'Just your family,' he said casually.

Just my family. *JUST* my family. 'Oh, shoot me now,' I said. My mother would come here and try to clean the place, in between crying and praying and wondering what she'd done to deserve this. My father would think I was wasting everyone's time and I was a wilful brat who he hadn't beaten enough when I was a teenager. Mary would sit and glare at me, resentful that I didn't do the job properly and that she'd had to take time out of her busy life to come here—like I'd asked her to come or something. And Peter would show up in a few weeks, probably after I'd been discharged, and would be genuinely surprised that the world hadn't waited for him to catch up.

'They were really worried. I told them to come in a few days, when you're feeling stronger.' I suppose that was something. 'I ring them every day and tell them how you are.'

'Have you told Nova?' I asked.

'No,' he said. 'I haven't told anyone except your family. I won't tell anyone else.'

'OK,' I replied, feeling my body relax. 'Thank you.' It was odd thanking someone for not gossiping about me.

'What about me, Steph?' he asked quietly, his voice as small and weak as mine was. I turned my head to look at him. He had shrunk in on himself a little, sudden anguish and torment were gouged deep into every part of him. 'I know you didn't want to be here any more for that moment, but

207

what about me? What am I supposed to do without you?' He pressed his forefinger and thumb on the bridge of his nose, tightly screwed up his eyes. 'How am I supposed to carry on if you're not here?'

I swung my head back to look up at the ceiling, his words were seeping into me like the grey had begun to do. What I did wasn't fair on him. But it wasn't about him. It wasn't about anyone except me. Like everyone else, he couldn't see that. He couldn't understand that. You never could until you were here. Where I was. Until the grey had so taken over, you had to stop it. And sometimes, the only way to stop it, to stop the slow, agonising suffocation, was to leave. To walk through the door marked 'exit', knowing gratefully that there was no way back.

It was the end.

'I need some sleep,' I whispered and closed my eyes.

I heard him stand, place the water back on the table on the other side of the room. He came back to me, pressed his lips on to my forehead. 'Love you,' he whispered and left.

When I opened my eyes again, I looked at the door, wondering how I'd be able to get out of here. He was still standing there. Tall, silent, strong. He stood by the door, staring at me. He smiled at me with his lips curled into his mouth before he turned around and left.

CHAPTER FIFTEEN

For two weeks I made him dinner every night.

I rearranged my shifts so I only worked days, so every night I could make him dinner. It was always a Ghanaian meal: beef stew; rice with kidney beans; plantain; fish soup; fu-fu; gari; black-eye bean fritters; jelof rice. The food of our childhood, the food Mum would feed us up with during good times and bad.

I did it because I loved to cook. And I did it because I could see that the smell of the food, the taste of it, would relax him. Would pull him out of the fog of fear that surrounded him when he arrived at my flat after having seen Stephanie. He didn't tell me what was wrong with her, I didn't ask. Instead we ate and we talked, and we fell asleep on the sofa.

On the sixteenth day he didn't turn up so I knew she was home. I knew she was fine.

CHAPTER SIXTEEN

'I want a baby,' I told him.

It had been bubbling away for a long time. It was the last trigger and I could see that I could prevent it happening again. Talking about this trigger would make it less scary. He could do what he always did, he could try to face it with me. Of course he couldn't, not completely, but knowing he'd listen and understand made me feel less alone in all of this.

'I'll pick you one up at the supermarket next week. Or do you want me to go down to that new delicatessen? They're organic and ethically sourced.'

I laughed, despite myself, and then punched him lightly on the arm to ask him to take me seriously. 'I'm being serious,' I said to him. 'I want a baby.'

His footsteps on the walking trail stopped and he paused. He said nothing for a while, just stared off into the vista, a breathtaking tessellation of green that made up the Welsh countryside.

'How long have you felt like this?' he asked.

'Six months, maybe a year.'

It clicked in his mind, behind his eyes: *What.*

Loss and disruption, two huge triggers for me. When I was thirteen our dog, Duke, died and six months later we moved from London to Nottingham. I was lost up there, I found it hard to make new friends and I missed Duke so much. Nothing was ever really the same after that.

'Is that why?' Mal asked.

'I think so. One of the reasons, anyway.'

He looked away again, replaying what had happened eight months ago now he could hang it all on a 'what'. Mal came back for me, took my hand and we started walking down the bumpy trail again.

'What are our options?' he asked.

'None,' I said. 'I can't have children. That's it. I only told you because I don't want to start slipping again, not if talking about it will help.' We navigated our way over the path, twigs snapping under our sturdy boots. It was a unique kind of peaceful up here, there were birds and other creatures, but they all made up rather than disturbed the backdrop of silence, so pure and uncluttered. 'I didn't understand what you'd given up until recently, you know. You gave up the chance to be a father to be with me, that's a huge thing to have done. Thank you.'

'Do you really want a baby, Steph?' he asked in reply.

When I thought of babies, I felt emptiness. It was something I couldn't do. But I wanted one. To have, to hold, to be mine. I wanted someone to take care of, to love. 'I really do,' I replied.

'Then we'll find a way to make it happen,' he said, as he wrapped his arms around me, drew me towards him, transferred his heat and strength to me with that hold. 'OK? We'll find a way.'

*   *   *

It all kept coming back to the same thing.

IVF was out. There was a waiting list on the NHS and it would cost too much privately. And how would all the hormones I had to take interact with the other medication I was on?

Fostering was not an option. I couldn't stand to take care of a child for only a few days or weeks and then have to lose them again.

Adoption was viable, Mal thought. But I was scared. Of the questions they'd ask, what they'd want to know. How closely they would monitor us if they found out about my medical history. What they would demand I do. I could see them making me jump through hoop after hoop so that I could fit their criteria. Mal didn't think it would be that bad, we should at least investigate it, but then *he* wasn't the one who always had to tick 'yes' to questions on forms about taking regular medication, *he* wasn't the one who had to regularly visit the doctor to have his blood checked, *he* wasn't the one who might have to inform the DVLA at any point that he wasn't allowed to drive. Mal didn't have what I had so he couldn't understand how it felt to be constantly singled out as 'other', 'broken', 'damaged'.

So, it all kept coming back to one thing: find someone to have a baby for us.

'Victoria is out of the question, obviously,' Mal said. We'd talked and talked about it for weeks and the conversation always went the same way.

'I don't know, two Wacken genes combined, it'd be a very cute baby,' I said.

'Stop it, stop it now,' he said. 'It's too heinous a thing to even joke about.'

'Mary would tell me that I was cursed and I deserved this. There's no way on earth I'd ask her,' I said.

'What about your cousin Paula? She was your bridesmaid, and she's had two children already.'

I didn't *really* like Paula that much, I'd only asked her because her mum was my mother's sister and I'd stayed with them once and it was expected. 'Yeah, maybe,' I said non-committally.

'What about your friend, Carole? Or Ruth? Or Dyan?'

'They're not those kinds of friends.'

There was someone else, of course, but in all the discussions, we never mentioned her. I hadn't because he hadn't. And I was surprised he hadn't. I didn't know why.

We lapsed into silence and it was at this point

212

one of us would say, 'We really need to get to know more people.'

'We could pay someone, sign up to one of those agencies,' he said.

'Yeah,' I said half-heartedly. 'Apart from the cost, I don't know, it wouldn't be the same as someone we know. I know you get to meet the surrogate first, become friends with her and everything . . . but I suppose I want someone I can talk to every day. Drop in and see her, be there with her. Be a part of the day-to-day rather than just seeing her for stuff like the scans and the birth. Do you see what I mean? A friend would let me do that, someone who I've become friends with for a specific purpose probably wouldn't let me take over so much of their life.'

'If we search for the right person through an agency, we can explain all that.'

'I suppose so,' I replied.

At this point he'd bring up adoption again and I'd have to explain why I didn't want that.

'Nova,' he said instead of 'adoption'.

'Nova,' I repeated.

'She's that kind of friend, she'd let us both be a part of the day-to-day, and the baby would be beautiful.'

'And half black.'

'Yeah, and . . . ?'

He really and honestly didn't understand. 'I know, Mal, in your wonderful, politically correct, rainbow-coloured world such things don't matter, but here on planet earth, they do. People will look at the baby and know it's not mine.'

He paused, thought about it, then said, 'So?'

'So? Mal, the baby would stand out at all our

family gatherings, walking down the street, when I take him or her to the park . . . The baby would always stand out, people would notice and they'd talk.'

'Why do you care what other people think?' he asked. He could ask that because he had the confidence not to care. He had the strength to fight anyone who said anything about him and those he loved. I didn't.

'I don't know, I just do,' I said. After I left home I had rebuilt my reputation, I had become the type of person other people didn't talk about, I blended in. This would be the opposite of blending in.

'Steph, things only matter if you allow them to. We all stand out in lots of different ways. That only matters if you let it.'

'Says the good-looking, white, middle class man with the white, middle class life. It's very easy to talk about things only mattering if you let them when you're in a position of privilege.'

'I'm working class,' he said with a bright smile. 'And I know things only matter if you let them because all those years that people gossiped about my mother, and the fact my father had been in prison, I only cared when Victoria would say things. Whenever she had a go at Mum for ruining her life, or when she accused me and the Kumalisis of sending her away because we didn't love her, that hurt. That mattered, because I care what she thinks. Yeah, I got in fights at school over the things people said about my family, but as I got older I realised it didn't matter. They can say what they like. And if they don't like something, fuck 'em, that's their problem. Not mine. If someone doesn't like the fact my child is half black, they can

214

fuck off out of my life.'

'I can't think like that. I'm not like you.'

'OK,' he said, leaning back in his seat. 'Say I had been married before to an Indian woman, had a child with her but got divorced. She gets custody, me and you get together. Then, one day, she decides to go off on a round-the-world trip and leaves our child with me. Us. So, what, you'd say no we can't look after her because she'd stand out?'

'Course not, but that'd be completely different.'

'Yeah, it would. Because you wouldn't have been holding her since the day she was born, you wouldn't have felt her moving around in the womb, you wouldn't have fallen in love with her from the moment she was conceived.'

When he put it like that, it sounded so possible. A baby of our own.

'Nova,' I said.

'She's the right choice.'

'If she's so perfect how come it's taken you this long to mention her?'

'Because you didn't,' he said.

'I didn't because you didn't.'

'You didn't because sometimes you think she and I are too close.'

'Only sometimes.'

'Fair enough.'

'Let me think about it,' I said.

For three weeks I thought about it, we talked about it, and it all came back to one thing. One person.

Nova.

CHAPTER SEVENTEEN

'We both know I didn't really like you when I met you,' Stephanie said.

Stephanie was about to ask me for something, I could tell. She was carrying out a classic move in trying to get someone to do something for you: lay all your cards on the table. Or, at the very least, appear to do so. She was trying to manipulate me in case I still hung on to any slivers of resentment for what she thought of me before she got to know me. Admitting to not liking me suggested that she was ashamed of it, therefore any hurt I still held wasn't going to be nearly as deep as hers. She was ashamed, I shouldn't hold that against her and hopefully we could 'move on' and find a new beginning, which would involve me doing whatever it was that she wanted from me.

'It wasn't you, of course, I didn't even know you,' she continued. 'It was me, my insecurities.' Her sea-blue eyes flicked upwards as though remembering that time, in a galaxy far, far away. She shook her head slightly, bouncing the waves of her cornsilk-coloured hair. Not natural. I knew that now. I knew all these things about Stephanie, the woman who had apparently become my friend over the past four years. I knew she assisted her hair colour, I knew she'd had a serious accident just over a year ago. I knew she stopped being office manager in a law firm just over a year ago and now was assistant manager of a clothes boutique. I knew Mal dyed her eyelashes and eyebrows every six weeks because otherwise she would look like she had neither. I knew she ran every day—rain or shine. If the weather was particularly bad, she would go to the gym and run on a treadmill. She practised yoga, she smoked even though she thought neither Mal nor I knew it was more than a sneaky one every now and again. She drank very little. She had kissed another woman in college. Her left breast was a half-cup size smaller than her right. She plucked the grey out of her pubic hair. She always wore bangles on both wrists, but had recently started wearing more of them.

I knew a lot of extraneous information about Stephanie, but if God was in the details of knowing a person, then we had a Godless relationship. She was a mistress of disguise; a regular Mata Hari. She put on whichever persona was appropriate for the person she was talking to, blending herself in to fit the background of their personality. With me, she feigned openness. Because I talked far too much for my own good, and tried to think the best of people always, she tried to be like that with me, too. She didn't realise that I saw through her disguise because I didn't simply listen to her, I could feel her. She was closed; her aura a tightly woven mass of energy with very defined, sharp edges that would never allow you beyond a certain point. You could spend hours with Stephanie and know very little. You could spend years with Stephanie and know even less.

'I can't have children,' she said. Her fingers revealed her anxiety. They laced together, they unwound from each other, they drummed on the table, they tapped on each other, they spun the base of her wine glass in a circle on the wooden

217

table.

'God, I'm sorry,' I said. Mal hadn't told me that. Not that he would ever reveal their secrets to me.

Her hands went to the bag that was sitting beside her on the red leatherette sofa. She rummaged inside, pulled out her pack of Marlboro Lights and lighter. 'Do you mind if I smoke?' she asked.

'No, course not,' I said.

Her body relaxed as she inhaled on her cigarette. As she exhaled, more tension was released.

'Where was I?' she said after two more draws. 'Oh yes. I'd just revealed my big secret.' Her flippancy wasn't at all convincing. 'I told Mal before we got married, when things became serious. I couldn't *ever* allow him to tie himself to me without knowing . . . Without knowing that.' She pressed her hand over her collarbone to show her sincerity and how much it had cost her to reveal her secret to another person. 'It's a medical thing,' she continued. 'A mishap . . .' Tears welled up in her eyes. The last—and first—time I saw Stephanie cry was on her wedding day. She'd been so overcome with happiness that tears cracked her façade. These, I could tell, were not as genuine as her wedding day tears. 'I'm sorry . . . Sometimes I feel like I've been cheated out of being a real woman.'

I nodded in understanding, wondering what she wanted from me. Under normal circumstances she would not be revealing this to anyone, let alone me. And her aura hadn't changed at all. The defined, razor edge was still there: get too close and she would cut me off. But she still wanted

218

something that she could only get from me.

'We've been looking into adoption,' she said, 'but it's unlikely we'll get a baby.'

'What, a professional couple like you two? Good-looking, successful, all your own teeth? I find that hard to believe,' I said. I knew nothing of adoption, but if I were ever to be responsible for advertising the concept, I would make Mal and Stephanie the poster couple. They couldn't look any less perfect if they wore matching T-shirts that proclaimed: 'We've cured cancer, ended world poverty and we're making great progress on reversing global warming.'

'OK, I admit, we might. But it'll take time. A lot of time. And form-filling and people prying into the very details of our lives.'

'As they should. They can't just hand over a baby to anyone.'

'No, quite . . . We also want a baby that is genetically connected to us.'

Her aura changed then, the edges softened, reached out to me. I felt a cold chill thrill down the side of my head, into my neck and along my spine. Without meaning to I leant back a little. They wouldn't . . . They certainly wouldn't—

'We've been through all the people we know and . . . We love you so much . . . There was no one else who would be suitable and who would even think about it. And we're only asking you to think about it. Nothing else. Absolutely nothing else.'

They would. They had.

She drew hard on her cigarette, the action hardening her: sharpening up the edges of her face and mannerisms. She was closed off again. As she expelled cigarette smoke, she ran her tongue over her upper teeth.

'We think you're amazing,' she said with a wide grin. 'And if there is anyone on earth we'd want to carry our child for us that isn't me, well, it'd be you. Every choice we looked at was no way nearly as . . . well, you as you.'

She's hiding something, crossed my mind. Followed swiftly by, *She's lying.* I pushed my thoughts aside. What was there to lie about? What was there to hide?

'I—erm—I . . .' I began, not quite sure what to say. I was surprised that it had come from her and not Mal.

'I asked because I didn't want you to say yes simply because it was Mal who asked,' she said, reading my mind. 'I know what the pair of you are like, you'll do anything for each other without a second thought. This is a huge thing, though, and I—*we*—want you to think about it carefully.'

'Oh, don't worry, I'll do that,' I reassured her, and grabbed my wine glass and took a gulp. Of course I wouldn't do it. This wasn't lending them money towards the deposit on their house (which she still didn't know about), this wasn't making an effort with a person who clearly hated me, this was growing a baby inside me and then giving it to someone else. Who could do that? I know people did do that, but who were they? How *could* they? I wasn't one of those people, that was for certain. And I was surprised that they thought I was.

'It'd be traditional surrogacy,' Stephanie said. Her eyes were poring over me, watching for my reaction. She should have tuned in with her other senses, because then she would know: the answer was no. 'That's when you use the intended father's sperm and the surrogate's eggs.'

I wouldn't be giving them their baby, which I had grown, I'd be— I took another huge gulp of wine. No way! Absolutely no way.

She rested her hand on my forearm. 'Please just think about it,' she said, a quiet, stilling plea. Our eyes met and for the first time she was open. I could see the emotion in her: sincerity. Her armour, her disguises, her deflections were laid aside and she was sincere.

When she had done that, had stopped playing the role of Stephanie for a moment and had *been* Stephanie, the least I could do was think about it.

Only think about it.

CHAPTER EIGHTEEN

She didn't say no.

She had looked shocked, but she didn't say no straight away. She didn't say no at all.

She was the logical choice, the perfect choice. I could see that now.

And she was going to help us.

She was going to help me.

I was going to be a mother.

I was going to have the family I'd always wanted. And the life I'd always wanted.

Everything was going to be perfect. I just *knew* it.

CHAPTER NINETEEN

Music rose up from the street below my window.

Not from a car stereo, not from someone's
Walkman being played too loud. I recognised the
tune almost immediately. The opening guitar
strains of 'Somewhere Over the Rainbow'. The
Hawaiian version, soft but faster than Judy
Garland's rendition. I went to the window,
twitched aside a sliver of net curtain. In the street,
below my window, Mal stood playing his guitar.
His eyes were fixed on my window and he grinned
as he spotted me. It was the mischievous smile he
used to give me when we were children and had
stolen biscuits from the cupboard, or sneaked out
of bed and sat on the steps listening to Mum and
Dad talking in the front room. It was the smile that
made what we shared special and unbreakable.
Few people who hadn't been there from the
beginning of our time together could understand
it.

He began to sing and even through the glass and
walls, the timbre of his voice touched the very core
of me. When he and Cordy used to sing together
when we were younger, it made everyone smile. I
hadn't heard him sing in years. Now he was
serenading me with his smooth voice at 11 p.m.
from the street outside my flat.

This would be so romantic if he wasn't married
and if they hadn't asked me to have their baby. I
knew why he was doing it—because we hadn't
spoken in over a week. He'd been round and he'd
called, but I was always 'unavailable'. I couldn't

speak to him after what Stephanie had asked, so had started to avoid them. He was forcing my hand, doing something that would get my attention.

I hauled open the window. 'OK, I get the message,' I said. 'Stop.'

The lights went on in the living room of the flat downstairs, suddenly drenching him in a yellow glow. He carried on singing, seemingly oblivious to the fact he was about to get seven types of hell kicked out of him by the body-building ex-bouncer-turned-Elvis-impersonator who lived below me. 'Quick, get inside!' I hissed.

Mal continued to sing, that grin on his face. He wasn't moving until I came downstairs to speak to him.

Jerking myself inside my flat again, I grabbed my keys from the side table and ran into the corridor. On the way out I threw on my poncho to hide my pyjama top and bralessness. Taking the carpeted communal stairs two at a time, I flung open the front door and ran into the night, to where he stood. All the lights in the four flats in our building were now on. Like a co-ordinated Mexican wave, the lights of flats and houses on our street blinked on one after the other; then people pulled aside curtains to see outside. It wouldn't be too long before someone would be calling the police or coming out to shove Mal's guitar down his throat.

In a book or film, all the people looking out would be won over by the romance of the situation: the women would be clasping their hands together and awwing at us, the men would be noting down the reaction such a grand gesture had elicited and

223

would be planning something of their own. Mal and I would have a talk, we would kiss passionately, and my neighbours would applaud our love.

In real life, Mal would be arrested for disturbing the peace and my neighbours would gang up and impress upon me how much I really did want to move. As soon as possible.

'Stop now, stop,' I said, placing my hand between his fingers and the guitar strings. 'Stop. I'm here, stop.' I liked living in this street.

He sang one more line and then lowered his guitar, resting the base on the pavement. 'Are you avoiding me?' he asked, with his head on one side, determination in his eyes—we were going to 'have it out'.

'What did you expect?' I replied, trying to keep my voice down. 'How can I speak to you after . . . ?'

'You only had to say no,' he said. 'You didn't have to blank me. Us. Steph's convinced herself that she's ruined things between us for ever. And, you know, I don't like it when we don't speak. It doesn't feel right.'

'How can I say no?' I flopped my arms up and down, all the despair, frustration and guilt I'd felt in the past week rushing to the surface of my mind, tumbling out in my words. 'How can I sit in front of you or Stephanie and say, "I'm going to put an end to all your dreams of becoming parents"? How can I do that? How can I face you after doing that?'

'This isn't the end of all our dreams. We'd find another way. We'd find someone else.'

'Yeah? Who?'

While I waited for him to answer, the lights around us were being extinguished. Now the disturbance had calmed down, people could return to their beds, their lives, their own complicated relationships.

'I don't know,' he admitted. 'But we'll find someone. We can't stop being friends because of it. That'd be stupid. You and me not talking. It's inconceivable. Excuse the pun.'

'OK. But you can understand why I can't do this, don't you? I could never give away my baby. Not something that had been a part of me. Look how upset I get when goldfish die. I couldn't . . . And how could I be friends with you, seeing a little boy or girl and knowing they were half mine? It'd drive me insane. I'd be . . . And what would we tell them? Do you think they'd understand why I gave them up? I couldn't do that.'

'No, you couldn't, could you?' he said. 'We shouldn't have asked.'

'No, no, I'm honoured in many ways that you asked. It shows how much you think of me. And you know I'd do almost anything for you. But . . . No. I'm sorry, no.'

'All right. I can understand that. But don't do that to me again, yeah? I can't function without you around. Don't ever shut me out again, Nova. I can't cope with it.' His honesty, his blunt frankness was disarming. I remembered suddenly the time Stephanie had been in hospital, the nights he spent at my flat, curled up inside, so scared and fragile. I knew he would have been brave for her, made her think her accident, whatever it was, was no big deal, but he would wilt once he was with me. He would come apart and stay that way until morning, when he would put himself back together and go back to his normal life. Few people saw the Mal I

225

did. Not even, I guessed, Stephanie.

'Be my friend again, yeah? Always be my friend.'

'OK.' I nodded. 'OK.'

He rested one of his hands on the back of my head and kissed my forehead, then my cheek. 'OK. Thank you.' He kissed my other cheek. 'OK, now, I can go home and I can sleep.'

*   *   *

'I can't wait to be a dad,' he said.

'So that you can boss everyone around and tell everyone what to do and stay up really very late?' I asked.

'Yeah. And so that I can get to look after people. Like your dad. My dad doesn't do that. But when I'm a dad I can do that. How do you get to be a dad?'

I shrugged. 'You have to get a baby.'

'Like the ones outside shops in prams?'

I shrugged again. 'I think so. I asked Mum the other day and she pretended she didn't hear me. And then I asked her all over again and she told me to ask Dad and he sent me to bed. Cordy laughed at me. So Dad sent her to bed, too.'

We fell silent as we thought about how to get a baby. 'It doesn't matter, I can get a baby,' Mal said. 'And I'll be a dad. You can be the mum if you want.'

I smiled at him, delighted.

'OK. You can be the dad and I'll be the mum.'

*   *   *

I had to do it.

I woke up twelve days after Mal's serenade and realised that I had to do it.

226

The same dream plagued me all night, every night. That memory reborn as a dream and I knew it was my conscience and my heart, ganging up together to tell me I had to do it.

Mal had been dealt so many bad hands in his life and he had played each one as well as he could, and he deserved to have a good hand now. He and Stephanie were incredibly happy, of that I was sure. He loved her, she loved him. I was convinced that the plethora of masks she wore were set aside with him and him only. No matter when she told him, he would not have walked away from her because she couldn't have children, he wasn't that sort of person. Once you were loved by Mal you were loved by Mal for ever. Even if he stopped liking you he still loved you. His relationship with his father was testament to that. He hated Uncle Victor for everything he'd done, but loved him enough to wear his watch, to always go to the cemetery on Uncle Victor's birthday, to never say a bad word about him to his mother. Mal deserved to be a father. To have the chance to do this.

I couldn't even begin to imagine what it must be like for Stephanie. To know the reason why you can't have children is because of your biology. Because something in you was preventing you doing what millions of people across the world did every day without a second thought.

Why did I train to become a psychologist? To help people. This was a way to help, to ease suffering. I wanted to ease suffering like the therapist Aunt Mer saw helped ease her troubles. These two people I loved were suffering, this could transform their lives. It was only being pregnant. That was no big deal. Women did it all the time.

Nine months and then I could give them the baby. They'd be happy, I'd feel great about myself because I had helped two people who were important to me. It was no big deal in the grand scheme of things. If you stood back, removed the emotions and thought about it, it wasn't as big a deal as starting a war, for example.

I picked up the phone beside my bed, dialled while the feelings from the dream still fuzzed around me, and while I was at enough of a distance to know without a shadow of a doubt that I was doing the right thing.

'We have to have STD tests, and HIV tests,' I said when the phone was answered.

'Nova?' he said.

'And we have to sit down and talk it all through. What—and when—we're going to tell our family, how we're going to do this. We have to talk about everything.'

He was silent.

'And we have to work out what we're going to tell him or her when they're older, or if we're going to tell them when they're young so they always know and it's not a big surprise.'

'OK.'

'And we have to . . . I don't know, there's more. But we need a legal contract or something.'

'Are you saying yes?' he asked, hope and excitement creeping into the peripherals of his voice.

'Um, I suppose I am, yes.'

For the first time in my life I heard Mal burst into tears. He'd only cried a handful of times in all the years I'd known him and those were silent, private tears that could be missed if you didn't look at him. 'Oh, God, thank you,' he said. 'Thank you so much . . . I'm going to tell Stephanie now and then we're going to come over. Is that OK?'

'Yeah, sure.'

'Thank you,' he said. 'You'll never know how much this means to us.'

I would know. And it would mean the world to me as well.

As I heard him snuffle back his tears, I knew, despite the unease and apprehension that being more awake brought, the dread that was crawling into the deepest recesses of my heart, I had done right.

This was Mal, after all. Of course I had done the right thing.

CHAPTER TWENTY

I shut myself in the bathroom at work and cried.

The only time I'd ever been so happy was when I got married.

I bought her flowers.

I bought her chocolate.

I bought her a little bottle of folic acid.

When I saw her, I noticed all over again how striking she was. She glowed with inner beauty. She was her actions and she was beautiful because she was doing a beautiful thing.

We talked and talked and talked and she said I could come and see her any time I wanted, as long as she was at home. She said it was going to be my baby and that I could be as involved as I wanted.

She was going to change my life.

229

I didn't like to think that it was going to change her life, too. But I'd take care of her. I'd make sure she was all right. She was doing something so wonderful for me, the least I could do was look after her in return.

CHAPTER TWENTY-ONE

Three minutes.

One hundred and eighty seconds. Your whole life could be altered in the same time it took to cook a soft-boiled egg. I never appreciated before the idea of living every second as though it was your last until I sat with a timer ticking away on the side table and the long white stick with two windows in front of me.

Waiting.

Waiting to see if my life was about to change. For ever. I hadn't appreciated that concept before, either. This would mean the end of a lot of firsts. I would never be pregnant for the first time ever again if this was positive. I would never be able to check the boxes on forms that asked if I had children, without asking if that meant having given birth to them or having had them live with me. I would never be able to say to anyone who asked if I got pregnant again, 'Oh yes, this is my first' and not feel as if I was lying, or without thinking back to this child.

After the tests, which Stephanie took as well so she wouldn't feel left out, and drawing up a contract through some of Stephanie's old work colleagues, I was provided with a sample. I wasn't sure how they'd produced it, I *never* wanted to know how it had been produced, but it was waiting for me in a specimen jar, wrapped up in a brown paper bag, when I arrived at their house on the appointed day. Everything else was at my flat.

I found out from the copious amounts of research I had conducted that the specimen was best kept at body temperature, so had slipped it inside the strap of my bra and fixed my jacket over it before I went back to the waiting cab. Mal had offered to drive me home, but it was best that I do it alone. They stood on their doorstep as I left, her moulded into his body, him with his arm around her shoulders, the pair of them looking like two parents sending their children off alone into the big wide world for the first time.

In the cab, I started to have visions of the taxi crashing and having to go to hospital and them discovering I had a jar of semen tucked inside my clothing. I could just see my parents' faces as the doctors explained, 'Your daughter received secondary injuries from a specimen bottle that smashed against her right breast on impact. It seems the bottle contained a rather large amount of semen. Do you, Mr and Mrs Kumalisi, know why your daughter might have almost two litres of semen in her possession?' Of course there wasn't that much of it, but the crash would have made the volume increase to an incredible amount.

Thankfully, I made it home in one piece and after running a bath, I—

I tried not to think about what I had done after that. I sent Mal a text saying, 'Mission accomplished' and then put it out of my mind. If I thought about it, all the doubts, the worries, the

231

anxieties would resurface. I was doing the right thing, I knew that. But when I thought about what potentially was happening inside me, I got scared.

I wasn't sure if other women who were trying for a baby ever experienced it, but the thought of it, separate to why I was doing it, was terrifying. I was leaping into a great unknown. I was changing my life and my body. Keith had already left me because of this; now it could be happening. Best to pretend it wasn't happening until my period was late. Which it was—by two days. Which was why I had to buy the test.

I'd told Mal and Stephanie we shouldn't talk about it, I'd let them know if I needed another sample, but they should put it out of their minds so that we could all get on with our lives as normally as possible until we got the result we wanted.

Ten seconds.

Ten seconds, then I would know. I would know if I was going to have to go through all this again. Or if I would be one step closer to doing this thing.

BRRRRRRIINNNNNNNNGGGG! sounded the alarm, and although I was waiting for it, I was still jolted. I stared at the stick. My hand shook as I reached out to pick it up. *One line not pregnant. Two lines pregnant*, I repeated in my head. *One line not pregnant. Two lines pregnant.*

One line another chance to get out of this, to change my mind.

Two lines . . . Two lines . . .

My breathing was shallow and fast as I looked down.

Two lines.

Pregnant.

I dropped the test, looked down at my stomach,

looked but could not touch. Could not quite believe.

I've made a baby. I'm going to have a baby.

I couldn't help but smile. We had done it. First time. One go.

I'm going to have a baby.

My eyes welled with tears. I was so overwhelmed suddenly with happiness. With joy. With an avalanche of such feelings gushing through me, I almost forgot. He or she wasn't mine.

This baby belonged to someone else.

*   *   *

Stephanie was wearing her work mask.

She had her hair piled up on top of her head, her blonde locks held in place with four brightly coloured and patterned chopsticks. She wore a yellow Chinese tunic dress made from real silk—she wouldn't wear it otherwise—and with a slit at the side that ended at the top of her thigh. She wore shimmery tights and yellow high heels that added more height to her frame. Her forearms, from wrists to elbows, were ringed with yellow and white bangles. For someone who worked in a fashion shop, I wondered why she didn't realise that yellow did not suit her. At all. It didn't suit most people with her pale colouring, and from all the pieces in the shop, it was the least successful one on her. But maybe that was the point. Show people that they could still look good even in clothes that didn't suit them. For me, clothes often reflected your inner state. And if I didn't know her, didn't know that this was one of the many ways she disguised herself, I would say she was trying too

233

hard.

The first time I met her she had been trying too hard. All of Mal's girlfriends had been worried about mine and Mal's relationship, but because of how enamoured he was with her, I knew she'd be particularly hard to get on with. So, I had not made any particular effort to dress up, not that I did anyway. I could tell instantly from the way her eyes swept over me when I met her that she took my lack of effort as a personal insult because she had tried so hard to look effortlessly beautiful and I, it seemed to her, didn't even think her worthy of slapping on a bit of mascara for. Having said that, if I had made an effort, the only way to make her happy would have been to get it spectacularly wrong so she could feel superior to me.

I navigated my way around the tightly packed rails, noting how truly 'individual' the pieces were. And expensive. I also noted that in a few months, I would find it hard to move between these rails.

'Hi,' I said to the back of her head.

She turned around and grinned when she saw me. It was a genuine grin, one of many I had been treated to since I'd agreed to do this thing for them. 'Hi!' she said, moving away from the copy of *Vogue* she had been poring over and coming to the counter. 'I was going to call you later. See if you fancied some noodles.' She opened her arms and did a little spin. 'Do you wonder why?'

'That'd be lovely. I'm not working today. Maybe we could ask Mal as well.'

'No need, he'll come because I've told him to,' she joked.

'I like your thinking,' I said, reaching into my bag, my hands closing around the sandwich bag I

234

had gently tucked in there before leaving my flat. It had been like carrying the Crown jewels in a carrier bag. I had kept wanting to take it out and look at it. Make sure it was real. That it hadn't evaporated.

'Now, how can I be of assistance?' she asked, back in work mode.

'I've got something for you,' I said. I pulled out the bag and handed it over. 'I thought you might find it interesting.'

She frowned quizzically at me and took it, her bangles clattering. Her eyes widened as she saw what was in the bag. Her manicured fingers pulled back the creases and folds of the clear plastic tightly over the test.

'OH MY GOD!' she screamed suddenly and loudly. 'OH MY GOD!' She threw herself across the cash desk, knocking aside the pink wrapping paper and the spool of ribbon and roll of tape, as she threw her slender, tanned arms around me, the bangles clattering loudly in my ears as they met around my shoulders. 'OH MY GOD!' She squeezed what she could of me. 'OH MY GOD!'

She let go and ran around the desk. 'OH MY GOD!' she screamed again and hugged me properly.

'Can I feel, can I feel?' she asked, almost bouncing up and down in excitement. I hadn't expected this reaction. I knew she'd be happy. I knew she'd be ecstatic, but not that she'd lose all semblance of Stephanie. I liked this person. I *loved* this person. It was a shame I had never seen her before.

'Yeah, sure, but there's nothing to feel at the moment.'

She dropped to her knees, pressed her hand inside my coat. 'Oh my God,' she said, tears welling up in her eyes. She pressed her cheek to the square of fabric over my stomach. 'Hello, little one,' she whispered. 'Hello, baby.'

At that moment, the owner of the shop appeared. She'd heard the screaming and had come to see what was going on. She was dressed far more soberly, in jeans and a cream twinset, obviously a woman who liked fashion but wasn't a slave to it. She stopped behind the counter when she saw her assistant manager on her knees, pressing her face against the stomach of a customer.

'What is going on here?' she asked. Her voice came from money. Probably how she could afford a boutique that never seemed to have any customers.

Stephanie got to her feet and grinned at her boss as she hooked her arm through mine. 'This is my best friend, Nova. And she's just found out that she's having a baby,' Stephanie said.

'I see,' the owner said. 'Congratulations.'

'Thanks,' I replied, feeling like a fraud. I was also overwhelmed by what Stephanie had said. Me, her best friend. Me. She had stopped being suspicious of me and was starting to accept me.

'We're having a baby,' Stephanie said, a huge grin lighting up her face.

The owner shook her head. 'I can see I'm going to get no more sense out of you today,' she said. 'Why don't you take your friend out for a celebratory cup of tea and some cake?'

'Oh, thanks,' she gushed. 'I'll just get my coat and bag.' Stephanie dashed out the back.

'Is this your first?' the owner asked me.

I nodded, feeling like a fraud again. I'd have to get used to this. When everyone could see I was pregnant, they'd quite rightly assume the baby was going to be mine. They'd ask about due dates, baby names, the sex of the baby, and all the other questions you asked a pregnant woman because of course she was going to keep the child. I hadn't worked out, yet, what I was going to say. To strangers and to the people I worked with. How I was going to explain what I was doing and why it was the right thing to do.

'Oh, wonderful. I don't think I've ever seen Steph so happy. That happens a lot, though. Friends become so happy and caught up in your pregnancy that it's almost as though they're having the baby, too.'

'Yeah,' I replied, 'I can understand that.'

When Stephanie returned, she hooked her arm through mine again. 'Thanks so much, Arabella,' she said. 'Come on, let's go tell Mal.' She stopped, looked at me, desperation and anxiety in her eyes. 'Or have you told him already?'

I shook my head. My first instinct had been, of course, to pick up the phone and call him, because he and Cordy were the first people I always called. But as I'd dialled his number I realised that I had to tell Stephanie first. Out of the three of us, she was the one who hadn't had anything to do with the baby so far. She had hovered like a moth around a flame, but she wasn't part of the flame. Telling her first would be a way to bring her in, reassure her that this was about her, too. 'You're the first person to know after me.'

'Really?' she said, then bit her lower lip as more

237

tears blossomed in her eyes. She hugged me again. 'Thank you,' she whispered against my ear. 'Thank you so much for doing this for me. I don't know how I'll ever be able to thank you.'

CHAPTER TWENTY-TWO

Pink, blue or white?

I held each of the Babygros in my hand in turn, trying to decide which one to buy. Yellow was out. No one should ever wear yellow, although I had to sometimes for work. Pink, blue or white?

White was the safe option, obviously, but it was sort of non-committal. Buying one of the other colours would show I fully believed in this.

Although we were only ten weeks pregnant and buying clothes could jinx it, I couldn't help myself. Every lunchtime, sometimes on the way home, I'd go for more baby clothes. My heart fluttering, my stomach dancing, with every soft piece of material I caressed.

I liked the attention, too. The way other women would assume that I was like them, that soon my belly would protrude and show under the pressure of my growing baby, my ankles would become swollen, I'd maybe have to wear my wedding rings on a chain around my neck instead of jammed on to my bloated fingers. No one asked when my baby was due, I simply noticed the surreptitious way they would glance at my stomach and back at my face, then would look away, their minds made up that I was pregnant. I belonged to their club. I decided to buy all three Babygros. I could always team the blue one with a pink bow and sew a football motif on to the pink one.

'I was thinking Malvolio for a boy, and Carmelita for a girl,' Mal said that night. Our legs were intertwined, the broad muscles of his limbs surprisingly light on mine. The bedside lamps created a pool of light around us, and piles of baby books shared the bed with us. We were as bad as each other, buying baby books, thinking about the nursery colours. (Mal didn't know about the clothes, I hid them in what would become the nursery.) He had a week-by-week planner splayed open on his stomach, and was nuzzling my shoulder, stroking my stomach as he spoke.

'*Why?*' I replied, genuinely mystified. I knew how he truly felt about his name, and Carmelita?! What the—?!

'Malvolio because it's tradition, and I like the sound of Carmelita. Carmie . . . Come on, Carmie, eat your sprouts.'

'Tradition? Since when have you been a traditionalist? Men are so arrogant, naming children after themselves. You don't get women doing it. You won't get a Stephanie Wacken Junior, for example.'

'We do it to carry on the name.'

'And it's not enough that your surname is usually carried on? If that was the case, then it should be women doing that. Because our surnames are obliterated by marriage and bearing children we should make sure *our* names are honoured by naming our first-born girls after ourselves.'

He pressed his finger on the tip of my nose before he followed it with a kiss. 'You're being silly. It'll never catch on.'

'Sadly, I think you may be right.'

'Besides, Carmelita is a wonderful name.'

'Yes, yes it is, but not for our daughter . . . Can you believe it? We may be having a daughter.'

'No, it's a boy.'

He spoke with such certainty, I raised my eyes to look at him. He was staring into space, a blissful half-smile smoothing out his features and unfocusing his eyes. 'Oh? Do you know something I don't know?'

'No, not really. Nova told me. She has a feeling she's carrying a boy.'

My heart dipped a fraction. Only a touch. Nothing horrendous. It was a momentary flutter that dissolved an instant after it touched my heart. Why hadn't she told me that? 'When did she tell you that?'

'The other day. I was asking if she was going to find out the sex and she said she didn't need to as she knew it was a boy.'

'But we agreed not to find out the sex during the scan,' I reminded him.

'I know, but just because we don't want to know, doesn't mean Nova won't want to know.'

I pushed myself away from him, looked at him. His handsome features, all strong and angular lines, still soft from his blissed-out mood, stared back at me. I frowned at him. 'It doesn't matter what she wants to know. It's got nothing to do with her, Mal.'

It was his turn to frown as he blinked at me a few times. 'She's having the baby,' he reminded.

'For us. It's *our* baby. We make the decisions about the scan and finding out the sex. She's only carrying the baby. Growing it. We're going to be its

240

parents, which means we need to make the big and little decisions.'

His forehead creased a little more. 'That sounds . . . I don't know, cold-blooded,' he said.

The heart flutter returned, lasted a little longer this time. Only a fraction longer, nothing to worry about. 'She has to be cold-blooded about this, Mal. Don't you see? If she starts making decisions like finding out the sex of the baby, or even if she's involved in those sorts of decisions, how is she going to be able to give him or her to us at the end of the pregnancy? The more involved she gets, the harder it's going to be.'

Mal shifted in bed, gently but precisely moved me off him, so he could sit up. I noted the movement, though, the slight pushing away. It wasn't me he was pushing away, it was the thought he hadn't completely explored before. The one thing he hadn't wanted to consider: how this would affect Nova. He'd just assumed it would be easy for her because she was doing this thing for us. That, her being her, she was doing it for someone she loved and there'd be no complications.

'I hadn't thought of that,' he admitted.

'If she starts to think of this baby as anything other than something she's growing then she won't want to give him or her up,' I said.

'You make it sound like she's growing a yeast infection and has to get rid of it at the end of it.'

'No, she's made it that way. I don't know how anyone could do what she's doing. I think it's wonderful and I'll never be able to thank her enough, but I could never give up a baby.'

A momentary look, a flitting through-thought, crossed Mal's face. The thought of the one I'd left behind, the baby that never was.

'That was so different to this, Mal,' I said, drawing my knees to my chest. One of the books toppled off the bed, landing with a loud thump on the rug. 'I didn't even know who the father was. It could have been one of three men and I don't even remember it happening.' I spoke quickly, loud and defensive, trying to remind him of the futility of my situation. 'I was *fifteen* and ill. I wasn't healthy and fit and capable of looking after a child. And I had no choice. They made me do it.'

'I know,' he said, reaching for me.

I moved out of reach, not wanting him to think for one moment that he had appeased me when he had just thought what he did. 'No, you don't,' I replied. 'You just thought I'd given up a baby. Like it's the same as this. But it wasn't.'

'Yes, I know, I'm sorry, I didn't really think you'd given up a baby, I just . . . I had a momentary fuckwit thought. I'm sorry.'

'I could never do what Nova is doing. I'm in awe of her, honestly. I'm in awe of any woman who could do that for someone else, but I'm not one of them.'

He nodded, rubbed at a spot behind his right ear. He was troubled. Worrying about Nova, worrying about what this would do to her. She wasn't one of those people who could shut off from something like that, either.

My eyes ran slowly over my husband's gorgeous, concerned face, each line a reminder of how and why I loved him. This hadn't occurred to him. Not even when he'd made her be our friend again, he hadn't thought that this could permanently damage her. While I, I had always known her love

242

for Mal would destroy her.

'We've got to look after her,' I told Mal. 'That's why I take her things. We have to make sure that she's OK. Not just for the health of the baby, but for her. So that she'll be all right with this. And we have to make sure she doesn't start to think of herself as the mother, because that will destroy her.'

I snuggled into him, let him put his arms around me now. I was suddenly scared that he might change his mind about all of this, that he might decide that Nova was more important than having the baby. Even though she was already pregnant, he might give her the opportunity to change her mind.

'She seems OK now, though,' I said.

'Yeah, she does,' he agreed.

'Blooming, apart from the sickness.'

'Yeah,' he breathed. 'It's bizarre that despite how sick she's being she still looks like she's doing really well.'

'And we can help her stay that way.'

'Yeah.'

'OK, so, as I was saying, Stephanie for a girl, Angelo for a boy . . .'

Mal smiled, and I ignored the flutter that him saying she looked like she was doing well caused me. It wasn't the words, it was the slightly wistful look in his eye when he said it.

CHAPTER TWENTY-THREE

I lay on the sofa listening to Mal move around my kitchen, making me dinner. He'd taken to doing that on his way home from work.

Stephanie had dropped by earlier, and stayed for a little while. She always called first to check if it was OK to drop round; Mal only ever called to check I was in—just like before I got pregnant with their baby. Stephanie would bring flowers, chocolate, a book or some essential oils she thought I might like. She would ask if she could put her hand on my stomach, and I would see the happiness soften her face, illuminate her smile as she obviously felt what she was feeling for.

Mal would kiss my cheek when I opened the door and his hand would immediately move to my abdomen, as he said hello twice—once to me, once to the baby. He'd then spend the rest of the night with his hand almost permanently on my abdomen.

I didn't know what they felt because I avoided touching my stomach. My natural instinct was always to reach down and place my hand there, to see if the skin was firmer—it looked firmer—or warmer because my body temperature seemed to have gone up. I was often hot, rarely needed that extra jumper I usually put on, my jeans were tight and my breasts . . . I'd bought six new bras in the last month. I had gone up three cup sizes and was flirting around an H cup. My back size hadn't gone up, just my breasts. I always resisted touching my stomach, instead lacing my fingers together under my head whenever the urge took me. I couldn't touch my abdomen; even when I was moisturising my skin in the morning I whisked over that area, not wanting to linger.

I couldn't engage with what I was doing. I always had to remind myself that I was growing this for someone else. If I allowed myself to think about it, even for one second . . . I wasn't sure I could do it.

Almost everything I had seen and read said that women who became surrogates should have had children already; should have 'finished' with children, should feel their families were complete. Your first child being one that you're having for someone else could cause problems: you might have separation anxiety, go through the bereavement process in a severe way. Have problems giving the baby to the intended parents. And, of course, what if something went wrong and you were unable to have more children afterwards? That could destroy you.

I couldn't imagine *not* going through all those separation feelings, whether my family was 'complete' or not, but I was doing this for two important people and I had to focus on that.

To do it, I had to stay detached. Removed. Uninvolved. Not do things like touch my stomach, nor give in to the temptation to stand in front of the full-length mirror in my bedroom inspecting every new development with my body. Even when Stephanie had held my hand during the twelve-week dating scan and she'd gasped when the image had appeared on the screen, I hadn't looked. I'd stared up at the ceiling, biting my lower lip, willing myself not to look as the sonographer pointed out the baby's head, the spine, the legs, the arms, which were waving, the heart. She'd asked me if I was OK because I wasn't looking and I'd mumbled something about having to concentrate on not releasing the contents of my extremely full bladder, which was why I'd brought my friend, who would remember every detail. Stephanie had been so overjoyed with it all she had hugged me for three or four minutes after I'd been to the loo. She asked if I wanted to see the photo, but I had said no, it was all hers. I couldn't bear to see him, it would be a connection that I couldn't afford—mentally and emotionally—to make.

The moment I indulged myself like that in any way, I'd be lost. I'd be tumbling into this fantasy world where I was going to be handed a baby at the end of the nine months. Where I would be living happily ever after with the father. Where I would have the things I had hoped for in life happening to me a few years early.

During the past three weeks, I had noticed, Mal had become incredibly attentive. Making me dinner, cups of tea, forcing me to lie down when I was sitting. He'd done things like that before, but something had changed in him, I could tell. I wasn't sure what it was, but he seemed to be even more concerned than normal.

I had started to wonder if he'd guessed that I planned to go away for at least a year once the baby was born. The only way I knew I could do this would be to leave afterwards, to get on a plane and see as much of the world as I could. I would need space—a lot of it—and that space lay out there, in the great beyond. When I returned, hopefully I would be able to look at the child as theirs and theirs alone, and would have found a way to put aside the fact I'd had a role in its introduction to

246

the world. I wondered if Mal had guessed and didn't want me to go. Hence the cooking, the constant reiterating his gratitude, and reminding me how much I meant to him.

After he had watched me eat the feast of steamed broccoli, beans on toast topped with cheese, boiled new potatoes drizzled with olive oil, and a white nectarine with natural yoghurt, he asked if he could listen to the baby.

'Sure,' I said and he climbed on all fours on the sofa, balancing himself between my legs, lifted my white T-shirt and pressed his ear against my skin.

I watched the top of his head, the blond curls that lay in a circular pattern. I had the urge to reach down and run my fingers through them. To gently stroke his hair like I wanted to do all those years I was in love with him. I wanted him to look up and our gazes to meet, for us to hold each other in a visual embrace. I longed for him to move up until we were face to face, for his fingers to start peeling off my clothes. I craved to start taking off his clothes. I wanted . . .

I threw my head back, started to take deep breaths to help veer my thoughts away from this. The hormones had done this. They'd made me incredibly horny. And, as I'd feared, they had unlocked and let loose in the world the feelings I'd shut away for so long. They hadn't died, those feelings, they were just incarcerated in a deep dungeon in my heart because whatever I felt was—at the time they started—one-sided, and now moot, because we had both made choices we were happy with. Admittedly, Keith had left me because I'd agreed to have this baby for someone else, but before that I'd been happy with him. Mal was happy with the love of his life, too.

I inhaled again, holding the oxygen in my lungs to help it purge my impure feelings. I brought Stephanie to mind. My friend. His wife. The woman I was doing this for. The woman who would do anything to be able to do this. I could not betray her by allowing myself to fall back in love with her husband.

Thinking of her, putting her in the picture, would usually be enough to stop my emotions and physical urges running away with me. Mal took his head away and I thought it safe to look up. He smiled at my abdomen as though the baby had been telling him something wonderfully insightful. I loved the way his smiles softened his face and sparkled his eyes. *Will the baby have his smile, his eyes, his nose?* I wondered before I could stop myself.

'Love you, baby,' Mal whispered before he lowered his head again and gently crushed his lips below my belly button.

My heart stopped, it actually stopped beating. Everything around us seemed to stop at the same time, suspended in my disbelief.

Stephanie often talked to the baby, said to it that she loved it, but she had never kissed my belly. She never would, I hoped. I never wanted to be that intimate with her. Mal had never done that before, either—and I did not want to be that intimate with him. It was difficult enough protecting my heart at the moment, I could not do that if he was determined to create more intimacy between us. I could always remind myself that I was having a baby for someone else, I would always be able to cope because I was doing it for someone special. There were only two people in the world I would ever even think of doing this for—Cordy and Mal. No one else. But I could not do this if Mal would not remain a friend. I was constantly fighting my feelings for him, consigning them to hormones—if he was going to act like this, I would go mad. I would start to believe that maybe, possibly . . . and once that thought started to grow inside me I would be driven insane.

I started to breathe, slow and steady, trying to ignore the pain my heart, which had started beating again, was causing me by speeding in my chest. I had to find a way to tell him that he couldn't do things like that to me, without revealing that it was emotionally difficult for me. I did not want him to say something to Stephanie and for her to take it the wrong way, for her to begin watching me from the corner of her eye, again; being suspicious of my every move and thinking I was in any way a rival. When she was like that before, she did not seem to understand that I had never been in her way, that he had come alive when he met her and I knew he would never love me or anyone else like he loved her.

Still staring at my stomach, Mal said, 'You know what I wish sometimes?'

'No, Mal, I do not know what you wish sometimes, but I am sure you are going to tell me,' I said, wondering how soon I could ask him to get off me. He was far too close, and I couldn't take much more of it, he was suffocating me just by being around me. I could feel myself slipping steadily down the slope of closeness into this moment with its quiet, soothing chat, this intimate pose, and if I did not change things, get him to leave, I would fall in, and lie back at the bottom of the slope and allow the feelings to consume me. I would forget about Stephanie, I would forget about telling him not to do this, I would start to indulge myself in him and I was scared of where that might lead. Not only with me starting to want Mal, but me not being able to distance myself from the baby.

He looked up at me, our gazes met as they often did in my hormone-induced fantasies, and he smiled, his mouth a crescent of wistful happiness.

'What?' I asked. 'What you looking at me like that for? And what do you wish sometimes?'

'That this was our baby, and we were doing this for real.'

I felt the physical punch as my heart exploded. I pushed my hand over my chest to ease the pain as the blood in my body ran cold in horror.

Mal immediately realised what he had done and scrambled back on to his haunches, cowering at the end of my sofa like a frightened, wide-eyed gargoyle on the edge of a church roof. 'I didn't mean that how it might have sounded. I, erm . . . You can never tell Steph that. Ever.' He spoke quickly, real fear in his voice, his hands raised in total surrender. 'It's really nothing to do with her. I promise. It's just . . . It's just, at one point I thought we'd be having a baby together, that's all and I shouldn't have said it, I know. But there's no one else on earth I could say it to. I'm sorry. Pretend I didn't say anything.'

Slowly and carefully, I swung my feet on to the floor, just as precisely I stood up, having to take a few seconds to check I was steady before I turned to him.

'Get out,' I said quietly and simply.

Mal closed his eyes in regret, shook his head and grimaced. 'Nove, I didn't—'

'I mean it, get out,' I said, talking over him. I was trembling, but my words came out firm and sure. 'Get out and don't *ever* come back here without your wife.'

Mal stood. I noticed he was shaking as he rolled down his shirtsleeves and buttoned up the cuffs. He reached down and picked up his discarded jacket, slipped it on. His lips were curled into his mouth as he chewed on them. I led the way out of my living room to the front door, my fingers bunched deep into the palms of my hands to hide how much I was shaking. I reached for the doorknob, and then realised that I couldn't let this pass. I had been turning myself inside out to distance myself from him and he had . . .

I rounded on him. He took a step back as he saw the look on my face. 'You never . . . You *never* wanted me. You've made it so clear over the years that you never wanted me, that you've never thought of me in that way, even though you knew how I felt. How could you be so cruel and say that to me now? Because I'm growing this for you? You think it's all right to say something like that to me? And what am I supposed to say? What am I supposed to do when you and Stephanie are playing happy families? How am I supposed to feel?

'Do you have any idea how hard this is for me? How I have to keep reminding myself that this isn't my baby?' I shook my head. 'I don't understand why you said that, Mal, why you would think saying something so cruel would be OK, but I can't see

251

you again without Stephanie, to make sure you can't say anything like that to me ever again.'

I looked him over, trying to forget all the reasons why I loved him.

He stayed silent.

'Don't come back without Stephanie, OK?'

Reluctantly, his lips mashed together, his gaze fixed somewhere to the side of me, he nodded. That day at the coach station the morning after he had rejected me and I had asked him without asking him to give me space, to let me get over him in peace, suddenly unfurled itself in my mind. Vivid and clear. His reluctance then as he agreed. My relief that he was going to let me go, set me free.

I opened the door wider and walked away, not wanting to watch him leave.

In front of the sofa I stood still as I stepped back in time and the pain from before resurfaced.

The sheer magnitude of it had engulfed me the moment I had locked the door of my room in halls. I had paced the floor with my coat still on, wringing my hands, feeling it all build up until I had to run to the sink and physically purge what I could by throwing up. In front of my bed, my knees buckled, and I had buried my face in the scratchy waffle blanket, dug my hands into it and begun to cry. I cried from humiliation. From knowing I'd never know love like that again. From wondering what would become of me if the one person on earth who was meant to love me didn't, couldn't.

In the present, I paced in front of the sofa, wringing my hands, feeling it all again. I didn't think it could hurt like before, but his throwaway line, something said as though it was nothing important, brought it all back, brought it all home. How could someone who cared even a little for me say something like that when I was already fragile? It didn't take a genius to see I was fragile, so why couldn't he?

I heard the click of the front door, and my stomach dipped. I did not want to see him again. With or without Stephanie, I did not want to see him again. Like any friend, he did my head in sometimes, and he knew it, but now he had changed focus, now he was trying to do my heart in again. And I did not want to see him.

'What makes you think I never wanted you?' He made me jump twice: once because he was still here, then again because he sounded so angry.

I stopped my pacing and looked up at him. He *was* angry: it criss-crossed his features and burned in his eyes.

'What makes you think I never wanted you?' he repeated.

'You told me.'

'*I* told you?' Mal was genuinely confused. His eyes seemed to search through time, his memories, for when he uttered those words. 'When did I tell you that?'

I blinked at him. Had I imagined it? Anyone seeing his confusion would think I had. 'I came to visit you in my first year at Oxford, remember? We went out, and I tried to tell you how I felt, that I loved you, and you stopped me by saying you could never be interested in a woman who was your friend. Friends shouldn't be anything else, you said. You shouldn't think about sex and certainly not talk about love in any other terms. Remember?

'This was three weeks after you'd been up to

253

visit me on your own for the first time and we almost . . . You touched me like that for the first time and then you changed your mind and couldn't go through with it. Then you said that thing about not being interested in a woman who was your friend. So, yes, it was you, *you* made me think you never wanted me.'

'That was years ago,' he said. 'I was eighteen, for God's sake. I'd just started having sex. I was surrounded by girls who noticed me for the first time in my life, I was experimenting, I didn't want to be experimenting with you when there was so much at risk.' He flopped his hands up and down. 'But it was crazy because all I *did* was want you.

'Every time I went near a girl I would wonder afterwards if it would be better with you. It started to drive me out of my mind, because immediately after sex I'd start thinking about you even though you were only a friend. I couldn't understand what was going on when I'd never thought of you in that way. And that weekend . . . I wanted to, God did I want to. I came to visit you without Cordy for that reason. When I saw you naked in the bathroom something clicked in me and suddenly you were a girl, a woman to me. I understood why I'd been so confused. That's when my obsession kicked in properly. I even called a couple of people I slept with Nova. So I came up to get it over with. To see if you were interested and to basically, well, I wanted you.

'But I had to stop because I knew it couldn't be a one-night thing with you. If we did that, then we'd be together for ever and I wasn't ready for that. And I couldn't let you tell me you loved me. I couldn't lie to you and say I didn't feel it back, but then I couldn't say it back. Not right then. But none of that meant I'd never want you. Who knows what they want at eighteen? Who makes a forever decision at eighteen and sticks to it for the rest of their lives?'

'OK, Mal, that was all when we were eighteen. But what about since then? You've never once shown me that you've felt anything like that for me, that you want me. In, what, ten, eleven years, nothing. Not one sign that you were interested. You never even went out with anyone *like* me. Not once. Every single one of them was thinner or larger, shorter or taller, prettier or more unattractive, but no one was like me. I had to put up with them—and let's not forget that all of them without fail hated me—even though they were reminders as to why you didn't love me.

'And then you go and marry someone who couldn't be anything less like me if she tried. We are such polar opposites it's like you sought her out to spite me and to prove that you could never stand to be with anyone like me. So don't rewrite history when it's been clear from your actions what you truly felt.'

'Maria had your smile but not your eyes. Angeli had your eyes but not your nose. Julie had your turn of phrase but not your wit. Claire had your ambition but not your charm. Alice sort of had your scent but not your laugh. Jane had your hands but not your arms. Do you want me to go on? Because I can list every woman I went out with for how she was and wasn't like you.

'And, yes, I married Steph because she's nothing like you. It was an end to my torture. Finally. *Finally*, I had someone who didn't remind me of you for all the ways she wasn't you. I could start from scratch with her. I could learn what love was about without it all coming back to you.'

I said nothing because I was astounded and doubtful in equal measures. It sounded plausible, but then implausible. We spoke almost every day, how could he have not let something slip in all that time if it was true? And why didn't I sense it? Because I didn't bother to try to read Mal any more? He had been such a fixture in my life I always assumed I knew what he felt, so maybe I didn't bother to do what I did with other people and try to experience him on every level.

'I came back early from travelling because it had started again. That obsession I had with you—I was meeting women, and wondering if it would be better with you. And I missed you. It drove me crazy but I knew it was because I was ready now. So I came back, ready to settle down. To get married, have children with you.

'I . . . I can't believe I'm going to tell you this after all this time. I had a ring made, platinum, inlaid with diamonds and rose quartz. Someone told me that rose quartz was the stone of love and romance, and I knew you were into all that, so I had a ring made with it. That's why I asked you to meet me at the airport. I was going to get down on one knee right there in the Arrivals area to ask you to marry me. When I saw you I knew without a doubt it was what I wanted. I had the ring in my hand, my heart was in my throat, but I was ready. I was going to do it. And then, there he was—your boyfriend.'

I was suddenly back there in the airport: the sound of the Arrivals area, the heat, the

256

excitement of people being reunited. I remembered the way he had held me so close, his lips lingering on my neck, the way he stared at me after he had kissed me on the mouth, the shock and horror that passed his face when he saw Keith. It was all clear: I understood it now. I'd always thought there was a vital piece missing from the jigsaw that was that memory, now I understood.

'Do you remember what I asked you when Keith went to pay for the parking ticket?' Mal asked.

We were back in the car park, standing beside Keith's old black Audi. Mal, more muscular than when he left, grey from the jetlag, unshaven and dishevelled; me, unable to contain my excitement because he was home.

'Do you remember what I asked you?' Mal repeated.

I nodded. I remembered. Of course I remembered.

Mal came closer, cupped his hand on my face, tipped my head up to look into his eyes. 'Do you remember what I asked you?' he asked for the third time.

'Is he what you really want?' I said.

'And do you remember what you said to me?'

I nodded.

'What did you say?'

I didn't want to repeat it. I didn't want to repeat the words that ruined it.

'What did you say?' he insisted.

I took a deep breath. 'I'd marry him tomorrow if he asked me,' I whispered. I hadn't meant it. Keith and I were back together and we were back in the first throes of giddy, giggly lust. If he had asked me, I would have dumped him. But I said it

257

because I wanted Mal to accept Keith. I wanted him to be happy, and thinking I was happy would do that.

'I was stupid to think that you'd be waiting for me to get my act together. But when you said that, I knew it was over. You didn't want me any more.'

'I didn't mean it. I thought you didn't like Keith. I thought if you thought me and him were serious, then you would be happy for me. I thoug—' We messed up. We messed everything up. 'Ohhhhhhhhhhhhhhhhhh,' I breathed.

The pressure of his hand on my face increased, and I moved my hands to his face as he lowered his head until we were a fraction away from each other. If one of us moved, even a little, our lips would meet. We'd kiss. It wouldn't be a quick hello or goodbye, it wouldn't be him larking about in front of our family, it would be a proper, love-filled kiss. I'd never wanted anyone to cover my lips with theirs as much as I wanted him to at that moment. I'd never wanted anyone to not kiss me as much as I didn't want him to at that moment.

His eyes slipped shut as he rested his forehead on mine.

Nothing could happen. Nothing could ever happen. We'd made our choices and nothing could happen.

'God, Nova, *God*,' he whispered as I closed my eyes.

We stood, unable to let each other go, unable to come together, prisoners of our own dishonesty.

CHAPTER TWENTY-FOUR

'Where've you been?' I asked Mal in a whisper.

I'd heard the front door open and close a few minutes before and had expected him to come up to bed, given the hour. But I'd waited and waited and nothing, no foot on the stairs, not even the sudden blast of sound as he switched on the TV and then sat down to watch the football highlights that I'd taped earlier (a sure sign that he was drunk). But nothing. For a few terrified seconds I wondered if it was a burglar, but then dismissed this because I'd definitely heard a key being used. I found him in the dark kitchen, leaning over the counter, staring down at the circular wooden chopping block as though it was giving him an important lecture on the theory of evolution.

'At Nova's,' he replied, just as quietly.

'All this time?' I asked. 'Shouldn't she have gone to bed hours ago?'

He turned his head to me then, confused, baffled. 'Why? What time is it?'

'Three o'clock.'

He frowned. 'In the morning?'

I nodded, worried. He seemed genuinely surprised. He seemed to have not only lost track of time, but everything: who he was, where he was, what he was.

'I didn't realise,' he said, turning back to the chopping board, 'it was so late.'

I watched my husband, with his head bowed, like a man bent in prayer, and searched in the gloom for what was different about him. He was still wearing the suit he was wearing this morning. His shirt was tucked neatly into his trousers, he hadn't worn a tie so his top button was open, his hair was all in place. But something was different. Something had changed. He reeked. That was what had changed, his smell. He reeked of her. Of Nova. Not of sex, not of anything physical, but he was drenched in her; I could almost see her flowing over him, like a slow-moving, powerful waterfall, dousing every part of him in *her*. Nova had been the one who was always going on about auras and energy fields and us giving off vibes and how simply being around someone could significantly alter your aura and therefore your mood. Which was why you had such strong physical reactions— good and bad—to certain people. Which was why you seemed to glow when you first fell in love. She had been trying to teach me how to read people, to see beyond their words, to look at them without your eyes, to tune in to how they made you feel when they did the things they did. I'd always had severe problems with it, because, basically, it was a load of nonsense—not that I'd ever tell her that.

Now I understood. Every lesson she'd tried to pass on suddenly came into sharp focus in the semi-darkness of our kitchen: Mal reeked of Nova. It was all around him. All over him: Nova. Nova. Nova. The woman who was carrying his child. The woman who was doing the one thing I couldn't.

'You know I love you, right?' he said, spinning to me all of a sudden.

It was like a sharp, invisible knife being slipped into the centre of my heart. He hadn't said 'I love you' like usual. It was a question, and one he didn't need to ask. Of course I knew. We wouldn't be

260

together if I didn't know. And this question sounded like the preamble to him telling me he was leaving me: *'You know I love you, right? But she's having my baby. She's the one I've wanted all along.'*

'What's happened?' I asked, my voice wavering.

He reached out, grabbed me into his arms, held me close. So close I felt the buttons from his jacket pressing through the thin fabric of my nightshirt, marking my skin. I realised after a few seconds he was unbuckling his belt, unzipping his trousers and then he was tugging me down on to the floor, encouraging me on to my back. We hadn't done this in an age. Why would we when we had three perfectly good bedrooms upstairs? And a comfy sofa in the next room. We even had thick carpet in the corridor, which would be more comfortable than this. In the early days of owning this place, sex anywhere and everywhere was fun. Now it was stupid. Especially if I was the one lying on the cold lino, not completely seduced to the point where I didn't care where we were as long as we were. His mouth covered mine in a deep kiss and then we were beyond the moment of relocating . . . I closed my eyes, arched my body, trying to relax into it. Enjoy it for what it was—an unexpected moment of passion. The type of thing that newly attached people did all the time and married people often complained about not being able to do. And when the baby came, we'd rarely have the chance to do this.

He was different. I could feel it. He was somewhere else while right there with me. I opened my eyes and his dark russet-brown eyes were focused through me, not on me. He couldn't see me. He wasn't with me. He was . . . I knew where he was. Who he was with.

'You know I love you, right?' he said again afterwards. We were lying side by side, staring up at the ceiling, waiting for our breathing to normalise.

I said nothing, felt the invisible knife twist, gouging out the centre of my heart.

He turned on to his side, his shirt rucked around his waist, and he was still hanging out of his splayed-open trousers. 'Right?' he asked, stroking a strand of my hair away from my face.

I could have told him right there that I knew. That I'd seen the look on his face, that I'd felt her on him. That I knew he was falling back in love with her. But I didn't. I rolled on to my side to face him.

'Course,' I said. 'Of course I know.'

CHAPTER TWENTY-FIVE

I was exhausted, but I could not close my eyes and go to sleep.

My mind was still swirling with what we had said, what I had discovered, what he had discovered, how the two of us, as close as we were, had managed to miss what was probably obvious to anyone on the outside.

In a daze he had left, and I had climbed into bed fully dressed because I was too tired to change my clothes, and tried to sleep.

Bleep-bleep. Bleep-bleep, sounded my mobile on the nightstand.

Without bothering to flick on the light, I picked up my mobile and called up the text message, knowing who it would be from.

Goodnight, beautiful.

It was over now.

We wouldn't talk about this again. I'd have this baby, I would go travelling and they would bring him up, and Mal and I would never talk about this again. We would bury it. I shut my phone, slipped it under my pillow and clung to it, like a precious jewel that I had found but had to return to its rightful owner. In the morning, I would delete the message. In the morning, when it was daylight, I'd return that precious jewel to whence it came. But for now: I'd cling to the first time in my whole life that Mal had called me beautiful.

CHAPTER TWENTY-SIX

It's much harder looking for evidence of an affair that isn't happening physically.

There's no telltale lipstick on the collar, no smell of her perfume, no unexplained absences or sudden preening. When it's a case of being unfaithful with your heart and mind, it's much easier to hide; it's much harder to uncover.

I took to watching him: noticing if he wandered off into a trance. If he did, I would bring him out of it by asking him something about Nova and the baby. See if he would blush and look alarmed or guilty before he replied. He did sometimes, and I'd know that's where he was when he was in the trance. Other times he'd reply without guilt or a blush and I would know that he hadn't been with her mentally. If we made love, I kept my eyes open, watching for that moment when he would glaze over, lose himself inside the thought of another woman for a few seconds. He always came back to me, came with me, but I could tell when he indulged himself in her.

From her, I found out something had happened. It was on her face the moment she opened the door to me when I went for a visit two days later. She smiled at me, said it was nice to see me as always, but now my senses had been opened to how to see someone without looking at them, I could feel that her aura had changed. She had changed. She didn't reek of Mal, like he had done of her, but she was saturated in guilt.

'Are you OK?' I asked her, after she'd thrown up for the third time since I'd arrived half an hour earlier.

'Yeah,' she said, tucking her hair, which she'd put back into plaits, behind her ears and slumping in the sofa next to me. She did not look OK. Her face was pinched, her skin a sallow shade of its usual dark brown. 'Remember how I said that it wasn't morning sickness, it was any-time-of-the-day-it-pleases sickness?'

I nodded.

'Well, it's that,' she said. 'I feel wrung out. And the more tired I am, the more sick I feel. It's not good when a restaurant manager keeps bolting to the loo to throw up. Hardly inspires confidence in the food. I thought it would have gone by now, but it's still here. Going strong.'

264

'What I wouldn't give to be able to feel all that,' I said. It was an evil thing to say, I knew that. But I had to know. Had to see how she would react to me hitting that particular emotional button. I hadn't even gone near it, hadn't thought I'd needed to. Now it was going to act like a lie detector.

I saw her stomach turn, the energy around her light up: guilt. Pure, concentrated guilt. I knew all about guilt. And I knew it when I saw it.

She clamped her hand over her mouth and ran for the toilet. I got up, went to the kitchen, slipped two pieces of bread into the toaster, flicked on the kettle, removed a white mug from the cupboard and dropped in a ginger and lemon teabag.

As I waited for her toast to brown and for the kettle to boil to make stomach-settling tea, I folded my arms and wondered how many times she had kissed my husband. How many times she'd stroked and caressed him. When she was planning to make love to him. How many ways she'd told him she loved him. How many times she'd listened to him say it back.

And as I doused the teabag in boiling water, the browned bread popping up out of the toaster, I wondered how I was going to make her pay.

*　　*　　*

I hated myself for it, but it was necessary, going through his things.

Through his pockets, his car, his desk at home. I took to turning up unexpectedly at her place when I knew he would be there, when I knew he shouldn't be there. Nothing. In three weeks,

265

nothing. If I showed up at her flat when I knew he said he'd be there, they didn't look surprised. They didn't look like they'd just struggled into their clothes, nor as if they'd been planning on taking them off. She would always put my hand on her stomach, same as his. If I turned up when he said he was working late, he was never there—he was always working late.

But I knew something was going on. He was still zoning into trances, drifting into her arms when making love to me. She was still wearing her guilt like a metaphorical hair shirt when we were alone together.

There was an affair. Or, the thought had been playing around my mind for a while, but was becoming more real with every passing day: they were going to keep my baby for themselves. They were biding their time; waiting for the baby to be born and then they'd run away together. Or move into my house. Him, her, my baby, my home.

He forgot his mobile twenty-six days after I realised they were making plans behind my back. He called me at work to ask if I'd check when I got home if it was there because if it wasn't, then he'd have to cancel it and get a new phone. It was there on the bedside table, all sleek and black and shiny. Holder of his secrets. I sat on the bed, holding it in my hand, and called him to let him know it was safe. 'Thank God,' he breathed.

'No, thank me,' I replied. 'I'm the one who found it.'

'OK, thank God, and thank *you*, especially, Stephanie, light of my life, keeper of my heart.'

'That's better,' I replied, wondering how many times he'd called her that.

I put the phone down and went to the bathroom to brush my teeth. It was what I did in stressful moments such as this. I moved from one foot to the other, moving the toothbrush over my teeth and gums, carefully avoiding looking at myself in the mirror. All the other places I had searched could, conceivably, have been done with the best motives: doing the washing, sorting the dry-cleaning, clearing out his car. But going through his phone, something he usually kept with him at all times? That was crossing the line. That was admitting to myself that I did think he was unfaithful. I felt it, I knew it on many levels, but if I searched his phone and found something . . . that would mean I had been looking. That would mean he would know that I didn't trust him.

Maybe you should leave well enough alone, I told myself.

Alone is what you're going to be if he is in love with her again, I replied.

Trust him, I told myself.

His face as he made love to me the night all this started flashed so vividly in my mind: his eyes elsewhere, his soul entwined with another. Using me as a vessel to make love to her; using my body to connect with her heart.

The phone was in my hand and I was pressing buttons in seconds. He had missed calls—almost all from me. The same with received calls. I opened the folder of little envelopes, text messages he called them, a bit like emails but on your phone. I didn't have a mobile. I wanted to avoid for as long as possible being tied down like that. And what if no one called? What if someone did call and I didn't want to speak to them? It was all far too stressful for me.

There was nothing unusual in his inbox. No text messages from Nova, only a couple from the lads he had shared a house with before he met me. Nothing. There was nothing. I put the phone down. My heart had been racing, my palms sweaty and my breath short. Like I was about to face the biggest horror of my life. But it was fine. There was nothing there to prove that he was with Nova. That they were in love and planning a life without me.

I don't know what made me think of it: she hadn't sent him anything . . .

Moving slowly and carefully, I picked up the phone again, went back to the text messages, and went to the outbox. There were seven messages, one to her. Sent *that* night. My heart palpitating in irregular beats in my ears, I opened it. I read it.

Goodnight, beautiful.

CHAPTER TWENTY-SEVEN

After Meredith leaves, I sit on the back step and smoke three cigarettes in quick succession, the only pause between them being the moments of stubbing one out and lighting the next.

Mal is working very late on a project so I have the house to myself.

I have been so wrong about Meredith. She isn't the weak, fragile person to be secretly pitied that I thought she was. She is strong, calm, fair. I suppose I have assumed, like everyone else, that being labelled as mentally ill makes you somehow less of a person. Someone to feel sorry for. That's always been my fear, why I want no one to know. I don't want to be labelled.

I light my fourth cigarette and rub my eyes.

I expected her to react, but not like that. I close my eyes and replay the moment: she had waited a few minutes after I finished speaking—confessing, really—before she placed her hand on my shoulder and said, 'It must have been so difficult for you.' I had told her the truth, even the bits in between that Mal doesn't know. I told her what I did, what I said, how I made it impossible for Mal to see his son, and her first thoughts were of me.

I didn't think it was possible to feel any worse than I have done all these years, but I do. If the people around me weren't so damn noble and nice and guileless, maybe I wouldn't feel so bad. Maybe I wouldn't feel so guilty all the time.

Inhaling deeply on my cigarette, I hold the smoke down in my lungs, trapping my breath like I would if I was submerged in the bath. I needed to do that when I was younger, especially after my mother sent me to stay with her sister so what needed to be done could be done without my father finding out. Mary thought it was incredibly unfair, of course, that I was getting sent on 'holiday' when I'd done nothing but bring pain and gossip and shame on the family. Even after our mother explained that I was a different type of ill, she still resented me. When I came back from my aunt's, the only place I could be truly alone was in the bathroom. I would run a bath, lock the door and immerse myself in the water. I'd feel weightless, as though I was floating in space and there was no sound, no feelings, no big gaping hole inside me where something had once existed that had been ripped out against my will. I probably would have made the same choice, but no one—not even the doctor, who had been so nice about everything else—ever *asked*. They just did. They just made me.

I got very good at holding my breath. At being weightless and not existing, until my father broke down the door because I had been so quiet in the bathroom for so long. Then I was ripped out of space, there was screaming, and shouting, and the water was red and I ended up in one of those places for the first time.

I was never allowed to lock a door after that. I started to live like a prisoner, where they held me hostage with open doors.

When I finally got to university, it took me a while to believe I was allowed to lock the door on my room and the bathrooms in halls.

I grind out the cigarette in the heavy glass ashtray.

Will she let me see him? In the flesh, will Nova let me see him?

I reach for my cigarettes again.

Every time I close my eyes I can see the easy loop of his smile, the sparkle of intelligence in his eyes, the joy he must bring to everyone around him.

I'd love to see him in the flesh. Maybe she will. That's the sort of person Nova is. Fair. I know that now, of course. Now. I know that she would never
. . .

Maybe if not me, then Mal. And if he sees him, then maybe he'll tell me about him. I'll get to know him through Mal.

I stop before lighting the next cigarette, resheathe it in the pack. I stand up, empty the ashtray into the wheelie bin, and then carefully hide it behind the evergreen bush and the fishing garden gnome that Nova's sister had given us as a moving-in present. Mal had laughed and laughed at the gnome, but I didn't get it. 'There's no joke,' he had said, 'it's just the most hideous thing and she knows I'll never throw it out because it's a present.' Now it helps to hide my secret. *One* of my secrets.

I sometimes wonder if other people are like me. If other people have so many secrets that they're not entirely sure all the time who they really are.

*   *   *

'I, er, I don't think I can go through with this,' I said to him.

'Go through with what?' He stopped lacing up his walking boots and looked at me cautiously. He could tell from the tone of my voice that I wasn't talking about this hike up the hills in the Lake District.

'The baby. I don't think I can go through with it. I didn't realise how hard it'd be to see someone else doing for you what I can't. I don't think I can go through with it.'

'She's not doing it for me, she's doing it for us.'

'I don't think there can be an us any more, Mal,' I said. 'Not with this baby. I think you should go and be with her. And your baby.'

He straightened up, his shoelaces still untied. He was frowning. 'It's our baby. She's having it for us. And I want to be with you.'

I shook my head, surprised at how calm I was, considering what I was doing. 'You don't. You love her. You want a family life with her. Not me.'

He stared at me, poleaxed, as though someone had struck him squarely between the eyes with something large, hard and solid, rendering him immobile. 'I love you. You. I want a baby with you.'

'That's just it, you can't have one with me. You can with her.'

'Stop this nonsense, Stephanie. OK? Just stop it.' He bent down to finish with his shoelaces, but I could see his hands trembling. It was working, I was getting through to him.

'What if I do something to the baby?' I asked.

'You're not going to do anything to the baby.'

'But what if I do? It's not mine. Women harm their own babies every day—how do you know I won't harm one I've got no genetic connection to? It'll be your baby with another woman. What if . . . What if I go a little . . . What if I hurt it?'

'That's not going to happen,' he said sternly. He'd finished tying up the laces on his left walking boot, but was still fiddling with it so he wouldn't have to deal with me face to face.

'You don't know that. You don't know what I'm capable of. You've never known what I'm capable of.'

He straightened up again, this time his eyes like laser beams aimed at me. 'What's this really about?' he asked.

'Really?'

He nodded. 'I know it's not because you're scared you'll hurt the baby. You would never do that. What's this really about?'

'I don't want to bring up another woman's baby.

272

Correction, I don't want to bring up *her* baby.'
There, I said it.

'It'd be our baby. She's having it for us. She is only pregnant because of us. It'd be our little boy or girl. *Your* little boy or girl.'

'But I can't even pretend it's mine. Everyone would know. And they'd think you'd fucked someone else and I was so spineless I let you get away with it. Or I'd have to lie and say it was something genetic in our family. But everyone would be looking at me, knowing it's not really my baby.'

'Why do you care what other people think?' he asked in frustration.

'I don't know. I just do. I don't know why, but what other people think matters. All the looks in the street, especially if the three of us are together. And I can imagine what my family's going to be like. I don't want to go through all that.'

'That's a stupid reason to not want the baby.'

'I knew you'd think I was stupid, that's why I didn't want to tell you.'

'I don't think you're stupid and I didn't say you were stupid. It's a stupid reason not to want our child. I can't see the problem.'

'Well you wouldn't, would you? It's your child. You can have children. I can't.' I felt the tears well up and I started blinking to get rid of them.

'Steph, I don't understand this. We talked about this before. Even before we asked her—'

'And you talked me round. Said it would be all right. But I don't think it is going to be, Mal. I didn't think I'd feel like this. On the one hand, I can't help but feel attached to him or her, but mostly, I feel empty. That you could walk away at

273

any time with her. I'd always be living on the edge, wondering at what point she might want her baby back.'

'BUT IT'S OUR BABY!' he shouted, his words ringing out across the hills, *'baby, baby, baby'* echoing back to us seconds later.

'NO, IT'S NOT!' I shouted back, waiting for *'not, not, not'* to echo before I lowered my voice to speak again. 'It's yours. It's hers. It's not ours.'

He stared down at the earth in front of me, his eyes seeking something. Just like I had seen him doing in our dark kitchen the night I realised what had been going on under my nose.

'Legally, I have no real standing. Despite that contract we all signed, if she changes her mind, she could get rid of me like that!' I clicked my fingers. 'I have no real connection to the baby. And emotionally . . . Emotionally, I can't get over the fact it'll never be mine. Always yours, never completely and wholly mine.'

'Have you been taking your pills?' he asked. A low blow. Unexpected, too. Mal never did that, never used that against me.

'Whether I take them or not, that's not going to change the fact that I won't ever be able to love this child like it's my own.'

'I can't believe that.'

'It's the truth, Mal,' I said. 'It's what I feel. So, that's why I think it'd be better for everyone if you went to her and your baby. I know a baby's what you truly want. I don't want you to miss out on your chance now, so go be with her.'

'I always said that it didn't matter about children.'

'It's OK, I know you didn't mean it.'

'I did mean it. Just like you've meant it all these weeks when you've been going round to Nova's to visit the baby. Telling it you love it. You've bought all those books. And I know you've been buying clothes, and hiding them. I know how excited you've been about this. That's why I don't believe you. That's why I think you're just having momentary doubts and that you'll change your mind back.' He nodded, as though convincing himself as he spoke. 'We're both feeling the pressure of it now, and I'm sure all parents feel like this before their baby is born. Worry and anxiety about how they'll feel. If they'll be able to cope. We've got the additional pressure of having to tell our families about the situation in a few weeks. It's all of that. Once that's all over with, you'll look back and feel really silly about feeling like this. We both will. Because I have my doubts and I'll feel even more stupid for believing you and shouting at you.'

I fixed him with a look. The one I used to give solicitors and partners in the law firm who, for a few misguided seconds, thought my role as office manager meant I was somehow a lesser human being and therefore didn't require them to be polite. 'You misunderstand me,' I said evenly. 'I am not having that baby in my life, let alone in my house. If you want to carry on with it, that's fine. That is your choice. And it'll mean I won't have you either.'

'You're making me choose between my baby and you?'

'No, Mal, the choice has been made. I don't want the baby and I don't want you.'

'You don't want me any more?' he asked,

horrified. He became a little boy inside, scared and alone. Terrified about what he had just heard. Scared of the monster who was standing in front of him, ending his marriage.

'Not as long as there's a baby out there that's yours, no,' I stated.

He tried to pull himself together. Scrabbling around for shelter and comfort. 'I love you,' I said, deciding to offer him a refuge. 'More than life itself. I don't want you to miss out on this. I've decided to accept that I'm not meant to have children, but you clearly are meant to have children. You are having one. And that's something I can never be a part of. Not completely. And you'll always be torn between us. So if I end things with you now, then you won't be torn. You won't have to make this choice in a few years.' *Oh, God, I'm going to start crying*, I realised. This was harder than I thought. I'd rehearsed this speech a million times in my head in the last week but this was the first time it had made me cry.

It wasn't hearing 'I love you' that had bonded me to Mal when we first met. It wasn't fabulous sex, and holidays and talking late into the night; it wasn't lying next to him and listening to him breathe as he slept, knowing he'd still be there in the morning. It was when he told me about his mother. About her illness. It was the intimacy that allowed me to give myself to him. As completely as I could. As wholly as I had ever done with another human being.

'I promised I'd never leave you,' he said.

'It's OK, I won't break without you. I'll be fine.'

Mal closed his eyes. He seemed to have stopped, like a battery-powered toy soldier, marching along

276

merrily and then halting because the batteries were flat. There was no more energy driving it, all it could do was stand still. Silent. Flat.

'I'll tell Nova we don't want the baby any more,' he said after ten minutes had passed in silence. With him standing as still and silent as one of the mountains we were about to climb.

'But—'

'When we get home I'll tell her,' he said, talking over me. 'I'll say that we changed our minds, that we can't take on this responsibility right now. I'll tell her.'

'You don't have to do this, Mal. I'm telling you that you're free to go to her. To have your baby. To have her.'

'I said I'd never leave you. Nova will understand.'

She wouldn't. Of course she wouldn't. How could anyone understand that? Not even Nova, the most understanding woman I'd ever met, would understand this.

'But what will she do?' I asked. 'You know her better than anyone on earth. What do you think she'll do?'

He shrugged. 'I don't know.'

'Do you think she might have an abortion?'

I saw the knife twist in his guts at the thought of it. That was why it had taken me a week since I found the text to say this. I needed time to assimilate the thought myself. To accept that possibility and that responsibility. 'Mal, don't do this. Not for me. Go to her, have your baby.'

'She might,' he said, as though I hadn't spoken. 'Or she might keep him.'

'If she does keep it, then . . .' I paused, suddenly

277

afraid of voicing this condition. 'Then we're back to that thing of you having to choose. Which is why I don't want you to do this, Mal.'

'What are you saying?' he asked, tiredly.

'If . . . If she does keep it . . . then . . .' I paused again. 'If we're going to stay together, then you can't see her. And if she decides to keep the baby, then you can't have contact with either of them.' I paused, watched him, trying to see him without my eyes. Trying to read his energy, his aura, anything. And I couldn't. I was suddenly blind to him in all respects but using my eyes, like I had done before I met Nova.

'She's a part of my family,' he stated.

'This is why I don't want you to stay with me. Because that's a terrible choice to have to make. If she keeps the baby and it's out there, you'll know he or she is out there but you won't be able to make contact. I'm not sure you'll be able to do that, Mal. I'm not sure I want you to be able to do it because that's not who you are. I don't want you to change, not because of me.'

'You can stop laying it on so thick, Steph,' he said, quietly. 'We both know I'm going to agree to that condition. I've made my choice. I choose you. OK? I choose you.' He reached into the open back door of the car, pulled out his rucksack and hoisted it on. He locked the car, then started striding down the path that led towards the hiking trail.

I said to him before that he didn't know what I was capable of. Maybe I was wrong, maybe he did know. Maybe he'd always known that when I started this conversation, I knew exactly what to say and when to say it to make sure that this would be the outcome.

Maybe my husband did know that when it came to keeping him, to eliminating all rivals, I would use every weapon at my disposal—I was capable of anything.

CHAPTER TWENTY-EIGHT

Four things that I love:
The beach.
The sky ablaze with red, gold and orange as the sun dips out of sight.
Putting on music and pretending to be an interpretive dancer.
The smell of freshly-made coffee.

*   *   *

Unfortunately for me, in the past four months, the smell of coffee, cigarettes, bleach and petrol made me feel sick.

I loved coffee, and having to limit it in my life was upsetting. And not ideal in my work. I would look longingly, jealously, at the customers sipping it, imagining the rich, smoky taste, tempered sometimes by milk, other times by sugar, slipping down their throats. Working its way through their bodies. On the tube, the way I salivated at the people clutching their white paper cups of coffee was bordering on obscene—I was surprised I hadn't been reported for lascivious staring.

I loved coffee; the baby didn't. This also meant that I had to sit outside in cafés; thankfully the weather was pleasant enough to do that at the moment. Mal had asked me to meet him at our favourite café in West London. He and Stephanie had been on a walking holiday—that was one of the best things about him meeting her, he had someone else to drag along to those activities—and he'd rung me, it seemed, the second they got back.

This had been our favourite place for years. I think we wandered in from the street one wet day and kept finding our way back here. It wasn't large, more cosy, and strikingly beautiful in its simplicity. It had oak wood floors, clean white walls, and chrome fittings. They'd squeezed a tan leather sofa in the back and small, round pedestal tables with stools in the rest of the space. The staff were always smiling and made wonderful small talk whilst they frothed up your cappuccino. I always wanted to kick off my shoes and curl my feet up under me whenever Mal and I sat here. This really was our place—since before he met her. *We* met her, I suppose. But we spent hours in here, even after he met her—she'd never been here—just talking and laughing and drinking coffee.

Outside, in front of the huge picture window of the café, they had placed small circular wood-topped pedestal tables with chrome chairs, and that's where I sat whilst I waited. Sipping at peppermint tea and trying not to mind that I couldn't sit inside on the sofa, nor sip a cappuccino.

Taking a sip of the tea, I replayed his voice on the phone. Involuntarily, my heart skipped a little. He sounded so serious. Maybe he was going to explain what was going on with Stephanie. She had been weird on every level recently. She looked tense and wary every time she crossed my threshold; cornered. That was it: cornered. As though her back was against a wall and she was waiting to pounce on me at any moment to free herself. Being around her had become exhausting. I had learnt about so-called psychic vampires during my many studies of all things esoteric: people who would—usually unintentionally—drain your energy as those undead creatures drained the blood of the living, leaving you wrung out or in a bad mood. Usually, I didn't allow people to do that to me, but for some reason my usual defences and tricks for distancing myself from people weren't working with Stephanie. She had become like Dracula, zapping my energy, and whenever she left I felt a great cloud lift from me and I would only be fit to lie down. All the excitement and happiness that had infected her in the previous weeks, had caused her to call me her 'best friend', had evaporated. What was left was a black hole into which anything positive was sucked and destroyed.

Hopefully Mal would explain it and things would get back on track. I closed my eyes, enjoying the feel of the warm and comforting sun on my face. There was little traffic on the street, and few people walked by. I could hear the sound of the air rushing past. This time next year, when I got to Australia, it would be the middle of winter—sun like this would be unlikely.

'Hi,' he said.

A slow grin moved across my face, and I took my time opening my eyes. 'Hi,' I said. The happiness I had felt withered in the deepest cove of my heart as I saw him.

I knew his expression well. It was the one he

281

wore when he was about to tell me Aunt Mer had relapsed: agony dressed up in a thin, watery smile and sleep-deprived eyes.

'Have you ordered a drink?' I asked.

He shook his head. Slowly, gently, he cleared his throat. 'I'm not staying long.'

'What's the matter?' I asked, sitting up straight in my seat.

He ran a hand through his hair, curled his lips into his mouth to moisten them. 'You know I love you,' he began. 'You're my best friend and no one is closer to me on earth than you.'

If we were going out together, I'd know without a shadow of a doubt he was about to chuck me. But people didn't chuck friends, did they? If you wanted to end a friendship, you allowed it to die, you stopped calling, you stopped seeing each other, you distanced yourself so much that the next time you saw them it was like you had been apart for decades and you had nothing real or meaningful to say to each other. You didn't ask a friend out to a public place to tell them it was all over. *Did you?*

'I . . . You've been so amazing to me all these years. Even when I truly didn't deserve it. We've had a lifetime together. But I need to make a lifetime with Stephanie now. That's what I committed to when we got married. It's only recently that I realised that I can't do that if you're still in my life.'

Apparently, you did ask a friend out to a public place to chuck them.

'We've been doing a lot of soul-searching these past few weeks and even more so the past few days, and we realised that we're not ready to have a

282

child. We haven't had any real time together. Just me and Stephanie. I've been torn a little, only a little, about my feelings for you, but it's been enough to mean I'm not a hundred per cent committed to her. It's not fair to her. It's not fair to our marriage. Bringing a child into this would be unfair on everyone. The pair of us just aren't ready for that kind of responsibility. We don't want the baby any more.'

'The thing is, Malvolio, if this was a meal that had gone cold in my restaurant, I'd understand why and how you could say, "I don't want this any more", but this is a baby. You can't change your mind. You know, what with it being a *baby* and everything.'

'I'm sorry,' he said, lowering his line of sight to the table top.

'You're sorry?' I asked. 'I'm having your baby, you've changed your mind, and you're saying you're sorry?'

'I can't say anything else.'

'Yeah, you can, you can tell me why.'

'I've told you.'

'You have talked a lot of nonsense. You haven't actually told me why you have changed your mind about something it took so much for me to agree to. And I only agreed to it because I knew how desperately the pair of you wanted this. Up until you went on holiday I couldn't keep your hands off my stomach, which leads me to believe that you don't mean anything you've said.'

Mal looked at me, his face set, his dark eyes fixed; it was clear he wasn't going to say anything else.

'What am I supposed to do about the baby,

283

Mal?' I asked him quietly. Because they may have talked about a baby not fitting into their lives, but I was sure they wouldn't have thought more beyond that. And they absolutely had to.

He lowered his gaze to the table top again. 'You . . . you could . . . abortion.' As he spoke, his voice was so quiet I had to lean forwards to strain to hear. 'That would be easiest.' He started to worry at a spot behind his right ear; he did that when he was anxious. 'That's what would be best.'

'Easiest? Best?' I repeated. 'What would you know about it?'

He kept his eyes lowered. 'Stephanie had one. When she was fifteen, she seems fine.'

Fine? Stephanie? Don't get me started on that one. 'There's a difference between having an abortion when you're young and have an unplanned pregnancy, and when you're in your late twenties and have gone out of your way to get pregnant.'

'Keep it, then.'

'Right, and tell everyone what? That you're the father? And you want nothing more to do with me? And, don't worry, I didn't shag him and his married butt to get up the duff, no, I used a turkey baster because I was going to have the baby for him and his wife. No, no, they didn't drug me, I did it willingly because I care about them so much.'

'That's what I meant about it being easier.'

'No, Mal, what would be easier is if you were to have the baby as planned.'

'We can't, I'm sorry.'

'At least look me in the eye when you say that, because otherwise I won't believe you,' I said.

He raised his eyes again and as they met mine, I saw that he wasn't there. He had dissociated from

284

this. I had learnt about this in my clinical training. A person would remove themselves so they could do something they didn't want to do, so they could survive a traumatic situation, so they could see through a deeply difficult decision. He had removed himself so that he could tell me this.

I'd only seen him do this once before. We were eleven. Mal, although tall, was sinewy, quiet and always with a girl—either me or Cordy—so a lot of boys took that to mean he was weak and an easy target. Billy Snow, who was large and bullish-looking, sat behind Mal and me in Maths, and one day called Aunt Mer a loony. He whispered it, knowing our teacher wouldn't hear but that it would needle Mal. And would probably provide a new line of bullying. Mal was out of his chair and on top of Billy Snow before anyone—least of all Billy Snow—could react. He knocked Billy Snow backwards out of the chair, and didn't say anything as he pummelled Billy Snow's face. Everyone in the class—including Mr Belfast—was shocked into inaction and we all watched in horror as Billy Snow's face became a bloody, pulpy mess. Eventually, Mr Belfast came back to life and hauled Mal off the unfortunate would-be bully. Mal's eyes, instead of being wild, slightly murderous, were blank. For the first time in my life I was scared of Mal. He was not the boy I knew, he was a person capable of severely hurting someone and looking vacant as he did it.

I hadn't been that scared of Mal again. Not until this moment. The fact that he had to remove himself to do something difficult meant that they didn't want the baby, and he didn't want to see me any more.

'I'm sorry,' he said. 'We shouldn't have done this in the first place, but it's best we tell you now rather than in a few months when it'd be far more difficult.' He reached out, held his hand over mine. He'd held my hand so many times over the years, and now this was the final time, he was telling me.

'Be safe, yeah?' He stood up, and walked away, leaving only the faint scent of his aftershave and the lingering impression of his warm hand on mine.

CHAPTER TWENTY-NINE

He opened the door, about two hours after he left, and shut it quietly behind him.

His keys jangled as he dropped them on the hall table, and he didn't put his head around the living room door to say hello, he went straight to the kitchen.

I heard the fridge door open and shut, and a chair being pulled out from the table. I waited a few minutes, gave him time to decide if he was going to settle there or come back to talk to me. When he didn't come back to me, I went to him.

He was sprawled on the chair facing the window, a beer in one hand, staring out into the garden. In front of him were four bottles of Sol and the bottle opener. He put the beer in his hand to his lips and knocked it back with a jerk of his head. I usually made him drink from a glass but right then, it didn't seem an important thing to enforce.

'How did it go?' I asked him from my place in the doorway. The sadness he was swaddled tightly in kept me at bay.

He didn't reply, but paused for a second in gulping down his beer, letting me know he had heard my question but wouldn't speak to me.

'What did she say?' I asked.

He put down the empty bottle, reached for another, flicked off its cap and began to drink.

I ventured into the room, deciding to put my arms around him. Love him better. It must have been hard for him, but it was for the best. In time he would see that. This would have come between us. Even if they hadn't been plotting to keep the baby for themselves, I would always be wondering if they had and that wouldn't have been good for our marriage. How would it impact on the baby, too, if I always blamed it for making him fall in love with her again?

I touched him, knowing he would stand up, fall into my arms and let me surround him with love; soothe and support him. Help him start the move towards putting this behind us.

His body flinched away from me in revulsion. I took my hand away, stepped backwards, scalded deep inside by his reaction. 'I did what you wanted,' he stated. I knew then we wouldn't talk about it again. He wouldn't be sharing with me the details. It was done. Full stop.

As he stood up, I saw his face. Torture branded into every pore. The image of it instantly imprinted itself on to my heart and mind, a permanent wound of what I had made him do. I'd never forget it. He swiped another beer from the table, took the bottle opener and went to the garden, slamming the door behind him to signify that he wanted to be alone.

287

It was going to take time. Slightly more than I had at first anticipated. I had slightly underestimated what this would do to him. But time would blunt the sharp edges of pain, smooth out the ragged parts. We would be fine. We would be happy again.

CHAPTER THIRTY

Mal stopped short outside the revolving glass doors of his tall office building when he saw me.

Something flittered across his face. Irritation? Fear? I'd never seen it on his face before when looking at me, so was taken aback. Every time he saw me he looked pleased to see me. Even when we were in the midst of rowing with each other, when he could push me into shouting and ranting and raving at him, he still never looked so . . . uncomfortable. That was it. He looked uncomfortable.

Inhaling deeply, he came towards me while securing a pleasant look on his face. *Pleasant.* As though he was going to speak to a client he didn't want to speak to. It was the look I put on my face when I had to go and talk to an irate customer about the food/service/ambience: a necessary inconvenience, one you had to endure to get your job done.

'Hi,' he said, his eyes skimming over me to focus somewhere else.

'Hi,' I replied, quavering over that one word, because I couldn't hide my anxiety. Pride had told me not to come here, to leave him to it, to decide

288

what I was going to do and get on with it. But pride was not pregnant, alone and, basically, terrified.

I waited for him to say something else. To continue the conversation. I thought . . . I thought when he saw me he'd realise what he'd done. That he couldn't possibly mean it. Even if they had changed their minds about the baby, he couldn't possibly mean it when he said he wouldn't be seeing me again. But he clutched his black leather briefcase, the one that I had bought him for his first day at work, in one hand, shoved his other hand in his trouser pocket. He had nothing to say to me. He had said everything there was to say ten days ago. That was why he hadn't called.

'Could we have a chat?' I asked him, suddenly unsure if this was a good idea or whether I should have listened to my pride.

He flinched, then lowered his line of sight to the ground. 'About what?' he asked eventually.

I blinked at him, surprised. When in twenty-nine years had I needed a reason to talk to him? 'I need a reason to speak to you now?'

He gave a half-shrug without raising his eyes.

'OK, *Malvolio*,' I said, folding my arms across my chest, resting my weight on one hip. 'You're my best friend in the world so I have to tell you about this problem I'm having. I'm pregnant. Don't worry, it was planned and I love the father very much. But now the father has told me to get rid of it. I don't know what to do because he won't talk to me, and I suspect he might change his mind. So, I was wondering, as my best friend in the whole world, if you wouldn't mind facilitating his mind-changing process by going round and beating some sense into him for me?'

Was that a small smile that played across his lips? It must have been because he said, 'Let's go for a coffee at Carlitto's.'

'I really need a glass of wine,' I said.

'Wine? You can't drink,' he said.

'Why?'

He frowned. 'Well, you're . . .' His voice trailed away, his mouth twisting as though angry at having been so easily caught out.

'Coffee it is, I guess,' I said.

I turned in the direction of Carlitto's, an Italian café bar we often went to when I met him for lunch.

'So, how've you been?' he asked after we'd walked a few paces, side by side in a strained, unsettling silence.

'How do you think?'

He looked pained for a second, his eyes flickering to focus on the mid-distance—away emotionally from me—before coming back to the present.

'How have you been?' I asked when it became clear he wasn't going to reply to my non-rhetorical question.

'Fine,' he said. 'We're planning a holiday. We were thinking of camping in the south of France. Maybe going over on the ferry and driving down.'

Was he talking casually about holidays when inside me grew his child? I began to glance sideways at him, wondering who he was. He even looked a little different: the bump on the bridge of his nose slightly more exaggerated, making his face seem off-balance. His eyes seemed closer together, narrower, meaner. His once soft, wide mouth seemed to have hardened into a thinner line.

'Steph might be able to get three weeks off work, but she's not sure yet. She's been covering for the owner whilst she's on an extended break. Steph loves it. It's been really good for her, having that extra responsibility. It's shown her she can do it. Hopefully the owner will give her the time off when she comes back. I've got holiday carried over from last year.'

'I thought you said neither of you could handle the extra responsibility,' I said. 'That's why you didn't want this baby any more.'

'I wasn't lying,' he said, his defences instantly bolting into place around him. 'And there's a world of difference between running a shop and looking after a baby.'

We arrived at Carlitto's to find the pavement outside cleared of tables and chairs, the blind pulled down over the glass door, the metal grills bolted over the windows. We should have known, few cafés stayed open late—this time was the preserve of restaurants and bars.

'I suppose we've got to go to the pub now,' I said. 'I'll just have an orange juice or something.'

The look of discomfort tinged with irritation flitted across his face again as he raised his wrist, looked at his watch. His father's watch. He never told anyone that, not even Stephanie I'd guess. 'I have to get going,' Mal said. 'We're going to a friend's place for dinner.'

'Don't you think this is more important?' I said. Why was he being so cold? In anyone else, it would have been upsetting; in Mal, it was devastating.

'Nova, I don't know what you expect from me. I've told you our decision. I don't know what else there is to say.'

'How about why?' I asked him loudly. A few heads turned towards us and I lowered my voice, took a few steps closer to him.

'I've told you why,' he said.

'No, you haven't. I know you, you've never been scared of responsibility in your life. You live with it every day. I don't believe that you can't handle the responsibility of a baby,' I replied.

'Did you ever think that's why? Because I've had responsibility, I've been looking after people my whole life, and I can't do it again?'

'No, I didn't ever think that because it's bollocks and you know it. Is this Stephanie's doing?'

He stared at me, a muscle twitching in his jaw. 'It is, isn't it? It's Stephanie. I should have known. She'd been so weird in the last few weeks, her energy was all over the place, giving off unsettling vibes—'

'Ahh, don't start all that bollocks,' he cut in. 'Do you really think that I'd let her dictate something like this?'

'Yeah, I do,' I replied. 'I know you, this isn't something you'd do. It has to be her.'

'Maybe you don't know me as well as you think you do,' he said simply.

Old pain doesn't completely die. Time may soothe it, stroke over it until it looks like it has healed, but it never dies properly. It stays with you, it lives in the cracks of your soul, waiting for moments when you feel true pain. Other people had hurt me several times over the years. I'd cried, I'd ached, I'd grieved with varying degrees of intensity. And I'd always known, after what had happened when I tried to tell Mal I loved him, that it only hurt enough to leave a scar when the person

292

mattered. When the person had managed to open up a path to the centre of your being. Few people had managed that. I never realised that the next person who would cause me as much pain as Mal had all those years ago, who would cause all that old pain to resurface with just a few words, would be Mal.

'Mal, this isn't you talking.'

'It is, you know.'

'What am I supposed to do about this?' I pressed my hand on my stomach, forcing him to look at me. Look at the space he could hardly keep his hands off the last few months. He fixed his gaze on that spot, and I knew, I *knew* that he didn't want to do this. I seized on that, stepped forward, reached for his hand to put it on my stomach. He didn't resist, allowed me to move his hand across the gap between us—then suddenly he snatched his arm back before his fingers came into contact.

'Nova,' he said quietly, looking some way over my head, 'please don't do this. We're not going to change our minds. That's the truth of it. We shouldn't have done this, and I can only apologise.'

'You can only apologise? I'm pregnant. It's not like you've accidentally smashed my favourite vase, I'm having your baby. I'm doing it for you.'

'You don't have to have it. Not any more,' he said.

'OK,' I said, fighting the urge to break down. 'If I do *that*, then you have to come with me. If you want me to go through with it, then you have to come and watch me do it.'

'I can't,' he said, still staring over my shoulder.

'You see, you see?' I replied. 'You can't face the idea of me doing it. You still want this baby.'

293

'No, Nova. If I come with you, you'll be thinking right up until the last moment that I'm going to stop you. And that's not going to be healthy for you. You'll need to be preparing yourself, not hoping that I'll come riding in on a white charger to save you. Because I won't. I can't.'

I disintegrated. All strength in me crumbling away. 'Please don't do this, Malvolio. Please. Please,' I sobbed, tears tumbling down my cheeks. 'Please.' I bent forwards, folding my arms over the pain that was expanding inside me. 'Please, Mal. Please.'

I heard his briefcase clatter to the ground, seconds before his arms met around me, pulling me upright and close. 'Please don't cry,' he said. 'I can't stand to see you cry.'

'I'm scared. I'm so scared. I can't do this on my own. Please don't make me. Please.'

'I'm sorry,' he whispered against my hair. Then he kissed the top of my head, and then he was gone. He picked up his briefcase and walked away, left me crying in the street without so much as a backward glance.

I saw him four times after that. I knew that if I could just let him see what this was doing to me, what the thought of not seeing him again was doing to me, if I could just talk to him enough, then he would change his mind. He would accept that he couldn't ask me to have an abortion. To not have his child. When it had taken so much for me to do this in the first place, he couldn't expect me to do that.

Each time—three or four days apart—I met him at work. Either at lunch, or after work. Each time he was a little more distant, a little more irritated, a little less moved by my pain. Until the final time, when he left his building, saw me standing on the edge of the wide pavement, waiting for him, and turned around and went back inside. I waited an hour and he didn't reappear. When I got home, he had left a message on my answer machine: 'Nova, please stop coming to see me.' He was cold, detached, hard. 'I have nothing else to say to you. I'm not going to say anything you want to hear. Leave me alone.'

CHAPTER THIRTY-ONE

Once she was out of our lives, I thought I'd find it easy. Easier. But it wasn't. It wasn't simply about Nova, was it?

It was also about our baby.

I hadn't only been buying clothes and books. I'd bought a couple of rattles, three teddy bears, a musical mobile for over the crib. And a change bag, which was square and white, covered in pink, blue, yellow and green daisies. It was so gorgeous I used to take it out and open it up, imagine filling it with nappies and wipes and nappy rash cream and a toy to keep the baby occupied while I did the deed.

I had kept everything in the second bedroom, the one that would have become the baby's room, and now I had to pack it all away.

I could have given them away, but I didn't want to. They were meant for *my* baby. I held each Babygro in my arms, imagining them filled with my baby's plump limbs, stretching and contracting at the chest with the gentle in and out of his breathing. He was a he, I was sure of it.

After I held each one, I folded them into the change bag until there was no more room. Then I got out my designer weekend bag. It was the most expensive thing I had ever owned—it cost even more than my car—and I had saved up for years to own that little piece of design history.

I put everything else in that. It seemed fitting, memories of the most precious thing I would never have, kept in the most expensive thing I would ever own.

Afterwards I braved the scary attic and tucked them out of sight. Not out of mind, of course.

Never out of mind.

CHAPTER THIRTY-TWO

I ended up in Brighton.

I had to come away because I couldn't do it in London.

Not in the city where I lived. I couldn't imagine having to walk past it every day, knowing. Or even looking on an *A–Z*, a train planner or a tube map and seeing the name of the place. The area of London where . . . where I did this thing.

I'd had two pregnancy scares in my life, both times because of a split condom and both times I'd known without a doubt what I'd do if I got pregnant. The thought was difficult, but I knew both times I wouldn't be able to cope with being a mother. I couldn't go through with it. Both times had turned out to be just that: scares.

This time was different in many ways, not least of all because I was pregnant.

I'd booked the hotel a few weeks after I got . . . got into this thing. I'd needed a few days to myself. Every year—even when I'd been with Keith—I went away on my own, to somewhere near the sea. Some days it was more spontaneous, I would wake up in the morning and would need to get away. Would need to not be in London, and I would get dressed, get on a train, destination: Brighton. I would walk on the beach, inhaling the salty air, loving the rush of the sea in my ears, the feel of the pebbles under my feet. On the way back at night, I'd feel calmer and in control. As though I'd had the chance to step out of my life for a while.

And now I was using this six-day break for . . .

I'd had the initial appointment after I got here, and in two days, it would be done. Afterwards, after it had been done, all I'd want to do would be to sit and stare at the sea. More than anything I'd need to lose my mind in the motion of the sea afterwards. It would take me out of myself and I would be able to get my head together, reassemble the pieces of my mind before I went back to London, back to work, back to my flat, back to 'normal'.

The hotel—four stars, no less—was horrible. The pictures the travel agent had shown me were of a pristine, elegant establishment resplendent with old-world charm and antique fittings. The room I was shown to had wallpaper that bubbled away from the walls, peeling in some places. The original sash windows sat in frames that had been rotted, cracked and peeled by the sea air, and the wind whistled relentlessly through the gap between

297

the new double-glazing on the inside. The shower had no temperature control; the television would only find three channels or encourage the viewer to pay for porn; the red, patterned carpet was worn in places, dirty grey in others.

Everything wrong with the room was tempered by the unhindered view of the sea. I lay on top of the bed, ignoring the suspicious stains on the duvet cover, and stared out of the window, watching the waves rollicking and rolling. Mal always thought he'd die at night in the sea, I remembered suddenly. He never had a reason to think it, nor could explain why he'd be on or in the sea at night, but he believed it with an unshakeable, fervent certainty. It wasn't something he had to convince himself to believe, he just knew it to be so. And despite all the times he'd dismissed my interests, my knowledge, my beliefs, he still held on to that one.

I watched an old man sitting on the bench beside a green-blue bus stop shelter with sea salt-smeared glass. The wind was howling around him, tugging, pulling, tearing at his pink skin, white hair and beige zip-up jacket. But he sat rock still. His hands, bunched into fists, rested on his thighs and he stared straight ahead. Unbothered and untouched by the battering elements.

What's your story? I asked him in my head. *Why are you alone? Why are you so numb to everything going on around you?*

He didn't answer, obviously. I moved my gaze further up the horizon, to the grey sea topped with white foam, fighting a battle with itself that didn't need to be won.

I looked down to find I was resting my hand on

298

my abdomen. The skin was taut and warm, I could feel the blood moving under my hand. In all the times Mal and Stephanie had done that, I hadn't. I knew it was important not to touch the baby, acknowledge it, engage with it when it was not going to be mine. If I bonded with it, connected with it, then how would I be able to give it to its parents? Now I was touching it.

And in two days, I'd be doing this thing.

My hand slid over the warm skin, and I felt it. Movement. Slight, fleeting, but movement deep inside. I snatched my hand away as all the different emotions that had been bundled up in a tight ball inside me unwrapped themselves.

I'm pregnant.

With Malvolio's baby.

I'm pregnant with the baby of the first man I ever loved.

It wasn't anyone else's baby. It wasn't a man I'd been casually dating for a few weeks. It wasn't Keith, who I'd only just split up with. It was Mal. I'd known him a lifetime. If we had been more honest with each other, this would be something we had planned and were doing together.

But he didn't want the baby and I had not intended to do this at this point in my life.

I wasn't sixteen, but I was on my own.

I was a twenty-nine-year-old knocked-up teenager. And I hadn't even had sex to get myself into this condition. I couldn't have a baby. I couldn't bring up a baby on my own.

But I couldn't lose the only little part of Malvolio I had left.

I moved my hand to my abdomen again. Felt it again. Deep inside, fluttering, small, little flutterings. Tears started to leak from my eyes as I waited to feel it for a third time. Just once more I would feel it, then I'd stop doing this. I'd distance myself again.

I had training to complete, a research paper to finish writing, a round-the-world trip to go on.

I couldn't do this. I couldn't have a baby on my own.

I couldn't. That was all there was to it. I couldn't.

CHAPTER THIRTY-THREE

By the time the baby's due date—a day burnt into my mind—arrived, Mal had completely shut off from me.

And he cried all the time.

Even when there were no tears, his eyes had the haunted hollowness of someone who was sobbing inside.

I wanted to help him but he wouldn't let me near. The crying he did alone, shut away in the room that was once going to be the nursery. He slept with his back to me, like a solid wall of flesh that kept the world out. He talked to me with empty words, in sentences that held no deeper meaning. He used to weave everything he said with the strands of the depth of his love. Now, he talked to me because he had to. Now, everything he said was flat and meaningless.

The grief was so huge, so immense that he was floundering in it. Swimming blind as he would in a raging sea at night. Swimming against the crashing waves and getting nowhere. Every day he was dragged further down, into those depths. Away from the surface. Away from life. Away from me. All he clung to was the loss. Nothing else mattered. I wanted to take his hand, swim us both to safety. To make him whole again; to soothe his wounds and help him heal.

But he would not reach for me. Instead, he flinched away, preferring to do this alone. He blamed me. He blamed himself. And he blamed me.

I blamed myself, as well. But I also blamed her. Nova. This was her fault, her responsibility, too. If not for her . . .

Mostly, I blamed myself. Mostly, I wanted him to stop crying, to stop hurting, to stop grieving with every piece of his soul.

I didn't understand the loss that he and Nova shared. I doubted I ever would. But I understood my husband. And soon, I'd lose him. The one thing I tried to stop by doing what I did, saying what I said, would happen. But this time I wouldn't lose him to another woman and her unborn baby, I wouldn't lose him to her and her child, I'd lose him to himself.

I could see it happening: he was going to drown in his grief, he was going to be pulled so far down he wouldn't be able to break the surface. He would be dragged down to those bleak, grey depths and would never start living again. And all I'd be able to do was stand on the shore and watch.

CHAPTER THIRTY-FOUR

I sat up in bed, exhausted, sore, flitting between complete despair and complete euphoria.

Every few seconds I would glance at the clear cot beside my bed. At him. *Him.* A living gurgle, wrapped up in a white blanket, lying two feet from me. I'd lost a lot of blood, the doctors told me, so I was to stay in an extra day. Every time I glanced at him—his face turned upwards towards the ceiling, his wrinkled eyelids resting together, his mouth open a fraction, his cheeks a reddened mocha—I wondered what I'd done.

Have I made the biggest mistake of my life? I kept asking myself. *Should I have done what I intended to do when I went to Brighton?*

I looked away from the little boy and found her standing at the end of my bed. Even though visiting hours were over and my family had just left (the poor beleaguered nurses had tried fruitlessly to get only two of them to stay), she was back. Standing there in her black overcoat, her blue scarf draped around her neck, her black bag on her shoulder.

She knows, I realised. *Aunt Mer knows.* The look on her face when she first saw him popped up in my mind: momentary shock, quickly brushed over by elation and delight.

'When Malvolio was born, his cheeks were so red,' she said, staring at my son, remembering hers. 'And he had these thick, thick curls. So blond.' With the gentlest touch, she stroked her forefinger over the tips of my boy's dark, curly hair. 'Your father walked all the way to the hospital to see me

302

the day after he was born because it was Sunday and there were no buses. Your mother wanted to come, but she was close to having you and could hardly move.'

She looked away from the little boy at me. 'He's so beautiful.'

I nodded, slowly, carefully. 'You can hold him, if you want,' I said to her. Out of everyone who had visited, she hadn't held him. 'I'm too shaky,' she had said; now I knew it was because she might betray herself and so betray me.

'Thank you, no. I wouldn't want to disturb him.' Her face, soft and gentle, creased into a deep smile as she stared at her grandson. 'When Malvolio was born, all you had to do was look at him a bit too hard and he'd wake up.'

'This one likes his sleep,' I said to Aunt Mer.

'Good for him,' she said. 'And you, of course.'

'Yes, good for me.'

'I told Malvolio you'd had your baby and that I was coming to see you today,' she said, her softness now smoothed over with regret. 'If I had known . . .'

'It's OK, Aunt Mer, you can tell him whatever you want. I really don't mind. And if you hadn't, Mum, Dad or Cordy would have.'

'Do you know what you're going to call him yet?' she asked.

'Yes. But I'm going to try it out just between the two of us before I tell anyone?' I phrased it as a question so that she wouldn't feel offended.

'I remember when I wanted to call Malvolio Malvolio. Everyone tried to talk me out of it. But I always knew if I had a son that was what I would name him.'

'Because that was the first play Uncle Victor

took you to see,' I said before I could stop myself. I had lived twenty years without repeating that to anyone.

'How did you know that?' she asked, looking a little upset. Uncertain. Scared. Aunt Mer didn't like to be startled. And if I told her the truth, God knows what it might do to her.

'I kind of guessed over the years that it must have had some sort of significance. It's so unusual.'

'It's at times like this that I miss Victor the most,' she said with a sad smile. 'I know how much he would have loved to be here. I know it doesn't seem important, but he was sad that he missed Malvolio's birth. Even being there at Victoria's birth didn't make up for it. He missed his firstborn coming into the world. That weighed heavy on him, I know it did.' Her grin grew. 'And it obviously meant he would have been able to stop me calling him Malvolio.'

I laughed.

A lot of people—Mal included—didn't think that Uncle Victor loved Aunt Mer, but I did. Aunt Mer did. But then, maybe that's because Aunt Mer and I were always hopeless romantics; we believed in the unending, redemptive power of love.

Uncle Victor did time for her. We weren't even born when he went into prison. We'd been told that he went in for fraud, but we found out years later it was far more serious: Grievous Bodily Harm with intent to kill. The person had called Aunt Mer a lunatic and said she should be locked up, not knocked up. Uncle Victor went crazy. Several witnesses all testified that the man in question had been goading Uncle Victor (who was of good character) for weeks, and had only hit

304

upon that particular button by accident. The reason Uncle Victor was sent to prison was that he showed no remorse. His 'brief' had told him to apologise to the man, to apologise to the court, to throw himself on the judge's mercy and reassure them it wouldn't happen again, especially since he had a baby on the way. 'I'd rather have the death sentence than apologise when I'm not at all sorry,' Uncle Victor had said. (I heard Mum and Dad discussing it years and years later.)

As a result he served five years; each one of them was hard and difficult and left him scarred inside and out, but he would do it again and again. Because no one talked about or to Aunt Mer like she didn't matter.

He never stayed with her, though. That was the deepest sadness. He loved her, but couldn't handle her illness and had to remove himself from her. He had been a builder before he was sent down—we were told originally that he was working away, then when the local grapevine put paid to that, they told us he was in prison for fraud and not to listen to what anyone else said—and when he came out of prison he decided to leave to find work. Everyone around our way knew what he had done so wouldn't hire him, so he travelled the country looking for work, living away, sending money home and returning every so often—usually during the quieter winter months—to live with Mal, Aunt Mer and Victoria. Winter was quieter in many ways—the dark skies, cold weather and general barenness in the world also quietened Aunt Mer. She was much more depressed in winter, and for Uncle Victor that meant she was easier to handle.

He had to watch her carefully, because the

likelihood that she would try to . . . went up. But he could cope with that. Much more than the highs. Which made her into a different person almost. She was still Aunt Mer but she would talk quickly, do unusual things, spend all the money they had and every penny they didn't have, clean maniacally, come up with fantastical schemes (like digging over the garden in the middle of the night looking for archaeological finds), not sleep, not eat.

Uncle Victor loved Aunt Mer, of that I was sure, but he could not live with her for any length of time. He just wasn't strong enough. Physically he was, emotionally he wasn't. I used to think it was because he couldn't stand to see her suffer and know that he couldn't do anything to stop it; I used to think that he hated himself for not being able to love her better, for not being able to give her enough to keep her well and stable. But I was an old romantic. And as I had discovered over the years, all relationships had their secret coves and hidey-holes, and no one on the outside could ever truly know what lay buried in them.

'I had better be going, dear, I told your parents that I had forgotten these.' She reached into her bag and pulled out her blue wool gloves. 'I don't like telling white lies, but I wanted to tell you he's beautiful.'

I smiled at her.

'Really—' Her voice caught in her throat, a silent sob she managed to choke back, '—beautiful.'

'Do you think I did the right thing?' I asked her before she turned away. Now that she knew a part of it, and she probably thought Mal and I had been having an affair, I had to ask. I wasn't sure, still, if I should have gone through with the other option.

Her face softened with the biggest smile I had seen her give in years. 'Absolutely,' she replied. 'I couldn't imagine the world without him. Can you?'

I glanced over at my son. My son. Holy God in heaven. *My* son.

'No,' I replied, a rush of protective emotions surging through me. 'No, I can't.'

CHAPTER THIRTY-FIVE

What Mal and I need is a holiday.

I'm washing up the tea service Meredith gave us, and I'm feeling more positive. What we need is a break from it all. To get away from the pressures of being here all the time, with only the two of us, everything always the same.

That's what childless couples are supposed to do: jet off on foreign holidays at the last moment, have sex wherever and whenever we want, spend copious amounts of money on frivolous things. We need to take advantage of the spontaneity being childless gives us. It's our duty.

Spain? Portugal? Dublin? Milan? Paris? Timbuktu! It'll be great, wherever we go. As long as we're together.

And, once we're both über-relaxed and blissed out, I'll bring up seeing Leo. Suggest that he talk to Meredith about talking to Nova about seeing him. She still cares for Mal, she must do to name her son for him. Only someone who loved him like I did would notice that, of course: Leo, Malvo*lio*. To do that, she must still have some feelings for him.

307

Which means she may let Mal back into her life, allow him into Leo's life. And me, as well. But one thing at a time. Mal first.

That will make him happy.

And that's what I want. So badly, for him to be happy again. To stop missing Nova and missing Leo.

A teacup slips from my fingers and drops the short distance into the washing-up bowl. It doesn't fall far, but my stomach turns at the sickening crack as it hits something submerged in the soapy water. This tea service is rare. Old, antique, rare. It cost Meredith a lot of money. I didn't like it, but I appreciated how precious she thought it was. It was meant to last us a lifetime. I pick up the handle, and it comes away with only half of the cup still attached. Without thinking I reach in with my left hand for the other half and pain shoots through my thumb as a jagged edge of porcelain pierces it. I jerk my hand out of the sink and run it under the cold water tap.

It doesn't mean anything, I tell myself as I transfer my lacerated thumb to my mouth without checking the wound first.

I'm not Nova, I don't read signs into everything, so this, it really doesn't mean anything.

part five

'So, do you have a best friend, Leo?' Mum asked.

'Yes,' he replied.

'Who is it?'

He hit the pause button on his controller so he could look at Mum without losing the game. She smiled back at him as if she didn't know the answer to that question.

Leo frowned at her. She was a silly mum sometimes.

He turned back to his controller, took the game off pause and tried to make Darth Sidious kill Master Windu.

'You, of course,' he said.

Leo, age 6 years and 9 months

CHAPTER THIRTY-SIX

Cordy is pacing the floorboards of my guest bedroom, wearing her knee-length, granddad-style flannel nightshirt and knee-length socks, while talking on her mobile. Her hair is combed around her head and wrapped under a blue satin scarf. She looks rather stylish for someone who is about to climb into bed.

She has her small silver mobile on speakerphone and one of her four-year-old twins, at a guess Ria, is crying loudly; the other one, Randle, is fervently banging something metallic. Over the noise of the two of them, Jack, Cordy's husband, is trying to conduct a conversation about Ria's missing

311

blanket.

'You've really looked everywhere?' says Cordy, pausing in front of the mirror to pout at herself. I sit in bed, watching her.

'Yes!' Jack shouts in frustration.

'I'm really going to miss our house, J,' she says, sadly.

'What?' he replies, thinking he's misheard.

'I'm really going to miss our house,' she repeats louder.

'What do you mean? Why?' he asks.

'Well, when you give up your job at the airline, we won't be able to afford it, we'll have to get something smaller.'

'Why am I going to give up my job?'

'We always agreed, the children have to know both their parents. It's not their fault their parents were stupid enough to take on all this debt, and if you're falling apart after, what, *four* hours alone with them, you obviously don't know them and they don't know you. So, less debt, more time with the children.'

Save the crying and banging, there is silence from Jack's end of the line. And then the sound of rummaging and things being overturned, his footsteps running from room to room.

'Found it!' Jack says triumphantly, and Ria magically stops crying.

'Thought you might,' Cordy says. 'Kiss the children for me.'

Cordy snaps shut her phone and climbs on to the bed, not coming under the covers with me. Mum and Dad are in my bedroom for a couple of nights, while they decide how long they're staying, and Aunt Mer is on the sofabed downstairs in the living room; Cordy and I are bunking in together here. Keith is at the hospital and, as always, gives me half-hourly updates on Leo's condition.

I thought I'd be overwhelmed by them all being here but a sense of calm order has descended since they arrived. Mum and Aunt Mer have been cleaning but have been careful not to disturb anything that Leo has left lying around, as if they know I'll want him to pick them up when he returns. Other than that, my house has been given their treatment. This would have upset me at one point, but I've accepted that this is their way of coping—Mum spent the afternoon cooking and freezing stuff, as well—they can't do anything to help at the hospital so they're taking their frustrations out on the dust and furniture and floors. Dad has been placidly following Mum's orders to go to do the shopping and have my car cleaned and take away the recycling and cut the lawn. Now there is a quiet in the house and I feel so much better. Less alone.

Keith doesn't make me feel alone, it's just that my family have always been the emergency unit. Parachuting in at times of crisis to clean and cook the bad thing into submission. This time is no different.

I have left the curtains open so, now Cordy has finished her call, I switch off the lamp and let moonlight illuminate the room.

'Where's Malvolio?' she asks out of the blue.

Is this a game, like those *Where's Wally?* books that I tried to get Leo to read when he was five and he'd had to break the news to me—gently—that he didn't care where Wally was because anyone who wore a hat like that should stay lost. For ever.

313

Where's Malvolio? 'Erm, in London?' I ask.

'Don't be facetious,' she says.

'Don't talk to me as though I'm younger than you,' I reply.

My sister is lit a shade of blue by the moonlight, it falls in gentle streaks on her hair, the right side of her face. She looks magical, as though she is some illuminated angel visiting earth, only visible to the human eye by the light of the fat moon—she would not appreciate me telling her that, though.

She shifts herself under the covers, nudging me aside so she can go top to toe with me, but instead of lying down, she props herself up with pillows.

'No one else is going to say this, even though they're all thinking it, so I have to,' she begins. 'Where is Mal? Why isn't he here?'

I shrug. 'I don't know,' I reply. I honestly don't know. I've never known, never understood why he decided to do what he did, so I don't know why he isn't here, why he isn't a part of my life any more. Just that he isn't.

'But he's family. He's always the one you called first about anything, how come you haven't now? Why isn't he here with the rest of us?'

Everyone in our family noticed that Mal and I didn't see each other any more, but Cordy has been the only one to bring it up in front of me. The last time, it had been the Christmas when Leo was eleven months old. We were gathered in Mum and Dad's living room after lunch, had finished opening presents when Cordy said, 'Why aren't you talking to Malvolio?'

Everyone—Aunt Mer, Mum and Dad— squeezed into my parents' living room stopped watching television or fiddling with their presents

314

and stared at me. There was no such thing as subtlety in our family once something had been voiced: that's what a lifetime of living out traumatic moments in front of the neighbours did.

'Who said I'm not talking to Mal?' I asked, stoically not looking at Leo, asleep in his cot beside the sofa.

'Well, not him!' Cordy went on. 'I asked him the other week and he said, "Who said I'm not talking to Nova?" and then changed the subject. But we haven't seen the two of you in the same room at the same time since before Leo was born.'

'It's not that we're not speaking,' I said, choosing my words very carefully, 'we've just got different, busy lives. He's married, I've got a child and the café, we just don't have as much time for each other.'

'Since *when*?!' Cordy screeched. 'All you ever have is time for each other. Most of us never get a look-in! Is it his wife? Is she the jealous type? Did she put the mockers on your friendship? Did she catch you at it?'

I don't know why, but my naughty little sister had the audacity to be surprised when the flat of Mum's hand connected with the back of her head.

Twenty-seven she may have been, but not too old to be reminded she was talking about Aunt Mer's son and his wife. In *front* of her.

'Ow!' she said, rubbing the sore spot. *What did you do that for?!* she wanted to add, but never would. Neither of us would talk back to our parents or Aunt Mer.

Mum had changed the subject by asking Cordy to come and help her with the mince pies, basically so she could tell her off in the kitchen. That was the last time they discussed it in my hearing. Cordy had effectively stopped anyone else asking the question and, as the years stretched out before and behind us like a long, windy road, I was grateful for that. I didn't have to explain, and I'm sure Cordy—who idolised Mal—wouldn't have asked him. Now, she clearly feels it is time to revisit this.

I stare at my sister; she stares at me. A battle of wills is starting. Who's going to give in first and speak? She thinks that if she can wait me out, I may give her the answer she requires. Unfortunately for her, I have had Leo for seven years—even when he was tiny he was the model of stubbornness—and I have had to hone my skills in waiting him out to get him to do what I want. I've spent hours sometimes, sitting on the stairs, waiting for him to agree to put on his coat so we can go to the park. This is small fry. But I know the best way to deal with a stubborn child isn't always to wait them out, but to deal with them on your level. I will not 'lose' this by speaking first if I am careful about what I say.

'*Min niem*,' I state.

Cordy instantly twists her lips into a displeased pout. Leo did that sometimes. *Does*. Leo *does* that sometimes. My sister wants to tell me off for being facetious again but she can't. The pout, the frown, make Cordy the little girl who used to glower at me when I wouldn't let her play with my toys until Mal would tell me off and make me share. He would always share with Cordy—his food, his toys, his time, even when he was really young. She was a baby, as far as he was concerned, and needed looking after.

'What?' I say to her. 'Me talking in English

didn't make it clear that I don't know, I thought trying in Ghanaian might.'

She shakes her head and suddenly looks distressed. 'What happened to you and Mal?' she asks sadly. 'We haven't seen the two of you together in so long. You didn't go to Victoria's wedding—'

'Because Leo got chicken pox a week before,' I clarify.

'But you refused to be a bridesmaid and were going to do the catering so you could hide. Mal didn't come to Leo's christening because of suddenly going on holiday. At my wedding you . . . I don't know, there isn't one picture of the two of you together. No one can remember seeing you together. He didn't come to the twins' christening cos he was away. Same with your wedding. We don't spend Christmas together any more. When I speak to him it's clear he hasn't spoken to you in ages. I don't know, it's like you're two strangers.'

I stare at her, wondering what I'm supposed to say. She picks up her mobile and starts opening and shutting it.

'You know what I found out recently?' she asks.

I shake my head. 'No, Cordelia, I don't know what you found out recently.'

'After Jack asked Dad for his permission to marry me, and Dad said yes and everything, Mal went to have a word with him. Jack, I mean. Mal drove all the way to the airport and waited for Jack's flight to come in and then sat him down and told him I was his little sister and that if he ever even thought of hurting me, he'd better change his identity and leave the country. He was very pleasant about it apparently, but very definite. My

317

big brother.' Cordy lays aside her mobile phone and draws her knees up to her chest, hooking her nightshirt over her knees and hugging her arms around them. 'I always hoped you and him would get together, so he'd properly be my big brother. I always thought you'd marry him.'

My subtle family—Aunt Mer included—had all thought, and therefore hinted at, that until he got engaged to Stephanie.

'I always thought I'd marry Keith,' I say.

'Really?' she asks, surprised.

'Ever since I met him, I thought I'd marry him.'

'Why?'

'Because no one has ever loved me like he has. He's always been very clear about his feelings for me. And when someone is so clear and open about how they feel for you, it's easy to let yourself go and to love him back.'

'You split up a million times.'

'And we always got back together. Like I say, no one has ever loved me like he does.'

'Not even Mal?'

'No one has ever loved me like Keith does.'

Cordy nods, and starts to rock slightly, summoning up her courage. She fixes me with a determined gaze as she continues to rock gently. She is building up her courage. 'Mal . . . Is he . . .' She pauses. She was going to ask, was set on asking, but now she isn't sure if she can. I know she has wanted to ask over the years, so have Mum and Dad. Every time Leo throws his head to the side and laughs, every time he rubs at the spot behind his right ear, every time he looks at them with his big, awestruck brown eyes, listening to what they're saying, *every* time he does something that is

318

obviously inherited from Mal, they have wanted to ask. Is Mal Leo's father? But they never have. They have always held their tongues because of what it would mean about me, about him and what we had done to his wife. They would have to think badly of us—even for a few moments—and my family would never want to do that. Better to stick to what I said when I told them I was five months pregnant—the father isn't around but I'm really happy and I'm more than capable of looking after myself.

'Is he . . .'

If Cordy asks me outright, I will tell her. That's the deal I made with myself: if anyone asks me outright, I will tell them.

'Is he happy?' she asks, sinking down into the bed, punching the pillow. 'Is he happy in his life? I know I speak to him all the time, but is he really happy?'

'The last time I spoke to him he seemed to be,' I say, sinking down too.

'Good,' she says. 'Good. He should be here, though. He should be here.'

BLEEP-BLEEP. BLEEP-BLEEP, sounds my mobile. I snatch it up and call up the text message.

All well. No change. Love you. K x

I text him back that I love him, relieved now I can sleep for half an hour.

'All I care about right now is Leo,' I say.

'Yeah, course,' Cordy agrees. 'Course.'

319

It was the coolest wheelie in the whole world!

Even Mum said so. She laughed and clapped and called him the wheelie king.

That was before it went wobbly and the front wheel went down too fast and he went flying over the top of the handlebars. It wasn't very far, it wasn't very high, but now he knew what it was like to fly. And he loved it.

But Mum would never let him do it again, of course. Not ever. She was probably going to start crying once they got the bleeding to stop. If she tried to get rid of his bike, he wouldn't let her.

'I don't know what else to do,' Mum said. She put another big bit of cloth under his nose and then another cold thing on top of his nose. 'I can't get the bleeding to stop.'

He didn't mind. Not really. It only hurt a little. But he flew. He actually flew. In the air and everything.

Mum stared at him, holding on to the cold thing on top of his nose. She looked worried. She was always worried. 'Hold this,' she said and put his hand on the cold thing. She went to the corridor, and came back with her coat on, her bag on her shoulder and her car keys in her hand. 'We're going to the hospital.'

Flying and the hospital. This was the best day ever! Maybe they'd make him have an operation. Like Martin had one once to get rid of his ton-seels. And all he had to eat was ice cream and jelly.

'It probably won't take long, I just need to be sure,' Mum said. 'Can you walk?' she asked as she helped him down from the stool.

He nodded. But when his feet touched the ground, they felt squashy like the bath sponge and he nearly fell over. Mum caught him in time.

'It's OK, mate, I've got you.'

She picked him up, like she used to do when he was a baby. And he didn't mind, not really. It was nice. Mum smelt of the café most of the time. Coffee and cake and biscuits. But when you were this close to her, when she hadn't been to the café all day, she smelt how she really smelt. She smelt of the garden, of talc powder and rain and sunshine all at once. She smelt of her.

She put him gently on his booster seat in the back of the car. 'We'll be at the hospital soon, OK?' she said.

He nodded. He was tired. He wanted to go to sleep.

She took away the red cloth and gave him a great big towel to hold under his nose. He closed his eyes as she shut the door and climbed in the front.

'We'll be there really soon.'

Leo, age 7 years and 5 months

CHAPTER THIRTY-SEVEN

'I see there's a family history of haemorrhaging, particularly in the brain,' the doctor says to my assembled family.

He had originally come into Leo's room to ask to speak to me alone, not realising that once we got a nurse to sit with Leo, 'alone' meant speaking to six people. We all crammed into the relatives' room, Mum and Aunt Mer sat on my right, Keith sat on my left, and Dad and Cordy stood behind us

321

as the consultant started to speak.

Knowing what I am about to unleash in the room, I hesitate before I say, 'His paternal grandfather died of a brain haemorrhage twenty-something years ago. An aneurysm that ruptured and became a fatal haemorrhage.'

Mum gives a small, fragile intake of breath; my father puts his hand on her shoulder to comfort her or to steady himself, I'm not sure which. Cordy takes a deep, deep breath and exhales loudly. Keith becomes a rigid form beside me at the reaction of my family—he hasn't realised until this point that my family don't know. He has always assumed that we don't talk about Leo's father because I changed my mind about the surrogacy and it must have hurt Mal, not because I have never told them.

I'm not a natural liar, and not owning up to something makes me feel as though I have lied. And spending the last eight years with this pact to tell only if someone asks directly has been difficult, weighing heavily on my conscience. I wanted to tell, but I couldn't because as soon as I did, they would have asked questions until it came out about the surrogacy agreement.

From there the conversations that would have started—the rebukes, the recriminations, the being silently told I was stupid to even agree—would have been unbearable. After that, I would have had to tell them why I kept the baby. Even after all this time I still found what he did, how he did it, something too hard to think about, let alone talk about. I had seen how hard he had become, inured to anything except going through with what he had decided. I didn't want to relive it, nor to visit it

322

upon my family. And knowing Mum, knowing Cordy, they wouldn't have left it after hearing the story. They would have known best; they would have tried to talk to Mal. They would have tried to set us up, thinking that this could all be fixed with a little staging, a few correct words and a reminder to him how much we mean to each other. I knew that wasn't true, I'd done all that: I had engineered those meetings, I had tried to talk to him, I'd broken down in front of him and none of it mattered. Mal and his wife didn't want Leo; Mal wanted nothing more to do with me. I did not want to expose that hardened, uncaring Mal I had experienced to Mum and Cordy. It was a decision I had made that was best for all concerned. I had basically decided to lie by omission, all the while knowing that the longer I avoided admitting everything, the more hurt it would cause them.

I have hurt the people who care about me most by trying to protect them.

'And his father?' the consultant asks. 'Has he suffered any sort of haemorrhaging?'

'About ten years ago he had a brain scan,' I reply. 'They found nothing.'

Aunt Mer probably knows the answer to that, however I don't dare look at her, which would implicate her in this. And I don't want my parents and Cordy to feel any more betrayed, which the knowledge that Aunt Mer has always known would do.

'He's fine,' Aunt Mer says. 'He had another scan last year, when he started to have headaches and blurry vision, but they found nothing.'

Another almost inaudible gasp from Mum, physical shock from Dad and Cordy. I hate what

323

this is doing to them. I never wanted any of them to find out like this.

The consultant, one I don't know, one I probably won't see again, makes a note on his clipboard with his expensive-looking black pen. He is writing down this new piece of medical information, and probably adding: 'Fucked up family, half of them don't even know who the child's father is. Mother clearly has been telling porkies.'

The doctor's sandy hair lays lightly on his forehead and I notice how young he is. I never realised that certain things, such as the age of the doctor whose hands in which the life of my son rests, would be important. He isn't seventeen, but nor is he that much older than me. Shouldn't he have lived a bit more to be able to diagnose things? Shouldn't he have seen more of life to be able to stand there and talk to me about things going wrong?

Which is, of course, what he is doing.

He began this conversation by taking me away from Leo. If he was going to tell me Leo was going to wake up soon, he would have told me in front of Leo, knowing that the knowledge would help the little boy. Would somehow filter through and let him know exactly what he is meant to be doing. Taking me away means what he has to say is for adult ears only.

It was like that when I brought him in with the nosebleed. They had stopped it, but then had taken me into the relatives' room to tell me that they needed to send him for an emergency MRI scan, because I'd noted down there was a history of haemorrhaging in the family and that Leo had mentioned he had headaches and blurry vision every so often. Then they'd said what they found on the scan, that they needed to go in and operate because one of the blueberry aneurysms was so close to rupture. Every time they told me these things it had been away from Leo, information they felt he didn't need to hear.

So I had known when the consultant, who is a stranger to me, asked to speak to me—to us—in here, that he wasn't going to deliver the news that I wanted. The news that I needed.

With his head still bowed, only the doctor's eyes move away from his clipboard and seek out mine across the room. His eyes are a deep, dark blue that house an old soul. He is young, but he has lived. Maybe seeing lives hanging in the balance day after day does that to you; maybe you age on the inside and only those who look close enough can see it.

'Mrs Kumalisi,' he says, straightening up and looking me in the eye.

'Yes?' Mum, Cordy and I all reply.

'*Doctor* Kumalisi,' the doctor tries again, after looking pointedly at Mum and Cordy, asking them silently, *Why on earth would I be talking to either of you?*

'Mr Consultant,' I reply, a small corner of my mind agreeing with him—whose son is in this hospital?

'We've been monitoring your son's condition for the past four weeks.'

'Yes.'

'He hasn't shown much improvement.'

' "Much" means none at all, doesn't it?' I reply.

I feel Mum, Dad and Aunt Mer stiffen: young

he may be, but he is still a doctor, and speaking to him as I would anyone else is not something of which they approve.

A little spark of respect ignites in the doctor's eyes. I suppose most parents would be hanging on to his every word, hoping he will tell them what they want to hear, all the while knowing that they probably won't get what they're longing for. I am clinging to hope, too. But I have also seen their repeated and failed attempts to revive him, I have seen the doctors' faces, I know he isn't improving.

'The current course of treatment doesn't seem to be as effective as we had hoped. Keeping him in the coma was not meant to be a long-term plan. However, attempts to bring him out of the coma have proved unsuccessful.'

He is recapping this, I realise, for my extended family, to make them understand that they haven't simply adopted a 'wait and see' approach; they *have* tried.

'Doctor . . .'

'Mr Consultant.'

His eyes hold mine, an intimate, unique type of understanding solidifying between us.

'Leo's condition is, in fact, deteriorating.'

Mum and Cordy both burst into quiet tears. Keith reaches over and curls his large hand protectively over mine. Dad moves to the corner of the room. Aunt Mer is the only person to react like me: to become completely immobile.

'There is no improvement, nor any constant stability,' the consultant continues. 'We're not sure how long it's going to take, but it seems, at the present, there is only one conclusion.'

Slowly, I get to my feet. The crying, the silence,

the attempt at comfort from my husband, is all too much. Stifling. Crushing down on my throat, into my lungs, into my arteries, into every blood vessel in my body.

Once, Leo dropped a rock on an earthworm because he wanted to see what would happen. He had called me out into the garden to show me the crushed beast. When I told him it was dead and that being dead meant it would never wake up and move again, Leo had stared at me in complete horror. 'I'm sorry, Mum,' he said, close to tears. 'I'm really sorry. Please don't let it be dead for ever. Please don't let it never wake up.' To calm him as much as I could, we'd had a funeral for it, with a matchbox for a coffin, and buried it at the end of the garden. Two years later Leo still visited the little grave to say sorry to the earthworm.

All I want is for Leo to be OK. It's only a little thing. In the grand scheme of things, wanting for a quiet, kind, beautiful little boy who hasn't ever hurt anyone to be OK doesn't seem too much to want.

There are millions of not very nice people out there. There are thousands and thousands of nasty people out there. There are hundreds of truly evil people out there. And they are OK. All of them are OK. But this boy, my boy, my Leo, isn't going to be. That's what this man is telling me. Someone who is sweet and kind and beautiful is not going to be OK.

Keith stands to come with me, I presume. 'I want to be alone with Leo,' I say to stop him.

He nods, sits down again.

The consultant has gone back to staring at his clipboard.

'You're wrong you know,' I say to him as I head towards the door. 'That's not going to happen. Not to my boy.'

CHAPTER THIRTY-EIGHT

When the door to Leo's hospital room opens I brace myself to tell whoever it is to leave. I want to be alone with my son, to talk to him, to sit with him, like it was for all those years when it was him and me.

The smell of fresh lilies and green Palmolive soap tells me that it is Aunt Mer. I relax a little, unable, like the rest of us, to be snippy with her. The only person who ever snipes or rages at her is Victoria, because she has her own unhealed pain and she never wants Aunt Mer to forget it. She actually wants Aunt Mer to relive and remember the hell she put them—Mal and her—through, as often as possible. Fair enough, I suppose. Despite all our best efforts to help her, Victoria clings to her hurt and thinks only Aunt Mer can ease it by feeling guilty every moment of every day for the rest of her life. No one can convince her otherwise.

The rest of us, Mal included, have always made allowances for Aunt Mer, would never be as harsh to her as we can be to each other, would never think of being offish or unpleasant. I wonder—for the first time—if she minds. We are constantly, unintentionally, treating her as though she is something fragile that the wrong word will break. Isn't that like what Victoria does? We don't mean it to hurt her, but it must in some way be a

328

reminder of her illness, make her feel singled out. It's never occurred to me before that she may mind.

'Everyone is pretty upset,' she says, coming to stand behind me.

'With what the doctor said or with what they found out?'

'Both,' Aunt Mer replies. 'Your mother and Cordy both haven't stopped crying. Your father's trying to comfort them, Keith has gone for a walk. I came here.'

'I'd rather be alone, to be honest, Aunt Mer,' I say, still staring at Leo. I am mapping his face, noting the way he has changed and stayed the same in the last month. His hair has grown back a little more, fine bristles covering the top of his head because they hadn't operated on him in two weeks. His nose seems a little bit wider so it looks even more like mine. His mouth hasn't changed. The creases in his eyelids haven't changed. The dark circles under his eyes, however, have deepened.

The doctor is wrong, of course. Leo is only sleeping. Look at him: his eyes are only closed because he is only sleeping. Like every night since he was born, he is only sleeping. Resting. Taking a time out. Healing. He will be back.

'I know you want to be alone,' she says. 'I just wanted to . . . You have to tell him.'

I don't have to ask who she means. Even though we have never properly, openly discussed it, always talking around it, knowing that any information, visits, and pictures I give her would be, at the very least, relayed or shown to Mal, we have never said to each other that he is Leo's father. The closest we have come to that was the time I asked her to stop giving me money and expensive presents for Leo. I knew Aunt Mer, like my parents, had very little—the odd two hundred quid she kept trying to slip me was obviously coming from Mal and I didn't want it. I might have needed it, but not wanted it. We had to struggle on because, as I had previously told Mal, if he wanted to give Leo money, he should put it into an account for when Leo was eighteen. I didn't want to accept cash from him that could be seen as condoning what he had done. Not even through his mother. That was the closest brush to that forbidden subject we had ever come. It was enough that she knew and to talk about it would be to further betray Mum, Dad and Cordy. If Aunt Mer and I never said it aloud, then we weren't technically lying to my family.

'There's nothing to tell anyone,' I say. 'He's going to be fine.' The hollowness of my words echoes around us, ringing loud and clear in my ears. She places her hand on my shoulder, just like Dad had done to Mum a few minutes earlier. Stillness and calm flow through me, from her to me. Peace. Calm. Aunt Mer has always had a raging soul; for as long as I can remember she has always been fighting the two sides of herself, I never knew that at her core she has this . . . this serenity. I never knew that she could be like the sea, could make me feel as lifted and tranquil as I did whenever I could sit and stare at the sea.

'He would like to know,' she says. 'He needs to know.'

'Mal hasn't needed anything from me in a million years,' I say.

'That is not true,' she replies. 'The pair of you were so close. I've never known two closer people.

330

Ask your parents or Cordelia, they will say the same thing.'

'Were. We *were* close. He hasn't wanted anything to do with me in eight years, why should he care now?'

'Of course he wanted something to do with you, he just couldn't.'

'Yes, I know, because I had his baby. So why would he care now?'

Aunt Mer doesn't say anything for a few moments, I sense she is wrestling with herself about something. Whether to say it or to keep it to herself. 'I saw Stephanie last week,' she says.

Every nerve in my body leaps up in protest. Her name . . . It is like running one long, sharp fingernail down a blackboard, it is like scoring my back with a red-hot blade. Every time—*every* time—I hear that name, every nerve in my body leaps to attention; my muscles tense, my teeth grit against each other.

That woman robbed me. She robbed me of being pregnant. Of enjoying that time at the beginning of being pregnant. Touching my baby, wondering at it growing, knowing that the any-time-of-the-day sickness, swollen ankles, exhaustion, miscarriage terrors would be worth it because at the end of it I would have a baby. I had been so careful not to bond, not to get involved, not to think of him as my baby because I was going to give him to his 'real' parents, I had missed all those months. Even later on, a little part of me was still removed, still thinking that maybe Mal and her would change their minds. She had taken that from me. I knew it was her who had changed their minds. Mal shouldn't have gone along with her, but she had been behind it. I didn't need a psychic to tell me that.

And she had done it because she never wanted me around. Despite my best efforts, she had never changed the decision to get rid of me she made when she first met me. I can recall the moment vividly in my mind because I saw it happen: I said to her I would like us to try to be friends, and she, rather than answer, had glanced at Mal. That had unsettled me, had made a cold chill slip down my spine—as it did again the day she asked me to have a baby for them—but I had dismissed it as paranoia. As me being silly. What I didn't do, as I should have done, is protect myself from her. She wanted to fill all roles in Mal's life and she did not like my place as someone important to him. The only time she had started to like me was when I agreed to do something for her, and even then, I realised over the years, that was because she understood a part of me better than Mal did. She knew that I would not be able to stay around too long after the baby was born, that I would disappear for a long while afterwards and I probably wouldn't be as close to them because of the baby. When she asked me to have a baby for them it was the perfect way to get the perfect life she wanted—Mal and a baby, with me gone. I don't know what made her change her mind about the baby, but she got the result she wanted in the end: Mal finished with me.

The irony, of course, was that the depth of her dislike for me was matched by the depth of my like for her. I couldn't help myself. Not only because she made Mal happy, like Jack made Cordy happy, but because underneath the disguises and masks, I knew there lay a good person. A person with a good heart and a troubled, but beautiful soul. Now, of course, I did not feel that way about her. After she had robbed me of being pregnant, taken my closest friend, almost forced me to have an abortion and manoeuvred me into lying by omission to my family for so long, I have nothing but dislike for her.

Sometimes, I think I hate her.

I certainly cannot talk about her, or hear about her.

Aunt Mer's hand curls into my shoulder, her thumb stroking along its brow, trying to get the knots of tension that name has caused to untie themselves. 'She . . . she told me everything. What you agreed to do for them. What they did to you.'

She didn't tell Aunt Mer everything. How could she? She didn't tell Aunt Mer that I had begged Mal, that I had lost all self-respect and had been so scared that I had begged him not to do what he did. She didn't tell Aunt Mer that I had almost gone through with the abortion. I didn't feel the baby move and then change my mind about a termination. I actually went to the clinic, changed into the gown, and was about to undergo sedation when I asked them to stop. She didn't tell Aunt Mer that sometimes—for months after Leo was born—I was slightly distanced from him because I had brainwashed myself so well into believing that he was their son. She didn't tell Aunt Mer that sometimes I would take Leo down to the seafront in the middle of the night and, with him asleep in the pram, I would sit and cry over how my life was such a mess because I had tried to do something I thought was right for someone I loved and I was

333

scared of being alone and I missed Mal so much I felt physical pain. She didn't tell Aunt Mer about the cavern that had opened up inside me when I realised that for someone I loved to be able to do something like Mal had done to me, love was not the be all and end all. That at that moment of realisation I stopped believing in love for a long time. Even when I got back together with Keith I was waiting for him to prove he didn't love me.

If she didn't tell Aunt Mer any or all of that, then she hadn't told her 'everything'. She had, in fact, told Aunt Mer virtually nothing.

'She hates herself for what she did,' Aunt Mer says. 'When I showed her pictures of Leo she started to cry.'

I don't like the idea that she has shown my little boy to *her*. Those are pictures I gave to Aunt Mer because of who she is. They are private pieces of our family, not to be shown to just anyone. And *she* is just anyone.

'To be honest, Aunt Mer, those two are the last things on my mind,' I say, to be diplomatic. I want to say that talking about them, not being able to reveal how I truly feel because of who they are to Aunt Mer, is painful.

I feel her inhale deeply, she is upset. I can understand that she is only doing what she feels is best for her son; I would be the same if it was Leo. 'You can tell Mal if you want,' I say to appease her.

'I couldn't do that, dear,' she says. 'He needs to hear it from you. And you need to see his reaction.'

'Why?'

'Because you need to see, when you tell him, how much he still loves you, and how much he loves that little boy.' She pauses. 'And, so does

334

Malvolio.'

He did have to have an operation!

Mum said it was nothing to do with his nose and it was in his brain. So cool. And he'd have to go to sleep for a while. And, right now, it was really really late, and he didn't have to go to bed. This really was the best day ever.

'Can I have ice cream and jelly when I wake up?' he asked Mum.

'Of course,' she said.

This was better than silly old ton-seels. It was in his brain! The nurse was coming in a minute to shave his head and everything. Dad was coming home from work so he could see Leo before he went to sleep.

'I'll be right there, watching you the whole time,' Mum said. She hadn't started crying, which is why he knew it wasn't serious. Mum only cried when it was serious. Or when she was cross with him. He never did understand that. Why would she cry when she was telling him off? But now, she wasn't crying, so he wasn't scared.

Leo, age 7 years and 5 months

CHAPTER THIRTY-NINE

The door of number 11 Pebble Street has not changed in over two hours.

I know, because I have been watching it. Mr and Mrs Wacken are in, but they do not know that I have been sitting in my car, observing them. Waiting for the moment that I will cross the road to go and see him.

The last time I spoke to Mal was about five years ago. Yeah, five years ago, six months after Cordy's wedding. I came to London on the train and talked my way into his office by saying I was Cordelia. I briefly flattered myself by thinking that he lit up when he saw me step into his office, but anything he did feel he hid straight away behind a mask of caution. Obviously fearing I'd break down or beg him again.

'I was wondering why Cordy would come to see me,' he said, standing up. 'Have a seat.'

On the low filing cabinet behind him and below the large, blind-covered window stood a host of pictures: his wife smiling radiantly at their wedding; Victoria and her husband on their wedding day; Cordy and Jack on their wedding day; Aunt Mer, Mum, Dad and Cordy in front of a heavily decorated Christmas tree in my parents' house. No pictures of him, no pictures of me and, of course, no pictures of Leo.

'Please stop giving me money,' I said gently, as I perched on the seat at the opposite side of the desk. I had come to see him because the week after Cordy's wedding, every month money had started to appear in my account. Whenever I returned the money it—and the next payment—would reappear on my bank statements. I wanted to see him face to face to tell him to stop; I wanted him to look me in the eye and know that I was serious.

'It's for—' He stopped, unable to say the little boy's name. Instead he stared at the mesh pot of pens sitting on the far left-hand corner of his desk.

'If you want to contribute to *Leo's* upbringing, set up an account for him to access when he's eighteen, buy him premium bonds, bury it somewhere and send him a treasure map for all I care, just stop giving it to me.'

'You could set it aside for him,' Mal said to the pen holder.

My eyes strayed again to the photograph gallery behind him, wondering how easy it had been for him to remove me from his life. I assumed that at some point I might have been there, with the rest of our family, but now I was gone. Erased, and easily forgotten?

The silence forced him to look at me, to check I was still there.

'Please stop giving me money,' I said, my tone as gentle as before. 'I don't want to be financially tied to you, I don't want Leo to be financially tied to you until he's old enough to make that decision for himself.' I softened my voice even more. 'It's what you said you wanted, so please don't mess us around.'

'OK,' he said.

'Thank you.'

Our gazes met, and stayed fixed together longer than was necessary. All sorts of memories of our life growing up blossomed in my mind. Mainly of us laughing. Clutching our stomachs and laughing, holding on to each other and laughing. That was what we had lost, not just each other, laughter. I'd never laughed with another person like I did with him. Leo made me laugh with the crazy things he did, I made him laugh, but we had yet to get to the point where just looking at each other could reignite an old joke and have us incapacitated with giggles in seconds.

I couldn't help but smile as I remembered Mum regularly telling us off for laughing too loud and too long, late into the night, and keeping everyone awake. Then Dad marching into our rooms—we were often talking and laughing through the walls—and saying we should go to sleep 'or else'. The sides of my body contracted as I was tempted to start laughing, and his shoulders started to shake. Suddenly, his face telling me he didn't want to see me again erupted in my mind, punching me squarely in the chest and removing my breath. I glanced away from him.

I stood up without looking directly at him again. 'Thanks for understanding,' I said, my voice tight and small.

'Do . . . do you have any pictures of him?' Mal asked as I reached the door. 'Not to keep or anything, just to see.' God knows at that point I could barely keep my purse in my bag for showing people pictures of Leo, but I didn't want to show him. I shook my head, and left without explaining that I wasn't angry, I wasn't punishing him, I was actually protecting him. He didn't need to torture himself by seeing how much Leo had changed in the six months since he'd seen him at Cordy's wedding. He had decided he wouldn't be seeing Leo again, and, difficult as it may be, he needed to stick to that.

'*OK, get out of the car now, Nova*,' I tell myself in the present.

'*No*,' the little rebellious voice in my head replies. '*Don't wanna. Wanna go home.*'

I am here because Aunt Mer is right. After saying her piece, she went back to the rest of our family, saying she was going to tell them everything so they would understand why I kept it from them, and I took a step outside of myself and the situation. I owed him nothing, I'd decided.

When he had walked away from me, he had said—he had showed me—that he wanted nothing to do with me. That anything that happened to me and the child I was carrying was nothing to do with him. He had no need to know anything now, because he didn't want to know anything. End of story.

Then I stepped back into the situation again: Mal cared about Leo. The fact he wanted to give him money said something. And, after Leo was born and I was going to register the birth, I sent Mal a text with the details of the registry office and what time I would be there. Unsurprisingly, he turned up. We didn't speak to each other, not even to say hello, we sat side by side and went through the process of giving our names to our son, and then parted without saying goodbye. The whole time we were there, I noticed the way his gaze kept straying to Leo, lying swaddled in his pram. I noticed the way his fingers twitched as though they wanted to gently trace the lines of his son's face. I could tell he wanted to reach into the pram and pick up his baby. Mal also thought that I didn't see him climb into his car, immediately flip down the sun visor to reveal the mirror, so he could examine each and every line of his face, checking for where the similarities and differences were between him and the child he'd just given his name to.

I knew he would have been frozen after that. That he would have sat in his car, staring into space, probably wondering whether he'd made the right choice. Mal had made some sort of pact with his wife to remove me and his son from their lives, but that didn't mean he didn't want to be involved in some way.

Aunt Mer was right, I had to tell him. He would want to see Leo right now. It wasn't about what I felt, it was about what was right. I have left Mum, Cordy, Aunt Mer and Dad taking it in turns to sit with Leo today.

They have all been reserved with me for the past two days, staring at me as though they are unsure what to feel now they know everything. Even Cordy, who would normally have asked me a million questions, has held her tongue. They want to know if I would really have given away my baby, *their* baby. Because Leo isn't only mine, he is my family's, too. He would still have been a part of our family, but not. With all the unasked questions and looks still prickling along my skin, I had set off for London. After a half-hour stop at a service station where I had to convince myself not to turn around and go home, I had arrived late afternoon.

I've been sitting here ever since. His wife returned first, rushed into the house—earlier than I would have thought, unless she no longer works in the clothes boutique. She practically ran through the door, her hair swinging, a bounce in her step. Ten minutes later he arrived. Involuntarily, my breath caught when I saw him. I hadn't seen him in three years. Not since I was coming to visit Mum and Dad with Leo and saw him getting out of his car to go into Aunt Mer's house and I had to keep driving. I didn't want to risk Mum and Dad ringing Aunt Mer and dragging the pair of them over. Leo had questioned me all the way back home about what had happened and I had to say I thought I'd left the oven on. He'd rung Mum and Dad the second we got in to tell them what I had done, with a very definite 'Mum's going mad' tone to his voice.

My pulse was still speeding long after I watched him walk into his house.

I have sat here for hours trying to get up the courage to do this. I couldn't have done it on the phone. It couldn't be this disembodied, disconnected voice telling him what the doctor had said.

I have been watching. I have been waiting.

This is a nice area, it is a wonder no one has reported me and my car to the police. Maybe they have and, even as I sit here, police officers are watching me, waiting for me to make a move, to drop a bit of litter on their pristine pavement so they can bang me up for life.

I've always been impressed that they can afford to live on such a nice road. But that was his wife's doing. She'd gone out every day for six months, pounding the streets, sometimes sitting outside estate agents' doors until they opened so she'd get the details of new properties first. This was in the days before the internet was so widely used, so it was necessary. She wanted to live in this area so much that she'd done that. She'd done whatever it would take to get what she wanted.

And now I am sitting outside in my purple Micra, gripping the cream leather steering wheel and staring at the house. Waiting for my nerve to catch up.

The front door opens and Mal's wife comes out of the house, hair tied back in a ponytail, wearing a

341

stylish black tracksuit with white piping and silver trainers. Under one arm she carries a blue yoga mat.

I watch her click open her sleek, silver car with the push of a button, and I slide down in my seat as she gets in, because she is effectively coming down to my height. If she looks diagonally across the road now she'll look straight into my car. She will see me. I suspect one of us will turn to stone if that happens.

The last time we saw each other was on the tube. The Victoria line between Pimlico and Oxford Circus. I'd been six months pregnant, really quite large, and travelling to see a financial adviser in town. She and I had stared at each other for a few seconds, two intimate strangers banged up together in a tin can. I suddenly thought that this was how a sardine would feel if it were caught with another sardine it didn't get on with—that horror of knowing for the foreseeable future you were stuck together. In the case of the sardine, you were going to spend the here and now, and then your afterlife with it. She'd dropped her gaze first and as I gathered my things, ready to exit the train and leave her be, I decided to never eat sardines again. And also to leave London. I was already near the end of selling my flat, so I would pull out of buying the place I had found and leave London. The idea of going through this again was too much. She beat me to it. She got up, went to the door and was first off the carriage.

She starts her car, and I finally let go of the steering wheel so I can slide completely out of sight while she drives away.

My fingers work independently of my brain, of

the urge to go home, and open the car door. My legs take over, propel me out of my car of their own accord. Then my hands take over again, lock the car door with the press of a button. And then back to my legs, walking across the road, and moving towards the front door. I can almost hear the swish of net curtains and the gentle clank of blinds being moved aside, the curiosity of a dozen or so people with nothing better to do watching me approach the black door.

Once there, my hands take over. Reach up towards the bell, then make a fist to knock, then reach for the brass knocker. My hand cannot do any of the things that will let him know I am here.

I can't do it. I'm not ready. Because when I knock, I have to repeat what the doctor said. Those words have to leave my mouth and become real. You can repeat a lie, an inaccuracy, a million times—or even once—and it can start to feel like the truth. The inevitable. As soon as I say it, I will be telling the world some small part of me believes it. The part of me that makes words, the part that communicates with the outside world will say I know it is a possibility. And then it will spread like a disease throughout my mind, my heart, my soul. And if I'm not using every part of me to will him better, how can he get better? By coming here, I have given in. I haven't acted out what I believe, what I know. I have betrayed Leo. I have betrayed myself.

I should not have come here.

I should not have given those doubts, those things the doctor was trying to tell me, the chance to infect me. I should not have come here.

My body turns away, ready to go back home,

343

back to that limbo we have been living in.

'Hello?' His voice moves through me like ripples on the surface of water. I stop on the path.

I cannot turn around but I cannot move away.

'Can I help you?' he asks.

Mal and Leo, the connection between the two of them unspools like a reel of ribbon before my eyes: Mal pressing his lips on my pregnant stomach; Mal's eyes straying to him in the registry office; Mal staring at him across the hall at Cordy's wedding; Leo showing me a picture of a young Mal, asking me why Mal looks like him; Uncle Victor holding Leo's hand, taking him away because, 'I'm ready to go, Mum.'

That's why I have come here. For him. For Leo.

'Nova?' Mal asks.

I may have all but convinced myself that it was for Mal, because it is the right thing to do, but that isn't the real, underlying reason I am here. I have come for Leo. Because he has too dads. One is a spy and livs at his huse. The uver one isnt ded.

The uver one is standing behind me and Leo deserves the chance to get to know him. No matter how briefly.

I turn to face him.

He is going on a trip. In one hand he has a pink suitcase, and over his shoulder is a large, black, many-pocketed holdall. In his other hand is a pink beauty case that matches the suitcase. His face breaks into a smile, one fringed with disbelief and happiness and surprise.

A silent beat passes and he sees it in my face. The beauty case slips from his grasp first, and clatters loudly on the black and white diamond-tiled path. The suitcase doesn't make as much

344

noise.

'Is it Mum?' he asks, his eyes full of sudden, naked terror.

I shake my head. 'Leo,' I hear a voice that could be mine say.

Mal takes a step back, as if he can escape from this back the way he came. His wary face continues to watch me and I continue to speak without being aware that I am using my lips, my throat, my words. 'Leo is in a coma. The doctors . . . I want you to see him. He needs to know who you are before it's too late.'

Dad looked like Dad when he came to see him before he went to sleep. He brought him the new Star Wars *game. It had only just come out in the shops and Dad had said he could only get it if Mum said it was OK. But now, he had it. This really was the best day ever. 'Bye, Dad, see you later,' Leo said as they began to move his bed towards the door. He didn't even have to walk to the room where they'd operate.*

Dad kissed his forehead. 'You're a brave boy,' he said. 'I'll see you later.'

Dad had been in the Army so if he thought Leo was brave then he must be.

Mum walked beside his bed, holding his hand and smiling at him. It wasn't her big, big smile, but it was the one she only gave to him. She didn't smile at Dad, or Grandpa, or Grandma or Nana Mer, or Aunt Cordy or Amy or Randle or Ria like that. Not ever. It was his special smile.

At the doorway to the room where they were going to operate, they stopped.

'I'll be right here, waiting for you,' Mum said, bending over him. 'I'll make sure they've got your jelly and ice cream waiting for when you wake up, OK?'

'OK.'

She kissed his forehead, she kissed his right cheek, she kissed his left cheek. She stroked her hand over his face. Still smiling her special smile.

'Goodnight, beautiful,' she said.

Leo, age 7 years and 5 months

CHAPTER FORTY

There's still time for him to make it. If he comes running through this airport right now and throws his baggage at the check-in woman and she checks him in in record time and we run to Gate 15, we'll make it.

But he has to arrive now. Right *now*.

I turn on the spot, scanning the crowd, the holidaymakers, the business travellers, the cleaners, the people dropping people off, those waiting for others to show up. They all have a purpose, they all know where they should be. They all know where they're going.

They aren't like me, stranded by a no-show husband.

I hit the redial button on my mobile, and it clicks straight to voicemail. He always turns his phone off when he's driving. Or maybe he's on the tube. So he must be on his way.

He was going to get the train here. I drove here after yoga and parked in a long-term car park so we could drive home when we got back from holiday. Thinking about it, I should have taken the bags, but for some reason it seemed more logical for Mal to take them. And now neither he nor they are here.

I hit the redial button again.

Voicemail.

'Mal, I have no idea where you are, but you had better have a damn good reason why you're not here right now. In fact, that reason had better end with "And so I'm lying in a hospital bed, bleeding", otherwise I am finding new uses for your balls.'

Knowing him, he received a call from work—heaven knows the thought of him not being there for five days plus two weekend days had been enough to send a few people at his office into a tailspin. And he probably tried to sort out whatever problem it was, which made him late for the airport.

I hit redial again.

Voicemail.

It's too late now.

Gate 15 is closed.

We're not going to get our holiday. Our fresh start, my chance to make amends, is currently waiting for take-off with neither of us on it.

'You bastard,' I say to his voicemail. 'You absolute sodding bastard.'

*   *   *

Eerie.

That's how the house feels when I get home. We were meant to be away so everything has that extra layer of clean, that extra formality of tidiness. All the appliances apart from the fridge-freezer are unplugged. In the centre of my body fear flowers. Our luggage isn't here.

There is no message on the answer machine.

I dial Meredith's number, but there is no answer. She never turns on her mobile despite the number of times Mal tells her to. Victoria wouldn't know anything.

I try Mal again. Voicemail.

I shouldn't have left those messages, I think as I sit on the brow of the third stair, my mobile in my hand.

I'm shaking. I have been since I walked in here and the coolness of a truly empty house swooped down upon me.

I have a very strong feeling that I am never going to see Mal again.

CHAPTER FORTY-ONE

He leans against the kitchen counter, his shirt tucked into his black pinstripe suit trousers, his top button open. The buttons on his shirt, I notice, are covered, and dice-shaped silver cufflinks hold his cuffs closed at the wrist. It's an expensive shirt. I do not know why this impresses itself upon my mind, but it does.

Silence slides between us like a sharp knife slicing into tender flesh, carving away even the hush of our unsynchronised breathing.

He is in my house. My home.

I inhale his presence. It is odd, so different from the way Mum, Dad, Cordy and Aunt Mer changed

348

the energy of the house when they first arrived. They were here to help, and that is what they filled the house with. Cordy has gone home because Jack was called away to cover a flight unexpectedly, and the others are now in a hotel.

Mal is here to get to know his son. He understood about not coming in when I stopped off at the hospital earlier, but now he is here and the energy in the house is slightly frantic. Forced. An unexpected sense of urgency surrounding us. We both want him to get on with it. Although we're not really sure how it will work, but the urgency hangs here. The need for him to go be there. *Start.*

His hands move first. His left hand reaching out, cupping my cheek, as the familiar-unfamiliar warmth of his skin spreads slowly through my body. And his body moves next, his other hand sliding around my shoulders, drawing us together, sewing up the long years that we have been apart by crossing the short distance between us.

Without thinking, my eyes slip shut and my body melts against his. Easy. Simple. My arms move around him and draw him close, trying to seal up all the tiny spaces that still gape between us.

It's still there, that unique place in the world where we fit together. If we do not think about everything else, everyone else, we fit here, so close we could be one.

I step away first. Push him back slightly and step out of reach. This isn't what we do any more. I may sometimes hate his wife, but I'll always be more hurt by what he did. Because he did it. He could do it. I can never forget that.

'The spare room is all made up, but I'll go find you some clean towels,' I say, avoiding eye contact.

His right hand goes up to finger the spot behind his ear. Leo did that. *Does* that. Rubs hard at the lump behind his ear, then runs his forefinger slowly over it. Usually he does that when he is trying to get something—a go on the PlayStation when he knows he is not technically allowed to play on it; the chance to climb into bed with Keith and me on a Sunday morning; a trip to the park even though it's raining outside.

'I'd better, erm, call Stephanie,' he says, 'she will have been waiting at the airport.'

I hate her name being said in my house. It is an irrational thing to be upset about, but I hate it all the same. It puts her here, makes her real in my life. 'Yeah, sure,' I say, the words choking in my throat.

I'm at the door, just moving through the doorway, when he speaks again, low and even. 'How long should I say I'm staying?'

I do not turn around. What he is asking is how long I think Leo has left. When I think our son will be leaving.

'However long you want to,' I say, before I walk on, when I should have said, 'However long it takes.'

CHAPTER FORTY-TWO

All my good make-up, my limited edition perfume, my best outfit and my most expensive underwear (the stuff that you pay more for the less there is of it), Mal has it all.

Fifty miles away in Brighton. And he doesn't

know when he is bringing it back. My plan to re-seduce my husband, to 'become a creature like no other'—I read that somewhere, I can't remember where—has spectacularly backfired.

'But what will I wear?' I ask him, cringing at the whine in my voice.

'The curtains from the spare room for all I care,' he replies. I don't blame him. I am being a brat because it is easier than saying to him I want to be there. That I am terrified of what will happen to Leo and I want to be there to help as much as I can. He'd have to tell me no, and I cannot stand to hear that.

'Are you sure you can't just drop my stuff home and then go back?' Ask any red-blooded man, behaving badly is so much easier than admitting you're vulnerable and afraid of something. Behaving badly or having sex.

'Do you want me to hang up on you?'

'No.' I sigh. 'So, will you be staying at Nova's the whole time you're there?' I actually want to ask how Nova is. How she is coping. But it would sound disingenuous. Mal doesn't know that after she was gone from our lives I regretted more than anything what I had done. When he was crying all the time over losing her as his friend I began to see the pair of them clearly. Yes, they probably had been in love, but Mal needed Nova in a way he would never need me. She was his foundation, the underpinning of who he was; like scaffolding erected around a building under renovation, she kept him up, she kept him going.

Because of her, he had the strength to be who he was to me. I wasn't as jealous about that as I thought I would be because that part of it wasn't about the love I was scared of, that was about habit.

In the months following what I made him do, I began to see that. I can look back now and see why she had been so important to him when we first met. Why he talked about her all the time. He needed her to listen to him. No one, I realised, listened to him like she did. I couldn't, I hadn't been there in the past. When his mother wasn't capable of listening to him, when his father wasn't there to listen to him, when his sister wasn't old enough to listen to him, when there were no real friends to listen to him, Nova always was. She praised, she congratulated, she sympathised, she disapproved, she told him off, she simply listened.

Many people don't realise how important it is to be heard. I heard him, I listened to him, but I wasn't a habit. Without Nova, he began to curl into himself, like the blossoming process in reverse. All the petals, the parts of him I knew, began to shrink away from me—almost as if he didn't have the confidence any longer to be himself. It wasn't simply that he was angry with me, he was, but it was that he had lost his footing, lost all semblance of who he thought he was, and was spending all his time holding himself together.

That was why he cried all the time, that was why he didn't intentionally touch me for more than a year after she was gone from our lives. He had lost himself when he lost her.

She needs him now, and I want him to be able to be there for her without thinking that I might have a problem with it. But I cannot say that. I am not able to say that to him.

'I'll be finding a hotel tomorrow,' he says tartly.

352

'Is that all right with you?'

'I was just asking,' I reply.

'Look, I'm going to go. I don't know why you're being like this but it's doing my head in. I'll talk to you tomorrow or something. Hopefully we'll both be in a better frame of mind.'

'Hopefully,' I echo. 'I love you.'

'Hmm-hmm,' he replies and hangs up.

The house is so empty.

It's too late to go to the gym. It's too late to call anyone to ask them over or to meet me for a drink. It's too late to call Mal back and tell him I'm sorry, and that I'm coming to support him.

I sit on the stairs looking around at my hall, realising that it is far too late to tell the truth and to make it all better.

CHAPTER FORTY-THREE

'I knew I'd find you here,' Mal says over the storming waves.

I thought he had gone to sleep hours ago. After I had shown him to the room Cordy and I had shared a few days ago, I couldn't sleep.

Couldn't rest.

Mal was in my house, which made everything seem final, as though Leo's health, whether he would wake up, was hurtling towards one awful, inevitable conclusion.

While I'd laid in bed, staring at the ceiling, waiting for Keith's next text, I had started to wonder if Mal being here would have a miraculous effect. Would bring Leo round. Or if this, what was

353

happening with Leo, was part of some big grand plan to bring Mal and me back together. To reunite us.

At which point I, the great believer in destiny and all that is out there, had known that I was going crazy and had thrown aside the covers and climbed out of bed. I could walk off the crazy thoughts on the seafront, I'd decided. I didn't walk far, just ended up sitting on the dark green iron bench, remembering the times I would sit here in the dead of night with my newborn baby and cry.

It is spectacular here at night. In the dark, in the stillness, when all there is around is a night sky and tiny, blinking pinpricks of stars. It's not like looking out of the window or at a picture—stand here and it's like standing on the edge of the world and feeling it carefully wrap itself around you to stop you falling off. It folds itself in front, above, behind, scooping you up to become part of its hugeness. I came here because I could become lost in the vastness of everything. There is no room for crazy thoughts.

'Why did you think you'd find me here?' I ask him as he lowers himself on to the bench beside me.

'I heard the door go and I saw your car was still there, so I guessed you'd head for the beach.'

'I had a sudden urge to see that sign.' I nod towards the keep off the groynes sign that sits on dark green railings (the colour of the railings revealed if you were in Brighton or Hove: aqua blue-green for Brighton; dark green for Hove). 'It described my love life for so, so long and I needed reminding of it.'

I am not looking at him, but I feel the energy

354

around him warm up as Mal smiles.

'How you doing?' he asks gently.

People are going to ask me that a lot in the coming weeks. And what am I supposed to say? A half truth like 'Bearing up', which will make them feel better? Something closer to the truth such as 'Falling apart', which will make them try to make me feel better? Or nothing at all, allow them to make up their minds for themselves and leave me to feel what I feel without having to factor them into the equation. 'How do you think?' I ask him.

'Stupid question.'

'Yes, it was.'

The waves fill the quiet between us, crashing almost violently against the pebbles and then racing away again.

'I'm sorry,' he says.

I'm sorry.

I'm sorry.

I'm sorry.

It is carried over the waves, filtering out into the majestic expanse of the sky. *I'm sorry*.

'Is that it?' I ask once the words have dissolved in the air around us. I spin slightly to look at him. 'Truly, is that it? No big emotional confession, no heartfelt plea for forgiveness dressed up as an explanation?' I shrug despairingly at him. 'Maybe a spot of self-flagellation at my feet? Don't I at least deserve a few tears and globules of snot as you sobbingly say that?'

Naturally, he doesn't respond, and I spin back on my bum to look at the sea. It's a much better view. Better, uncomplicated. 'You know, anything less than something you've put your back into is, quite frankly, an insult.'

'God, Nova, if you knew how sorry I was—'

'I would, what? Forgive you? Feel bad for you? Just so you know, in case there is any lingering doubt, you are not the be all and end all of my life. Especially right now.'

Mal's demeanour beside me relaxes suddenly. 'I just replayed what I said,' he says, 'and now I can hear what a wanker I sounded like. *Sound* like. I abandoned you, I abandoned our son and now I think two words are going to change everything. Make it better.'

'I suppose it's a start,' I reply.

'No, it's not. It's pathetic.'

My eyes slip shut and I squeeze them tightly together as I massage my temples. 'I said self-flagellation, not self-pity. Christ, Mal, do we have to do this now? Couldn't it wait until some other critical moment when we should be talking about something deep and meaningful and then it all comes out how sorry you are, how I've never managed to hate you properly, how our friendship forged so long ago in pain and joy is unbreakable, so I have, in my heart, already forgiven you? Can't we just wait for all that to come up at the appropriate moment in the script rather than forcing it now?'

I feel his face soften in a wry smile. 'I forget that you're a psychologist and you don't fall for the things people say as easily as they think you do.'

'It's not from being a psychologist, it's from knowing bullshit when I hear it.' I inhale, the salt in the sharp, cold air shoots through me, quick and delicious, tinglingly painful.

'I think about you every day,' he reveals. 'And I think about him. Leo.' That's the first time I have heard Mal say his son's name. It sounds strange, unnatural somehow, because it's the last part of his own name and he rarely says that. 'Some days it gets so bad I want to jump in my car—even in the middle of the working day—and come down here and see you. Sometimes to watch you, sometimes to throw myself on your mercy.'

He is telling me that he didn't live happily ever after having erased me as much as possible from his life. I—we—were there somewhere, niggling away at the back of his conscience. That sort of thing can weigh heavily on a person's happiness. Their life.

'Nova, if at any point in my life up until eight years ago someone had told me that you and I wouldn't talk every single day and we'd have a son that I never see, I'd have told them they were insane. How could we not—'

'Don't say it like I had any choice in the matter. That you didn't make a decision that I was forced into accepting.'

'OK, how could I ever do that—'

'Tell me why,' I interrupt as I turn to him. 'Tell me why you did it. Because all this chat about thinking about me every day means nothing really. Tell me why.'

'I told you, we changed our minds.'

'That's an excuse you came up with,' I say. 'I need to know the *reason*. I have never known the reason and I need to know.'

His defences come up in an instant: he sits up straighter, his body, once fluid, now rigid and poised to deflect an attack; his eyes as hard as brown diamonds, his face an unreadable mask.

Shaking my head, I glance away. 'Until you can

357

tell me why, the real reason, Malvolio, we have nothing to talk about on this matter.'

He is as still as the Sphinx, and as inscrutable, too. I did not come here for this. I came to escape the crazy thoughts, to ground myself in the motion of the sea and magnitude of the world. I did not come to not understand Mal all over again.

'This is where I first kissed my husband,' I say. 'The last time we got back together, we had our first kiss here, down on the beach.' I stand.

The railings by the steps leading down to the pebble beach are cold under my hand as I move down the uneven, slick concrete steps. I hear Mal follow me, his footsteps crunching loudly over the dewy pebbles, following me to the water's edge. 'Amy was babysitting and because he said we were going for a wild night on the town, she was going to stay over. We went for tapas down in the Laines— it's the best tapas in Brighton, you should go there one day. Then we went to the Pier.' I grin as I am swept along in the memory and it unfolds in my mind like images on a cinema screen. All the colours were bright and wonderful, our soundtrack was laughter and familiarity. 'Turns out dancing was on a dance machine. He fed coins into the machine and then challenged me to do it. I love dancing but it was so hard and I could hardly keep up. We were suddenly surrounded by a group of teenage girls, arms folded, all resting on one hip, like they do. With that look they get on their faces. That one that says, "What are you doing, old woman, why aren't you hiding your face in shame, what with you being so *old*?" I kept at it until the machine ran out of money.

'I virtually fell off the platform, completely out

358

of breath and all sweaty, and those teenage girls pounced on it. And, my God, they hammered that machine. Jumping and twisting and making a total show of me. They'd clearly been practising and had all the routines worked out. I slunk away in shame. "It's OK," Keith said as we left, "you obviously just dance to the beat of your own drum. It's not that you're past it at all."' I narrow my eyes, like I did then. 'I gave him a dead arm, cheeky bastard. We walked back to mine along the seafront, until we got to here. This spot. And he tried to point out Orion's Belt and Cassiopeia. He didn't have a clue, and obviously didn't think me having a name like Nova might mean I have a knowledge of the heavens. When I was doing my duty and putting him right, he kissed me. To shut me up.' I drift back to that moment. How wonderful it had felt. Being back in his arms. Being kissed by someone I liked, after all that time. 'I knew that this was it. I was finally ready to get married, like he'd always wanted, and we'd raise Leo.

'Six months later we had a small service—despite our long, drawn-out battle because he wanted to wear his Army uniform—and he sold his place in Shoreham and moved in with us. And we just got on with it. Our lives weren't remarkable or overly exciting, but that was what I wanted. We had a normal, happy life.'

I turn to Mal, he is listening intently to what I am saying, although what he is thinking is a mystery. 'It's all gone. My life is all gone and I can't work out why. I keep looking back over my life, even way back to before Leo was born, and I can't work out where it all went so wrong. What I did to make this happen.'

'You didn't do anything,' Mal says with quiet certainty.

'Then why is this happening?' I ask. 'Why do I have to spend every moment wishing and hoping and wanting Leo to wake up and be OK? Why do I know if I don't spend every second doing that—'

'It'll be in that moment, that one tiny moment when you're not using every part of your soul wanting it to be OK, that it goes even more wrong. That something already awful becomes unbearable. It's in that moment that the world will collapse.'

'Your mum?'

He is agonised all of a sudden as he nods.

I used to think I knew how Mal felt about Aunt Mer, that I felt it, too. All those years of being around her, living with her problems, her highs and lows, made me think I was right there with Mal. That his pain was my pain. But I only shared a fraction of it, the most minuscule amount of it. I could leave it behind for a while, could go to sleep at night not worrying about Aunt Mer, Mal couldn't. He had never been able to, he never could. She consumed his life.

Stephanie. Tall, blonde, blue-eyed Stephanie. An image of her is suddenly in my mind. So vivid, so clear, it is almost as though she is standing beside Mal. The feeling of her is so strong, I can smell her sweet, heady perfume, I can hear the clank of her bangles, I can feel the sharp edges of her aura. She is on the beach with us. The wind is blowing her hair across her face, tugging at her clothes.

Being with her consumes him like taking care of Aunt Mer consumes him. Maybe I didn't

360

understand what not being able to have a baby had done to her. How it had shaped her. Maybe I shouldn't sometimes hate her because maybe she isn't simply troubled, maybe she is damaged. Maybe she has been hurt and she needs looking after, like Aunt Mer does. And *maybe* I should stop being so understanding. She went out of her way to hurt me, she never liked me, she never tried to like me. Maybe all the times I have given her the benefit of the doubt should stop. They should always stop when someone sets out to deliberately harm you.

'She's been so much better recently,' Mal says, and for a moment I think he means his wife. But he doesn't, he means Aunt Mer. 'There hasn't been a major incident for years and years, but still, I cling on. Part of me believes that's because I've been—how did you put it?—wishing and hoping and wanting so hard. It's not simply the medication, the stability, the weekly trips to the psychiatrist; it's me using every second to will for her to be OK.'

'I know,' I reply. 'I know now, I mean. Except I'm not doing a very good job, am I? Leo's not . . .' I can't say it. I've said as much as I can to Mal, I can't do it again. I can't make it even more solid by repeating it. Because that would be saying I might one day have to live in a world without Leo.

Is there a world without Leo?

'Yes, there is,' Mal replies. I hadn't realised I'd spoken that aloud. 'But I don't know if it's one any of us will want to live in.'

Unbidden, the corners of my mouth turn downwards, the horror of that rips through me like a single, focused laser beam, cutting me in two. As the two sides of me start to fall apart, Mal is

361

suddenly around me, holding me close, holding me up. He cradles my face in his large, warm hands, as though I am something precious, made from fragile glass that will shatter under even the slightest pressure.

'But, that's the thing about all of this,' he says gently but urgently, 'we survive. After each knock down, each earth-shattering blow, we get up again. Even though we walk through hell, and we walk through hell, and we walk through hell, and it feels like all we do is walk through hell, we do eventually make it to the other side. Scarred. Mostly broken. But we survive. And then we start to rebuild ourselves. We're never the same, but we do rebuild ourselves. Because something like this is just another way in which we change. We all have to change.'

'I don't want to change. I don't want to walk through hell. I just want things to go back to how they were. I want him to be constantly asking his questions. I want him to wake me up and pester me to play on the computer. I want him to call me "Marm" like he's an American. I want him to tell me that I could be a better mummy but I'll do for now. I just want things back how they were. I don't need change. I don't need hell.'

'I know, I know,' he whispers the whole time I am talking.

'I want my Leo back. Whole. Perfect. Just like he was.'

Mal's eyes search mine, like I had been searching the dark horizon, desperately seeking something that would make everything all right, before he came here.

'Let me make love to you,' he says.

362

'*What?!*' I screech. His hands on my face aren't a gentle comfort any longer and I push him violently away.

'Let me take you to bed, let me make love to you,' he repeats.

'*Are you on drugs?!*'

'No—'

'I haven't let my husband touch me in God knows how long, why would I let you? You of all people. Is that why you came here? For sex? Because if it is, you can go straight back to London.'

'It wouldn't be sex,' he says quickly and earnestly.

'Oh, really? What would it be, the inevitable joining of two souls cruelly separated, or something equally unique and beautiful?'

'No, no, it's a way to forget. A coping mechanism. I used to do it all the time—especially when I was in Australia. If I started to worry about what was going on at home, I would . . . I'm not proud of myself, but it was a way to forget. For a while, you feel something else, and unlike exercise or drinking, for a while the pain is gone but you're not alone and you're still conscious. It's still there, it's still waiting for you on the other side, but for a while you forget how to hurt about that thing. I still do it, I'm not proud of that fact, either, but it's the truth. Sometimes doing that is the only thing that can stop the pain, even for a little while. Let me do that for you.'

I search his face, his eyes, explore his energy, and all I can feel is truth, sincerity. He means it. He is offering me the only thing he can to try to help. He wants to take my pain away in the only

363

way he knows how.

For a moment I waver. I want this to stop. I desperately want this agony and fear and the waiting to stop. I want respite, freedom from what has become my life: hospitals, medical journals, eyes wondering who I am. Being offered a few minutes of normality is tempting, like being offered thick-soled shoes while you're walking on a path of broken glass. You'll accept almost anything to stop the pain.

Are you crazy? I ask myself, shaking my mind like I would shake my shoulders if I could. 'Thank you, no,' I say. 'No. All this is awful, but it's the hand I've been dealt and I'm still playing it. Doing *that* will mean that I know everything is over. And it's not. It's far from over. Besides, Keith and I would do that for each other.'

'I'm sorry, it was a stupid thing to offer,' he says, 'but I couldn't think of anything else . . . I was being selfish, too, I suppose, because that's what I need right now. This is one of my worst nightmares. I'm going to lose someone I love even though I only know him from the things my mum has told me. How come I turned into my dad without even trying?' He runs his hands through his hair, his whole body shaking as he does so. 'I was offering for us both. Truly, I am my father—a completely selfish bastard.'

'Oi, Wacken,' I say, shoving him slightly with my shoulder. 'I ain't gonna shag you so give it up, all right? And begging is highly unattractive.'

The sound of his laugh is steady and loud over the waves and the schlink of the pebbles moving over each other.

I startle him by slipping my hand into his, but

after the momentary shock, he closes his fingers around mine, clamping us together. It feels so solid and safe, holding his hand, that one of the chains of anxiety belted around my chest loosens and I can breathe a little more.

'You want to know about Leo?' I ask him.

'Absolutely.'

We stand holding hands, watching the stars, looking at the white-foam-topped black sea while breathing in the saline air as I tell him everything I can about my most favourite person in the world.

CHAPTER FORTY-FOUR

'You'll back me up, won't you, Nova, when I call the police and say I've hit an intruder with a wok and he's out cold on the kitchen floor?'

Mal is pressed up against the worktop beside the cooker, a pan has been removed from the heat but what looks and smells like porridge is in it, and two pieces of browned toast sit up in the toaster just behind him. Cordy is standing in front of him brandishing in one hand my heavyweight wok and it is aimed at Mal's head, while four-year-old Randle is holding a little silver milk pan in both hands like a rounders bat, aimed directly at Mal's left kneecap.

Mal looks surprisingly calm, or maybe it's resignation to the knowledge that he could expect nothing less from Cordy. He's probably been waiting for this day since the day he finished with me. Out of everyone, he knew Cordy would always be the one who would react most violently to him breaking up our family.

His body is leaning as far out of reach as possible, though—resigned he may be, but not overly eager to get a dual panning.

A commotion, raised voices, had drawn me out of bed and I'd come downstairs to find this scene. Four-year-old Ria is standing in the doorway beside me, hopping from one foot to the other in delight, the ribbons at the ends of her twin black pigtails bouncing in delight as she jiggles. I can see why this is fun. A small part of me is laughing inside because this is what Cordy would like to have done to all her ex-boyfriends, all my ex-boyfriends and all of Mal's ex-girlfriends—and probably her Jack a few times, too, if she could have got away with it. Better out than in is her way of expressing herself. I respect it a lot. She and Amy are similar in that respect—they rarely experience an emotion they don't immediately expose to the outside world. It must be liberating to be that wanton with your feelings. I talk too much, they emote too much.

'Why are you trying to hurt Malvolio?' I ask Cordy, conversationally.

'Why?' she asks in incredulity. '*Why?* Are you serious?' She doesn't take her eyes off her quarry, not for a moment.

'Yes, I'm serious, why?'

Mal's gaze flitters between Cordy's weapon of choice and me, probably trying to work out if I'll let her hit him.

'I come here to make you breakfast before we all go to the hospital and there he is, large as life, making himself breakfast as though it's his house.'

'I was making Nova—' Mal begins.

366

'*Who said you could speak?*' she shrieks at him, while jerking the wok dangerously higher.

Mal raises his hands in surrender and leans his long, muscular body even further back.

'I don't even know how he dares show his face around here,' Cordy says, as though Mal is in another room. The emotion she is feeling the most of is betrayal. She has always idolised him because he has always taken care of her. Put her on a pedestal, treated her as though she is indeed his little sister, his little princess. She's always been able to rely on him and now she's wondering if she can. Now she thinks he is someone she doesn't really know.

'I asked him here,' I say, leaning against the door frame and folding my arms across my chest.

'*Why would you do that?*'

'Because it's my house and I can invite whoever I want here.'

'After he got you to have his baby and then left you?' she asks.

Mal's jaw clenches at this, his features tighten, his body tenses. I forgot that as far as he knows, everyone is only just recovering from the knowledge that he is Leo's father. He doesn't know that his wife told his mother everything. And Aunt Mer has told everyone else. Now everyone knows something about him that he'd rather they didn't. And they'll probably be asking him why, as well. Like me, they won't settle for the excuse he trotted out, either.

'It doesn't matter,' I say to Cordy. It does matter. It matters a lot. I would love to believe it didn't, that there are bigger issues that negate all that . . . There are, but they don't erase the rest of it, they don't stop what he did still being the cause of a painful breach that has never healed. But, just as I had to show people how to react when I told them I was a twenty-nine-year-old knocked-up teenager without the father on the scene, I had to show others how to treat Mal.

Back then, I said I was really happy, it was what I wanted, I preferred to do it without the father because he and I would never have worked out and wasn't it great news? So they all knew that was how to react: with joy, elation and happiness. I was happy so they had to be as well.

With this, I have to act as though I have set aside my hurt, because the most important issue could become everyone else's anger at him and that will hijack what this is all about. Which I cannot allow to happen.

'How can it not matter?' Cordy asks, uncertain suddenly if I should be getting whacked around the head to have some sense knocked into me.

'Mal is Leo's father. I want Leo to know that at a time like this everyone who cares about him—his father included—came to see him. No one forced Mal to come here, he wanted to come. So, in the grand scheme of things, what Mal did does not matter. The fact he is here now, when Leo needs him, does. If I can put it all aside, I think you should be able to as well.'

'I'm not a pushover like you,' Cordy says, although she has clearly understood what I have been saying because the lines of her slim body have softened, the line between the wok and Mal's head not as direct and inevitable any longer.

'No, you're not. But you are wonderful and you are sensible and I know you're the best person to go to the hospital and explain to Mum, Dad and Aunt Mer that Mal is here, and why they shouldn't smack him on sight either.'

'And what will you be doing?'

'Getting Mal out of here before Keith arrives home to get ready for work, and finding somewhere for him to stay.'

Cordy still hasn't lowered her wok.

'It's OK, Cordy, truly, I've forgiven him. Which means you can, too.'

'I suppose so,' she says to me. 'And you—' she says, swinging the wok under Mal's nose suddenly, using it as a pointer.

Randle thinks the hitting has started and swings the milk pan with all his considerable, four-year-old strength and connects with Mal's knee with a loud, crunchy crack.

Ria jumps beside me, Randle drops the pan and immediately bursts into tears, Cordy is shocked and frozen for a second then she moves to comfort her wailing son, dropping and denting my wok in the process. Mal crumples and falls to the ground, clutching his knee and gritting his teeth to stop himself howling in agony. Ria runs to her mother, not wanting to miss out on the cuddles being dished out. All three of them ignore Mal.

My family are insane, I decide. It comes to something when I, the person who hasn't slept more than a few hours for the better part of a month, who has been living on the edge of a mental and emotional breakdown for weeks, is probably the sanest person in this room.

*   *   *

369

'You haven't really forgiven me, have you?' Mal asks as we head for the café later.

'Not for one second,' I reply without hesitation.

CHAPTER FORTY-FIVE

'Amy, this is Mal,' I say. 'One of my old friends. Mal, this is Amy, my business associate.' I don't call her an employee because her friendliness, sunshine soul and hard-working nature are all reasons why Starstruck is such a success. And she isn't simply an employee. She is an amazing friend who has gone above and beyond the call of duty in the past few weeks. She has opened up on time, closed on time, served customers, cleared tables, pandered to the usually ridiculous requests of the psychics, sometimes done readings herself, cashed up, locked up, visited the cash and carry. All without a word of complaint. She also visits Leo whenever she can.

'Shakespeare!' Amy exclaims, her eyes running all over Mal's face, as though she wants to use her fingers to forage into his skin, looking for something. 'You're Shakespeare!' she grins. Excitedly, she claps her hands, secures a lock of hair behind her ear and turns to me. 'He's Shakespeare! I wasn't going crazy all those years ago. I didn't get it wrong.' She waves her finger excitedly at him (if she were Leo, I would be telling her not to point). 'He's your connection to Shakespeare.'

Mal eyes her up suspiciously, wondering if the tall woman with the waist-length hair, pierced

370

tongue and tattooed belly button is a little bit crazy.

'When Amy and I first met she thought I was an actress,' I explain.

'Oh,' Mal says.

'She's psychic,' I elaborate.

'Right,' he says, nodding sagely, as though I have just said, 'She's a bit slow.'

'No, she is, actually,' I reassure him. 'One of the best I've ever met.'

Amy's eyes widen, and an even broader grin splits her face. She also blushes furiously. I've never said that to her. Mal looks like Keith does whenever I bring up this subject—as though he's wondering if some sort of psychiatric help will make me stop this nonsense.

'When she met me she thought I was an actress because she could see me surrounded by stars. She didn't know my name at this point.' I trawl through my memory to recall it accurately. 'She said I had a very strong connection to Shakespeare. And when I said most people did because we learnt it at school, she said that both Leo and I had a very strong connection to Shakespeare. And then she said it was something to do with twelve or the twelfth. And then she said I had a connection to the Old Vic. Or was it a person called Old Vic?'

I know that last bit will get to Mal. Most of his dad's workmates called him Old Vic. Mal's face pales and he looks over Amy again, now unsure of her and her abilities.

'Amy only reads for people if she gets something from them. If she doesn't have a connection with them when they sit down in front of her, she won't charge them or read for them,' I say. 'That's why I respect her. That's why I only allow people that scrupulous to work here.'

'But you're Shakespeare!' she exclaims, clapping her hands again. 'I love that I've finally met you.' Even when Amy is sixty I'm sure she will still delight like this in the world. 'Every now and again I'd wonder what that connection was. Especially as it's so strong with Leo. Hey, was Old Vic your dad?'

Mal draws himself in tight, and he becomes cold and closed off, his face a hard expressionless mask. Clearly his policy of not talking about his father is still in place. His eyes, now as flinty as unwieldy diamonds, drill into Amy.

'Amy, I was wondering if you would do me the hugest favour?' I say, to deflect this conversation for now and not allow them to alienate themselves from each other before they have valid, quantifiable reasons to dislike each other.

Her head moves towards me, but her eyes are firmly fixed on Mal. Eventually she brings her brown, whirlpool-like eyes towards me too, but I can tell they are dying to return to him. 'Hmmm?' she asks.

'Mal's just arrived and we haven't had time to arrange a hotel or B&B for him yet. My house is not the place for him, so I was wondering if he could stay at your place for a couple of days? Just until we can find a hotel.'

I expect her to say yes; she is that kind of person, that's why I asked her. Instead she swings her head back to Mal and stares at him for a long, silent, tense moment before she returns her gaze to me. Her long fingers curl around my bicep. 'Can we have a quick word, over there?' She indicates to the door that leads to the back of the café, and before I can answer she is dragging me away.

Mal's thoughts are unreadable as he pulls out a chair and sits down.

'That's Leo's dad, right?' she asks.

I nod.

'And he broke your heart, right?'

I nod again.

'So what's he doing here? Why does he need somewhere to stay?'

I haven't told her. In all that's been happening, I haven't told her what the doctor said. Everyone else was there and she was here, as always, holding the fort for me, saving me from financial ruin, and she still doesn't know.

Amy has seen Leo nearly every day for all of his life. The only person he has seen more frequently than her is me. The pair of them are great friends and he loves it when she talks to him in Japanese and attempts to play PlayStation with him. This isn't the sort of news she should hear from me. Someone more detached, more objective, should tell her. Even though I hated him for what he said, the doctor telling everyone in my family at the same time what he thought saved me from having to do it. Saved me from having to go through the worst case scenario with a person who loves Leo.

'You'd better sit down,' I say to her.

'Just tell me,' she says, aware that if Mal is here it isn't going to be good news.

In halting, jumbled, mumbled words I tell her what the doctor said. I try to repeat it without saying what I said in between. As I speak, I watch her, waiting for the moment when she will do what Mum and Cordy did and burst into tears. Or what

Dad did and move to another part of the room. Or what Keith did and reach for me. Or even what Aunt Mer and I did and become incredibly still.

Amy surprises me: she nods slowly when I stop speaking, then she faints clean away.

*   *   *

I lock up the café without bothering to cash up—I just put the takings from the early morning rush in the safe. I have more pressing matters. Mal is taking care of Amy so that I can go to the hospital. I haven't seen Leo since I dropped in on my way back from London last night. That's a long time away from him. Mal said he'd drive her home, even though she lives very close—just the other side of Poets Corner—make sure she is safely in bed and will stay with her until Trudy gets back.

She was virtually catatonic and I envied her. I have—at various points in the last few weeks—wanted to do that. To simply check out of reality and sit quietly, safe and removed by a protective force field my mind has erected. Sadly, I did not, do not, have that luxury.

My current life is like a machine, it has many parts, all of which need tending or it will break down. The area in most dire need of a service, of love and attention, at the moment is my marriage. Keith is not talking to me. He has stopped speaking to me unless absolutely necessary since Aunt Mer revealed to everyone everything about the surrogacy. But I cannot focus on him—tending to Amy, getting Mal to come here, actually getting to the hospital are the parts of the machine that get cleaned and oiled first.

374

I pull into the hospital car park, there is a special one for parents and carers of long-term sick children, and a sense of relief is wending its way through my body. I don't have to worry about Amy and the café for the rest of the day. The relief of that is so deep and syrupy and delectable, I decide, as I walk towards the looming grey-brick building, to keep Starstruck closed for a few more days. There it is, that delicious relief. I want to dive into it, drink it in, swim in it, stay there for a lifetime. I want to drown in something I do not have to worry about.

There's an odd scene in Leo's room: Mum is crocheting, sitting in my chair, facing Leo with Randle asleep on her lap, his head resting on the shelf of her impressive bosom; Aunt Mer is in Keith's chair, reading to Leo; Dad is in another chair, a new one to the room; Cordy has laid out a tartan picnic blanket on the floor and the children have an array of toys on it, although Ria is rapt, listening to Aunt Mer. Cordy is sitting cross-legged, reading a magazine.

This is why the hospital rules stipulate that only two people are allowed to visit at one time. If there was an emergency now, they'd be tripping over people to get to Leo, but I love that my family are here. That they've made their lives around him as they do when he's in a school play, a football match, or when it's his birthday. Everyone descends upon Hove, ready to watch him, to be with him, to praise him.

'Hey, Leo,' I say to him. 'It's me.' I sweep my eyes around everyone else as I say 'hi' to them. They all smile at me in their different ways: Mum's is bright, Dad's is hidden, Cordy's is brighter than

Mum's, Aunt Mer's is like she knows a secret, and Ria's is curious.

Cordy has worked her magic. She's told them whatever is necessary so that they've all stopped looking at me as though they are not sure how to talk to me, and that I have been wronged and that I should have told them years ago so they could have carved the offender out of their lives. She's soothed them, possibly by saying he's here now and I've forgiven him and he wants to make amends. Maybe she's even told them that Randle had all but kneecapped him and that has sated their thirst for blood. Whatever, Cordy—PR woman extraordinaire that she is—has calmed my family. Mal might get a stern talking to, but he won't be skinned alive and they won't make this about him. I love my sister for that.

'There's no change,' Mum says quietly, as she holds out her intricate crochet web to Dad. Without having to be prompted, he puts aside his crossword and picks up her cloth bag and stows the crochet and the hooked plastic needle into the bag's depths. Cordy is packing the toys away into one of her large bags, with Ria's help, and then folds up the picnic blanket. Mum weighs Randle in her arms, then works out how to stand without waking him.

'Where's Malvolio?' Aunt Mer asks as she stands, shutting the book.

'He's taking care of Amy,' I say. 'She fainted when . . . Earlier on. Mal took her home and is staying with her until Trudy gets back.'

'Poor Amy,' Cordy says. Mal has gone up a notch or two in everyone's estimation because he doesn't even know her.

'But call him,' I say to Aunt Mer. 'He's looking for a hotel to stay in.'

'OK, we're off then,' Mum says.

'I'll see you tomorrow,' I say.

'You aren't going to go home tonight and see us on the way?' Dad asks.

'No, I'm staying here. I want to keep Keith company.'

After a round of see you laters and hugs, they leave. Cordy and the twins are going back to Crawley; Mum, Dad and Aunt Mer make noises about going to look around Brighton.

And then I'm alone. With Leo.

How I like it.

When I'm not here, I like him to be surrounded by our family, but at times like this, I want it to be just me and him. Like it always has been.

CHAPTER FORTY-SIX

Last night, the first glass of wine made things feel less empty, especially because I put on the radio in the kitchen, the CD player in the dining room and the TV in the living room.

The first bottle of wine made me decide to sleep on the sofa because the bed was too far upstairs and too vacant of my husband.

The second bottle of wine must have convinced me that the attic was a wise place to visit: I woke up to find all the baby clothes I'd bought all those years ago laid out flat on the floor around me, like cut-outs from a model-free, three-dimensional children's clothing catalogue.

I don't remember doing it, but I must have. My thick, gummy eyes told me I'd been crying as well.

Sobriety, shame and a shower (long, hot, lots of soap) have brought me here. To the back garden, a cigarette clamped between my lips, as I smash every single piece of the tea service Meredith gave us on the concrete path that leads from the house to the wooden shed at the other end.

All this started when I broke that cup, didn't it? I need to finish what I started that day by accident. It's clear to me now: the tea service, wherever it came from, has a hex on it.

I need to remove every cursed item of it from my house and my life.

CHAPTER FORTY-SEVEN

The knock on the door startles me.

I've been dozing, not sleeping—no dreaming, which is a blessing.

I automatically check on Leo: no change, then stumble to the door.

My heart forgets to beat for a few seconds, and my lungs stop: Mal.

Oh, yeah, I invited him here. He's all out of context—over the past few years I haven't seen him as someone you deal with close up, it's always at a distance.

'Hi,' he says; he's clearly seen the shock register on my face.

'Hi,' I say. He's had a shower and combed his hair so it now sits pushed back from his face in tamed curls. I'd forgotten how angular but strangely soft his features are. For so many years I'd wanted to kiss his plump lips and to have his eyes, a shade darker than the brown of fox's fur, stare down at me as they are now: gently, carefully, probing me, as though trying to peel back my outer layers and see inside me.

Whenever we'd been apart for extended periods—like when I returned to London from Oxford, when he came home from Australia, when I went on holiday with Keith—he'd do this, would want to reacquaint himself with me physically, mentally and emotionally. He'd stare at me, reach out to touch me to confirm I was real. Now, after all these years, his need is even worse.

I have an urge to slap him. Just like that. Slap him to snap him out of it, remind him why he is here. Someone already has, I see: a florid red streak sits proudly on his left cheek from where someone has repeatedly hit him. 'What happened?' I ask, pointing to the mark.

'Huh?' he asks, touching his cheek. 'Oh, Mum.'

Aunt Mer did that?

'She slapped me the first time because of what I'd done. Then she slapped me a second time because I hadn't told her the truth all these years and let her think what she did. Then she slapped me again because she said no matter how much anyone else wanted to slap me, they never would. Then she slapped me because she said if I'd seen the look on everyone's faces as she told them the truth, I'd slap myself. After that, I stopped counting.'

Aunt Mer?

'Then she started crying and said she'd never thought the first time she'd have to smack one of her children would be when he was in his thirties. And then she said in all her life she'd never been ashamed of anyone and this was the first time, and I wouldn't believe how painful shame was. To be honest, I preferred it when she was hitting me.'

'I didn't tell them, you know,' I say. 'I didn't tell them any of it.' It must have cut him deep that Aunt Mer was ashamed of him.

'Steph told Mum. I don't know why, but she did,' he says. 'Amy's fine. Trudy came back and put her to bed. She's still not talking. I found a hotel, too. It's near where Mum and your parents are staying.'

I nod at him.

'I was hoping to see Leo now?'

'Yeah, sure.'

'Really?' He is surprised.

'Did you think I'd get you all the way down here to not let you see him?'

'I wouldn't blame you.'

'Mal, this isn't about you, it's about Leo.'

He crosses the threshold and becomes frozen. Everyone does the first time they come in here. The machines that surround the bed are daunting, they bleep and make drip-drip noises, while lights flash and lines move across monitors. A white hose leads from one machine to the bed, to Leo's mouth. Sometimes they take the hose out because he can, mostly, breathe on his own. A drip is linked to his arm. When you enter the room for the first time, the machines dwarf Leo, make him seem small and fragile and easily breakable. This scene reminds you how amazing the human body is because it can do all these things and more on its own. And reminds you how weak you are, because the smallest thing can put you here.

Mal is terrified, his eyes wide, his body rigid as he looks at me. I gently take his bicep and lead him to my chair.

'It's all right, just sit down,' I say to him, 'tell him who you are, and talk to him.' Gently I push him into my chair.

'Look who's here,' I say to Leo. 'It's my old friend, Mal. He's Nana Mer's son. Just like you're my son, he's Nana Mer's son. And he's your other dad. Remember? You wrote down that time that you have two dads. He's the other one.'

I rub my hand reassuringly up and down Mal's arm, then leave him to it by retreating to the other side of the room, standing by the door.

'Erm, hi, Leo. I'm Mal. I saw you when you were a few days old. I thought you were so small. I wanted to pick you up because I was sure you'd fit in the palm of my hand. I've also seen you at your Aunt Cordy's wedding. Your Nana Mer shows me pictures of you all the time.

'Actually, do you know who I am? I'm the boy in the picture you showed to your Nana Mer and asked her why I looked like you. That's me.

'Your mum told me that you love PlayStation and football. Well I love those two things, too. So we'll have to play one day, see who out of us will win. I'm pretty good as well, you know. Very few people can beat me, but I'm sure you'll try.'

I love Mal's voice. The way he speaks, the intonation of his words. I love it all the more because he's having a long-overdue conversation with Leo.

CHAPTER FORTY-EIGHT

'We should be careful when we tell lies,' I say to Carole. 'They're alive. Lies are alive. Once you've told them they need looking after, feeding, nurturing, attention, companionship . . . love and affection, I suppose, like any other living thing we're responsible for.'

Carole stares at me. She is on the other side of my wooden kitchen table, a cigarette in one hand, her cup of tea in the other, staring. She has no real idea what I am talking about. But I need her. In a moment of clarity after I had smashed the tea set and repeated the same drinking ritual with the baby clothes, I realised this was a sign and I needed to talk to someone before things got out of control. She is it. From our group, she is the person I am closest to, I suppose. In the first few weeks of college we'd shared a room in halls until a few of our fellow students realised that university life wasn't for them and left, so freeing up rooms. Carole slept on the top bunk, and was the one who moved when the girl next door decided that she'd rather go home and start a family with her boyfriend than spend three years away from him, studying. It should be awkward and weird between Carole and me, given that I went out with Vince for two years and then she went on to marry him, but it isn't. Vince and I were a car crash from the start, it only took us two years of tears, tantrums, visits to casualty and threats of being thrown out of college for us to see that. Carole is steady, sweet, suitable. Everything I'm not.

Carole lifts the cup to her lips, and I realise my mistake. I've made tea in the coffee cups. I really haven't been thinking straight, and hopefully in a few minutes she'll understand and won't bring up this tiny transgression in front of the others. We're a pack of bitches, yes, but it's been known for us to 'discuss' these sorts of mistakes we each make behind each other's backs.

My eyes run over the white crockery with a thin, candy-stripe pink line around its base. *How did I miss that it is a different shade of pink to the one surrounding the base of the saucers and the teapot, milk jug and sugar bowl? How?*

I lured Carole over saying I wanted us to go jogging; instead I had a cup of tea, cake and packet of cigarettes waiting for her. I'd been too cautious, too shy, to ask her to come over to talk. She might have told one of the others before I'd impressed upon her the need for secrecy, the need to not share with anyone what I am about to tell her. Carole is nice. She likes Mal and she likes us being together. Smoke obscures Carole's face as she blows out a plume of it. Under normal circumstances we'd never smoke in here, but these are not normal circumstances.

'Carole, I'm going to tell you a secret about a lie I once told. The one that needs love and attention and companionship,' I continue, drawing my eyes away from the crockery. Maybe she won't have noticed. Maybe she won't tell everyone how I've messed up. 'I'd— Please keep it to yourself. I— *Please.*'

She takes a draw on her cigarette, frowns a little as she nods, and wraps her arm around her stomach as though steeling herself for what I am about to say. 'Of course.'

'I lied to my husband. To Mal. I lied to him. Once. A long time ago. It was only the once, but that lie needed a companion to keep it alive. It needed lots of companions. And as a result of that lie, and its companions, Mal's son is going to die.'

Carole's frown deepens and her eyes flicker for a moment as her mind goes back to her son and daughter. Safe with their father, she hopes. I'm sure all parents do that: whenever they hear about a sick, missing or hurt child they flash to their child and hope they are OK. OK and where they should be.

'It's all my fault that the boy is going to die,' I tell her. Suddenly, gorgeously, the weight of guilt lifts a little. That part of the confession has eased my guilt. The rest will hopefully ease me more and more.

She shifts back in her seat a fraction, only a fraction, as she wonders what I've done, how I've hurt the boy, how she is going to react to finding out I am someone who is capable of hurting a child. Her voice quavers over every word as she asks, 'What happened?' I've chosen the right person. She has asked me what happened, instead of 'What did you do?', which suggests that she thinks it might have been an accident. Not something I would have done on purpose. She doesn't believe me to be evil. Which means she might understand when I tell her the rest.

'Years ago, not long after I met Mal and it looked like it was serious and I sensed he was going to ask me to marry him, I told him I can't have children.'

Carole's anxiety softens a little, her shoulders

384

loosen. Then her mind goes back to the dinner party and shame crawls across her features. 'You can't?' she asks with such sympathy that I'm almost unable to tell her the rest.

Maybe she will think me evil after all. 'I can't. What he didn't realise is that what I meant was, I *won't* have children.'

The cigarette stops on the way to Carole's waiting mouth. She is wearing pink lip gloss even though we were meant to be going jogging. 'How do you mean, won't?' she asks cautiously, lowering her cigarette over the crystal ashtray.

I watch the end of the cigarette burn, unable as I am to look her in the eye. 'I mean, I decided long ago not to have children because it would mean a huge sacrifice and it's one I just can't make.'

CHAPTER FORTY-NINE

Keith is definitely not talking to me.

It hurts like a punch in the chest every time I think about that. We have always talked and this is causing me immense distress.

We have barely exchanged more than two hundred words in six days. He comes to sit the night shift, to spend the night with Leo even though each member of my family has offered to do it so that he can come home with me. Always he refuses so he doesn't have to sleep next to me. His texts are signed 'Keith', no 'love you' any more, no 'x' kiss. I suspect he wants to type 'I don't know you'. Last night, I had tried to insist that I stay with him and he had said, 'No, just go home, Leo will need you to be awake tomorrow' and refused to speak to me after that.

He is still floored by what I have become in his mind: someone who could give a baby away. Someone who would have given her own child away if the intended parents had not changed their minds. Keith does not believe that anyone could do that and be able to live with themselves; he believes every surrogate—paid or not—is actually every intended parent's worst nightmare because she will ultimately decide to keep the baby. Knowing that I had been prepared to give the child who became Leo to his 'real' parents after nine months has shaken him. Keith does not like to be shaken. Leo being in hospital is bad enough, this revelation is one shake too many. So he has taken to ignoring me, speaking to me if and when it is absolutely necessary.

'You think I'm going to stand by while another man's baby grows inside you?' he shouted at me all those years ago. Talking and talking at a normal volume hadn't got us anywhere; now he was trying to shout some sense into me. 'It's not like I can pretend it's not there when you'll be getting bigger every day. We'll be walking down the street and everyone will look at us thinking it's ours and ask us questions and, what, we're going to lie?'

'I've told you, I don't care what other people think. What you think is important, not what anyone "out there" thinks.'

'I think it's a bad thing to do.'

'How can doing this to make someone happy be bad?'

'It'll be bad for you. You'll be a mess afterwards.'

'You mean it'll be bad for you if I'm a mess afterwards because you won't want to look after me.'

'Why do you say that like I haven't got a right to worry about how this will change everything between us? You won't be able to drink, you'll be sick, they'll always be round here to see you. Your body will change, you won't be able to do as much. I'll be watching this baby move, and we'll only be able to have sex in certain positions. And after all that, we won't even have a baby at the end of it to make it worthwhile.'

'Is that what this is about? Sex?'

'Lucks, if you think I'm going to be able to fuck you when I *know* you've got someone else's baby growing inside you, then you don't know me very well.'

'We're getting nowhere with this,' I said. He was right, there was no denying it. I hadn't considered him when I'd agreed to it. I hadn't thought I needed to, I'd assumed he'd understand, when in reality I was asking him to put our relationship on hold for the best part of a year, while I put two people before him. I should have consulted him or have been prepared to lose him.

'Let me lay it on the line: if you do this, then . . .' He stopped because he did not want to do it. Not when it wasn't his fault. They weren't his friends, he hadn't grown up with one of them, why should he drastically alter his life for people he had no real loyalty to? And why should he have to be the one who ended our relationship?

'I'm doing this. I love you, but I'm doing this. I said I would and I'm going to. So I guess it's over.' I wanted to cry. When he was gone, I was going to collapse into tears.

Slowly he looked me up and down, like he was trying to remember details about me. 'I'll go and get my stuff.' When he returned with two holdalls of clothes and books and CDs and other things he'd left at my place, he looked me over again. 'I keep telling myself not to get back together with you,' he said. 'Because every time we break up, it takes me that bit longer to get over you.'

'Me, too,' I replied, feeling the corners of my mouth turn down. I wanted him to get out before I cried. Because every time we broke up and I cried he would comfort me and we would end up in bed and I'd cry again afterwards.

The next time I saw him, he'd decided to look me up because he found out that I was living in East Sussex and he was living in West Sussex. I told him straight away I had a son, and when Keith found out his age, he assumed that I had decided to keep the baby.

'Please talk to me,' I say to him later. Everyone left a couple of hours ago and I've been reading to Leo and trying to work out how to fix things with Keith. He is back in his suit this week, and for the first time ever I'm tempted to ask him about his job so he'll go into an elaborate explanation as to why he can't and won't tell me. I want to hear his voice, to have him direct his words at me for more than a few seconds. He stops in the middle of shedding his jacket and shrugs it back on. I'm scared suddenly he'll walk out again. Instead, he stares at Leo as he asks, 'About what?'

'About anything. Talk to me, please stop ignoring me.'

He turns slowly to face me and I see that he isn't

388

angry with me, he is confused, uncertain. He doesn't know how to talk to me. He sighs with his whole body, and I'm reminded how strong he is. Muscular, tall, quiet, confident, strong—in such a different way to most of the men I dated. He is honest and that gives him strength. Nothing he says is dishonest, or untruthful, or spun, which gives him fortitude. That's why this has upset him—I haven't lied to him outright, but if I am able to keep the whole truth from him it makes him unsure about who I am.

That is why he stopped talking to me: he has been trying to work out what else I haven't been completely honest about. He nods his head towards the door. 'Outside.'

He doesn't want to do this in front of Leo. He doesn't want to—what, say it's over?—in front of Leo.

In the wide, brightly lit corridor outside Leo's hospital room, I lean against the wall opposite so I can still see in through the open doorway, can keep his bed and him in sight. Keith swamps me, though. He stands over me, one arm resting on the wall above my head, his body shutting me off from anyone who might approach. Men do this to women in clubs and bars to mark out their territory, to show a woman belongs to them.

'I keep trying to work out if I'm a bad person because I have a problem with what you were going to do,' he says.

'Course you're not. It's something I had to do,' I reply. 'Not everyone could do it.'

'But it was Leo. How could you have watched him grow up with someone else, knowing he was yours?'

I shrug. 'I don't know, I just would have.'

'You'd have broken your heart to make two other people happy,' he says. 'But you don't want to have our baby, what am I supposed to think? What am I supposed to say to you?'

'I do want our baby,' I protest.

'If we could make love right here, right now, you'd panic. And you'd do whatever you could to avoid it.'

My heart is galloping, it is echoing in my ears, I'm convinced he can hear it, can feel it because he is so close to me, and then he will know that I am scared of having another baby.

'Am I wrong? Because we both know this began way before Leo got sick.'

Now he knows what really happened, that being pregnant lost me my closest friend, I could explain the fear I have. I know it is irrational, I know in time I'll be able to overcome that fear, but right now I can't. And I can't explain to Keith because he won't understand. He will think I am being silly, and I can't stand the thought of revealing my fears to anyone and having them dismissed.

'I do want more children with you, but I'm not ready.'

'When will you be ready, Lucks? You're thirty-seven, I'm forty-six, time isn't on our side.'

I look into his eyes, deep and dark, an almost-black brown. When we first met and I had that crush on him, I used to forget what I was saying when I looked into those eyes. I had to stop making eye contact because the resulting muttering and mumbling were incredibly embarrassing.

'I don't know when I'll be ready,' I say. 'But I do

390

want it. I promise you.'

'Let's talk about it again. When Leo is better, we'll talk about it again, and you can maybe tell me what you're so scared of. All of your fears, and we'll see what we can do about them. Does that sound fair to you?'

I nod. I forget sometimes that he may have been in the Army, he may work in the police force, he may seem like a typical bloke but he loves me. And because he loves me, he tries to understand me. It is my fear that stops me talking to him. Because even if it is irrational and it isn't what he wants to hear, Keith has loved me for so long, he'd find a way to make what I feel work for us both. I would do the same for him. That's what our love is about.

He kisses the centre of my forehead, a wonderful, chaste blessing. He kisses my nose, another touch of his love. He kisses my lips. And he doesn't want anything more. He doesn't want sex, he doesn't want me to be on the same page as him physically, and that is what I need right now. I just want him to love me without expectations. Without wanting me to deal with Leo how he does, without wanting me to start planning a future, without him wanting me not to have been able to give my child away. This is wonderful. Being with him like this is a little piece of heaven we haven't had in so long.

We have heaven, so that is when all hell breaks loose.

Machines start frantically bleeping in Leo's room, the lines and numbers on the monitors start flashing. A nurse comes running, followed by two doctors and another nurse. I move to join them, to go to Leo, but Keith's strong hand holds me back.

He wants me to leave them to do their job.

'Not yet,' I want to scream, but there is no sound. 'Not yet, not yet, I'm not ready.'

CHAPTER FIFTY

You probably think I'm selfish. That I don't deserve to have a loving husband and a good home if I could lie to him about something like not being able to have children. You might think that having contraceptive injections on the sly every three months and doing the odd pregnancy test in the toilets at work are no ways for a woman who claims to love her husband to behave. But you don't understand. I told the lie and now I can't take it back.

I . . . I have an illness. A disorder, they call it now. They have a nice name for it now, and every other celebrity seems to be talking about how they are suffering from it, but when I found out what I had, it didn't seem so glamorous. It has never been glamorous and I don't understand how those people who have it don't seem to suffer like I did. Like I do. When I found out that I had this disorder, it was the beginning of the end as far as I could see.

I was always aware that I was different, that I didn't fit in. I didn't see the world like the other girls I went to school with, but I wanted to so badly. When I was thirteen Duke, our family dog, died, and we moved to a new city. And the differences became more obvious.

I found life so hard sometimes. Little things—a

C grade, a cross word from my mother, the troubles in Poland—would literally leave me lying on the floor unable to move because it hurt so much, it hurt so physically. I'd cry. I'd spend hours in my room crying because Mum had told me not to leave my bag on the floor by the door. I didn't know what was wrong. My mother kept taking me to the doctor to find out what was wrong with me. Why I wasn't like other children, not even my brother and sister, but the doctor kept saying it was just teenage hormones, or simple naughtiness. Something I would grow out of at some point. They'd talk about me as though I wasn't in the room. I soon learnt that I wasn't me, I was a set of behaviours that no one liked.

If I was down all the time, it might not have been so bad. Bad for them—my parents, my siblings, the few people I could vaguely call friends at school. If I was down all the time, they could explain it as simple moodiness.

No one could understand the other times as anything other than wilful misbehaviour. During the other times, the times I lived and longed for, the world was an amazing place. Everything was vibrant, colours were rich and deep and you could almost touch them they were so tactile.

I used to dance in the back garden, I would throw my arms up in the air, throw my head back and dance to the music I heard in my head. I'd want to write this music down or sing it out loud and have it recorded in the air. Anything so other people could hear it, could move to it, could be as happy as I felt. I had so much energy. I could run for ever. I would draw and paint. I was in love with the world. I was in love with everything and everyone.

Euphoria ran through my veins. Add a few tins of cider and some cannabis to euphoria and you got me, at fifteen.

At fifteen I got pregnant.

I didn't know when exactly. That's the thing about those times: I vividly remember the feelings, but rarely the specifics. The edges blur away into nothing in my mind, I have huge gaps in my memory; patches of recollection.

I do know, though, that the father could have been one of three men, because over the course of a month, three different men approached me. I was back down again, feeling awful, barely able to get dressed every day to go to school. One of those men must have seen me going into school because he waited for me outside the school gates, calling my name, blowing kisses, touching himself. He only left when the PE teacher threatened to call the police. Another one came up behind me in a sweet shop, rubbed himself against me and whispered things in my ear. The third man I saw when I was waiting at a bus stop and as he came towards me, the grin of recognition on his face told me he was another one. I knew what I'd done. The disgusting things that the second one had whispered in my ear. I turned and ran.

After that I started to get flashes of things. I was in a car while a man's hands tore at my clothes and crawled over my body. I was in a strange house, with my face pushed into a bed while someone behind me was doing something that hurt more than I could imagine. I had someone on top of me, almost smothering me as he moved back and forth. It was one of those times that I lost my virginity. I never did remember which.

My mother guessed I was pregnant when I skipped two periods. She was too scared of my father finding out to be angry. She took me to the doctor to find out for sure. Our usual doctor was on holiday and the replacement was a rare thing in those days—a woman doctor. When my mother, who I'll never forget was white as a sheet and shaking all the time, told the doctor that she thought I was pregnant, the doctor asked my mother to leave us alone. You could tell my mother, in her best coat and carrying her best handbag, didn't want to go, but she's of that generation that will do anything anyone in authority tells them.

'Could you be pregnant?' the doctor asked kindly.

I nodded.

'Have you told your boyfriend?' she asked.

'I don't have one,' I replied.

'Do you know who the father might be?'

I shook my head.

She changed then, became all concerned. 'Did somebody hurt you? Force you?'

'I don't remember,' I told her. 'Nothing. I don't remember things. I don't remember this happening.'

'Do you forget a lot of things?' she asked.

I told her everything. Once I started talking, I couldn't stop, it came tumbling out in a jumbled mess, the crying, the dancing, the happiness, the way drinking would be like pouring pure, potent joy down my throat, the gaps in my memory, the flashbacks to those times with those men.

When I finished she asked me more questions.

So many questions.

And I thought . . . I don't know, I hoped, I suppose, that at the end of it there'd be a simple prescription for antibiotics, or she would say that in a couple of years I'd grow out of it, like the other doctors had said.

Instead, she ended my life. She told me, told my mother, in words that we could both understand, that I wasn't 'normal', that I was ill in the head, that I was a freak of nature. No, she didn't say that, of course she didn't. She went out of her way to say that it wasn't my fault, more people than we could imagine had what I had, that this wouldn't stop me leading a normal life.

I was fifteen, all I wanted was to fit in, be like everyone else, and now she was telling me that would never happen. I was marked. Branded.

She wasn't a hundred per cent sure since it wasn't her area of expertise, but would refer me to a psychiatrist, they would do more tests, they would be able to tell for sure—as sure as they'd ever be—and they could prescribe the right medication.

I was willing to go along with it then. I had heard the word medication, and I knew then that I would get better. This would all become a horrible memory, something to lock away in my past. All I had to do was be a good girl, go along with this, get the tablets, get better. My father was willing to pay to see a psychiatrist because it would all happen quicker. We could get the tablets down my neck and I would stop being the thorn in his side.

My parents waited patiently outside the psychiatrist's office, knowing it was worth it. I waited patiently inside the psychiatrist's office, answering question after question, doing everything he asked because then I would be normal again.

I don't know who out of my parents and me was more upset when we discovered that 'medication' was for ever. Medication meant regular blood tests, constant visits to the doctor, the possible need to add more tablets as time went on. Medication wasn't a quick fix. Or even a fix. It was maintenance. It was to stop it—me—spiralling out of control in either direction.

On top of that, they wanted me to talk about how I felt to this man, this psychiatrist.

How are you supposed to feel when you've been told you're mentally ill and you've been handed a life sentence of pills, pills, doctors and pills?

My mother sent me to live with my aunt so, she told my father, I would have the chance to get used to all this. But it was really to take care of the other problem. To further empty me out.

And because my father was more loath to pay a psychiatrist ('quack') than I was to talk to one, he agreed.

When I came back, another term was introduced into my life: 'suicide watch'. After that, I started to live in a prison with no locked doors. My every move was scrutinised. I had to take tablets in front of my keepers. Everyone knew what was best for me but no one ever asked what I thought. What I wanted.

I know they were just looking after me, but no one seemed to consider that I may well have agreed with them. I may have needed them to watch me carefully, but once in a while someone should have *asked*.

No one was more shocked than me that they let me go to London to college, but all those years of learned dependence and its resulting docility must have convinced them I was safe to unleash upon the world. I made it. I only came close to the edge a few times, I only tried to stop the grey a few times. I was fine. A routine, exercise, medication, looking after myself, not doing too much or hoping for too much paid off.

I was extra careful with sex. I had boyfriends and we always used condoms because I never told them I was on the Pill. I never wanted to risk getting pregnant again. If I did, I might have to sacrifice my medication, my equilibrium, fragile as it was, for nine months to ensure the baby was born healthy. Or, worse, it might turn out like me.

I told Mal I couldn't have children because it was easier than explaining that I didn't want to risk having children. He knew all about my condition, all about the things I had done while I was in the manic phases, but I didn't want him to hope I would change my mind. I would change my mind, obviously I would, but if I had a lie to keep me locked to my decision I wouldn't be tempted to try to have a baby.

What I have is passed on genetically, they think. Or it runs in families. Whatever it is, however it is explained, I did not want to pass this on to someone else. It was a chance I did not want to take. Even if it was the smallest chance, I didn't want to take it, especially because it runs in Mal's family, too. The odds were not in my favour.

I saw what my illness did to my parents. How it dragged peace, happiness and certainty from my mother; how it coiled resentment, bitterness and fear into my father. It cleaved them apart with every incident. I did not want that for Mal and me.

Then I saw the woman and the boy in the supermarket and I wanted a baby. I couldn't have one, so back to suicide watch. When I told Mal, he tried to fix it because he always tries to fix things. Even the things we should not try to fix.

'I'm the person who desperately wanted a baby,' I say to Carole.

'Pardon?' she asks. She has been so still and silent all this time, revisiting my history without a hint of judgement crossing her face. I have been studying her carefully, waiting for the moment a revelation will shock her into judging me, but it hasn't happened. It hasn't come.

'At the dinner party, remember I said someone close to us wanted a baby? That was me. I was the one. Mal's friend, his best friend from childhood—'

'The black woman you introduced me to at the wedding?'

'Yeah. She agreed to have a baby for us. And then I got scared and jealous and I changed my mind and I changed Mal's mind and forced him to choose, but she had the baby anyway. She moved away and had the baby.'

Carole frowns, her face a corrugated mass of confusion. 'And he's going to die?'

'The doctors think so, yes. Very soon by the sounds of it. Mal's there now, to see him before . . . before it happens.'

'You've never met this boy?'

I shake my head.

Her frown deepens all the lines of her face as she stubs out a cigarette. 'I still don't understand, how is any of this your fault?'

399

Why can't she see what is so obvious to me?

'If I hadn't lied, Nova would never have had Mal's baby and then he wouldn't be about to die. If I hadn't lied, none of them would be going through this because Leo would never have been born.'

'Oh, Stephie.' Carole scrapes back her chair as she gets to her feet and comes to me, enveloping me in her arms and bosom and musky scent. 'If up was down we'd all be living in Australia.'

'But—'

'You're feeling guilty, that's all. None of this is your fault. I hate to break it to you so bluntly, but you're not omnipotent. You don't control the order of the universe. We could all go back and "if" better all the things we've done. If I hadn't felt so insecure about my looks and being a frumpy old housewife, I wouldn't have let myself be seduced by Vince's best friend and I wouldn't always be looking at Sophie and wondering who her daddy really is.'

My jaw hits the table. 'You and Dan?'

'Yup, but let's not talk about that. Ever, actually. Stephie, babe, you must be twisting yourself up in knots over this because you feel so powerless. Being here all alone all day can't help. It's really not your fault.'

'I don't want him to die.'

'Of course you don't.'

'I still miss him. Even though I never knew him, and it's my fault he isn't mine, I still miss him. Almost every day. I pretend I don't, but I do. So much.'

'Oh, sweetheart.'

'He's the hole in our lives. And if he dies . . . I couldn't bear it. It'll destroy Mal and it'll do the same to me.'

'I know, babe, I know.'

'I want him to be all right.'

'This is what we'll do,' Carole says, suddenly all business. 'You'll ring Mal and ask him how Leo is. That's his name, right, Leo? Right, you ring Mal and ask him and say you're worried and is it all right if Mal calls you the second there is any change.'

'He won't. I was such a cow to him on the phone the other day that he hasn't even called me since because he's so angry.'

'No, Mal's not like that. He's probably just confused and scared, too. Just tell him how scared you are. And then pack some stuff up and come and stay with us until Mal comes back.'

'But I don't know when that will be.'

'Doesn't matter. The last thing you need right now is to be on your own.'

I sniff back my tears, and let her stroke back the strands of my hair that have become matted with the wetness on my face. 'Does that sound like a plan?'

I nod.

'Good.'

'Thank you, Carole. Thank you for listening and for being so nice to me.'

She shakes her head. 'Shut up thanking me. That's what being friends is all about, you don't have to thank me for it.'

Is that what being friends is all about? The closest thing I had to friendship that went beyond dinner parties and jogging and exchanging the odd phone call was what Nova tried to create with me. And that was always one-sided—she shared with

401

me but I would never dream of sharing with her. I kept her at arm's length for obvious reasons.

'We may seem a bit shallow in our group, but we would always be there for each other in a crisis,' Carole says. 'You know that, don't you?'

I stare at her, blankly, I've never considered it a possibility. I would never even dream of telling them things that were a bit unpleasant, let alone sharing a crisis. Under normal circumstances, if Mal was here, I wouldn't have told her about myself to help stop what I could see was happening. I would never have told anyone.

'*Don't* you?' she repeats, horror spiking in her eyes and on her face. 'My God, Stephie. I've always thought you were the most sorted and settled person out of everyone, but you're just as fucked up as the rest of us.'

'You don't have to sound so pleased about it.'

'Oh, yes I do. Now I can stop thinking everyone out there is better off than me. Everyone, and I mean *everyone*, is messed up in their own way. I love that. Come on, now, chop, chop. Get some stuff together. Let's hit the road.'

Normally, I hate people taking over, telling me what to do, but at this moment, when all around me is falling apart, there is nothing better. Nothing sweeter and more soothing. All the more because she doesn't seem to care what I told her about myself. I told someone and she didn't change how she felt about me. She isn't even worried about having me around her children. She thinks I am as fucked up as her. She thinks I am what I've always wanted to be: normal.

'On the way back to mine,' she says as she loads our tea things in the sink, 'I'll stop off at church, light a candle, say a prayer. I'm sure his mother will appreciate it.'

CHAPTER FIFTY-ONE

I haven't been praying.

Mum has, I know. I think that's all she does when she isn't talking—crochet and pray. Everyone else probably has as well, but not me. I haven't been praying, because I haven't reached there yet.

If I pray, I won't be asking God to make Leo better, but for Him to do what is best for Leo. Not best for me, but best for Leo. And for Him to look after Leo when he leaves here.

Most people are surprised that I am a clinical psychologist who has such a strong interest in the esoteric world *and* a belief in God. 'But what about all those awful things religion has caused?' they'll ask as if I have all the answers to everything. For me, my belief in God is separate to 'the church' and to 'religion'. Separate to all the 'my god is better than your god' stuff that happens in the world.

My belief in God is personal, I do not need to browbeat anyone into agreeing with me, because I believe what I believe and I try to live by it. My belief in God is about trying to be the best person I can be in this life, and knowing that in the next life, whether it is as a reincarnated soul on earth or as myself in heaven, I will see the people I love again. That's what life and the afterlife is all about for me: it is about being with the people I love.

I need to start praying.

I stand in the very corner of the room, watching them work on my son, trying to get him back, trying to stabilise him, and I know, in my soul, that I need to start praying. To ask for what is best for him at this critical moment and to ask for him to be looked after if what is best is for him to leave.

I need to start praying for the little boy who was never meant to be mine. Who I was blessed with for nearly eight years. I shouldn't have had him for even one day, but I got him for more than seven years. It isn't enough. It isn't nearly enough. I am being robbed.

I need to start praying.

But I can't.

I'm not ready.

I probably never will be.

It can't be now, though. Please not now.

I close my eyes, feel the storm around me: the noises from the machines; the shouted instructions with words I recognise from journals but do not understand; the professional, controlled panic. It feels like it has been going on for hours. It's probably only been ten minutes, but every one of those minutes feels like long, protracted hours. Where they cannot get him back. Where he is gone for real and they cannot bring him back and keep him here.

The stillness at the centre of the storm is Leo. *'I'm ready to go, Mum,'* I hear him say.

That is what the dreams have been trying to tell me; that is what my mind has been trying to tell me with the dreams: what is best for Leo is not going to be what is best for me. I may be keeping him here, by clinging on so tight because it's what I

404

want, but it is not what he needs. I may need to let him go and see if he still stays. But letting go is too much to ask of me right now. I need more time.

Please. That is my prayer. *I need more time. Not even a forever, just more time*.

I open my eyes because all is still again, there is the forced hush of inactivity. The doctors and nurses have stopped, they are waiting. Waiting to see.

Bleep-bleep-bleep, go the machines. *Bleep-bleep-bleep*.

Counting out his heartbeats. Counting out the time.

When I was about twelve, I said to Mal and Cordy wasn't it weird that your heart was only going to beat a certain number of times and then you would die. And no one knew how many times your heart would beat before that happened. Mal nodded and agreed it was weird, Cordy burst into tears and ran to tell on me because she thought I was saying 'you' to her and was saying that her heart was going to stop beating.

I watch the lines on the monitor tell the world that my son's heart is still beating, that he hasn't reached the final number, yet.

When I look away from the monitor, from the jumpy, glorious lines that say he is still here, there are only four of us left in the room: Leo, Keith, me and the doctor with the young face and old soul in his eyes.

He stares at me across the bed, I stare back at him. We're back to being two intimate strangers locked in visual combat.

I know he's going to do it again, he's going to say something I don't want to hear.

He knows I'm going to tell him he's wrong. Only this time, he'll sound a little more certain, I'll sound a little less convincing. And only Leo will be able to tell us who's right.

'Doctor Kumalisi,' he begins.

I hate you, I think at him across the sleeping form of my son. *It's not often I can hate a person, but I hate you.*

CHAPTER FIFTY-TWO

Keith thinks I should call my family, even though it is late now, and tell them what the doctor said.

We are standing in the corner of the hospital room, rowing in whispers about it.

By not calling them, he thinks I am lying *again*. My husband thinks I am a liar because I choose to not say things. He's probably technically right about that, but I never omit things for personal gain. If I do not tell something, it is to protect someone else. But for Keith, lying is lying, no matter what your motivations. This is where his view of the world—that wrong is wrong and right is right and there is no middle ground—differs from mine. This is where his view of the world, which gives him such strength of character and conviction in everything he does, creates a gnawing irritation that reminds me why Keith sometimes pisses me off.

'You have to tell them.'

'You want me to get on the phone right now, and tell a group of half-asleep, already upset people what the doctor said? That the coma is so deep now that he'll never wake up? That we're looking at forty-eight hours at the most? I'm supposed to do that to the people I love?'

'It's the truth,' he states.

'Yeah, well, fuck the truth.'

'Nice,' he replies, the word double-dipped in disdain and disgust.

'Forty-eight hours, Keith, yeah?'

He nods, reluctantly, looking down upon me from his high horse, letting me know I'm honoured that he has even bothered to acknowledge me now that I have stooped to swearing in the same room as my son about something so fundamental and pure.

'How do I want them to spend the next forty-eight hours? Crying, grieving, wishing there was something they could do but feeling powerless? Or full of hope? Thinking that it's possible for things to be OK? And how do I want them to spend tomorrow, probably their last day with him? Sitting around here, crying and talking quietly, bringing gloom and sorrow in here? Or chatting and playing and reading and crocheting like it's just another day in this bizarre situation?

'And am I supposed to allow all that anguish to surround Leo, before it's necessary?'

Mr Truth says nothing. He knows I'm right, but like me, he'd rather have his nipples removed than admit it straight away.

'No one is going to say goodbye before they absolutely have to. I want them to look back on the last day and think of it with happiness, not sorrow. I'll tell everyone Monday morning and they can all go in one at a time and say goodbye.'

'You're going to have to lie again about when

you found out,' Keith says, which means he definitely knows I'm right about this.

I glare at him in the gloom of the room. 'It's a really good thing I love you because I fucking hate you sometimes,' I tell him.

'And I sometimes wonder with the way you can hide things, if I know you at all,' he replies, to get the final word.

'Well we're even then,' I add, to usurp him, and march across the room before he can say anything else and sit down in his chair just to further needle him.

'You know what, Leo,' Keith says to our son as he sits in my seat, 'you've got a really silly mummy.'

I pick up Leo's hand, imagining how he'd roll his eyes at how childish we're being, even at a time like this. 'You've always known how "difficult" your dad is, haven't you, sweetheart? Well he's being really very difficult today. I think I might ban him from the PlayStation.'

Keith jerks his head around to me with such horror on his face, and a protest on his lips, I actually laugh at him. It is such a Leo expression of injustice. Keith starts laughing, too, at his reaction. We keep on laughing until Keith's laugh becomes breathy and hiccupy, and light from outside the room catches the tears on his face.

As his hiccupy laughter subsides, he gets up and stumbles over the chair as he leaves the room.

I keep laughing, long after he has gone to find a quiet corner where he can cry in peace and solitude, where he can stop being a big strong man with principles and a failing marriage and just cry his heart out.

I keep laughing because once I stop, the only

sound I'll hear is the bleeping machine, counting down the heartbeats Leo has left.

CHAPTER FIFTY-THREE

All I can do is wait.

Smoke and wait.

Mal accepted my apology by dismissing how I had been on the phone and saying he was sorry, and that he missed me. He is going to call when there is any news.

All I can do now is wait. And smoke. And hope that it's going to turn out all right.

CHAPTER FIFTY-FOUR

I've had that song, 'Perfect Day', lodged in my head since this morning.

It's all rather corny, really, hearing that on loop and watching all the important people in Leo's life gathering round his hospital bed, carrying on as normal.

Mum has been crocheting and trying not to tell Cordy how to mother Randle and Ria—Mum thinks they're a little bit on the spoilt side and she should know since she's done a hefty amount of the overindulging.

Dad has been completing the stack of *Times* crosswords he has brought with him in between beating Mal at cards. Every hand Mal loses he puts a look on his face that says he's let Dad win, but we all know it's not true. Aunt Mer, Keith and I have been taking it in turns to read aloud; there aren't that many chapters left and Keith and I both know that we've got to get it finished today.

Randle and Ria have been remarkably well behaved, and have been either rapt listening to the story or playing with the array of toys on the floor, with Amy and Trudy, who have focused on the children all day.

Cordy has been tormenting her Jack. She has been sending him out on missions to find things she doesn't want—like stripy rock that doesn't have writing imprinted all the way through. Whenever he thinks of protesting, she raises an eyebrow, slides her gaze threateningly over to Mal, her big brother—Jack is usually on his way in minutes, sometimes taking a child with him. He came back in the afternoon with pizza for everyone.

In many ways it is a perfect day. Yes, we're all crammed into a small hospital room, yes, the nurses and doctors all disapprove, and yes, Leo, the focus of attention, is deeply asleep, but it's as close to perfect as we're ever going to get again.

When they look back, I hope they remember this as a happy day. And I want Leo to hear his family around him, being themselves, being exactly as they always were.

The song is still playing in my head as they all start to drift away, back to another evening before they come back again and do it all again tomorrow.

The song is still playing as I turn to Keith, now we are alone. 'Do you mind staying here while I go away for a few hours?'

He lays the book face down on his lap. 'It was a

good day,' he says. He grins at me like he did the first time I asked him about a job in the bar in Oxford. *'I thought you would be my undoing from the moment you spoke to me,'* he said in his speech at our wedding. *'And I smiled because I thought there couldn't be many better ways to become undone.'*

'Yeah, it was,' I say, smiling back. *Such a perfect day*.

'You were right, we all deserved it. It's just what we needed.'

'Did you just say I was right? Pass me the phone, I need to call hell to tell them to expect cold weather.'

'Don't bother, hell isn't going to freeze over until you've said I'm right about something,' he says with a laugh. 'Sleep?'

'Sorry?'

'Are you going to sleep?'

'No. I need to get some stuff from home for Leo. Walk around. Find a way to empty my head. I'll come back later and you can go home and sleep till morning. I'll do the night shift.'

'Yeah, sure, anything you want.'

I slip on my denim jacket, hook my bag on to my shoulder and then go to him, sitting so tall and upright in his chair. I pour myself into his lap and loop my arms around his neck.

He stares at me, a little confused. I take the time to enjoy his face: his big, black-brown eyes, his wide, flat nose, his full lips, his smooth, mahogany-brown skin, and the wonderful, perfect lines that make up his face and shaved head.

The wide spaces between the small moments of great irritation are filled with such an

411

overwhelming love for him. And that's why I can be irritated with him: I know that at the end of it, I'll still always love him.

I close my eyes and wait for the gentle press of his lips on mine. When he kisses me, it's as simple as falling through time. This is how it's always felt to kiss him. Easy, uncomplicated, honest. His tongue finds mine and I know the exact moment he closes his eyes and drops himself completely into the kiss.

We used to kiss for hours. Just kiss. Lie together on the sofa in my flat in London, kissing and luxuriating in it.

I'd love to do that now. To spend the next few hours kissing and kissing him, but we can't. *Then* it was a wonderful way to spend our time together, now we both know the longer we kiss, the further apart we'll feel once we stop.

CHAPTER FIFTY-FIVE

When he opens the door to his hotel, he knows. Mal knows why I have come to him. He knows what it means.

But he's known all day. He caught my eye once and held my gaze for a few seconds before looking away, and then avoided looking directly at me all day. Out of everyone, he worked it out.

I need to forget. He offered me a way before and I need it now.

He stands aside to let me in, clutching the door frame momentarily for support and briefly closing his eyes as he does so.

The room is large, larger than I expected. The double bed is neatly made and he's obviously been sitting in the armchair, watching television with the sound turned down because the subtitles are crawling up on to the screen one at a time. His mobile and BlackBerry are on the desk, both flashing with unread messages. As the door clicks shut, I stop examining his room and turn to face him. My arms are wrapped around myself, my bag hanging off my shoulder, my hair probably blown wild by the wind on the seafront as I walked here. I no longer have to be strong in front of Leo, with Keith, with my family, in front of doctors and nurses, so I am the dishevelled wreck on the outside that I am on the inside.

He hasn't bothered to throw on a jumper before answering the door, because I think he has been waiting for me. He suspected I'd come and hoped I wouldn't. But here I am, so he stands in grey jogging bottoms, bare-chested in front of me.

Fear is implanted in his eyes, on his face; fear and agony and understanding, but quickly they are gone, brushed aside so he can do this. His chest lifts and expands as he takes a deep breath, steeling himself as he crosses the short distance between us. Even though he has managed to hide his feelings, his hand trembles as he reaches out for the buttons on the red and white flower shirt Leo picked out for me the last time we went shopping.

He undoes the small pearly buttons and with both hands pushes my shirt and my denim jacket off my shoulders on to the floor. His hands are still shaking as he peels off my white vest with the sparkly pink smiling skull and crossbones motif—

another Leo choice—and lets it fall away. He pulls me towards him, allowing me to feel the solidity of his body. As I feel his heartbeat, absorb his heat, he undoes my black bra, slips it off.

It's still there.

I can still remember. It plagued me every step from the hospital to here. And even though I'm doing this, I haven't forgotten, it's still there.

Leo—

Mal's fingers are on the top button of my jeans. I focus on that. On him unbuttoning me. His hands tugging open my jeans. On kicking off my trainers, on him pushing down my jeans and taking them off and managing to take off one of my socks in the process. I concentrate on taking off the other sock, while he stands again.

—is—

Mal's hands hook into the top of my plain white knickers and tug them down.

—going—

Mal stops, then. Tenderly, he stares down at me, silently asking if I am sure. If it has truly come to this. If there really is no hope.

—to—

My body quails. The next word will shudder through my body and cement it in my mind. Make it real. Confirm what the doctor said. I don't want it to be real. I want to forget.

Reading my mind, reading my body, Mal's mouth comes down hard on mine, erasing the next thought. His hand digs into my hair, the other grips the base of my spine, clutching me close to him as he kisses me.

I plunge into the kiss with the passion that comes from grief and terror and heart-searing

414

pain. Our skins meld together, almost becoming one as we kiss. I can feel him, firm and ready, against my stomach and I reach down to touch him. He takes my hand away, kisses me even harder, all the while walking me backwards towards the bed.

—*d*—

The word wells up in my mind and I kiss him more urgently, expelling it from my mind. His mouth still on mine, his tongue still in my mouth, he pushes me down on to the bed, climbing on top of me in one move.

He pauses for a second to tug free the tie of his jogging bottoms and push them off, and then his mouth is back on mine. Slower this time, deeper, but just as unyielding. Constant. Concrete.

—*di*—

He stops for a moment, stills himself on top of me. Everything stops with him. Our eyes lock and I am lost for a moment. I forget. I understand why he offered to do this. I'm not me. I'm not a mother. I'm not a wife. I'm not me. I am a mass of atoms. Only tethered together by this moment.

Now. It has to be now. Before I come back.

Mal thrusts so hard and forcefully into me, I cry out, and his mouth comes back down on mine, taking the sound, that little escaping expression of pain, into himself.

I dig my ragged nails into his back, clinging to the muscles that move on top of me, puncturing his skin. His lips close around my right nipple and he bites hard, spreading shards of sweet, physical pain through my body; I sink my teeth into the flesh below his collarbone and he moans loudly. He buries his hands in my hair and clings on tight as he moves; I claw again at his back. He is rough, far rougher than he needs to be.

This isn't about pleasure and desire and lust. Every brutal thrust is a peeling back of the layers of reality. A shedding of this earthly agony. A quest for that black, hot state of pure, blissful oblivion. We are hurting, so we hurt each other to forget; to become a mass of unknowing, ignorant atoms.

His mouth covers mine again, swallowing my groans, pushing his moans into me. I can feel its approach. The end. The point of no return. It rises up from between my legs, the space Mal fills, and rushes through my bloodstream. I am racing towards the edge, he is racing inside me . . . I am on the edge . . . I am teetering on that precipice . . . And then I am falling. I am exploding and I am plummeting, and then here it is: the void. I am nothing. I am untethered. I am free.

Free.

* * *

We come apart so easily, I realise, as he rolls off me on to the bed, flopping back to stare at the Artexed ceiling. It felt like we were one for a forever, and now we are two again. Separate. Unwhole. Even our laboured breathing is unsynchronised.

'I'm sorry,' he says.

I know. In my head, I say it. I can't speak aloud. I can't do anything aloud. I have to stay perfectly still, not ruffle anything by speaking or moving, because I can still hang on to the forgetting if I am careful. My scalp tingles from how tightly he clung

416

to my hair, my mouth is still bruised from how hard he kissed me, my nipple still smarts from his bite, the space between my legs still aches from how rough he was inside me. If I hug these small agonies close, I can still forget.

'I couldn't leave her. That's the reason why. When she said I had to choose, I knew I couldn't leave her. I promised I wouldn't and I couldn't. She's like Mum.' He stops. 'She's bipolar.'

Well, of course she is, I say in my head. *Of course she is*.

He explains it all then. How she first told him. The way she tries to control herself. The crises she's had over the years, the worst being the time he found her in the empty bath with her wrists slashed and an empty bottle of paracetamol, and an empty bottle of her lithium, after which she stayed in hospital for two weeks. The abortion at fifteen. How no one can ever know because she is so scared of being judged and labelled a loony.

I listen to his words and with each one Stephanie finally comes into focus.

'She got scared that she would hurt the baby, that's why she changed her mind,' he says in his tumble of words.

No, she didn't, I say in my head. *Stephanie knows that the only person she'll ever be a danger to is herself. Just as we all are dangers to ourselves whenever we take risks. Stephanie got scared that you would fall in love with me. I would have your baby and you would fall in love with me and you would leave her for me. You would take the baby and go.*

'I knew you'd be OK, that you were so strong, much stronger than Steph is. You had all these people around you who would take care of you,

417

and you would survive. Steph has no one but me. So when she said to choose between her and you and the baby, I had to keep my promise. She had no one else.'

She was never going to let you go. There was never any choice, because she knows you would never leave her. But she had to be sure, when the fears about you falling in love with me started, she had to move quickly. She had to make sure the choice was made before the baby was born. Afterwards, you might have wavered. You might have seen that there was someone out there who needed you more than she did and you might have gone. That's why you had to shut me out: if you got to know your son, you might have wanted to be with him.

Stephanie was scared. And because of that, because she didn't trust how much you love her, she had to do what she did. I don't hate her. I feel sorry for her. Not for her condition, but for her lack of trust in the one person who would always love her. Even if you did want to be with me, you would never leave her.

'Every day for the last eight years I've seen your face, heard your voice as you begged me not to do what I did. It's tortured me. I want you to know that. I couldn't ever forget. And every time I heard about you, or saw your mum and dad and Cordy, I would feel sick at what I'd done. I knew you were strong, but I still hated myself.'

'It's OK,' I say, breaking the spell, allowing the residual pain that has kept me removed to evaporate now that I have spoken and stepped back into this world. 'I understand. You should have told me back then, but now I know, I understand and it's OK.'

'Really?' he asks, turning his head to me.

'Yeah,' I reply. 'I understand so I can let it go.' I close my eyes for a moment. 'And right now, it doesn't matter. Nothing matters.'

He rolls towards me, and I see the mark on his chest—vivid, red and raw—from where I bit him. His back will still have my deep scratches, which drew blood. Stephanie will see them. She'll see them and she'll know. *I don't want her to know.* And I don't want Keith to touch some newly sore part of my body and know. I don't want anyone to know. I don't want anyone to be any part of what we did. It's ours, ours alone.

I don't want any of this, I think. *I just want normal.*

He takes me in his arms, cuddles me up, holds me to him. This is what I need Mal for. 'I'm sorry,' he whispers. He's not apologising about eight years ago. He is sympathising about now. 'I'm so, so sorry.'

Die.

The seams of my mind burst wide open. My pain flooding outwards, the torrent of tears coming thick and fast; my cries loud and uncontrolled.

Leo is going to die.

I cling to him as my sorrow becomes a tsunami, the pain flaying my heart, decimating my mind.

Leo is going to die.

'I know,' Mal whispers into my hair, his voice strong and reassuring as he rocks me in his arms. 'I know I know I know I know I know.'

CHAPTER FIFTY-SIX

Mum and Dad are first.

Their fingers are intertwined; their hands clasped together as they open the door and step inside. This is the first time I have seen them hold hands. I know my parents have a deep affection, a limitless love for each other, but this is the first outward display of it. They bicker, constantly. Being irritable and mildly antagonistic with each other in public comes easily to them—in fact, the past ten days at the hospital have been the longest they have gone without sniping at each other—but they rarely express their love.

Some time later, they come out, no longer holding hands: Mum's head rests on Dad's shoulder, Dad's arm is locked around Mum. They are supporting each other, holding the other up. They don't look at anyone as they leave, they simply help each other down the corridor and turn at the corner; suddenly disappearing from here as though magicked into another realm before our very eyes.

Cordy is next.

She takes her entourage, as she likes to call them—Jack, Ria and Randle. Before she reaches for the door handle, she turns to me. Her eyes are already red, her face scored by guilt and remorse. I know what she is thinking, because if I was her, if I was a mother of healthy children looking at me, I would be thinking it, too: I'm sorry this is happening to you, but I am glad my children are well and I hate myself for being glad. I do not want my sister to feel an extra burden, this is awful enough. I smile at her, telling her I know it isn't her fault. That I would never resent her for having and keeping everything I once had. In response she presses her fingers to her lips and blows me a kiss. My little sister still does that because, as I say, she has never experienced an emotion she has not expressed. I try to widen my smile, before she turns back to face the door and they go inside.

They emerge, each parent carrying a child, each child's head buried in the comforting hollow between their parent's neck and jaw. Both children are crying; the adults' eyes are red and swollen, their bodies stiff and cowed, they meet no one's eye as they move down the corridor and then vanish, like Mum and Dad.

Amy is next.

Trudy stays frozen where she is, terror streaked on her gamine face, her hands pressed against the wall while panic rages around her. She has known Leo since he was five, at which point she wasn't enamoured with children. Leo, of course, sensed this and befriended her. They got on because they both have a no-nonsense approach to things. Glancing to her side, her hand ready for Trudy's, Amy realises that she is alone. She turns to her and Trudy shakes her head. Amy smiles at her, gentle and understanding as always, she raises her slender hand, her bangles tinkling together, and holds it out for Trudy. Suddenly calmed, as though a wild horse tamed by secret words whispered in her ear, Trudy comes forward, reaches for Amy and they enter together.

They are holding hands when they return. Amy is dry-eyed and upright, but I know her, I can see she is held together by nothing more than the desire to not collapse in front of me. She and Trudy wander away, into the realm of the vanished like the others.

Mal and Aunt Mer move towards the door next, and at the same time Keith rises from his seat. I hold him back. He wants the waiting to be over, to go in there and say what needs to be said, but he has to wait a little longer. He is Leo's dad, it's only right his be the second to last voice Leo hears.

Mal is steeling himself: like a man about to leap from an aeroplane without a parachute, he takes deep, deep inhalations as he stares at the door. He wraps his arm around Aunt Mer's shoulders as they walk in. For some reason, I remember that for years I called Aunt Mer Aunty Merry, and she would always smile at me as though I knew a secret no one else had stumbled across. I only stopped because Mum said it made her sound like a drinker.

Keith takes my hand, and kisses a lingering moment into the well of my palm. Jolted, confused, I turn to him and, for the first time, see, experience his grief. Deep and wide; unfathomable. He has been holding it in all this time, not only to protect me, but to protect himself as well. He has been consciously denying it, hiding it, cowering from it because he is terrified. A kind of terror he has never known before. He was in the Army, he works in the police force, he has seen death, he has lived through incredible acts of evil, and yet none of them have been capable of felling him like this. Nothing has been as immense as losing a child he loves; nothing has been capable of removing his future and replacing it with a void. That is why we haven't been able to help each other, both of us have been keeping ourselves strong separately.

Leaning forwards, I kiss him, filling it with as much of the love I have for him as I can. I want him to know I love him. I want him to feel that we both tried, but this was way too big for us: we aren't going to survive this. Even if I hadn't done what I did with Mal, almost all the strings of our marriage have been severed; waiting together to say goodbye is the last one. Once it has been cut, only love will remain. And it takes more than love—no matter how fervent, deep and passionate—to keep two people together.

The door to Leo's hospital room opens and Aunt Mer steps out, shutting it behind her. Her eyes glisten, but she is calm. Calmer than when she went in: as if all fear and worry have left her. She tugs her bag on to her shoulder and walks a little way down the corridor before she stops and leans against the wall with her back to us. When we were allowed to visit her in hospital, sometimes she used to do this: stare into space, her body unnaturally still. It was the medication, Mum and Dad reassured us, but I wasn't scared. Mal and Cordy always were, but I knew she was there. I knew we'd be seeing her again sometime, that the standing and staring were just a rest.

After some time, Mal comes out of the room. He is broken. He was my rock last night—he held me for hours while I cried for the first time, drove me home so I could shower and change and pick up some new clothes for Leo, and he had driven me back to the hospital—now he is diminished; devastated and broken. He shuffles a short distance, then stops, falls back against the wall, his head tipped upwards, and then his knees give way and like a stone dropped into a pond, he sinks quickly and heavily to the ground. He draws his knees to his chest, jams his fingers into the blond waves of his hair and begins to cry. Loud, uncontrolled sobs. He rocks as he sobs, whipping up his anguish, losing all grip on himself.

Out of all of us he's the only one for whom it's too late. He never got to talk to Leo, never got to hold him, never had a Leo moment he could call his own. Aunt Mer comes to him, all the calmness she radiates suddenly explained: he is her baby, her little boy, and he needs her. For the first time since he was a baby, she is able to completely support him. She brings him to his feet with gentle coaxing, then she allows him to swamp her with his large frame as he throws his arms around her and cries, all the while saying he is sorry. He is really sorry. She rubs his back and hushes him, says she knows he's sorry, as the calmness she has diffuses slowly into him. Once he is able to stand alone, she takes his hand like the little boy he will probably always be to her, and she leads him away from here. I watch them go and then vanish like everyone else.

Keith's goodbye is the shortest.

He has a lifetime of things to say to Leo and no time to say them in. So he says goodbye, and retreats.

Before me, the doctor with the young face and old soul and Nurse Melissa go in to check on Leo. To make sure things are going the way they think they will.

On his way past the doctor says it will be a few more hours yet, but I know for a fact he's wrong. I know Leo. It won't be long now.

424

I step inside the room, sealing us in together by shutting the door, and I can't help the grin spreading across my face. It's Leo after all. How can I not smile when I see him?

'Hey, Leo, sweetheart, it's me.'

CHAPTER FIFTY-SEVEN

I pick up his right hand, measure and weigh it in my own.

Chubby and childlike, four perfect digits and a thumb. I made those, in my body, I made them. I kiss each one, lingering as I press my lips on to the tip of every perfect finger. I turn his palm over, press a special star magic wish, as he used to call them, into the well of his hand. He would curl up his hand and close his eyes and make a wish. He never told me what he wished for or if they came true, but he always did it so it must have given him some rewarding returns. Or maybe he was always hoping the next time it would work.

I pick up his left hand, the mirror image to his right, press kisses on to those fingers, that thumb, the well of that hand.

This is the last time I will be able to do this. The last time.

We say last so many times, but never consider the gravity of the word. How final it is. Binding.

How soon will I forget? I wonder. I have virtually no videos or films of him. After he was born I used to take copious amounts of photos, but even their number dwindled after a while because, with only two of us to take pictures, I preferred to spend

425

time on the other side of the camera, with him, doing things. I can hear his voice in my head and the words are clear, but some of the intonations are slightly fuzzy. How soon before his voice is completely gone? With nothing etched in stone to remind me, how will I remember? He is on my wedding video, of course, but that was over two years ago and his voice has changed since then, as he worked his vocal cords around his ever-increasing vocabulary.

How soon, too, before I lose the full range of his expressions? Some were captured on film, frozen in photos, but they weren't the same as seeing him. I can close my eyes now and remember how he would turn his nose up at broccoli ('You know it's poison, Mum') but would devour spinach as though it was nectar. I can bring up so easily how he would look up to the heavens as he searched for an answer to a question, how his eyes would widen and he'd stick the tip of his tongue out the corner of his mouth as he battled to reach for the newest level on the PlayStation. I can luxuriate in his frowns at injustices—like not being allowed a dolphin. I can lose myself in the memory of his huge smiles. But how long will they last? I thought they were etched into my mind and heart, but are they? Won't time erase them as it softened and blunted all memories?

He's wearing his green Teen League Fighter power suit. It's his favourite thing. If he could choose the one thing to put on every day, it's this. Because then he can legitimately go out and fight crime. I haven't put on his mask.

I lean down, touch a kiss on each of his eyelids. Each one closed, the long lashes resting gently on the area under his eyes. I press my lips to his forehead, lingering there.

I stroke my fingers down one side of his face, marvelling as I always do at how soft his skin is. I stroke my fingers down the other side of his face. My baby. My beautiful, beautiful baby.

I sit down in my chair, take his right hand and hold it in mine again. He held my hand almost every day—while we crossed the road, while we walked along the promenade, while we strolled through the park, while we ambled along the road. Sometimes while we watched TV and he got scared at something and would reach for me because, he said, he didn't want me to be scared on my own. I hold his hand against my cheek.

'You know, Leo, I realised something. You always worry about me, don't you? So, I realised that you might still be here because you're worried about me. I'll be fine, though. I want you to know that. Remember that, always. There are so many people who will look after me. Grandma, Grandpa, Aunty Cordy, Nana Mer, Dad, Amy, Trudy, even your other dad. I'll miss you, of course I will, but I want you to stop fighting this if it's hurting you. I love you so much that I never want you to be in any pain.'

I hold on to his hand as I lay my head down on his chest, still feeling the warmth of him, the outline of his hand against my cheek.

'I love you and it's OK to go now. I'll see you again so I won't say goodbye. OK? I'll see you again. I'm going to say goodnight, instead. Sleep tight, Leo, my love. Goodnight, my beautiful boy. Goodnight, beautiful.'

The rhythm of the machine is changing. The

427

bleeps are slower, the gaps in between them longer.

I close my eyes. I wish I could go to sleep. I wish I could go to sleep and be with him and hear him speak to me one last time. Have him hug me, roll his eyes and ask if I'm going to start crying now.

I keep my eyes closed, allow myself to drift away.

'I love you,' I say to him.

The bleeps of the machine slow. Slower. Slower. Slower. And then . . . Bleeeeeeeeeeeeeeeee-eeeeeeeeeeepppppppppppppppp. Steady. Slow. Continuous.

Over.

His hand is cold by the time I sit up. My face, cold. Everything cold.

'Goodnight, my beautiful boy,' I whisper to him. 'Goodnight, beautiful.'

CHAPTER FIFTY-EIGHT

Meredith is the one who calls me.

She tells me with gentle words shaped by her soft voice.

She asks me if I am all right, if I need her to come and be with me.

She explains that Mal has been sedated by a doctor and is asleep in her hotel room.

She doesn't know when they'll be home.

She doesn't talk about a funeral.

She wishes me goodnight; blesses me with her love.

She hangs up.

And I realise then how quietly the world can come to an end.

CHAPTER FIFTY-NINE

I sit by the beach.

Surrounded by the expanse of stars scattered all around me in the night sky, I absorb the sound of the wash of the sea.

I watch the sun come up.

I listen to the world come alive: the seagulls swooping into the waves to catch breakfast; the disciplined joggers following their routine; the not-quite-awake dog walkers doing their duty; the all-night partiers stumbling home.

Home.

I don't have one of them any more. Not when he's not there.

part six

CHAPTER SIXTY

We held on to each other as we slipped, slid and clambered down the steep bank of pebbles.

The sea lay before us. Foaming and fizzing as it gushed towards us, bubbling as it was sucked back. We kicked off our socks and shoes, stood beside each other, our feet cold, waiting for the sea to try to gobble them up, seeing who could wait the longest before running away.

The sea went away, he and I stood firm, shivering in the cold, our legs close together, giggling with anticipation, waiting for the tide to come for us. And then it was racing towards us. The tremors of excitement thrilled between us as the water came and then I was squealing, running backwards, I was the one who caved first. The chicken. He stood his ground, let the sea come and come, until his feet were completely submerged by the grey, foamy water. His face grimaced at the coolness of the water, and he screamed in delight and didn't move.

He turned towards me, to see where I was when I should have been beside him.

I laughed at him and he laughed at me, his childish giggle bubbling up and out of him.

Playing chicken with the sea was our favourite game. I always ran away first. He was the one who stood his ground. The bravest boy in the world.

*   *   *

Someone is watching me.

I know everyone here is watching me, wondering

433

how I am, how I'm coping, whether I'm going to break down, whether I'll finally let them comfort me, but these eyes are different as they study me. They aren't concerned, they are curious. Trying to read me, to see what I am thinking as well as feeling; trying to burrow into the hidden places of my mind.

I slowly open my eyes and find her staring at me. Like the last time we both saw each other on the tube, the day I decided to move away from London, our eyes lock.

She looks appropriate: dressed in a simple, straight-cut dress, the long, honey-blonde locks of her hair pulled back into a low ponytail, flat black shoes, pearls around her throat.

I hadn't told Mal he couldn't bring her, because it hadn't occurred to me that she would want to come. Nor that she'd find enough courage to do that.

She is startled, a deer caught in fast-approaching headlights, by the fact I have caught her staring at me. Colour rises in her cheeks, but she does not look away. She knows I know what she was doing. She was trying to see if she could work out my frame of mind so she could come and talk to me. She was trying to work out if I would turn my back on her, shout at her, tell her to leave me alone, or politely listen to her hollow words.

She doesn't realise that whether she speaks to me or not, none of this means anything.

Every day I wake up, lying on his bed. I sleep in his room, with his favourite sheet—one I used to have on my bed—scrunched comfortingly under my cheek. I don't sleep under the covers, I'm too warm to do that. I need to be in his room for as long as it smells of him. I want to capture every molecule of his scent before it evaporates into the air of time.

Keith and I hardly speak when we are in the house at the same time. We dance around each other, making each other cups of coffee without asking if the other wants one because initiating conversation is too much. He went back to work two days after and stays away for as long as he can—until he knows that I will be in his room, with the door shut, curled up on the single bed, pretending to myself I can sleep. Even though I know I'll see him again when I die and that I will one day find him in my dreams, I cannot sleep for long enough to find him. I drift in dreamland for half an hour at most, and then I'm awake again until dawn. As I close my eyes, I always hear him ask me why he doesn't have a large bed like me. 'I need lots of space, too,' he always says in my head. 'Just because I'm smaller than you, doesn't mean I don't need space.'

When I wake up, I hear Keith in the living room. Playing PlayStation games. One after the other. I don't know if he gets any enjoyment from them, but he plays until as late as possible, then he climbs the stairs to bed. Always he stops outside the white panelled door with the big picture of a lion on it ('All lions are called Leo'). I always hope Keith will come in, share this with me, breach the gap between us, but he never does. After a few seconds he moves on, goes to bed. In the morning I creep around our bedroom getting dressed and leave for Starstruck while he is still asleep.

I make the cakes, cookies, pies, flapjacks as usual; baking is something I can do without thinking. I make the ordered coffees, teas and smoothies but Amy gives them to the customers. I don't serve customers any more. People talk to me otherwise. They ask me how I am, they ask after my son if they haven't been in for a while, they try to comfort me when there's nothing they can do.

I usually sit at the back, in the seat where I used to sit with him when he was a newborn, before I bought the place, and I stare out of the window.

I sit and order my thoughts.

I sit and attempt to smooth out the raw edges of my pain.

I sit.

I return to an empty house, one that echoes with permanent loss, and I make dinner that neither Keith nor I will eat. I sit alone in the kitchen, I push food around my plate for what feels like hours and seconds at the same time, then I scrape the food into the bin, wash the plate. I sit in the living room to watch television by staring through it, my thumb pressing buttons on the remote control until I get to a channel that doesn't hurt my ears and my brain and then I stare through it.

Every day, *every* day I'm surprised that the world has carried on. News is still happening, newspapers are still being made, people are still walking and talking and making mistakes and creating wonderful memories. Every day I'm surprised anew. Every day, I wonder if anyone realises that time has actually stopped and they're fooling themselves that it is moving forwards.

This is my life.

It has nothing to do with Stephanie.

Keith's strong, solid arm slips around my shoulders and his full, soft lips press against my right temple. He hasn't touched me in nearly two weeks. Not since the day after, when I finally went back to the house, and he tried to hold me, tried to let me collapse into his arms, and I couldn't stand to be touched. Not when the feel of my son was still fresh on my skin, was still gently impressed into the curves of my aura. 'Love you, babe,' Keith whispers.

'Love you, too,' I reply.

We both mean it.

We both fear it. When you love someone you risk losing them. Like we have with our son, like we have with each other. He moves on to another part of the room; he can't stay near me too long because it reminds us that we don't talk any more.

That is why Stephanie's concern about whether to speak to me is so laughable. She doesn't exist for me right now. No one exists for me right now.

Time is standing still.

Only for now, though. It will start ticking again. Something will happen to make my life start ticking again. I know I will fall asleep and find him again and I will want to go out into the world again. But for now, nothing can rouse me from where I am.

Especially not you, Stephanie.

I shut her out by closing my eyes. I want to go back to that memory on the beach. I want to go back to where I was with him before she came creeping in.

part seven

CHAPTER SIXTY-ONE

As always, she's wearing her red duffel coat.

I watch her kneel down beside him, not seeming to notice or care the ground is damp and cold, as she runs her fingertips over the gold engraving on the cool, cream marble, like I did a few minutes ago. Then her long, slender fingers move over the yellow, velvety petals of the roses I laid there.

She never suspects it's me.

She always looks up and around, wondering who it is that has left yellow flowers every few days for the past three months, but she never suspects—but why would she? In all the world, I'm the last person she would think would do this. No one knows I do this. That I work part-time hours so that I can come down here.

I'm always careful. While I talk to him, clear away any weeds or leaves, I always keep an eye out for her, watching to see that familiar flash of red that means I have to move away and keep my head down or, like today, I have to hide behind a tree and stay pressed up against the trunk until she's gone.

She looks different. She is still incredibly beautiful, but she is different. Maybe it's that her hair is back in plaits, like when I first met her and when she was carrying Leo. Or maybe it's because she looks so grown up. Grief has aged her, she seems so removed, aloof, untouchable, like grown-ups always seemed to be when I was a child. It's haunting.

What I want to do each time I see her is this:

throw my arms around her, tell her I'm sorry. For her loss, for her pain, for the end of the world. But most of all, for not being her friend when she tried so hard with me. Since my friendship with Carole has become so real and open and supportive, I know now, properly, what my fears did all those years ago. I wouldn't let her close, but I took away her closest friend. I robbed her. I finally have a friend who isn't Mal but who I can rely upon, so I understand how harmful that was. How she didn't deserve it.

And I know that it should be me sitting where she is.

It should have been me who spent day after day at the hospital, sitting by his bed, holding his hand and willing him better. It should be me coming here every day, talking to him, sharing with him, missing him like no one else could. It should be me walking around with my heart removed and a bottomless hole where the centre of my soul once lived.

I'm sorry. That's what I wanted to say at the funeral. That's what I want to say now. I'm sorry. I'm sorry. I'm sorry.

CHAPTER SIXTY-TWO

'I won't keep you long,' I say to Mal.

We're in a small café overlooking Brighton marina, far enough from Hove, from Starstruck, from the hospital, to make this an anonymous, neutral meeting place. We sit in a window booth, opposite each other, the sea is on one side of us and we can see it but not hear it.

Everything about him says he doesn't want to be here, but when I called him earlier asking if we could meet up some time soon, he said, 'I'm on my way' and two hours later he arrived. Now he sits stiff-backed and tense across from me in the café.

He's tried constantly to talk to me in the past three months, like everyone else has, but I haven't been able to speak to him or anyone else properly. Talking reopens the wound, it makes me want to comfort other people, it makes me feel guilty that I sometimes want to scream in their faces to show them how I'm really doing. Show them that inside, that's what it feels like most of the time: a constant, unrelenting, one-note scream.

I can speak to Mal now, and it seems I might be too late, because he doesn't want to be here.

I smile inside at the way half a lock of his butter-blond hair sticks up just over his right ear, at the crystal of sleep that sits in one of his eyelashes, and at the hairs that lie the wrong way in his left eyebrow. Instinctively, I lick my thumb and reach across the rectangle of the table and start to smooth his eyebrow hairs into place. Mal jerks away from me, backwards in his seat, startled and reproachful at the same time.

'Sorry,' I say, digging my fingers into my palm and resting my hand beside my cup. 'I keep forgetting, as Leo used to say, "don't want your spit on my face".' I can say his name. I can talk about him in little increments before the urge to scream takes over.

Mal covers my hand with his, a warm and gentle cocoon. I raise my gaze to meet his as he lifts my thumb, cradling my hand in his palm, and, our eyes locked the whole time, he runs my thumb over his eyebrow before returning it to the table. As soon as he sets my hand down, we break eye contact: I return my gaze to the table, he stares at a point over my shoulder.

'I . . . I won't keep you long,' I repeat. 'I know this is probably the last place you want to be.'

He refocuses on me, stares with his warm, rust-brown eyes. 'What I want, is to be on that side of the booth,' he says in a low, even voice. 'With you. I want to rest my head on your lap and have you talk to me for hours about everything and nothing because that's your way of telling me it's all going to be all right. I want to put my arms around you, hold you close, stroke your face and tell you that it's all going to be all right.'

I've almost forgotten what it's like to be held. How the feel of another person's body can so completely surround you, you lose the point where you begin and they end. When being with someone suddenly means you have the strength of two.

On the nights Keith and I sleep in our bed, we don't touch. We want to, but it seems we have forgotten how; we cannot remember the way to reach out for another and become a part of them. If our bodies accidentally brush, we leave them there, barely touching, hoping that the memory of how to be together will come rushing back to us, until it becomes too painful a reminder of what we have lost and then we slide away to the very edges of the bed. Mal was the last person to hold me. In that bed, in that hotel room, the night before Leo left.

'This is the biggest crisis we've ever had and we're not facing it together,' Mal says. 'Which is

444

what I want to do. That's all I've wanted for three months. So, you're wrong, this isn't the last place I want to be; it's the closest to the place I want to be as I can get.'

I inhale through my nose, exhale through my mouth, calm my panic at what he has said. I haven't let anyone close enough to tell me that. I know that Mum, Dad, Cordy, Aunt Mer, Amy, Keith and Mal all think they lost me too when we lost our little boy. But I cannot help that. I cannot cope with their grief as well as mine. I have needed to do this alone.

'It's good to see you,' I say to Mal.

'Yeah?' he breathes, as his face relaxes into a beautiful smile, crinkling his eyes, widening his jaw, illuminating him from every possible angle. I have to look away, fighting down the lump in my throat. I haven't been able to find Leo in my dreams, yet, but there he is, sitting opposite me, smiling.

'Yeah,' I say to Mal, my eyes still averted. 'It's good to see you.'

After a silence that could go on for ever if we let it, I have to speak. 'I wanted to see you for a reason,' I say, looking at him again. 'Two reasons, actually.'

He waits patiently for me to explain.

'I'm pregnant,' I say.

His eyes widen in shock but he does not speak.

'Turns out what we did was sex after all and I'm pregnant.'

He still does not speak.

'Anyway, you must excuse me, because right now, I'm going to go throw up.'

He has ordered me lemon and ginger herbal tea and a piece of dry, white toast by the time I slide back into my part of the booth. He's remembered that was what had kept the any-time-of-the-day sickness at bay last time. He's also had his coffee taken away. It isn't as strong a coffee-smell-induced nausea as last time, but once I've thrown up, the smell of it at close quarters makes me more sick.

I sip my tea, nibble a crust of the toast. 'Thanks, for this,' I say, indicating to the food and drink.

'I was thinking,' he replies, 'that I must have super-sperm.'

This makes me laugh, the first time in months, a proper full-bodied laugh.

'Don't laugh,' he protests, his eyes dancing. 'Hear me out. I, Malvolio Wacken, have super-sperm. Twice now I have knocked you up with one lot of the stuff. I mean, the first time I was trying, the second time not so much, but still it happened. I reckon I have super-sperm and maybe I should bottle it and sell it.'

'Good idea,' I laugh. 'But the flaw in your plan is that it seems you can only knock me up. And believe me, I won't be buying it. Not when I can clearly get it for free. You big sperm tart.'

It's his turn to laugh, to throw his head to one side and guffaw so loudly a couple of people turn around to look at us. I remember suddenly why I loved him for all those years. Why I still love him. All the reasons that come from moments like this.

'What are we going to do?' he asks, suddenly serious. His eyes are now fixed on the area of my body that is hidden by the table. 'Are you going to have the baby?'

I nod. Since I did the test last week, I've known without a doubt that I'm going to go through with this.

He nods also, relieved, openly happy. 'OK, all right. So I need to tell Steph. It won't be easy, especially at the moment, but I'll do it.'

'Stephanie is already so hurt and damaged, so scared of losing you, do you think telling her what we did and then about this,' I place my hand over my stomach, 'is fair to her? She was always paranoid about our relationship; what will confirming her fears so soon after all this has happened do to her?'

'You think I should lie to her?'

'No, Mal, I think you should wait until you've heard everything I've got to say before you decide who you're going to tell and when.'

'You're not going to tell Keith?'

I shake my head. 'No. It will hurt him more than I could bear. Before he'll be able to tell, I'll be gone.'

'Gone?' he asks.

'I told you I had two reasons to see you. The first is that I'm pregnant. The second is that I've decided to see the world. To do some travelling. I'm going in a few weeks. Keith doesn't know yet. If I told him, he'd think we were going together and he'd make himself come. But he wouldn't want to. Our marriage is over and I don't want him making himself cling to it.'

'Your marriage is over?'

'I love him, I always will. But he, like the house, like Hove, like England, I suppose, reminds me of

447

what I've lost. They're all a part of it. I walk into the house or a room, and I expect to see some new sign that he was there. But the toys he left lying on the floor are still there. His blue controller on the PlayStation is still sitting on top of the box. The book he was reading before he showed me the ultimate wheelie is still open on his bedroom floor. It's all the same. And I can't change it because if I do, I get scared that I'll be losing another little bit of him. It's agony going into the house. And it's agony being with Keith. I can't go to the beach without breaking down. I can't do it any more. I need to get away from here. Make new memories in a place that isn't full of the old ones.'

'You're pregnant.'

I shrug. 'Yeah, I get to be pregnant somewhere else. Which is why you should think carefully about when you tell Stephanie. Because I don't want you to tell her thinking you're going to be a regular dad to this one.'

'I could come with you.'

'Even if I thought you could leave Stephanie, why would I want you to do that to her? What sort of a person would that make me? If you and she split up, that's got to be because that's where your relationship is at, not because of me or the baby.'

Mal stares at me, and I can feel his grief. I do not want to take another child away from him, but I cannot stay here. I have to put myself first.

'I don't want you to go,' he states. 'Please don't leave the country. Please don't leave me.'

'I wish . . . I have to go. For my sanity. So I can start to get over this. So that Keith can find someone else. For a million and one reasons, I have to go. I'm not saying I won't be back, but I have to go. You do understand, don't you?'

He nods. 'I don't want it to be like this, but I understand.'

'I want you to be her dad. This one's a she. I want you to write to her, send her pictures, call her, I want her to know you from the start. We'll work it out. Somehow, we'll work it out.'

'Yeah, we will,' he agrees. 'We will.'

I stand, shrug on my coat, pick up my bag. 'I'll see you, Mal.'

'Isn't that the point, you won't?'

'I don't like goodbyes, so I say I'll see you, then it makes it that little bit easier.'

'OK, I'll see you.'

I nod. 'I'll see you.'

Standing in the cool, fresh air outside the café, watching seagulls swoop into the waves, I realise I have forgotten something and go back inside.

I slip my arms around his neck, hug him close and kiss his cheek. 'Thank you, Mal. I forgot to tell you that. Thank you for Leo, and for that last night. Thank you.'

'You know I love you, right?' he says to me.

'I love you, too. Maybe in our next lifetime we'll get it right and get it together.'

'I don't believe in all that nonsense,' he replies.

'Yeah, but I do. Enough for the both of us.'

'There's no point fighting it, is there?'

'None whatsoever.'

Without thinking, without hesitating, our lips come together. And we kiss for the first time because we love each other. Because, unfortunately for us, we've always loved each other.

The bell behind the café door tinkles as it shuts

449

behind me. I button up my duffel coat, and pull my bag over my shoulder.

That was the second most difficult parting I've ever had. When you love someone as much as I love Mal, leaving them is never easy, even if you both know it is the only way for you both to start all over again.

CHAPTER SIXTY-THREE

'Hi,' he says as I enter the kitchen. 'You all right?'

I stop in my tracks, startled and cautious. Is he talking to me? *To me?* He hasn't asked if I'm all right in three months. He hasn't asked me a non-rhetorical question in what feels like a lifetime. Usually he talks at or through me. Not to me. Usually he's been crying and he can barely form words.

'Yeah, fine,' I answer, resisting the urge to look behind me to double-check he isn't talking to a random stranger who has followed me in from the street. His eyes are even looking at me, not through me. 'How are you?'

He raises and drops his broad shoulders in a brief, dismissive shrug. 'You know,' he says.

I don't. You don't talk to me so I don't know. I can try to imagine, but I don't know. I can try to put myself in your place, but I cannot fully comprehend.

'Where've you been?' he asks. His handsome, loving face is interested. He isn't crying, I realise, even on the inside. He is here, in the room, waiting for an answer from me.

'I've—' I'm going to lie. The last thing he needs,

when he seems to have made so much progress in such a short amount of time, is to hear his name, to be reminded why he was crying, to be reminded why he doesn't want to be with me any more. 'I've been to take flowers to Leo.' I've lied enough. They end here. I cannot change the old lies without destroying everything, but I can avoid any new ones. From now on, no more lies. I owe him, and her, and Leo, and myself that. 'Yellow roses. I always think yellow is his favourite colour. I don't know if it is, but every few days I take him yellow flowers.'

Mal's russet-brown eyes study me for a moment. I cannot read them, nor his face. I cannot tell what he is thinking. If I have pushed him back a few steps, or if he wants me to remove myself from his sight.

'It was green,' he says. 'His favourite colour was green.'

'Oh.'

'But I'm sure he liked yellow, too.'

'Maybe.'

'Do you want to know about him?'

I nod. Of course I do. I want to know everything I can about him. Even the trivial, seemingly insignificant details, such as if he would brush his teeth before bed, I want to hear, so I can create a person, a memory that is more than the photos. So there is someone real I can picture at night before I go to sleep, when I visit him. 'Yes,' I say quietly. 'Yes, I do.'

'I don't know that much,' he says, his eyes flicking to the chair opposite him, an invitation to sit down, to stay a while. 'Not as much as I'd like.'

I pull out the chair, settle myself on it as I drop

my bag on the floor beside me.

'I only know what Mum and Nova and the rest of the family told me. But it's enough.'

I nod at him, link my fingers together and prepare myself to listen.

'I sometimes wonder if it's possible to love someone you didn't even know,' he says. 'But that's how I feel about Leo.'

This is it. The lifebuoy I've wanted to throw him while he has been drowning. Mal's way safely back to shore. I didn't realise it was mine, too.

'Over the years, as Mum has been telling me things, I've felt an incredible bond with him. As though hearing about him, seeing his pictures, being with Mum after she's been with him has bridged the gap between us.'

Mal and I have been drowning for more than eight years.

'Mum said Leo once showed her a picture of me as a child, and said that Nova had told him that the boy in the picture looked like him because God liked to play jokes on her sometimes. But Leo told Mum it was because he knew that the boy in the picture grew up to become his dad. He was only five at the time. Mum was thinking how clever he was when she realised that he was hustling her. He wanted to find out where babies came from and thought she'd tell him if he said he knew about dads.' Mal's smile is wide, proud, woven with deep sorrow. 'Nova said that's what he was like: far too clever for his own good. And for her own good.'

I reach across the table and lace my fingers through his, for the first time in a lifetime he clings back. Holding on to each other, we begin to navigate our way back to dry land.

EPILOGUE

I want you to know that I'm all right.

Yes, *you*.

Now you've heard my story, you may think that I'm still in that place of pain and sorrow, but I'm not, truly, please don't worry about me.

At this moment, I'm sitting in a park, watching Dolly dance. She's twenty-one months old but she insisted in her stubborn way on wearing a thick cream jumper, a blue denim skirt, yellow Wellington boots and a pair of sparkly, silver fairy wings that are far too big for her. Her black-brown corkscrew curls are flying in all directions as she dances to the tune she's making up as she goes along.

We live in a town outside Braga, in Portugal, and I teach English lessons on a one-to-one basis to children coming up for their exams. I know some of the people in the town describe me as *inglesa preta com o sorriso grande e olhos tristes*, which means 'the Englishwoman with the big smile and the sad eyes'.

So, you see, I can smile again. I don't know when I would have been able to do that if I had stayed in England, if I hadn't started all over again.

I still hurt. I'll always hurt, but I had him for seven years. I feel a little sorry that you didn't know him. You never heard his laugh. Listened to the questions he asked at the most inopportune moments. Saw how his obsession with the PlayStation paid off in the number of points he could rack up. Heard his theories on life. Watched

453

his face open up with delight whenever I bought him something he wanted, or he heard a song he liked. Became his co-pilot in the car submarine. Reasoned with him about getting a dolphin/shark/lion/_____(insert wild animal as appropriate). Cried because you'd made him cry. I had all that. I had more.

I wish I still had him. But I had Leo for seven years. And I know I'll see him again. I've always believed that and I believe it even more now.

So, like I say, please don't worry about me. I am all right. Dolly and I are all right. She makes me laugh, she keeps me going and one day we're going to go back. At the moment, I love watching her play in the sunshine, I love just being with her. I love that we've found a new place called home.

And, I don't want you to worry about me because I promise you, we're having the time of our lives.

'I love you. And it's OK to go now,' he hears her say to him through the quiet. It's dark here, but light too. He can't see but there is light.

He knows it's Mum's voice because no one else sounds like her. No one else is as great as his mum.

'I'll see you again so I won't say goodbye. OK? I'll see you again.' She isn't crying. There aren't tears in her words so he's not scared. If Mum's OK then he isn't scared. 'I'm going to say goodnight, instead. Sleep tight, Leo, my love. Goodnight, my beautiful boy. Goodnight, beautiful.'

'Goodnight, Mum,' he replies, and then goes to see what's going on in the light.